Mallory Square
April 10, 2008

To
Grace and Bill,
Only your heart
can hear the Rhapsody
Playing. Enjoy the dance.

KEY WEST RHAPSODY

Pamela Pinkholster

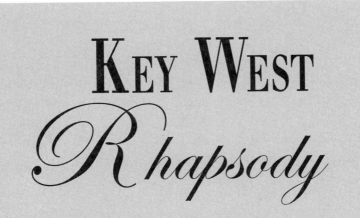

KEY WEST Rhapsody

The Anomaly

A Novel by

PAMELA PINHOLSTER

KEY DEER PRESS
BIG PINE KEY, FLORIDA

ISBN: 978-0-615-16834-0
LIBRARY OF CONGRESS CONTROL NUMBER: 2007905911

Printed in the United States of America

For my loving husband, Peter.
Always and forever, my miraculous gift.
And to my children, Patience, Province, Pristine,
Peter, Jr., Paul, Prescott, Poetry and Preston.
God's legacy to me and the eight, precious jewels in my crown.

Acknowledgments

First and foremost, I want to write a "thank you" to my Mom and Dad, who are living in Heaven. Sadly, they will not be able to read their daughter's first book. They always encouraged me to write and use my artistic gifts, since my early, childhood days. I am eternally grateful to them for instilling those dreams within my heart. It has brought much joy to me to fulfill their previous desires.

Also, I want to thank, my youngest child, Preston, for being the primary inspiration of this book. I could not have written it without him. He was always there for me.

I thank my sweet husband. He listened faithfully to me and waited good-naturedly, as I invented this imaginary world of old Key West. He cheered me on and always said that I was a "good writer" from the beginning. I thank him for his belief in me and his steadfast patience.

I thank my sons and daughters, who have prayed and encouraged me, along the way. I am grateful for the great faith that they have shown in their mom's literary quest.

I express much gratitude to my only brother and my only sister for their hopes and prayers, as well, as any person who prayed for the completion and success of my book.

Finally, I thank God. He is the true author and finisher of my faith.

"*I am the good Shepherd, and know my sheep, and am known of mine.*"

— BOOK OF JOHN 10:14

"*The Lord's mercies are new every morning. Great is His faithfulness.*"

— LAMENTATIONS 3:23

Awake! Pretty Morning Glory of blue,
Look! What the dawn has left for you.
Your silky petals wear sparkles of dew.

But, hold on tightly, my soft, strong one.
You'll be weary, by the day is done,
From wind, rain, hail and the sizzling sun.
Never forget your name, valiant flower . . .

— Pamela J. Pinholster

KEY WEST

Rhapsody

Prologue

Always too busy thinking, I found myself, gently being drawn by the soft tinkling sounds of a drowsy wind chime hanging outside my open window. The soothing, fairy-like tinkles seem to arrest my very being. The clarity of their song saturated my deep thoughts in a tinkling waterfall. Comforted by the sweet notes, they caressed my mind and touched my busy world, reaching into my inner most soul. I soaked in their pure essence and enchantment. Like cool, cascading water, their peaceful tones washed over my mind. They lured me farther away from time, while singing a healing lullaby to my aching heart. I watched the lacey, grey shadows of the suspended chime swaying gracefully against the bright, sun drenched wall. The gentle breeze unhurriedly stirred these musical reflections deep into my heart, filling me with great wonder and hope of an expected end.

One

Thinking back to that cool, January evening in Key West a year ago, I envisioned the cracked sidewalks and the smell of expensive Cuban cigars burning, as I walked up Duval Street with my guitar slung over my shoulder. I was a man still in my twenties, young and talented and energetic. I could make enough money in the evenings playing and singing at old Mallory Square to guarantee eggs and grits at Carmalita's every morning and still make my rent on my small Conch cottage over on Higgs Lane. For now, I was satisfied how things were going.

I had written some new songs lately and I found great pleasure in trying them out on the curious people that gathered at Mallory each evening at sunset. This was a pattern I held to for several winter nights in Key West Old Town. I think a few of the locals liked my songs, because they would stand there longer and more often to hear my music, making me feel like an accomplished student of a famous music school, which I wasn't. It was just me, sharing my thoughts and mind through my songs. No worries and no cares was how I perceived my world. I wanted to control my environment and sometimes I got stressed out, just trying to keep it from getting out of my control. I didn't like that part. This was not the part I bargained for. Just stepping on the pop tops and blowing out my flip-flops was about as far as I wanted to go in my quest for unexpected adventure and problems of the day. Maybe a broken guitar string, I could handle, but really, my life in Key West, I felt was not to be any more complicated than that, so to speak.

I was wrong when I thought I was right. It all seemed right, but my predictable world that I stroked like a purring kitten, evolved into the constancy of change. My cradled cat became a scratching feline.

The sun was setting right on time this particular January evening. Purple clouds, etched in gold, floated above a fiery orange ball sinking below the blue horizon. I felt very excited about some new arrangements I had written. I couldn't wait to try them out on the audience that night. Some of these songs were really good, I thought. I only played my own original music and never did songs by other artists. Actually, I was disappointed with musicians that always played someone else's songs. I tried not to be too judgmental, but I guess I struggled with pride.

I was just getting settled in my regular spot between the fire-eater and the magic pie juggler when a balding man of about forty came up to hear me play.

"It will be a minute," I muttered, trying to get the guitar strap untwisted from around my neck. I had opened my guitar case wide on the pavement in front of me, so as to cast off any negative expectations. "Hope to fill her up with hundred dollar bills tonight," I joked, as I adjusted the guitar under my arm. I started to strum a few chords of a new song I had been polishing up that past week, when the man, rudely gestured a handshake, as I continued to strum. "I'm Rod Castellano from

Hanover, New Jersey. What's your name?" I hated giving my name to strangers. So I made one up, for the heck of it. "My name?" I asked, "My name is Dannon, but people call me Dan." I had just finished a yogurt and thrown the empty cup in a plastic, grocery bag.

"Dannon?" the man glanced down at my garbage bag, with the cup sitting in it. "Isn't that the name of a yogurt?" he asked wryly. "I guess it is, but you can call me Dan," I replied, while giving the yogurt cup a hard stare. This guy was getting on my last nerve. It was time for him to move on down to the fire-eater.

"I've been out here the last couple of nights and liked what I've heard. Sounds like original stuff," he commented, holding out his hand again. Ignoring his hand and him, I began to sing. "Don't you have a card or something?" he shouted loudly over my battery-driven amplifier. I stopped playing and gave this person a very hard look. Startled, he frantically waved his hands back and forth protesting with "Sorry! Sorry! Keep playing, I know you're working now, I'll stop with the questions."

"I'm not working, I'm entertaining. And why should I have a card?" I shot back at him. He gave me a nervous grin and shuffled backward, to the side of the gathering of people who were anxiously awaiting my first song. He stayed there for almost all of my performance, than glancing up, thankfully, I saw he was gone.

The sun had lazily set and disappeared under a still, green blanket of sea, as if too tired to stay any longer. The street lights illuminated faces of lively sun-loving vacationers. Everyone out at Mallory seemed to be celebrating the exhilarating sunset, by the sound of their thunderous applause.

I never saw Rod Castellano depart, but after I was winding it down for the night, I could still feel his presence close by, in a weird sort of way. What a freaky guy, I thought, as I gathered my money up out of the black velvet lined guitar case. I was really thanking God for the generous number of five dollar bills in my hand. This was a rewarding sign, I mused, as I beheld a fifty dollar bill in the pile. The memory of the New Jersey man's face dissipated like a vapor, with the elation I felt over my bursting pocket of money. Tonight's fans stayed the whole time. I smirked to myself, as I pictured them drinking much and paying lots.

It was growing late, and stopping off at Sloppy Joe's bar down on Duval Street for a relaxing beer seemed like a great idea. I was only a few blocks away from there and I was thirsty. I was finished playing by nine and I had scored a satisfying evening.

I entered through the wide front door of the bar. Peeking over, I noticed my favorite small table in the far corner was taken up by a couple of locals that appeared to have been there a long time, by the numerous, empty beer bottles lined up in front of them. I slid onto a nearby barstool, using my guitar case for an armrest.

"What would you like, baby?" I heard a husky voice inquire, as I turned to see who was laying their hand on mine. I pulled my hand back and ordered. "A Bud Light, please." Her bleached hair frizzed around her fatty cheeks and toothless smile. "Alright sir, I'm a friendly girl and just being helpful. One Bud Light for you," she rasped.

I didn't know anybody at the bar. The barmaid set my beer down without conversation and I was glad. Cool air moved slightly through the open windows where the wooden shutters were cocked open. I wondered how often Ernest Hemingway had gone back to his old typewriter to write after downing a few brewkies at Joe's. His famous photos, scattered around the bar, brought life to the old landmark. Tired now, I was ready to hit the rack. I motioned for my waitress. While I waited for the bill, I glanced at the full tables and crowds of strangers, staring in through the window casements, from outside on the sidewalk. I stopped suddenly, with a jolt. There was that jerk, Rod-what-ever-his-name, was at one of the open windows. I turned my head quickly. The jolly barmaid returned with my check and said, "I know who you are, now. I seen you on the square playing your big, git-fiddle."

I replied, "Great, here's ten dollars. Keep the change. I gotta get myself." I climbed off the high, wooden barstool, leaning on my guitar for a brace, as I got down. My eyes followed the narrow path, winding through the filled chairs, as I made my way to the entrance of the bar. The band had just started cranking when I stepped out onto the sidewalk.

"Hey Dan," I heard a man's voice shout over the loud music. I glanced up in time, and weaving his way over toward me, among the throng of revelers, was Rod. This was a person I knew I wanted to avoid. There he was smiling and shouting at me, "Dan, over here. Over here," pointing at himself, above the crowd. I nodded a knowing nod, taking notice of two rather large, dark-haired men with him. Those must be his body guards, I said, pondering to myself. I put my head down, slung my guitar case over my back and made my way through the ensuing crowd, heading down Duval toward home, as fast as I could. When I crossed the next street corner, I ducked into a dimly, lit bar and watched out through the open air windows. It was sort of hard to make out the passing walker's faces, but after about five minutes, I felt they probably didn't follow me. As I was stepping out of the doorway, I suddenly froze and pulled back inside. I leaned back against the door frame, clutching my guitar tight up against my thumping heart. I could hear their riled voices as they passed right in front of me.

"This little Dan, the music man, has not been an easy . . ." the biggest man was saying as they went by. But, then their voices trailed off, as their leather shoes swiftly beat up the walk. There was no sign of them as I looked out, down in the direction in which they were headed. I felt relieved, but anxious, as I started down Duval toward Higgs Lane again. I was puzzled why these three men were so concerned about me, to the point of hunting me down in the dark. It made no since to me at all. My life was my music and I hoped my future, too. Writing and composing my own lyrics and recording them and then, hopefully soon, getting the thirty or more songs copyrighted, was all I thought about. My spare time was usually spent performing at the square. As far as friends, I had a couple of really good ones and absolutely no enemies that I knew of. Finally, I had reached my cozy Conch cottage over on Higgs.

After a good night's rest, things would look better in the morning, my mom always said. I laid down on the futon and listened, as the soft tinkling of the wind chime lulled me into a peaceful sleep.

The next morning, I woke up refreshed and ready for a day of developing my newest creation. Shortly, evening arrived. Feeling relaxed, I eased on down to the square. The cruise ships had come in, docked and dumped off a bunch of tourists from foreign countries, at the end of Key West. The passengers loved the radiant sunset over the gold-glinting water. Time stood still as the glorious sunshine waved goodnight with its luminous translucent rays held high above its head.

"Thanks for that song," a young woman whispered, as I ended my last song, an hour or so later. Bending near my face,

I could smell the alcohol on her breath. Her steel-grey eyes looked through me. I stepped back. "Thanks, glad you liked it. I was just packing up to leave."

"I really wish you would sing that song alone to me, some-time," she suggested, in broken English."

"Well, I'm really busy myself, but maybe you can buy my CD, when it's made."

"Oh, you're making a CD?"

"Well, after I get all my written music copyrighted, I plan to release lots of CD's . . . ." I paused and stared at her pretty face.

"What's your name?" speaking without thinking, and then catching myself, I hurriedly added, "I gotta get going now."

"My name is Danielle Stodard from Sweden. I heard your name was Dan," she smiled at me intuitively.

I tried not to over react. My face felt flushed. I pretended to adjust my guitar over my shoulder. "Yeah, that's my name. How did you know that?" I asked, wondering where she got her information.

"The word gets around, I guess. You're so popular out here."

"Yeah, I guess it does," I agreed. I began walking in the direction of Duval Street, she walked along side of me and than abruptly stopped, "I have a rental car parked nearby. Would you like a ride?" she asked.

"No thanks. I enjoy walking."

"I can drive you wherever you want to go," she protested.

"No thanks," I dashed across the street with her at my heels. *Where is she going?* I wondered. Then she asked, "Where are you headed? Mind if I walk with you?" She sure was determined, I thought, as I maintained my course. Amazed, I answered, "I'm meeting a friend at the Green Parrot," hoping she would get the hint.

The Green Parrot Bar wasn't exactly close by, so I was moving out pretty fast.

"Well, don't let me hold you up. It was great hearing you play." And she said good bye, disappearing into the colorful fusion of people and lights.

Two

I made my way to the Green Parrot bar. The band was jamming. Morgan was sitting at a table where we could hear each other talk. He was drinking a glass of wine. "Hey, James," he called to me, as I approached the table. "My name's Dan now!" I quipped. Morgan studied my face, than laughed and retorted, "Well, have a seat, Dan, and relax awhile." He poured some red wine into a waiting goblet. I didn't feel like relaxing, but I drank the wine anyway. I told him about the New Jersey trio and about the mysterious, Swedish girl with the British accent, trying to hit on me.

"Well, all I think you need, is for me to protect you from the beautiful girl," Morgan kidded. I protested with, "How could she have known my name was Dan? I had only given that name to Rod Castellano last night. And Morgan, why would three, strange men be trying to track me down on Duval?" Puzzled, I set down my empty glass, feeling quite perplexed.

Morgan added, "Yeah, I know," he stared at me, "What would they be after you for? Duval Street can sure be a place of strangeness, sometimes." I picked up our tab to pay it, but

Morgan grabbed it from me and grinned, "Legendary locals, like me, take care of their bills at the end of the month. Now let's walk over to my place and I'll drive you home."

We headed over to his mom's house, on Caroline Street, where Morgan lived, taking care of his disabled mother and helping maintain their tropical paradise. Exotic birds in ornate cages composed a symphony of color and song, as we strolled into the torch-lit gardens. Colorful, rare orchids and lacey, green ferns hung gracefully from several of the tall, lush, flowering trees. Blossoming foliage burst in pastel profusion, along each balcony railing and winding walkway, filling the air with their sweet fragrance. As Morgan came out of the back of the house, from checking on his mother, I called out, "How do you create this massive masterpiece of nature?" I was totally overwhelmed by Morgan's landscaping artistry.

"I just kind of throw it all together, and as usual, expectant-ly, perfection grows," Morgan chuckled. "As you well know, James, I'm easily impressed with myself. It's the impressing of my friends that challenges me most!" Morgan shot a presump-tuous glance at me.

"Actually," I responded, "it's your humility that impresses me most." Morgan's artificial composure crumbled. Attempting to cover, he recklessly tried punching me in the arm. Laughing, I quickly spun out of reach.

"Jamie-boy, you're lucky I'm a compassionate man. I'll take it down a notch. I wouldn't want to bruise that playing arm, anyway. I like your music too much." He gestured a fake jab in my direction, finding glee in my unplanned flinching. I natu-rally ignored his immaturity.

The night air was balmy with freshness. I paused and silently, gazed up at the dark sky, "Check out all those millions of stars! Have you ever seen so many stars at one time?" I got really caught up in that lofty Key West moment. My spirit soared adrift in timeless space. If Morgan answered, I never heard him. Without a whisper, a brilliant star streaked across the horizon, blazing a golden, dusty trail.

I rubbed my eyes and glanced over at Morgan's indifferent expression. My gaze returned to the glittery, black heavens. "Time seems to stand still when I look up at the stars sometimes. What seems like eternal seconds are really fleeting moments on earth," I reflected, pointing up to the curtain of stars, stretched like a canopy, across the small island.

"You took the words right out of my mouth!" Morgan exclaimed. "I was just gonna say that!"

"Really?" I sneered. "Come on, Galileo! Let's get going."

"Hope you've got some good espresso, when we get over to your place, James. I want to hear that new song that you've been working on, too." Morgan yawned, as he spoke. "No worries shipmate. Get in the car," I said, confidently.

We turned on Higgs Lane and eased into my drive. A car suddenly came up and parked, snuggly behind us, blocking us in. Morgan intuitively glanced my way, asking, "Expecting company?" We opened our doors and climbed out, leaving our car lights on. A figure approached me, on my side of the car. As it drew closer, I knew who it was, as her car lights lit up the baffled expression on my face.

"Surprised to see me here, Dan?" Danielle asked, as her eyes penetrated mine, in the bright, headlight beams. "Yes, as a matter of fact I am," I sighed, "How did you find me?"

"I went to the Green Parrot and followed you when you left."

"Why did you follow me?" I asked her, in a sharp tone.

"Because I like you."

"You don't even know me!" I stammered.

"Who is this? Your friend?" she mused.

"I'm Morgan. You must be Danielle."

"Dan must have been telling you about us," she gushed. I rolled my eyes in dismay. "Hey, it looks like you may have more unexpected visitors," she said, her voice sounding suddenly serious, as she pointed at a big luxury car pulling up to the curb. "I will see you again," she assured me, tossing a kiss in the air. *A kiss meant to fall on me.* She hopped in her car without explanation, backed out of my drive and sped away.

"Who's that?" I asked, out loud, mostly talking to myself. Morgan was still staring at Danielle's car, as it slowly faded out of sight. He slammed his car door and came around to my side. "Who do you know in New Jersey?" he asked, as he pointed to the New Jersey license tag, reflected by the headlight beams. "Big car, big men," he mumbled, under his breath, watching their three doors fly open all at once.

It was clear to me who these visitors were, as soon as, they got out of their car. "Hey Dan, remember me?" Rod inquired, after he and his buddies walked up next to us. "We need to chat with you boys, a bit." He motioned us to go inside. I noticed the biggest man of the group, purposely stood up extra tall, next to his crony, Castellano. Immediately, we saw that he was holding a small gun in his massive hand.

"Okay, we'll all go inside," Morgan agreed, with wide eyes.

All five of us filed up the wide, wooden stairs onto my small, tiled porch. Crowding us, big boy waved at us to open the front door. Everyone packed into my front room. Rod looked around, giving orders. Threatening me, he yelled, "I'll tell you what I want and I want it pronto, Danny Boy, or you and the captain here, may be singing the blues." I was stunned. "Lloyd! Start bagging it up," he snapped. "Give Lloyd all your files, papers, CD's, tapes, digital recordings, videos and anything else you got that has your songs on it," Rod demanded of me.

14

After getting all my material together and handing it to Lloyd, I nodded toward the bulging bag, "Stealing my music isn't going to get you anywhere."

Rod sneered, "When we get it copyrighted, it will!"

I sighed, "How do you know there isn't already existing copyrights?"

He laughed maniacally, "Let's say a little green parrot told me," then added, "tune us in on your radio and hear your favorite song, Yogurt Boy." They roared at Rod's stupid pun. Bowing and curtsying, lost in their dim witted hilarity, I asked myself, what the heck they were even doing. Looking over at Morgan, my rolling eyes confirmed that we were dealing with some real weirdos here. His eyes mirrored what I was thinking. I could tell he was assessing an escape plan and appealing to me for one, too. I tried to recall some defense moves I had learned in my early Coast Guard days, but those memories had long ago, evaporated into an unidentifiable mist. *Why was I giving into these joker's demands?* Seething, my temper flew, "Why does your kind always end up down here in Key West?" Furiously, I answered my own question, "When your toilets in Hanover get flushed, New Jersey sewers just dump the worse load down in Key West. And here you three are, ripe and stinking, fresh out of the sewer-pipe-express."

Rod snarled, "Maybe you don't realize whose in charge here, big man," gripping my arm forcefully. "I got better things to do, than listen to your smart mouth."

"What's that?" Lloyd asked, as I put the last of my property in his big bag. "It's what you wanted, but what you don't get, is that all my music is locked in my brain, where not even three losers from New Jersey can have it." Lloyd smiled a twisted grin and then winced, "I mean, who tipped the cops off?" he cried, pointing out the window. Rod grabbed me by the throat, jerking my head up close to his. He sprayed my face with his saliva, while sadistically cursing me and restricting my breathing. Blue lights were flashing all over the street, up and down and in front of my house. Their reflections showered my living room walls with a chilling, blue radiance. Banging at the door, the Key West cops poured into my small Conch cottage. The time it took for them to make the arrests, get our statements and eventually, give our testimonies in court, was nothing, compared to the time it has taken me to, finally, get all my songs copyrighted.

And now, months later, here I am, basking in the calming atmosphere of a consoling wind chime, thinking back, but yet, looking forward and lately, thanking God more than ever. I just pray God will help me figure out what the heck this message says, that arrived today, on the back of a picture-postcard from Sweden.

Three

The sky was greyer than most rainy days, on an October morning. Sort of elephant-grey. Puddles collected under the downspouts, strapped against the soaked, red, brick buildings lining the city sidewalks. Off in the distance, as if crying to be found, a fog horn bellowed a low and lonely call across the misty river. Wind gusts burst through the dripping tree limbs, shaking and clattering their spindly branches. Shuttering and quivering, the wet, turning leaves hung on tightly by their wrenched, tiny stems, clinging for life to their home.

Amber could relate with their stormy struggle, as the damp, cool air breezed against her wet face. This was the kind of overcast, bleak day that brought a welcoming change to her and a feeling of not wanting it to do anything different, than what it was doing.

The gentle raindrops softly soothed her aching heart. Dappled skies were covered with soft, flannel blankets of grey clouds that enfolded her in showers of hope. The depth of this comfort, her words could not express, but she knew it as an unfathomable knowing, flowing from a river that ran deep within her soul. Amber was waiting for God to change her mourning into dancing, and faithfully, she believed He would.

Amber's darting steps skirted the splashes from the passing cars. Being a part of the weather, felt so healing to her, she lost herself in the colorful umbrellas that dotted the rain-drenched walkway, of hurrying passersby. She watched as they moved together in their own vibrant rhythm. The raindrops drummed loudly, hitting and splattering against their taut, vivid cloth. She was glad she didn't own one. *Think of all I'd miss hiding under an umbrella,* she mused, dodging a vast puddle, that reflected the sky and trees above it, like a mirror. The two canvas tote bags, she was lugging, were now soaked and so was the beige trench coat she was wearing. Aware, that she looked a sopping sight for her arrival at the hospital, she wished she had found a closer parking space. *Maybe the rain will slack up a little,* she pondered. Amber was thankful for her long, auburn hair, kept dry under her snug hood. It cascaded down her back, keeping her warm. The untucked, wet tresses that whipped wildly with the wind, bordered her rain-streaked face. Thrusting them back out of her eyes, she saw the prominent, brown-stone building looming before her, just ahead. She could feel her heart beating harder, as she approached her destination. Ascending the steep, wide steps of Washington, D. C.'s Veteran's Hospital, she felt a burden being lifted from her slight shoulders. She hesitated. *I am finally here. I hope the Colonel is ready for all of my questions.* She stopped and caught her breath atop the high steps. As she entered the heavy, glass doors, into the beautifully decorated lobby, vases of colorful, fresh fall flowers, met her gaze.

Dripping water on the white marble floor, Amber removed her drenched, hooded coat. She noticed the puddles of rain-water she was making on the slick marble. Oh well, she resigned, I guess I'm a whole lot wetter, than I thought. Flopping her soppy coat over her bare arm and readjusting the water-logged, tote bags, she decided, her soggy shoes were another adjustment she would have to deal with, too. "Lady's room straight ahead" the sign read, just beyond the congested hallway. She knew where she wanted to go, and she set out in that direction. But, as she began maneuvering her way, through the streams of people coming and going, Amber felt a tender touch on the back of her shoulder.

"Excuse me, Miss. Are you Amber Albury?" Surprised, Amber wheeled around. "Oh, I'm sorry, I didn't mean to startle you," the quiet voice of a curious lady, gently offered. Her clear, delft-blue eyes brimmed with overflowing kindness.

"Yes, that's my name. Do I know you?"

"No, I am afraid not, but I knew your husband, Peter, over in Iraq. Colonel Benson said you were coming to visit with him today and he invited me here so, I could meet you, too." Her black, silvery streaked hair curled around her serene face. The endearing lady took Amber's cool, damp hand into her warm, dry one. "I knew Peter would have a lovely wife. He told me so many wonderful things about you and what a special relationship you both had, together."

"I know who you are!" Amber exclaimed, "You're Marsha Gordon, the editor for *World Outlook* magazine, aren't you?"

"Yes, I am. I've waited a long time to get back to the states to finally, meet you," Marsha held out her caring arms and gave Amber a reassuring embrace, "I was sad to have missed Peter's memorial service. Being in control of the most popular news reporters on earth, has allowed me to see, that I really can't control when I may or may not take a leave of my post."

"Peter wrote to me so often about the many articles you worked on with each other. I read many of them. He said he learned so much from you," Amber remarked.

"We were a good team," Marsha affirmed, looking far off,

picturing in her mind, the last day she was with Peter. "On our final assignment together, the day before he was killed, we were leading a group of Iraqi reporters into an overcrowded, refugee compound in the heart of Baghdad. We accomplished what we intended to do by giving the Iraqi newsmen invaluable knowledge, even to the extent of allowing them to use our special broadcasting equipment. I remember, Peter instructing them in the use of our digital cameras and laptop processing. They loved him. He was so patient in dealing with their technical questions, considering the language barrier and all." Marsha realized she had opened a floodgate for Amber's tears, but she felt the need to continue. "The English interpreter we worked with had us laughing most of the time. He was from India and was very fluent in French, English, and several Hindu and Moslem dialects. Peter operated with Madi full time. He lost so much hope with Peter's death. He had a very special trust in Peter."

"How is he doing now?" Amber asked, sniffing sympathetically, "It has been three months since Peter's passing and I've never heard any news of Madi?"

"Fortunately, there have been many positive signposts along the way, showing me that Madi is better. You know, when your best friend dies, it takes much time for inner healing to take place and to forgive those who killed your friend. This is what Madi is working through." Amber reached out and gripped Marsha's arm, knowing so well, herself, what he was dealing with. Marsha consoled, "I know you have been through so much grief, Amber. And another thing, I know that Peter cherished you. He would want you to forgive and be happy. He loved God and America, and that is why we are here together, today."

Tears ran unreservedly down Amber's pale face. Marsha shared some tissues with her. "Would you like a cup of hot coffee or tea before we go up to see the Colonel?" she asked. Amber dabbed her watery eyes. "No, thank you. I'm feeling like I should go on up immediately, but, I would like to make one stop at the lady's room, along the way, if that's okay with you?" Marsha smiled endearingly, nodding her head.

The elevator doors opened up at the fifth floor. Marsha explained that this was the floor for homebound patients, as they walked down the hall. Marsha put her hand out, "This is his room." She slowly pushed the door opened. Colonel Benson was sitting up in bed, reading the *Wall Street Journal*. Amber had imagined him looking so different, when they spoke on the telephone a few days ago. She was surprised by how handsome he really was. His graying hairline came across as quite distinguished. Although, it was hard for Amber to tell, Colonel Benson looked tall and lean, lying stretched out in his hospital bed. She thought he resembled more of an outdoor, clothing model, than an Air Force Colonel.

"Hello, Colonel Benson," Marsha called from the doorway. "Who do you suppose I have with me?"

"I can guess!" he cried, "Peter's lovely bride. Welcome to my home-away-from-home." Amber crossed the room, extending her graceful hand. His handshake was strong and friendly. "It is so good to finally meet the woman, who sacrificed so much for our country and her husband's career. Peter meant everything to me. On the field or off, he remained my devoted friend and trustworthy confidant. We could be anywhere and his loyalty to the cause was extraordinary. Peter Albury was an incredible news reporter." Amber went limp. Her body felt like Jell-O. May I sit down?" she asked weakly. "Of course, you can! Please!

Please! Sit here, next to me." He motioned to the padded chair, beside his bed. "I want you to feel right at home with me, today. I feel like I know you already from all the bragging I heard from Peter for almost a year. My desire is to help you in any way, I can." He patted his wounded leg and commented, "Just because the Air Force shipped me back, I'm still in the service of helping others. Any questions you have about Peter and the explosion that took his life, I hope, I can answer." His smoky-grey eyes sparkled. "I'm so sorry, that there were no remains or proof, with which our government could come up with, to send back for Peter's honorary, memorial service. Lord knows, the search and rescue teams explored for several days, just to locate any remains they could find of him, but extensive investigations brought no positive results. We are now pretty positive, that Peter was near the power-head of the explosion. No living creature, without a miracle, could survive such a forceful blast. Any hope for Peter's remains were destroyed after that. But the SAR team never wanted to give up. They searched until every team member was satisfied, that there was nothing left to find."

"I am so sorry you were hurt in the violent skirmish that followed, Colonel Benson. It was a miracle you were not killed, too," Amber wept. "Just knowing, you were with Peter the morning he died, is such a comforting thought for me," she quietly paused in retroflection and blotted her tear-filled, green eyes, then continued, "I'm so glad you're going back to your home in Williamsburg, soon. Peter told me that we lived near your old home in Virginia. It's even possible, that we could have bumped into you, while we were shopping at a grocery store in Williamsburg and we wouldn't have even known it!"

"Isn't that the truth," he chuckled. "I'm so anxious to return home next week, that I'm actually counting the days." Marsha then remarked, "Life won't be as exciting for you, as flying fighter jets, but your sweet Virginia plantation will certainly bring a peaceful change. It will be a calming retreat that you much deserve and greatly could do with. Heaven knows, you're ready to enjoy a well-earned retirement."

Colonel Benson, thoughtfully, nodded in agreement. "You must both come visit me and help me sort out my post-war nerves, while drinking fresh-squeezed juice, from my own vineyard of home-grown, Concord grapes. I promise you both, that lemon-silk pie will be regularly served on my sweeping veranda, overlooking the James River."

"Sounds inviting," Marsha said, "I may just have to do that. A vacation in Virginia, lazing around and immersing myself in the peaceful views, may be just what I need."

"Well, you both are very welcome any time and I look forward to your visits. Let's face it, an old military bachelor, such as I am, would love to be able to test my culinary skills out on somebody, other than myself." He laughed and added, "Even though the results may turn out to be a gastronomic experience! I will make sure that I keep plenty of frozen TV dinners in the freezer, just in case."

"My leave time is classified, but labeled as very indefinite, right now," Marsha remarked. "A leave of absence is what I'm calling it, although, my magazine associates call it something else. It seems, out on location, they can hardly function without my presence. I don't miss Iraq in the least bit and Williamsburg is sounding more alluring to me, with each passing moment."

"Well, we'll talk about this southern repose later, because I know Miss Amber, is anxiously waiting with many questions, that I've promised to answer, especially about Peter's last days in war-torn Iraq." Colonel Benson's eyes twinkled with a comforting smile, as he took Amber's delicate hand and held it in his.

"Thank you Colonel for all you have done for Peter and me.

My new plan is to return to Charles City, Virginia in a few days and close on the sales of my Meadow Dew Farms and my small art gallery in Williamsburg. After they are finalized, I will be taking a long, relaxing sabbatical in Key West, Florida. I don't know where I'll be staying yet, but happily, I have already purchased my plane ticket. I'm flying out next Friday morning." Amber shifted in her chair and cleared her throat, conscience that she was getting ready to bare her sole to her two new friends. She shyly smiled at them both, saying, "Recently I made a promise to myself that I would always try to remember that God's Spirit continuously fills me every day, enabling me to handle every situation that comes my way." With that said, she took a deep breath and sighed.

Amber had waited a long time and she had many questions for the Colonel that needed to be answered. With yearning and anticipation, this important day, had at last, arrived for her to hold and cherish. Now, meeting with Colonel Benson would unearth the answers that she longed to find. The fullness of this epic moment was, now, directly in her grasp, to transform mysteries into history. Not even the relentless storm raging outside could hold her back.

Four

The phone rang relentlessly. Lying in the dark in his snug bedroom, James was now awake, and his agitation was mounting like a monster thunderhead on the nearby horizon. He drew out his noisy yawn, grumbling at the irritating telephone caller, "When do you get it? No one's answering the phone. Is this so hard to get? Only a really bored-out-of-their-mind reject would continue this . . . Ummm . . . ! What the . . . ," his drowsy voice trailed off, drifting back into a sleepy stupor and trying to block out the phone's incessant ringing again and again. "Forget it," James snapped, "That's it! I've had it with you," feeling more awake than he wanted to believe he was. He rolled over to the other side of his comfy, full-size waterbed. It heaved and swayed, making slushy, swishing sounds under his firm body. Fumbling for the telephone speaker button, he hit it hard with the heel of his hand and a red light pierced the darkness.

"Yeah?" he asked, sighing in surrender, "What's your all-so-fired-up emergency?" He squinted his dark, brown eyes tightly, trying to make out the time on the dull, glowing face of his dive watch. The blue light faintly reflected three o'clock in the morning. No one spoke. *Just what I need, a bored phone stalker that wants to play games with me. This person is easily entertained, that's for sure.* James slammed his fist against the phone button, hanging up on the caller. He flipped on the bedside lamp and shoved the answering machine plug into its phone jack. Turning the light off, he rolled back over, flat on his stomach, squeezing his two pillows down tightly over his head. The phone began to ring again. *This time, I'm ready*, he thought, as he snickered quietly to himself under his feather pillows. Relieved that his machine would do the talking, his elevated stress-level had dropped and sheepishly, he closed his sleepy eyes. Finally, after several annoying rings, the message machine clicked on. James laid still and silent in his dark room, waiting and listening, assured that a peaceful sleep was in the offing, following this last attempt to harass him.

"Hello, please leave your message," the same stranger, who made his home in the message machine, answered the call, as usual, with his lifeless, recorded greeting and his familiar, deep booming voice, followed by an obnoxious, squealing beep. Then, James heard a slight pause and some light, frustrated panting. *Obviously, exasperation is taking over. And, oh yes, here comes the heavy breathing part. How did I know that?* James grimaced agonizingly, beneath his pillows, waiting for the nuisance to give it up, but the voice that began speaking on the message machine startled him and his eyes popped wide-open and he was wide-awake.

"Hello. Hello . . . . Is anybody there?" A hopeful pause. "Is this the Island Hop Taxi Service run by a Mr. Island Joe? I desperately need a taxi to pick me up at the Key West Airport and take me to the hotel where I'm staying. My cell number is 757-300-0077. I hope you are open and hear my message. Please, call me back. Thank you." Click.

James pushed the play-button, again. He listened intently,

then, played it once more. He started to wonder if he should call her back, explaining to her that the Island Hop Taxi was defunct. He knew he had their old phone number assigned to his telephone, when he got his landline hooked up. *Why did I choose that stupid number? I knew that I should have picked another phone number. Just had to have four eights at the end of my number.* He sighed, reluctant to think about his contrary choice. Running both of his hands back and forth through his shaggy, thick brown hair, he wondered if he should call her back. *She really sounded like a damsel in distress.* He pondered some more . . . *I'm awake, now. Maybe, I should drive to the airport and look for her. I could give the poor lady a ride to her hotel in my truck.* James knew there were no taxi cabs running in the middle of the night in Key West. Struggling with the guilt thing, he stared out his open French doors. Contemplating the whole situation, he viewed the silver sliver of moon that was hanging in the star-sprinkled western sky and setting right on time. Considering the strange woman's predicament, he weighed it all up and he reached his final assessment with some serious rethinking about her plight and its destined outcome.

This is not a big deal. She probably has lots of friends here in Key West. And why would she ever want to get in a truck alone with some guy she doesn't even know? If she flew into the city by herself, then she no doubt, knows someone here to call. She can wake them up to come pick her up. She's really good at that. Waking them up is a whole lot better then getting me up out of bed. Soon, some help will arrive and she will be rescued. And besides, there is always the remote possibility that she is not alone! An option that I should never overlook! He smirked wistfully. *There's always that option!* With the problem irrevocably resolved, James fluffed up his two, fat feather pillows, laid his head back on them and fell into a deep sleep.

The sun was beating down on his hot, pickup truck the next morning, as he got into it to drive to Old Town's Carmalita's Restaurant for breakfast. He flipped on the air conditioning switch, thinking about how much he needed a cup of coffee. The night before seemed like the blur of a bad dream plus a sad loss of sleep, he determined, pulling into Carmalita's parking lot. Morgan was inside waiting on his arrival.

"Have a cup of simulating java, my friend! Man! You're looking rough," Morgan chimed, filling a waiting mug and setting it on the table, across from James, as he approached their booth. "I ordered for you. The usual." He paused, then added, "Maybe you should have looked in the mirror before you left home."

"Well, it wouldn't have done any good, because there's a reason why I look like this. I didn't get hardly any sleep last night. I'll be able to think and talk clearer, after I drink this coffee. I would love a plate of eggs and grits, right about now, and this coffee gives me hope." Clasping the warm mug with both hands, he lifted the cup up to his lips. He meditated upon the moment, as he blew his soft breath across the surface of the dark liquid. Entranced by the tiny, swirling waves he made, the moist, warm steam rose and caressed his face with a calming touch. James sipped it and pensively, savored the soothing effect it created.

"Cat got your tongue, Jamie?" Morgan asked, breaking the sweet spell with way too much cheerfulness. He reached over and placed the morning *Citizen* in front of James's face. Pointing to the entertainment section, he said, "You're in this, today." Morgan beamed proudly over his outstanding accomplishment.

James, by habit, pulled a white, plastic guitar pick out of his orange, tee shirt pocket. Rubbing it between his thumb and fingers, he studied Morgan's eager expression.

"It's like this, Ol' Captain," James addressed Morgan by his infamous title. "I am suffering from some very serious sleep-deficiency."

"So, does this mean, you're phoning the Green Parrot and canceling your gig at the last minute?"

"No! I had not planned on doing that . . . ." James glared. He was in no mood for any humorless suggestions. "You are really a weird cat, aren't you Meredith?" He emphatically called him by his last name. James stared at him hard from his side of the table. Morgan knew he had crossed the line. Qualifying his statement, he said, "Look, I was just joking. Why don't you eat and go back to your place and sleep?"

"I would, but I need to do a bunch of stuff to get ready for this evening. My equipment has got to be dropped off early and set up. There are just a lot of loose ends I gotta take care of." He drained the last drop of coffee in his cup and set it down harder than necessary. "I don't have time to sleep!" He signaled the waitress for a refill, since their carafe was getting seriously depleted, "*Café, por favor?*" A short, robust Cuban woman of about seventy years old came bustling over to their booth with a steaming pot of strong Cuban coffee.

"*Mucho gracious, Señorita* Theresa!" James quipped, displaying a gleaming smile, as she lowered a straw basket of pressed, hot, buttered Cuban bread onto the table. The famous bakery at Carmalita's made long, hot loaves to go, from early morning until noon, each day, but Sundays. The two guys devoured the whole basket of warm bread in no time at all. Each bite melted in their mouths, as they waited for their customary breakfasts to be served. Soon, Theresa was back with more

Cuban pan and the enjoyable aroma wafting up from the heated platters she set before them. The large plates held steamy Spanish, egg omlettes, smothered in fresh salsa and oozing with soft, melted cheese, Spanish, yellow grits swamped in pools of warm, golden butter, and plenty of fried crisp bacon on the side. "Life is good, isn't it, Morgan?" James clucked, holding up his fork, poised and ready.

"I got a great idea, James," Morgan exclaimed, blissfully biting down into the loaf's crunchy, rounded end-piece. "Since you're so worn out from a rough night without rest, I'll help you go and set up after we finish breakfast. P.J. is a good friend of mine and I know he will let us in early. I'm in tight with the management that runs the bar, too and they are all my good buddies, as well. After they've seen what an invaluable help I've been in arranging everything for you to play there, I'm sure, I will be more than compensated for all that I've done. No doubt, they will reward me with a few, complimentary brewkies at my own little table, on your opening night. Now, how can you pass up a deal like that, Mate?"

"Great, Cap, you're hired!" James suntanned face was awash with relief. He lately had been just a little nervous about this weekly, three-night engagement that he had committed to do over at the "Parrot" and he was glad for Morgan's support. The bar was always a favorite hangout that they both frequented, enjoying the music and playing a game of pool, once in a while. He had Captain Morgan to thank for using his weighty influence as a seventh-generation Conch in the showing off his musical talent to the right contacts. As Morgan had expected, there was no contest when they heard James sing and play his own arrangements. The audition was over after the first song. Locals from all around knew him from the Mallory Square Sunset Celebrations and recently, most of the many free newspapers in Key West printed a weekly picture of him sitting and playing by the water's edge, but especially now with the stir of his up and coming appearance at the Green Parrot, they were including interesting, short, news-blurbs about him, too.

"Come on, partner! Let's rock n' roll," James threw out his trite, worn-out cliché. "You've got work to do. I'll even pay the check as part of the deal, this morning!" He laughed and motioned to Theresa that they were done eating and ready for the bill.

"Okay, take it down a notch, *partner*." Morgan narrowed his blue eyes and gazed at James, as if under a magnifying glass. "You know, I have to say one thing. That's the first time I've heard you laugh today." He smiled, casually showing concern for James's fragile state.

"Well, you'd understand better if you had experienced what I did last night." Morgan grinned at him curiously. "No, Captain Crazed, I was not out partying until dawn, like some people I know." Glancing down, he tried to hide a smile, "You know how to really get on a guy's last nerve, don't you, Meredith?" Morgan slowly nodded his head.

"Believe me, James, I do understand. Say no more." And he didn't.

Five

A cool breeze sailed through the open air windows of the Green Parrot bar. It was dark and the sunset crowd was drifting in on the coattails of a gentle wind. The occasional gusts alerted the local revelers to the old familiar story that only whimsical Key West could tell, without ever speaking a word. Key West's breathtaking sunsets and blustery headwinds were only some of her *carte du jour*. Her temperamental ways continued to amaze the flocks of tourists, known as visiting "Snow Birds." They always complained about her stormy, unchangeable habits and surprising inclement weather. But locals, known as Conchs, born right on the Island, identified with Key West's unreliable and transforming unpredictability. If the tendency of change was stable, then Key West would not be Key West. By weathering her storms, the character of the resilient Conchs exemplified strength and her obsessive changes became their second nature. Survival granted them the essence of their past and gained the hope for their future. Key West was moved by her own passionate rhythms, never tiring of the enduring beat that the spirited Samba played for those who could feel her song.

The intoxicating tempo throbbed on endlessly, enamoring the devoted dancers to follow her captivating lead. Alluringly fresh, Key West would always play an endless rhapsody.

James had settled himself on a tall, ladder back bar stool up on the compact stage at the Green Parrot. Wooden backless stools were scattered throughout the extended room and a long, green fold up table in front of the stage was collapsed, to make room for him. "Thanks for coming out tonight. I have just completed my summer tour at Mallory Square," he said, quietly into the microphone, followed by a contagious chuckle. The crowd rippled with laughter, as some loyal fans related to the camaraderie they held with him in his past, at the Square. Gaining his composure, James screwed up his mouth into a reserved grin and shot a glance over at Morgan, who was sitting high and comfortably at his favorite, tall table. His clear, frosty pitcher of free beer prominently set in the middle and in his hand was a brimming glass of the liquid gold. The foamy, froth overflowed down the sides of it, as he held it high. In a gusty salute, Morgan could stand the wait no more, "Come on, James!" He thrust his glass higher. "Sing us the mermaid song!"

James laughed, "It's not called the mermaid song, but I'll sing it anyway," he joked, as he corrected his ecstatic, confused friend. All stools were packed at the broad, wooden square-shaped bar at the front of the big room, near the open front door and yawning windows. It was standing room only, with the smaller, back bar filled up, too. Some people got unusually quiet, as James began singing his song, "*Under the Sea*".

The message was riddling with mystery and intrigue. Unexpected, several spontaneous faces turned to hear the lyrics of the melody. It continued to hold their attention until he was finished singing. Nothing pleased a small club's crowd more, than to be entertained by a new musician that played his own music with such intimacy. James understood the passion and the depth of inspiration behind each of his songs. The soulful music and heartfelt words came from his very spirit. This was the core of his unique message, not to just entertain, but to awaken the listener's inner-self, provoking deep reflection of their own lives, as seen through his eyes of inspiration and enlightenment.

As the Bahamas fans whirled, the sail-cloth that hung in billows against the ceiling fluttered and ballooned in the light wind. A misty fog laid beneath the luminous glow of the bright track lights that lit up the stage. James concluded his seventh tune and decided to take a break. Thanking the audience, he gracefully excused himself and rested his guitar on its guitar stand. He stepped down off the compact stage and scooted around the standing on-lookers, winding back to Morgan's table. He was amazed at the pretty, young woman sitting with him, on one of the two, elevated chairs.

"Oops! Sorry to interrupt." James stumbled over his words.

"You're not interrupting anything, but a very good perform-ance, Bubba."

"Your music sounded so great," the mysterious lady gushed. "I came in the bar right after you had started playing. Your ocean song made me feel right at home here in Key West. It kind of described my deeper feelings, right now. I wouldn't mind just living and breathing under the sea, like the girl in your song. It has beautiful message. Your music is really different and you really do a great job."

"Thanks. I appreciate your enthusiasm. It seems to be my favorite diversion in life. I don't quite call it a job." She smiled, agreeing with him, as Morgan got up to offer James his seat. "I can't take your seat. Where are you gonna sit?"

"I'll stand."

"Taking your offer, Captain!" He flourished a friendly affirmation to Morgan and climbed upon the stool. Leaning back against the contoured, slatted, ladder-back, he relieved the tension in his shoulders by resting his elbows on the backside of his lofty chair.

"Does playing like that stress you out?" The girl asked, leaning over and studying his sparkling, coffee-bean colored eyes.

"No, I love singing my songs to people. Entertaining is fun. It's the holding my guitar in the same position that seems to tense up my back muscles." He stretched his arms up above his head and then out at each side, relieving the tightness.

"How would a chilled, frosty mug of icy-cold beer taste, right about now, James? That'll relax you."

"Sure, I've got a few more minutes until I gotta get back to my "job" up there," he joked and winked flirtatiously at Morgan's new friend.

"Of course, I have your glass right here waiting for you, as usual, but I'll order the frosty mug, if you prefer." James rolled his eyes at Morgan and shook his head, knowing that he wasn't going to be waiting around for any frosty mug to appear any time, any too soon. Morgan held the glass at a slant, while slowly filling it with the cold brew.

"So, where do you live? Here in town?" James asked, admiring her cute features over the rim of his glass and drinking in the moment.

"Right now I'm staying at the Gardens Hotel, a couple of blocks away from here."

"So you're new to Key West?" She nodded, almost appearing embarrassed.

"Well, one thing I can see, if you ever get out on the water, you'll need to use a lot of sun block to protect the fair skin that you have. The sun can be wicked out there on the water."

"I haven't ever been out on the water here. So, I wouldn't know about that. It is so incredibly beautiful. You must love living down here."

"The water is what it's all about," Morgan interjected, "and James has the sweetest little Boston Whaler on the island, if you would like to see it up close."

"What is a Boston Whaler?" she asked hesitatingly.

"You explain it to her, Morgan, because my break time is up and I need to get back up there and play, again." He set his empty glass on the table. "Thanks for your chair, Captain."

"You better sing more than seven songs this time," he replied, laughing.

"What were you doing? Counting them, you weirdo?" James reeled a bit backwards, shook his head and then added, turning toward their new acquaintance, "Hope to see you again." He paused, than hastily remarked, "Get the Captain to tell you about my boat!" He gave Morgan an approving grin. With that, he turned and headed back up onto the stage.

After the music session was over, Morgan helped James pack up his equipment and drove him home. "I'm beat." James sighed, as he slumped down in the passenger seat of Morgan's car. Taking the weight off his feet, he propped them up on the dash and nuzzled the back of his head against the soft, leather headrest. "Man, this is great. Thanks, Morgan, for all of your help today. I didn't realize how last night's loss of sleep had caught up with me.

"Anytime, my friend, glad I could be of service," he answered, turning the car down Higgs Lane and stopping in front of the dark cottage.

"Thanks, again, Captain. I'm taking you out in my whaler tomorrow. Plan on it! I haven't been out to my best ledges for awhile, and they should be loaded with lobsters. See, old buddy, I'm making it up to you, already. I'm sure we'll catch our limit of crawfish. One dozen tails, between the two of us, and before you know it, we're back at the dock." Suddenly, he hesitated; obvious to Morgan, he was rethinking the girl situation. Contemplative for just an instant, he cheerfully suggested, "She can go, too, if you want to invite our new friend that we met, tonight. Her name? Name? What is her name? You never told me her name."

"She never told me her name. I was just being the nice guy and giving her the seat I was saving for you. She looked lonely, standing by herself, leaning against one of the pool tables. I felt sorry for her and being the sociable guy that I'm known for, I motioned for her to come over and take your seat. So she did."

"You irresistible dog, you, but I'm amazed you drank a pitcher of beer while chatting with the girl and you never even ask her who she was?"

"She wrote her cell phone number on this paper towel, so I'll give it to you," he handed the folded paper to James.

"You want me to call her, since it's my deal, is that it?"

"Yep. You got it, buddy."

"Umm . . . okay. I'll call this number in the morning, but I've got just one last favor to ask of you, Cap. Help me get my stuff out of your car, so I can get some sleep."

Six

James jumped over the three wood-planked, porch steps, easily clearing them, landing on the grass below. Without hesitation, he whipped around, tore back up the stairs and into his house, to catch the telephone on its last ring. He grabbed the cordless from the kitchen counter, "What's up, Cap? I knew it was you," he gasped, as he caught his breath, "I was out in the backyard, putting some extra dive gear into the boat. Why didn't you call me on my cell?"

"Well, I didn't think about it, but I wanted to call and make sure you were up and getting ready to go out in the boat. Also, I was wondering if you called our new friend."

"No, I haven't had a chance. Actually, I just got up twenty minutes ago."

"She might not hang around the hotel all morning. She'll want to get out and see the city sites. So, maybe you should give her a ring now, before she heads out."

"Boy Morgan! You're the anxious one."

"I'm not anxious! I just want to bag some lobster for dinner and was thinking that whoever-she-is, might enjoy Key West, local-style."

"Okay, okay . . . you're right, it would probably be an experience she might not forget. I was just gonna hitch the boat up to the back of my truck, but I'll give her a call first." James held the phone up to his ear while he walked into his bedroom. "I've got the paper towel you gave me right here, on my dresser. I'm unfolding it, as we speak. Ummm, and . . . okay, here it is . . . the numbers are little faint but, readable. Call you back in a few." Click. James purposely rubbed his chin, as he looked down at the phone number. Pensively, he closely studied the legible inscription written neatly upon the soft, paper towel. He lifted it to his nose and inhaled. A slight, *frangipani* flower fragrance filled his nostrils. *Ummm . . . Key West Fragrances.* He recognized the smell as a locally-bottled perfume. *She got the best perfume in town.* He smiled. *She must be a snow bird that knows where to seriously shop.* Curiously, he held the towel up to his nose again and sniffed in the recognizable scent. *Well, she picked a good one. Smells like the red flower, not the pink, white or yellow.*

This phone number just seems so familiar. I know this phone number from somewhere. It's a number I've heard before, he thought. "Heard recently, as a matter of fact!" he cried aloud, as he suddenly bolted over his squishy waterbed and smashed down the button on the message machine. Screeching back past previous messages, he then, fast-forwarded to the very one he

"Hello. Hello. Is anybody there? Is this the Island Hop Taxi Service? I desperately need a taxi to come to the Key West Airport to take me to my hotel. My cell number is 757-300-0077. I hope you are open and get my message. Please call me back. Thank You. Click.

"What the heck! Man! I knew that double 07 rang a bell," he mumbled to himself. "I can't believe this is happening. Why, Morgan do you have get so extremely inebriated?" He dialed him back. Morgan answered, "Yea, what happened? She's busy, right?" James cleared his throat, "I don't know if she's busy or not. A weird thing is happening, right now." Morgan chortled, "That's nothing new." James, frustrated, qualified the statement, "I'm not sure how to explain this and make it clear, but the reason I didn't get my sleep, the night before last, was because of the girl you had sitting-pretty with you, at the Green Parrot, last night."

"James, if you only met her last night for the first time, that sure doesn't make any sense." Morgan, thoughtfully puzzled, added, "Unless there's something you're not telling me."

"Well, there is something I didn't tell you before, but I'm telling you now, because it wasn't that important to me at the time. Except for the major fact, that I lost a bunch of sleep."

"Are you sure you want to share this, James? You don't owe me any explanations. But I have to say, I'm a little shocked that you both did such an excellent job of pretending not to know each other. I guess I should have counted on something screwing up the situation, when we both decided to take the same chick out, at the same time."

"No! No man, you're the one who's got this all screwed up. Listen, I didn't know her at all before last night. I never saw her in my life, until I saw her with you at your table." James let out a big sigh, and then continued, "What happened was this . . . this lady was stranded at the airport in the middle of the night, after her plane landed and she needed a ride to her hotel. She kept calling me, thinking I was that stupid, Island cab company with the flamingo-colored taxis that went out of business. My new phone number is their old one. She must've got a hold of an old phone book at the airport and found my number in there, thinking she was reaching them to send a taxi. Finally, she left a desperate message on my message machine, for a taxi to come get her, leaving no name, but just her cell number. But, the worse part is, after hearing her problem, I made the decision not to help her, thinking she'd figure something out. I knew, somehow, she would get a ride, be rescued and that would be the absolute end of it. Wrong! Can you believe it? Her cell number that she left on her message is the same one as the number she wrote down for you on the paper towel. I feel like a total jerk. There I was, last night, singing to her, drinking with her, joking, laughing and flirting with her and now, today, arranging to take her out in my boat and teach her how to dive for crawfish."

Morgan gleefully seized this opportune moment, "See James, I told you I could count on something to screw things up, and you are, 'the something'!"

James was silent for about three seconds. Crestfallen, he fervently retorted, "Okay, Morgan, you made your point and I know you're thinking you're the righteous and noble one, right about now, but can you possibly understand, that I'm probably, going to feel a little guilty and maybe, even a bit convicted to confess this whole thing to her? That is, if she really wants to go out in the boat with us, today." His voice deflated and trailed off painfully.

"Hey, James, cheer up. No worries, shipmate! I heard they're hiring full time workers at the Welcome Station, here in Key West and greeters at the Key West Airport. You know, handing flowers out to the arriving tourists, except, you probably wouldn't want to work the night shift. Or maybe you could run a taxi service. One, of course, that doesn't do night calls. Or, I can see you with a rescue service helping deserted damsels in distress, particularly, those left marooned on a dark island. That would be your specialty." Morgan laughed harder with each imaginary scenario.

"I'm glad you're getting such a kick out of this, Morgan. You're a real riot, encouraging, too. For a second there, I thought you were making fun of me." He assertively bit his lower lip, heaved a resigning groan then asked Morgan, sarcastically, "Now tell me again, how bad you want fresh-caught crawfish for dinner?"

"Okay, you've made your case, but you know I'm just joking. You need to get over this whole, dumb deal and move on." Morgan snickered, "Oh, by the way, when you get her on the phone, how about asking her what her name is. It sure would be nice to know, who the heck, we're both taking out."

"Alright. Meet me at Carmalita's in thirty minutes and I'll tell you what's up."

"See you there with all my gear." Click. James closed his eyes, took a deep breath, and reached for the telephone.

Seven

Carmalita's was closed in the morning for a family funeral. Sad, Morgan drove over to another favorite eatery and patiently, waited for James, leaning against his mom's car. He had parked directly across the street from the Sapodilla Lounge. There, in front of this old, struggling landmark, grew a giant, ageless sapodilla tree. It cast wide-spreading and far-reaching shadows, below its enormous, green, leafy branches. The deep, breezy shade that swallowed up Morgan's car enveloped much of the short, narrow, unpaved road, meandering through the sleepy neighborhood. Threading past the Sapodilla Lounge, the road was pleasantly sheltered from the scorching sun.

The expansive shade provided cooling relief for both man and creatures alike. Lazy Conch dogs, with their short, black furry coats, sometimes bothered raising their characteristic gold eyebrows and cropped, pointed ears to passersby, as they sprawled and slept on the dappled, shady street, under the massive tree. Far-reaching in all directions, the invasive limbs furnished more than deep, cool shade. In a few months, golden brown, sugary sapodillas, the size of tangerines, would be ripe for picking. Making their showing in early January, the small, fuzzy fruits would grow browner, sweeter and softer, by the day. The old Sapodilla Lounge had rested lazily under the ancient tree for many years. Overhanging boughs served as a natural canopy, for the open-air commons. Built in the late thirties, following war-torn years, it gave the Navy sailors, stationed in Key West at that time, an offering of fresh air and fresh fish to eat. Many hurricanes had pounded her structure into a weakened and dilapidated state, but the old building never doubted herself and fiercely embraced her ground, ever-attempting to hold her feeble, head up high. She still, proudly, presented a variety of favorites to the faithful few that still darkened her door regularly. And the squeak of that same screen door, continually brought music to the ears of the elder and portly, Cecilia Medina. She bubbled a zealous greeting to each visiting customer, while her smiling salutes sang throughout the friendly cantina and streamed out the windows, to invite others to come in and join her.

The Sapodilla's gaudy, turquoise, wooden walls and her shutters of the yellowiest of yellows, shouted "notice me" to all who passed, by her way. But, sorrowfully, the shrill party whoops, that once were heard nightly, had died to a whisper years ago. The lusty nightlife had vanished and seemingly, washed out to sea. In those days, as the golden sun melted into the deep, green Atlantic Ocean each evening, the iced-down, Cuban beer was as plentiful as the hot, golden-fried conch fritters dripping in fresh-squeezed Key Lime juice, that the young Cecilia Medina once served. But now, only the locals dribbled in, to sample the everyday staples, along with ordinary, domestic beers and never seemed to tire of listening to the ancient stories the aged-proprietor told of the wealthy pleasure-seekers in Key West long ago. Cecilia winked a brown, wrinkled eyelid, when she described how the patronizing elite gathered to hide away at the Sapodilla, from publicity and prying eyes. Imbibing, incognito, drinking their choice Cuban beers and smoking fine Cuban cigars—the privileged could be found—sitting and frolicking about the brightly-covered outdoor tables scattered under the ancient tree. They shared their sordid secrets as they puffed away, ladies and gentlemen alike. The great tree's majestic, black-barked trunk towered above their heads, witnessing everything that was said or done.

Since, those days-gone-by, tales have been heavily veiled by the ageless hands of the immortal, "Old Man Time" and laid to rest. Pressing on, unyieldingly, hour by hour and in no way loosing a minute or having a second to spare, he persevered and took the underground plans of lawless proposals, laced with unspoken influences and intertwined them with twisted, political tactics, burying them deeply beneath the big sapodilla's black, twisted roots forever, never to surface, again. Old Man Time marched on before and he marches on still, without a single stop. And, as for the sapodilla tree's best-kept secrets, that's what they shall always be.

Morgan's curiosity about the place went only as far, as his concern for the sapodillas that might happen to fall off the branches and hit his car. He climbed up on the hood to check it out. Satisfied there was no ripened, sugary sapodillas on the loose; he peeked inside one of the pub's open-air casements. The bright, morning sun poured through the large, front windows. Paths of golden light spilt over the worn, polished, planked floor. *Man, those men must be hot in there.* He noticed four men dressed in business suits. *Who would wear clothes like that to the Sapodilla Lounge?* He glanced down the road, searching for James, knowing it was heating up out on the water. Again, from his high perch, he continued to study the four men leaning over the bar. The Bahamas fans were rotating at high speed, as they tried extra hard to stir the motionless air of the sun-lit lounge. The men seemed preoccupied with something black, sitting in the middle of a table, positioned at the back of the lounge. He hoped they wouldn't discover him staring in through the window at them, huddled close together. He observed that they appeared to be intently interested in an open leather satchel.

Morgan jumped down to the ground, as he saw them close it up and walk toward the screen door. *Well, guess I must be really bored, if I'm all alone, entertaining myself, by standing on top of my car, spying in windows and snooping on people I don't even know.* He opened his car door and hopped inside. Starting the engine, he flipped the air conditioner on high and then, fumbled around under the passenger seat, until he retrieved the cover of James's new CD. He removed the silver disc and placed it into the car's player, as he observed the backs of the four men in the dark suits, walking with a vigorous step down the side of the narrow, shady street. A short guy, wearing a black, flannel hat, carried the briefcase. The small group finally stopped and climbed into a black, four-door, Mercedes sedan, sitting just a bit more than a stone's throw away from Morgan. The driver had carelessly parked in the flowerbed of someone's yard. *Out of state tag. It figures. They sure look overheated and out-of-place. Guess they don't know how brisk the towing business is here, in Key West.*

Turning down the volume of the music, Morgan waved as James pulled up close beside him in his Ford truck. The boat was following behind, on its small trailer.

"Got your message about the funeral. Wonder if it's for

someone we might know?" James asked, shrugging his bare shoulders. Then, reaching over, he lifted his shirt up off the truck seat and slipped it on over his head. "Been waitin' here long?"

"Long enough to spy on the darker customers of the Sapodilla Lounge."

"You really need to get a life, Meredith." James squinted his dove-brown eyes through his long, black lashes, and peeked over the top of his dark, polarized sunglasses, scrutinizing his friend closely. Morgan ignored him.

"Well, I'm sorry it took so long. I got to talking to Amber and time just got away from me." James rubbed the end of his nose with his hand, to conceal a mischievous smile.

"Amber, is it?"

"Yep. That's the young lady's name. Amber Albury. Like it? It kind of goes with her auburn-colored hair, don't you think?"

"Well, I haven't had too much time to think about it or her hair, like you have, James. But, now that you mention it, her hair did seem to shine with an amber color, under the lights of the bar, last night. Did you inform her that there was an Albury Street here in Cayo Hueso named after the famous, old Albury family? And, that they are at least, fifth-generation Conchs from the Bahamas?"

"No, I never thought of that, but I'll save that one for you to tell her. We're supposed to meet her at the Gardens Hotel in about a half hour." He glanced at his diving watch.

"I can see I'm going to be the third wheel, today."

"What? Are you serious? You can forget that garbage. I'm not getting involved in any serious relationship right now. I've got far too much going on in my life. A lot more than I'd like, actually. As simple as it might seem to other people, my days are plenty full. She's all yours, Captain! As beautiful as she is and as sweet as she seems, I'm passing on this one. And besides, she might not think we're so great and wonderful, by the time the day is over."

"Speak for yourself." Morgan pulled down the car visor to admire his lengthy, light-blond hair in the mirror. James leaned out his window, trying to catch a glimpse of him in the mirror.

"It's useless, Cap," James quipped, turning his eyes heavenward.

Morgan laughed in reply, "Think so, huh? We'll see, man. You know, I'm the chick-magnet of this town and . . . "

James interrupted and snapped back, "Do you mean chicken-magnet of this town?"

Morgan flipped the visor back up, retorting, "Come on, bozo, we better get going. We can grab something to eat on the way to the boat ramp. Too bad, Camalita's is closed today for a family funeral."

"Yeah, when I saw you sittin' over here under the sapodilla tree, I figured you probably didn't want to eat breakfast in the Lounge. Suits me just fine. Too slow service, dished out with too many stories, for me, this morning. I drove by just to read the sign on the front of the door at Carmalita's. I was a little curious, since they're rarely ever closed. You can leave your mom's car at the Gardens. It'll be safe there. He pointed at the car, "Maybe one day, I'll buy a BMW, midnight blue, just like that one and I'll chauffeur you around for a change, Captain."

"Chicks dig your truck, James. It's just finding room to sit among the guitars, amps and diving gear."

"Yeah, you're right, man. I plan on decluttering the front of my truck, soon." He slammed the gear shift in park and leapt out of the truck. "I forgot you're riding with me. Might as well, start now!" He began hauling out music amps, speakers, microphones and a bunch of diving gear off the long, pleated, leather cab seat. Lifting the truck-topper, back-window and lowering the tailgate against the trailer winch-post, he deftly squeezed all the stuff into the back of his truck. "Well, that should do it!" He slammed the tailgate closed. "Let's get going."

"Good job, old man. I think even I can fit in there, now."

"I sure as heck hope so! You may be over six feet tall, Captain, but you're just about ready to turn thirty pretty doggone soon, and when you do, I will still be twenty-eight." He smirked and climbed back into the truck. "There are a lot of advantages in being younger sometimes," he smiled a sideways grin at Morgan, as he shut his truck door, "and shorter, too."

"Except when it comes to bar bouncers. Or have you forgotten how they use to drag you out of the bars in Old Town when you were under twenty one. I guess you can't forget the night you scaled two roof tops and leaped across a balcony in a single bound, to sneak into Ricky's dance club. Two body-building-bouncers drug you out, while the band played on. One had you in a pretty hard headlock."

"Yeah, well I went limp and told him I wasn't fighting and that I could walk. The fat sucker believed me and I slipped out of his grip, as soon, as we hit the door." He paused in reflection. "Man, was I ever embarrassed in front of those older girls we were with. I'll never forget that. And I never went back there again, either. I didn't need that scene in my life. It wasn't worth any of the stress I put on myself or my job."

"Well, sorry I brought the painful memory up. Hard to believe that it's been almost a decade, since I met you. You were clicking off the remainder of your service time, to the second, on your dive watch, as I recall. Stationed here in the Coast Guard, living on your sailboat at Boca Chica, would be only a dream for some people. I was home on spring break from college in Gainesville. You had just turned twenty in April and I was, of course, the older man that passed with the legal age of twenty one." He noticed, at this point, James was yawning extremely loud, while dramatically, pointing at his watch. "Okay, I can see I'm boring you. I'll follow you over there. Let's see if Amber falls in love with the Lakes, today."

"Is that where you want to go? Not the reef?"

"Nah, lets save that for a calmer day. It'll pound her too much getting out to the Sandbos, or anywhere else on the ocean side, for that matter. It's supposed to blow ten knots and gusting to fifteen this afternoon, with three-foot seas. Besides, I brought my boat grill to cook some small steak tenderloins and baking potatoes for lunch. Not to mention, the best red wine my mom had in the fridge, cooling for who-knows-who."

"For us, of course!" James responded, with enthusiasm and feeling quite motivated, he motioned for him to follow. "Sounds good to me—right now. I'm starving!" He shifted the truck into first gear, his Boston Whaler trailing behind.

Eight

The narrow sidewalk was soaked with washed shades of grey, resembling the final brush stroke across a wet, cement canvas. Sprinkles, left over from an early morning shower, took their turn, falling from the heavy banyan-tree leaves, drip-dropping onto Morgan's head, as he stood on the damp walk. The soft, gentle, rain drops offered a refreshing reprieve from the early November heat. He waited anxiously in the humid surroundings while James parked his pickup and boat, up the road on Angela Street.

"Hey, I parked my mom's car under the tree above us, on the other side of this wall," Morgan called to James, as he joined him in the cool shade.

"So?" James responded, feigning distraction.

"Think it will be alright parked there?" Morgan continued to fret, his brow creasing with worry, as he pointed to the drooping branches overhanging their heads.

"Yeah, it should be okay, I guess," he responded, but thoughtfully, paused, "covered with bird crap when you get back, but it should be fine." His mouth turned up at the corners, as he took special delight in taunting Morgan.

Morgan backhanded James's broad shoulder, then shaking off the self-inflicted sting that he was feeling in the ends of his fingers, he sourly retorted, "Thanks for your insight. I forgot about your expertise on those types of things," he bit his bottom lip, trying not to show the pain he was experiencing. He tossed his silky, blond hair out of his blue eyes, watching James's brown eyes, clearly dancing with amusement.

"Don't mention it," James mumbled, as they headed toward the hotel.

"Now, Amber? Didn't you say she would be out by the pool?" Morgan gingerly inquired, changing the annoying subject. "Follow me, James," he sneered.

They wandered through the front entrance of the Gardens Hotel winding their way outside. They followed a crooked path of white seashell-shaped stepping stones that wrapped through the lush, tropical vegetation, leading to the pool area.

"Did you get her room number when you talked to her?" Morgan asked, turning his head from side to side, searching the deck chairs. "I don't see her out here waiting for us."

"She can't be too far," James hesitated, "wait," he directed Morgan's attention, "isn't that her sitting there beside that big, yellow, hibiscus bush?" In the distance they could see her petite figure, delicately defined by her distinctive silhouette.

"Yea, that's her. Come on."

"Looks like she's talking on her cell phone," Morgan observed.

They walked around to the other side of the glittery, sunny pool, passing an inviting white-latticed gazebo. As the two of them drew nearer to her, they overheard Amber speaking in an excited voice. She was sitting in a brightly-flowered, cushioned chair with her slender, graceful back facing them. Her shapely legs were draped across another cushioned chaise and opposite of her was the old, historical, Cuban cigar-maker's cottage. James put his hand out to hold Morgan back from advancing any closer, realizing she was unaware they were coming up behind her. He then motioned him to be still, so as not to interrupt her private conversation. With the best intentions of appearing to be polite, helplessly, they stood as silent statues, growing more curious, by the second, as they listened to her exchange.

"Yes, Colonel, you are right," Amber cooed into her phone. "I am definitely trying a new thing here in Key West. Aside from getting stranded at the airport for almost the whole night when I arrived, and learning my lesson about the nighttime taxi service in these parts, everything seems to be just what the doctor ordered for me. Actually, I'm even going diving today, or snorkeling is a better word for it. Some new friends I met at a local pub are taking me out in their boat." Pause. "I know . . . I know . . . I just got here. I will be cautious." A long pause. "Yes, I will call you or Marsha each week, I promise." Another pause. "I know . . . I know . . . You are right, Colonel Benson, about my grieving time being a lonely time. I know I could be an easy target."

Morgan threw his head back, with his long, sun-streaked tresses flying, trying to hold back his laughter at her suggestion. James jabbed him in the side with his elbow and put his finger to his lips to shush him up.

Amber continued. "Your calls do help me so much, Colonel. I appreciate you and Marsha watching over me. With no family to help me, it is hard to grieve Peter's loss, alone. God has assigned His angels to work overtime, watching out for me, too."

James raised his dark, expressive eye brows and glanced over at Morgan. They stood stone still, feeling a tinge of guilt for eavesdropping on her private conversation. Morgan motioned for them to pull away and step back toward the gazebo. James hesitated, still interested in what she was saying.

"I hope Marsha will enjoy Williamsburg as much as you do and I once did. Iraq can wait a little longer. There is too much danger for her there, at this time and I'm glad her leave-of-absence can be extended. Under the trying circumstances and all the duress of her stressful, overseas field-work, she deserves a break." Pause. "At the Gardens Hotel," she answered. She listened closely, and then nodded her head. "Yes, I will call you, as soon as I have my new address. I only hope I can find a house for a decent price here in Key West. The hurricanes have helped the prices come down a little and there are plenty of homes on the market, so that's good for me. Then, you and Marsha must come and stay sometime."

James realized she was ending her call. Silently, he signaled Morgan to walk back toward the pool.

"Talk to you soon, and please give my best to Marsha. Thank you for calling. Bye-bye." Her voice trailed off. She sat motionless. Pensively, she stared across the lawn at the puddles on the Cuban-tile pathway sprawling before her. Vibrant flowers with hues of glowing-pinks and neon-oranges, entwined themselves, to make a vigorous hedge, lining the twisting, natural corridor. In the distance she heard the gushing tripled-tiered fountain spilling with flowing water. Her mind journeyed back to a past time. For an instant, she pictured herself zipping around the tight curves of the Blue Ridge Park Way on her annual October birthday trip to the colorful, tree-covered mountains of Virginia.

Snuggled up to Peter in their small burgundy sports car, she felt happy and settled for the rest of her life. They had wished the yellow, orange and red leaves would never fall off of the trees. Then perhaps, their ride could last forever. She saw his face, smiling lovingly down upon her, as they wound their way up and around the next mountain and on up the next steep incline, each memorable view seeming more spectacular than the last.

Autum would always be her favorite time of year. Amber heaved a heavy sigh, stretched her willowy arms high above her head, and dreamily snatched at something imaginary that only she could see, floating in the sky. Tipping her long, burnished brown locks backward, she shook them care-freely over her fair-skinned shoulders. The ambiance of the gardens filled her heart to overflowing. A peaceful aura streamed over her cameo-shaped face, saturating her soul with unfathomable hope. Amber stood up, slowly turned and walked, as if on air, toward the swimming pool.

"Hey," she called, catching a glimpse of her two, new friends, relaxing and sitting on the side of the pool. Their feet trailed lazily in the sparkling, sun-lit water. "Been waiting long? I'm sorry I was not out here, like I said I would be." Her coral lips expanded into a glistening, white smile. She casually dropped her tiny phone into the side pocket of her fawn-colored shorts. Her lavender bathing suit top was edged with forest-green lace around the borders and along each thin strap, giving away her taste for Victorian colors.

"We just got here a bit ago," James beamed nervously.

"Well, it wouldn't have been hard to find you, since there's no one else outside here but you," Morgan piped. Realizing what he said, he saw James's big brown eyes widen and look up at him. So, flashing a wide exaggerated grin, he redirected his careless banter, "Hey, I love the landscaping they've done here, don't you?"

Amber looked around, thoughtfully. "Yes. It's breathtakingly beautiful. I love it here," she agreed, her jade-green eyes twinkling. Feeling as if she just found the door at the end of a long tunnel, Amber breathed in the crisp morning air, "Yes, yes! It is incredibly beautiful here. It's practically intoxicating!"

Affirming her statement with a nod and a smile, they studied her angelic countenance. Morgan then broke the awkward silence, with a glint in his eyes, "Well, that's a subject I could tell you about!" Morgan joked. "Are you ready to dive in the ocean and catch a spiny lobster?" Amber's reply bubbled over with high expectation, "I can't wait to meet the ocean or a thorny lobster!"

"Well, get your stuff and let's get going. We gotta hurry and get out there." James exclaimed. "All the big lobsters could be lined up in a crawl, as I speak!"

They drove down Truman Avenue towards the Garrison Bight boat ramp. Amber was sitting in the middle, between the two guys, on the wide, leather truck-seat. The disc player was playing a soft, Samba rhythm. James flipped it to a faster beat.

"I like your music, James. Can we hear some?" she inquired.

"We haven't eaten yet, have you?" James asked, as he handed his newest recording to Amber to play.

"I have, but I could go for some coffee. How about that Burger King up there?" she pointed up ahead.

"Yeah, that sounds really good," Morgan approved. "I'm starving."

"Let's pull in. I need a cup of coffee right away," James gasped while holding out his trembling hand as a joke, to make his point.

"We'll get the food to go, if it's alright with you guys," Morgan said, "so we can get the boat launched before other boats and trailers show up at the ramp. It can get really congested over there."

"Yeah, sure, let's just go through the drive-through and eat in the skiff, as we motor our way out the channel," James fired back, "but the coffee, that's another matter. We drink that now!"

After a small delay at the Garrison Bight boat ramp waiting for a couple of early morning fishermen to launch their boats, they were soon motoring out of the deep channel. While wolfing down their breakfast and becoming more informative with each sip of their king-size coffees, James and Morgan indicated different points of interest to Amber, that passed by on the shoreline. Amber huddled on her seat taking it all in with x-ray vision. Under the protective refuge of the teal-colored canvas, Bimini sun top, she absentmindedly smeared a thick layer of sun block lotion all over her arms, recalling James's serious warning to her at the Green Parrot. She was captivated by the pristine, white, frothy foam of the boat's wake flying and spraying up behind them as they cut through the emerald-green saltwater. Amber studied the transparent surface that mirrored the golden sun. Immeasurable shimmers of glinting lights sparkled brilliantly like scattered diamonds over the endless, bottle-green sea. This was a day she would want to remember, she thought. Her heart pounded with excitement as their little boat rose and fell on the choppy, untiring waves.

Morgan glanced back at her from his shifty perch on the bow, and shouted over the engine, "How do you like it so far?"

"I love it! Can we go faster?"

James face radiated, as his smiling brown eyes shown in the soft light that filtered through the dark lenses of his shades. He pushed the gear shift down and gunned the outboard into high gear, shouting, "I'll see what I can do!"

Nine

"What are the names of these different islands we're going by?" Amber called over the whine of the outboard motor. She pointed toward the three green isles stretched out like a napping cat, resting lazily in Key West Harbor, under the bright sun.

"The first big one we passed coming out the harbor was Fleming Key. Only military personal are permitted on that island. Everything is kept top secret at that place. I'm not sure if even our own CIA can get in there," James scoffed.

"This island is Tank Island, on the left," he pointed to the built-up formation of priceless real estate. "At one time, it was really barren, but now the island has been developed and is home to the affluently rich and famous. The other one is called Christmas Tree Island, because it was once covered with Australian pine trees that resembled a solid grove of Christmas trees. The whispering pines you see growing there now, were in the past, much denser. Back in the day, as my dad says about any time period that goes back more than a decade ago, the government wanted to get rid of all the trees because they were not native to Monroe County, but it didn't exactly work out, as you can see. They did, unfortunately, succeed in removing them up the Keys, on the shoreline at Bahia Honda State Park. My mom said several feral cats and their kittens lost their boroughs in the old hollowed out trunks, when the tree assassins attacked. She liked going over to the park to paint pictures of the raccoons, on driftwood planks. They lived up in the old whispering pines. It made her really sad to see how barren and hot the beach became after the tall, shade trees were destroyed," James commiserated.

Soon, the three islands were fading in the distance, leaving them behind. The calm water stirred and rippled as the refreshing northeast breeze kicked up a bit. The breezy air blew a cool caress against their warm faces. James gripped the steering wheel securely as the boat skimmed over the washboard-like surface. Amber braced her feet up on a bulky cooler sitting in front of her. Suddenly she felt her wide brimmed sun-hat being lifted off her head. With both hands she snugged it down tightly over her ears, surprised by the forceful gust of wind.

"Yep!" Morgan called back to Amber, who was sitting staunchly on her seat, pulling the sides of her hat down, hoping the wind wouldn't catch her unaware again. "Back in the day, as James calls it, a bunch of hippies—as thick as the pines—lived and did some partying on that island," he declared, excitedly brandishing his bronze-tanned arm back in the direction of Christmas Tree Island. His brawny back glistened with fragrant, tropical coconut oil, reminding Amber of the perfectly-sculpted man embracing a flawlessly beautiful lady with his strong, muscular arms, on the cover of the romance paperback novel she had found in her room the night before. She enjoyed scrutinizing Morgan, as he motioned to the port and starboard sides of the small boat, with his big, expressive hands.

"They were happily gathered on the island's high-ground,

living in tents and driftwood shacks. They even had picnic tables down on the beach, and rumors were flying that a lot of them were growing small yields of the green stuff out on outer, more remote islands. But, of course, those were just rumors! Hippies that lived on the island either wore clothes or didn't wear clothes. It was optional, and they believed in 'it's all good' . . . all the time." Morgan chuckled, but then he gave Amber a quick warning that the waves were going to escalate and become quite bumpy, as they crossed the Middle Ground, leaving Key West Harbor's protected water and the shelter of the mangrove islands.

"When my dad went out diving almost daily, or to work as he called it, in the Lakes, he'd usually see something bizarre going on, as he passed by Christmas Tree Island," James chimed in. "Once he and his diving buddy, Waldo, were frantically, flagged down by an extremely distressed hippie-chick, standing in ankle-deep water off Christmas Tree Island. They got really concerned when they spotted her waving at them, so they thought they should help her out. They got in, as close, as they dared without running aground in the shallow water, and hollered for her to wade on out to the skiff. And she did."

"The water got deeper and deeper, the closer she got to their boat, yet never much past her knees, but this didn't stop her from hiking up her dress higher and higher. Eventually, as she neared the boat, with the water still remaining only slightly above her knees, the hem of her dress had passed over her thighs and continued up passed her waist, until finally she held her gathered dress up around her neck. Shocked to see this strange, loose, unembarrassed woman walking naked—except for her neck of course—out to their boat, they both wondered what they had gotten themselves into. Dad and Waldo tried not to stare or look at her, embarrassed for the woman. Finally, after waiting patiently and wishing they had never responded to her beckoning, they pulled her over the side and on board the boat."

"What was her problem?" Amber furled her soft, arched eyebrows, growing suspicious of the lady's wiliness. Lowering her sunglasses, she studied James's face inquisitively. She wondered what his dad was really like and asked, "Did she get the help she needed or was she tricking them?"

"Yep! They helped her alright, but only to my mom's dismay and Waldo's wife's disbelief. My dad, of course, made sure that both wives appreciated the fact that he had ordered her to pull her dress down and leave it pulled down as she neared the boat and before they would allow her into the skiff. She complied willingly, and they got her aboard, and delivered her to shore in Key West, where she wanted to go. Waldo confirmed Dad's story. They alleged they were 'helpless' and the situation was a 'you know how it is' problem."

"Dad claimed she was a poor lost soul who really did need a helping hand. Of course, my mom didn't see it that way at all, but my dad assured her that this hippie-girl was not at all attractive and was a dirty, bedraggled mess. Waldo claimed she wasn't the least bit bothered by having salty, sandy seaweed matted in her unwashed, stringy hair. Her trendy, hairy legs didn't impress Dad or Waldo, but she convinced them both, before they off-loaded her near the Front Street boat ramp, that she was considered above 'star status' on Christmas Tree Island."

"Well, I have to say, I can understand, why your mom was put out with Waldo and your dad, too. I've heard it was pretty loose down here back then," Amber commented, wistfully.

James leaned over the steering console, so he could hear what she had to say. Agreeing, Morgan and he nodded their heads, but James interjected, "Things change every day here in Key West, that's the most constant thing about her." He turned the skiff in a circle, taking note of the changing sea-bottom, and then pointed the bow out again, maintaining their same course and continuing with his story.

"The drug-runners smuggled pot into the Keys by boat, as if it was just a load of crawfish. Some of the 'Flower Children' in Key West considered Columbian Gold too expensive, but very 'far out, man,' if they could get a hold of a twenty-five dollar baggie of lower grade stuff, tied off with a rusty-wire twisty. And some of those poor hippies, who couldn't afford anything just grew homegrown weed back on a mangrove island somewhere. My parents claim pot was as abundant, as coconuts. Sometimes, abandoned bails of it, wrapped in big, black garbage bags, floated around here on the tide. Which reminds me of a different time my dad took part in another gallant rescue. Do you want to hear it?" He politely called to Amber over the motor's noisy roar. "I don't want to bore you all."

Morgan blurted out, "Oh, come on, James, go ahead and tell it. You know you have a captive audience! Where are we gonna go?"

Amber grinned, the sun was lighting up her pale face, as she motioned with her graceful hands for him to continue. Her peachy, polished fingernails glistened in the sunlight like shiny seashells.

"Alright then," he began. "This unexpected occasion happened in the day of really authentic hippies, not wannabees, like today. My father rescued two, car loads full of hippie guys and hippie girls off a beach, by the old, but very much used, Bahia Honda bridge, in his hand-brushed and hand-painted, nineteen-fifty-four, Easter-egg-purple Buick sedan. The cops had discovered the group down on the beach and warned all of them that they had less than one hour to break it up and get off the beach. So, they took the time to bury their valuables in the sand and then aimlessly headed up the embankment onto U. S. One, hoping somehow to hitch a ride. Back then, it was legal to hitchhike in Monroe County, so this was not a problem. But the group was very large and that happened to present a big problem. There they all were, lined up on the highway, anxiously thumbing a ride in the pitch of night, when my dad came driving across the dilapidated bridge, returning from seeing a movie in Marathon. My mom was out of town and he was bored, so he had spent the evening in town doing dinner and a movie. He couldn't help but see the throng in his car's headlights, there were so many dang hippies! Without a second thought, he stopped to see what they were doing out there on the road.

When they explained their plight to Dad, he saw their urgency, felt compassion for the group and told them they could all jump in the car and come spend the night at his house on Big Pine Key. They whooped with joy, ran back down through the darkness to the beach, and dug up whatever they were hiding. But it ended up, Dad didn't have room in his purple Buick for everyone. He realized, he would have to hurry and make two trips. One half would go on the first trip and then, he would get back quickly to rescue the rest of them and drive them safely to his place.

He said there were, at least, twenty hippies needing help and standing out there on U.S. One. When he finally got them all to his small house on the Avenues, he told the whole group to make themselves at home. But, he informed each one, that he had to get up very early and go diving off of Key West the next morning. All that he asked of them was to please be gone when he returned that next evening, clean up before leaving and not use his bedroom for any reason. His bedroom was off-limits! He explained that his wife would be arriving home that evening. In addition to those requests, he told them that when they left the house, not to bother locking the door because there wasn't a key." He paused and exclaimed, "Two weird things happened from that particular rescue. The first thing that happened was when my mom returned home that night. She climbed into their king-size bed and discovered the sheets were covered with beach sand. That's when my dad knew the hippies hadn't bothered obeying his bedroom rule, and that he needed to tell Mom about his unexpected house guests. And the second weird thing that happened was about an eon later after my dad rescued those grateful hippies. Through an unusual course of events, one of those hippie-guys ended up later becoming his good friend."

Morgan reacted, "I never heard that story before. How did he meet the guy after all that time passed?"

James studied Morgan's eager face and Amber's intense expression, amazed that they both were so interested in his dad's past exploits. She riveted her attention on James, while tipping her paper cup and draining the last drop of the sweet, creamy coffee. Swiveled around on the white boat cushion, she sat sideways, facing James, not wanting to miss a word. She held her delicate hand up over her eyes, making a shade-visor above her rosy face, as he told the story.

James continued on, "In an evening discussion many years later, when my dad had a group of friends over for dinner, this older man, named Ben, was visiting at our house. He was in another room, other than where my dad was sitting, telling someone about the time he got rescued many years ago, by this guy with an old purple Buick in the Keys. This grabbed my dad's attention, as he heard him expounding about the incident. From where my dad was sitting at the dining room table, he somehow, overheard Ben's conversation coming from the living room. He tuned in as he heard Ben colorfully describing how one dark night back in the day, he was hitchhiking through the Keys. While out on a beach, partying with a bunch of hippies, he was almost arrested and ordered by the cops to vacate the beach. When out of nowhere, God sent His angel to rescue him and his nomadic companions. This man drove two separate trips, taking them all to his little house on Big Pine Key. That's when I remember my dad shouting, 'I'm the angel who picked you up and brought you to my house!' The man went into a big shock. They were both in shock! Dad even remembered what Ben, who was known to young, fellow-hippies as the Doc, was wearing that night. A sandy, faded Army jacket! Ben laughed, agreeing that he remembered right and realized he had made quite an impression on my dad. Out of the entire horde of hippies, my dad remembered just Ben. Both young men had gone on from that eventful night with their complicated lives, raising their families and later on, many years later down the road, they miraculously found each other again and became Christian friends, never realizing until that moment, they had known each other before, in another time."

Morgan looked hard at James and asked, "What other exciting things did your dad do? Like I said, I never heard that one, before."

Amber quipped, "I'll bet he has lots of good old Key's stories. He ought to write a book. I'd buy it. It would be fun to meet your dad and mom!"

James laughed and spouted, "Yeah, they're a trip. They enjoyed the Keys when hitchhiking wasn't outlawed, like it is now. It was a poor man's paradise and transients without much money, flooded in here, especially in the wintertime and slept anywhere they could find a safe spot. Under bridges was a favorite freebee.

A fisherman could actually make a living in those days, too. Nowadays, the fishing laws are passed fast and furiously and often, without enough research. Combined with inadequate knowledge about the fishing industry, the new laws put many fishermen in the poor house. Even now, one radical group, wants to ban catching fish altogether. They think of all the fish, as little friends and want to stop all fishing in the Keys. Many local fish houses have gone out of business every year, because of more and more enforced regulations. There are only a few of them left. Someday, the local-color of the Florida Keys fish houses will just be history."

Morgan broke in above the roaring engine, "Transients poured into the Keys, back in the day," he shot an approving glance at James. "They arrived from everywhere. Old broken down step vans, painted with psychedelic colors parked just about anywhere, on any island, for a quick shelter. Hippie communes and nude beaches were the "happening" thing back then. Traditional, old fashioned families were shy of the hippie movement. If you were married and a young parent, you felt like some kind of alien down here, was what my mom told me. Names like Rainbow and Hummingbird were cool. Dosing on pink sunshine was a badge of honor for some who insisted that "tripping" was "groovy." My mom met a young hippie-mom living on Stock Island at a crapped-out trailer park, who smoked grass with her kids, after they got off the school bus. The mother thought it was all good, but my mother got freaked out. My parents, both opposed the free lifestyle that saturated the Keys back then, but they also told me that the hippies who wanted so much to be the "free-spirits," back in the so-called day, usually burned out or joined the establishment's rat-race, eventually, anyway. Even at my young age and growing up here in Key West, I realize this island will always draw different people down to check it out. Some will stay and some will go.

That's why they call it Paradise, no matter who comes along to try and change things, it will always be paradise to someone new."

"That's right," James agreed, "the water will always be a beautiful green, the sunsets ablaze with glory, and the night sky bursting with twinkling delights!" James slowed the boat to an idle.

"How poetic you are, James! I love poetry. I write sonnets often. Would you like to hear my latest poem, sometime? It's about the trees in the fall season." James grinned, entertained by Amber's suggestion, as Morgan looked on, quite nauseated by it all. "This is totally amazing. Look at all the small, colorful fish swimming," Amber giggled, as she leaned over the side and peered through the crystal-clear water.

"Well," Morgan mused, tossing his empty coffee cup under the seat. "The water is usually always calm and smooth as glass out here. I can see why someone named it the Lakes. It's like a mirror, isn't it?"

"Yes, it is. I can't believe I can see everything on the bottom so clearly!" Amber squealed, "It's like another world."

Morgan threw out the anchor and tied it off on the bow cleat. James cut off the annoying motor and silence broke.

Ten

Keeping time with the gentle lapping of the water, the little boat drifted languidly in the light current. The small Danforth anchor, dropped overboard, scooted and inched its way across the rippled, white, sandy bottom, as if trying to sneak away. Dark, round sponges, looking like giant, sturdy mushrooms, dwelled beneath the boat's listless shadow. Spotted among the hard, coral heads and rising up sporadically, here and there on the silvery, reflective sand, the huge sponges delighted Amber. Streaming rays of sun pierced the translucent surface, dispersing radiant light beams throughout the Lakes in all directions. Vibrant hues of darting tropical fish flitted in and out from Amber's view, magnified in size, by the water's surface. Anxious to get into the water with the tiny fish, she patiently listened, as James instructed her on how to keep her diving mask airtight against her face and the self-clearing snorkel clear.

Finally, after the lesson, she lowered herself slowly over the skiff's edge and slid down the starboard side. James quickly hooked a little plastic fold-up ladder at the stern of the Whaler, just in case she needed a boost getting back into the boat. They watched from aboard, as she plunged into the pleasant, cool water with a spirited splash and a shriek that echoed throughout the peaceful Lakes. Kicking her feet through the tranquil surface and treading water, Morgan handed her a pair of small fins that he had borrowed from his mom's vigorous supply of various dive gear. She floated with her back curled up tight in a circle, resembling a jellyfish, as she held her masked-face under water and slipped a bright, orange fin on each foot. Fortunately, both fins and mask were a perfect fit.

After, squaring her away and making sure she knew how to breathe through the snorkel, the guys geared up and jumped overboard. They each took her by the hand, leading her out to the nearest mammoth, loggerhead sponge. Together, all three friends steadied themselves, gently standing and balancing on its firm, four-foot, wide surface. Holding their heads up above the water, Amber kept putting her face back under, looking down through her mask and staring at their colorful fins, lined up on the dark, smooth rim. She was amazed that they were all three, standing on one, giant sponge, with room to spare.

"Look," she squealed, with the snorkel muffling her shrieks. "A snake! A big green snake!" Morgan tilted her head up out of the water with his large, gloved hand.

"No! That's a giant Moray eel. They sometimes live under the ledge of the sponges." Morgan laughed, "We just disturbed him from a plan he was working on." They watched, as he unhappily swam in a wavy motion away from them.

"Gosh, he looks like a six-foot-long, fat, lime-green ribbon, wiggling through the water like that. Can they bite?" Amber winced with curiosity.

"Ah yes," James sputtered, spitting the out the snorkel from his red out-lined lips with a sputter, "They have razor sharp teeth. But if we don't mess with them, they don't mess with us."

He grinned reassuringly, as he shoved the snorkel back in his mouth. "Come on. Follow me. I'll show you where spiny lobster like to party."

Morgan kicked off in another direction, leaving the teaching to James. Their nets and yellow, lobster bags, streamed along the sides of both guys, as they swam. Each bag was clipped to the buckle of their light, lead, weight belts, filled with a long tickle-stick, extra, heavy, rubber gloves to protect their hands from the spiny, prickly crawfish and a measuring gauge. Soon, James caught a glimpse of a pair of long wiggly antennas sticking out from under a dark, bulky, wool sponge, growing on the shimmering, white, sand. He dove down, about five feet and stuck the end of the tickle-stick under the black, leathery, coated sponge to scare any lobsters out. Six crawling and jumping crawfish danced out immediately. Two shot off, resembling detonated missiles, out toward the deeper water. James hurried and grabbed the other four that were cautiously tiptoeing off, stuffing them all into his net bag. Clipping the metal handles shut, his jubilant smile outlined his mouthpiece and he winked up at Amber, on the surface, through the clear glass of his face-mask.

She lay outstretched on her tummy, softly kicking the water with just the slightest motion of her flippers, as she studied his every move. Her lips curled up at the corners into a mystical mermaid's smile around the bulky mouthpiece of her clear, silicone snorkel. Tiny air bubbles escaped from her lips and covered her exultant expressions. She nodded at his beaming face, and gave him a gratifying approval by lowering her long slender arm down through the water and turning her petite thumb up in the air. Then confidently, she turned away and fluttered off, her fins cutting through the transparent water, heading toward the next big sponge.

Obviously, she's clearly getting the hang of this fast. Wonder how she'd do with grabbing the next lobster? He smiled a secret smile and followed close at her heels, watching her delicate feet thrust her stiff fins up and down. Amber glided nymph-like through the sunlit water. She stopped over a huge, black logger-head sponge, but this time she held her breath and dove down by herself, to examine what was living in the underwater habitat below. James inquisitively followed. Screeching in a muted tone, she pointed to a French angel fish staring at her, face to face. It was about two inches long with brilliant, vertical yellow stripes going down its tar-black body. The French's rounded, black tail, waved gracefully back and forth, as others of its kind, scooted out from underneath the big sponge to observe their new visitors. The little angels were as curious about Amber, as she was about them, as they watched her unfamiliar, but interesting animations. Limberly kicking her feet, suspending her small body, upturned and upside-down, in the translucent water and standing on her head, she became a part of their mysterious, underwater world. James got her attention and motioned her to the top. They both broke the surface together, gasping for a breath of fresh air.

"Those are immature French angel fish. The other two on the other side of the sponge that are staying together look like Frenches, but they are black angels," James huffed and puffed, panting for a lungful of air.

"How can you tell the difference?" Amber removed her pliable, rubbery mouthpiece and massaged her slightly-sore jaws.

"The black angels are also immature. Their tail is straight on the back-edge, where the French angels have rounded tails. The sergeant majors are the small yellow and white fish with black vertical stripes, swimming, unafraid, in schools around us."

"Military fish. That's cute. And the half royal blue and gold?"

"Those are called a beau gregory. Let's give this area a good check, then go find Morgan and see what he's got." Amber nodded than lowered her head in the water and eagerly swam next to him.

He observed her, as she gracefully dove down and lurked about, picking up shells, bending and extending her lean torso. She reminded him of the mermaid in the song he wrote, who lived under the unruffled, green surface of a tranquil sea. Amber's fins treaded through the saltwater, effortlessly behind her. Her long, auburn hair surged gently over her soft, contoured back, like burnished corn-silk, fluidly waving in an underwater breeze. Again, entranced by her willowy ballet, he compared her to the sweet mermaid she had heard him sing about, just the night before.

She pointed at some waving antennas poking out from under another large sponge. Her green, eyes danced with adventure, as they squinted through her mask. Gasping for big, deep breaths of air and holding it, they kicked down toward the sandy bottom. Again, they stood on their heads, as they scared the spiny lobsters that were within James's reach. His powerful kicks maneuvered him right on target. He grabbed the biggest lobster around his hard, brown-shelled body, right behind his shiny, black, periscope-eyes.

Both divers quickly kicked to the top. James held his struggling trophy high above his head, as he broke the surface and shouted with victory. The angry crawfish wildly waved his long antennas in the air. His tiny swimmer-fins connected to his tail, quivered back and forth, trying uselessly, to get away. James paid no attention to the lobster's squawky protests and gleefully pushed him down deep into his crawfish keep, snapping the lock closed. *No need to measure these guys. They're all keepers, for sure!*

He and Amber headed back toward the boat. James threw his bag of lobster into the skiff and onto the deck, with a loud thump.

"Morgan is just over there," he pointed at the churning water the Captain was kicking up, about forty feet away. The hot sun that was at high noon and the glare on the water was blinding after being under so long. James shielded his mask with his big, red, rubber glove, saying, "Those beautiful, lavender gorgonians and purple sea fans you see swaying in the current down there, are live, soft corals." He hung on to the side of his boat, resting and catching his breath. She continued to look through her mask at the bottom, as he explained several of the colorful, ocean plants and corals in her field of vision.

"And the soft, green, purple and brown gushy things with all the water-filled tentacles are sea anemones. They gather food with those tentacles. They can attach themselves with the soft, hidden foot, located under their bodies, to about anything. Getting them off bone coral is really hard. They stick like cement."

She tossed her head back up out of the water, asking, "But why would you want to get them off?" Salt water was starting to fill the bottom of her mask, right under her nose. She tilted her mask up with her fingers and let the leaky water run out.

"My dad and I use to collect those things and sell 'em when I was a kid. He always made sure that I was careful not to rip their delicate foot, when I slid my fingernail underneath and lifted it around the edges to make 'em detach. That was work to Dad."

"Sounds like a fun to me!" she replied. "Wonder where Morgan went to now? I can't see, the glare is so blinding."

"I see the ol' Captain. I'll swim over and get him. Maybe he's ready to make us lunch."

76

"Alright. I'll just hang around the side, here, so I can still look down at the fish."

"Good. We'll be right back in a while. Just relax and enjoy yourself." James kicked off to catch up to Morgan. Amber's feet felt surprisingly light in the water, after she slid off her bulky flippers. Dropping each fin over the side of the boat, she heard them thunk onto the deck below.

They returned in about thirty minutes to find Amber playing in the clear water. Morgan and James pulled their slippery fins off and thrust them aboard, dragging their dripping bodies up over the edge and into the Whaler. Amber continued to paddle about nearby, as the boys dumped out their two bags of lobsters and measured their catch with a metal, lobster gage.

"Well, Morgan you beat me by one, but I do believe my five crawfish are running bigger than your six keepers. Plus you had two shorts that you threw back and I didn't have any."

"Yea, well we'll see who eats the most, too, won't we?" Morgan snorted. He threw the crawfish into a wooden fish-crate with a hefty thud and dragged the slatted box over to the side of the skiff. Above the grating noise of the box against the deck, they heard a loud scream out behind the boast's stern.

"What the heck?" James exclaimed, as he dove off the side of the boat and swam quickly to Amber, who was shrieking and crying when he reached her. She was holding onto her foot with both of her hands and pulling it up close to her chest. Her face was frightfully white with fear and pain, as she squeezed her foot with one hand until it was a beet-red color, and dug her fingernails into James's broad shoulders with the other. Amber's gripping pain distinctly translated through her white knuckles, clenched against James's dark, tanned skin.

"What happened, Amber?" James cried over her screams. Her green eyes were filled with tears, behind her mask, as she held on tighter to him.

"Something bit my foot down there. The pain . . . the pain . . . my . . . my foot is paralyzed."

"Let me see it. Hold it out of the water, so I can see it." She obeyed and held it up, wincing in pain. It wasn't bleeding. He examined it very carefully, as his bare feet tread the water and supported both their bodies.

"What happened?" Morgan called, "Can she make it to the boat?"

"No. Pull the anchor and get over here quick. She's been hit by a black, spiny urchin." Morgan motored over to them. Turning off the engine, he helped pull Amber gently aboard. She sat in a small puddle of water, in the bottom of the boat, where she landed, still gripping her foot with both hands. He lifted her foot and studied it closely. It was very red and swollen. Black lines like pencil-lead marks, drawn on her skin, etched along the sole of her petite foot and up around her ankle. Morgan pulled her mask carefully from her head, tying hard not to entangle the long, wet strands of hair around the mask strap.

"The spines are broken off in your foot. You kicked up against a cluster of long, needle-like spines. The spiny urchins like rocky ledges and you were snorkeling right over a small ledge. Those sea urchins have brittle, sharp spines that can go into your skin and break off and hurt like heck, because of the poisonous sting that enters under the skin. With these guys, when the spines break off, you don't try digging them out. That can cause a really horrible infection."

"Here put your foot up on the seat," Morgan said, placing a bag of ice on the side of her foot.

"Hey, didn't I see meat-tenderizer in the cooler with the steaks?" James asked.

"Yea, now the ol' brain is kickin' in. We have the perfect answer for your pain, Amber. Hang in there," Morgan cried, as he opened the cooler lid and fished out the bottle of meat tenderizer and held it up high for her to see.

"Morgan, I'm in too much pain to eat steak right now. I'm sorry. I'm being such a baby." She gritted her white teeth, attempting to bare the pain. Her rosy, bottom lip trembled, as she rocked back and forth in the bottom of the boat, clutching her throbbing foot. Bravely, she defied the excruciating pain.

"No Amber," James offered compassionately. "We're not talking about cooking steaks. We're going to put the meat tenderizer on your foot to alleviate the pain. It will draw out the poisonous sting. We know what you're going through and you're not being a baby, at all. We've both been there." Hoping she would receive comfort from his heartfelt words, he glanced at Morgan and ordered, "Dump the whole thing in this towel, while I hold it open."

"Do it! Do it!" she cried and writhed, as another jolt of pain shot through her foot. James smacked the cool towel down on the stinging area of her foot and ankle, holding it tightly against her swollen skin, to restrict the stinging. He searched her face for a reaction and encouraged her with his caring smile. His black, expressive eyebrows curved with concern over his warm, coffee bean-brown eyes, while Morgan held her cold, clammy hand in his. Morgan tried to position a couple of boat cushions underneath her body, with his other free hand, while lifting the bleak mood with a few humorous remarks. The distractions, unfortunately, were not effective.

"It'll take a few minutes to take affect," James consoled her tenderly, as he wrapped her foot up in the damp towel, "but it will work, I promise." He winked at her. She flipped her salty, wet hair back with her hand and her pouting, pink lips grimaced in agony, releasing a final, audible cry, while waiting impatiently for the promised cure.

"You know, over there," Morgan squeezed her hand, attempting to entertain her, "people have claimed that Papa, Ernest Hemmingway, that is, had an old stilt-house of his own, out here in these Lakes." He pointed in the direction of the broken, old pilings that were thought to be the foundation of Hemmingway's hideaway. "My mom and dad use to have their own stilt-house on the Lakes that we shared with a Cuban family, out here," he paused. "Right near Ernest's old place, as a matter-of-fact."

"Yep," James jumped in, "my mom and dad went boating and fish collecting down here for many years, and used the stilt-houses, too. After a long day of fishing or diving, my dad said, he would play dominos with a group of old men on Sunday evenings, following a Cuban dinner at the home of Moondo, his old friend, who lived here in Key West. The old men built the stilt-houses when they were younger, but the state, evidently, couldn't stand the thought of all that freedom and fun that every one was having, back then, so, they tore all of the houses down. Some of the platform pilings still exist and are marked on the ocean charts today."

"Hey! I can't believe it! The pain is starting to ease up," Amber smiled faintly, dramatically exhaling, as she pressed the towel really hard against her small foot. Lifting it off again to assess the progress, her sprite smile spoke volumes to James and Morgan. They held their breath, looking for anymore signs of discomfort. Morgan whooped, releasing a great amount of pent-up stress. James slowly removed the moist towel from off her foot and again, searched her face for any possible, distressful sensations. Amber grinned impishly at his sympathetic expression. She caught Morgan by the hand, and said affectionately, "Steak on the grill, suddenly, sounds really good to me, Morgan, and possibly, maybe even a glass of your mom's healing, red wine." She laughed teasingly, as she saw the relief in their surprised, but puzzled eyes. "Actually," she qualified her statement, with a deliberate toss of her sun-dried, salty mane, "I feel like it may be just what the doctor would order for me!"

"Now, that's a medicine even I can prescribe," Morgan snickered, as he playfully extended his hand out toward James. "Corkscrew, please, sir."

James paused and looked intently at Morgan, squinting his glinting eyes in the bright sun, "For some reason, I knew, not only could you prescribe it, but you could fill the order, too," and he grinned at Amber, with a sideways glance. She surrendered, declaring, "Today, I will follow my doctor's orders," and a peaceful, but tired smile, spread over her mouth enhancing her conspicuous, sun-burned cheeks.

Eleven

"The sunset was so beautiful out there on the Lakes. It must be heavenly to live on a sailboat down here and see the sunsets every evening of your life," Amber surmised, as they returned from the dive trip and pulled up in front of James cottage on Higgs Lane. "The mother dolphins and their babies were so cute, as we came back into the harbor. I've never seen friendly dolphins feeding in the wild like that. They actually turned their heads and looked up through the clear water, right in my eyes, when they swam next to the boat. Is that not the most awesome thing you've ever seen?" she exclaimed, oblivious that they were backing the boat into James's side yard. "I mean, we really connected, the dolphins and me. We made eye contact, locked eyes, eyeball to eyeball! I think I'm going to learn dolphin-talk, so I can communicate with them." She gave a candid chuckle, but yet, seemed quite serious about the idea.

"We get to experience stuff like that all the time, don't we, James?" Morgan bragged, with not even a trace of humility. His blue eyes twinkled.

"Well, not all the time, but pretty frequently. Morgan has a certain way of exaggerating things out of proportion. But, especially, running out toward Boca Grand in the deep channel, you see a lot of sociable dolphins in schools," he turned off the truck engine, dropped the keys down into a side-pocket on his door and flung it open. "Well, welcome to my little piece of Paradise!"

She slid off the truck seat and dropping her tote bag to the grass below, she cried, "I love all those purple and red flowers hanging over the porch railing and from your roof, too. They're so brilliant and outrageously wild."

"Those are called bougainvillea. Guess that's French, right Captain? He's the landscaper, not me. I just do music, but I will take a whack at cooking dinner for all of us, tonight." Amber's eyes widened with apprehension.

Morgan yanked the front door open for Amber. James followed, with the two, wet, salty bags of crawfish, slung over his shoulder. "Make yourselves at home, guys," James offered, as Morgan lit a few candles on the coffee table, then scattered them here and there throughout the snug, living room. "The bathroom is down the hall, next to my bedroom. It's a little cramped, so you may want to use my room to get changed. Florida Keys Aqueduct just got my money, so if you'd like a long shower, use all the water you want." He nodded Morgan's direction, "I'm gonna get these lobster into the kitchen and start ringing their tails, while they're still alive."

"You go on ahead, Morgan. Watching James ring the lobster will be a first for me," Amber declared. "I'm learning so much from you guys today. I don't want to stop now."

"You may not like what you see, but you're welcome to watch," James warned. "The kitchen is this way." She followed behind him. He flicked on the wall switch to the overhead, ceiling fan. The dark-blue, wooden paddles began to whirl, vibrating the glowing, cobalt-glass, lamp shades, suspended below the rotating blades. The navy blue and white, tile counters and walls were suddenly mirrored with springy flickers of dancing lights. He dumped the thrashing and snapping crawfish into the cold, stainless sink. They soon settled down, resigned that their box-time, boat-ride was over and their new relationship with Morgan and James would soon be history. The end was near. James dug a pair of red, rubber gloves out of a side-cabinet drawer.

"James," Morgan called from the bedroom, "I left some shorts and a couple shirts here a while back? Do you still have them?"

"Yeah, they're folded up in a plastic Winn Dixie bag, on my night stand next to the phone," James yelled back.

"Thanks. I see it."

Morgan grabbed the bag off the night table, accidentally, hitting the message-machine button and clicking it on. "Oh great," Morgan grumbled aloud, as he heard the recorded messages booming throughout the cottage, "how the heck do I turn the thing off?"

"Hello. Hello. Is anybody there? Is this the Island Hop Taxi Service? I desperately need a taxi to come to the Key West Airport to take me to my hotel. My cell phone number is 757-300-0077. I hope . . . the message trailed off. James froze where he was, standing next to Amber at the sink. They heard the familiar words echoing into the kitchen, as Amber turned her head and stared incredulously at him. Confusion laced her puzzled voice, "That's me on your message machine, isn't it?"

"Yes, that . . . that is definitely you talking on my message machine." James studied her troubled, jade-green eyes. *Are those tears, I'm seeing?*

"How did my message get on your machine? This is so

surreal," she marveled. Thoughtfully, she set her glass of drinking water down on the tile counter. James's bewildered brown eyes followed her glass.

"You called me accidentally, the night you flew in, thinking I was the Island taxi service. They don't exist anymore. I was given their old number when I got my phone, because they went out of business." He methodically rinsed his hands under the faucet, thinking about what to say next and reached for a dish towel to dry them on.

"But, if you heard my message, why didn't you call me back? I know! You were asleep and perhaps, you didn't hear your machine playing my message." He feebly looked at her and miserably shook his head from side to side. "Then, why didn't you call me back and explain to me about the taxi service, since it was the middle of the night? You knew there were no taxis running at night, I presume. Plus, I know, you knew that I was stranded in a strange place, James . . . you could tell that by my urgent plea." She placed her hands on her hips, demanding, "How long have you known, that I was the lady on your answering machine?" At this point, Morgan was leaning hard on the door frame in the kitchen doorway.

"Sorry, buddy. I didn't mean to check your messages. I hit the button by mistake." Morgan droned, glancing sympathetically at Amber and knowing the game was up, by the expression on James worried face. "Sorry. This is my fault."

"Morgan, this has nothing to do with you." James held up his hand, gesturing for him to shut up. Morgan cringed, fully regretting his blunder.

"I have known since I called you this morning and, as soon as I saw the number that you had written on the paper towel. I felt really sorry and embarrassed, when I realized that you were the same person on my message machine. I'm sorry I didn't help by returning your call at the airport. I just assumed you would get a friend or somebody you knew to come pick you up and take you to your hotel," James lowered his eyes and studied the white, ceramic-tile floor. "Believe me, Amber, I was really wrong to have ignored your phone call, no matter who you were, trying to call for a taxi," he raised up his head, appealing to her with his sad eyes. "Would you, please, forgive me? I am truly sorry."

She blinked back the tears and curled her arms around his neck and whispered, "Yes, I forgive you, James. I know you were concerned, even though you screwed it all up. I understand your mistake and I'll never bring this up again or let it ever come between us." He sighed in relief and smiled. "Let's forget that night ever happened. Believe me, I have been through a lot worse things than this, in my young life," she laughed compassionately at him. Then, without warning, Amber mischievously turned her eyes toward Morgan, who was standing motionless, as if he might collapse against the door frame. "I can tell Morgan is dying to know how I finally, got to the Gardens Hotel on that eventful night." He stood up straight, rolled his china-blue eyes and pretended not to care, but she knew better. "I'll tell you how I got to the hotel, if you'll solemnly promise me one thing. Just one thing, Captain. May I call you Captain?"

He nodded thoughtfully, *how hard can this be?* And chirped, "Sure, Amber, what do you have in mind?"

"Would you, please, promise me, that James will not be permitted to cook the lobster dinner, tonight?" Her question was stripped of all superficiality and she immediately, noticed James fabricating some sort of animated rejection, as his pursed mouth concealed a relieved grin. Amber, peacefully, held out her fragile hand. Morgan wrapped his big, comforting arm around her shoulders and grabbing her small hand, he eagerly shook it up and down, gingerly commanding, "James, my man, stand aside! I believe a good and delicious deal has been struck with the little Lady of the Lakes." James, with haste, gladly handed the rubber gloves to Morgan.

Twelve

"**M**y life reminds me at times, of the incoming waves surging in on the beach," Amber remarked, whimsically, while stretching her arm out and setting a mug of frothy mocha on the rattan, glass-top, coffee table in front of her. "You know the ebb and flow-type stuff." She sat next to Morgan, who appeared puzzled and had no idea what she meant. He offered no comment, but certainly was paying close attention, hoping to learn something from her chatter. The colorful, rattan sofa intrigued her, momentarily, as she gushed, "I love this couch fabric," she bubbled. "I've never seen coverings like this before. In Virginia, it's got to be either bluebirds or pineapples. So beige, so blue, so boring!" She ran her polished fingernails over the vibrant, smooth cushions. Splashes of bright, multihued, tropical birds and flamboyant flowers covered the printed material.

"James, bring your coffee and join us," Morgan hollered to him in the kitchen, attempting to be heard over the loud hum of the aged dishwasher. "Forget the dishes."

"Well, Morgan that's easy for you to say, now that they're all done," he retorted, embellishing the statement with a hand-gesture of 'what did you expect,' as he walked into the room, where they were relaxing. He clutched a steaming cup of mocha in his other hand. Carefully, he fell into the fat, stuffed recliner opposite the couch. He pushed out the foot-rest with his large, tanned, bare feet. The brimming, hot liquid sloshed from side to side in his purple mug. "I'm so full," he moaned, rubbing and examining his bulging stomach. "Those were the best lobster I've ever had, Morgan. Grilling them is your secret, isn't it?" he grinned, nodding his head and prompting Morgan to finally agree.

"You say the same thing every time I fix crawfish," Morgan commented proudly, pretending not to be impressed by the flattery. Lifting his sizable, red-rooster-embossed mug to his lips, he sipped his hot coffee, and asked smugly, peeking over the rim of his mug, "What can I say? A master chef has many secrets, right Amber?" Morgan turned to her, looking for back-up.

"Absolutely! And I respect you for guarding all of your cooking secrets," she giggled. "I know better than to pry. That was truly one of the finest meals I have ever eaten in my entire life. Thank you both so much, for inviting me to go out in the boat and dive up those pokey lobsters. Morgan's wonderful feast will be an experience I'll always remember."

"Well, I guess she knows which side her bread is buttered on, Captain, or should I call you Master Chef?" James mocked, glancing at Amber and shaking his shaggy, brown hair. "He'll be difficult to be around for the next week. All I'll hear about is his bragging for days, after tonight's dinner," James rubbed his chin thoughtfully, "but, considering I'm the lab rat he uses for testing all of his new, exotic dishes, I think I'll try to put up with his inflated ego."

"Just keep me in mind for taste-testing purposes, too, Morgan. You might need another opinion," Amber interjected.

"I may almost be your best critic!" She smiled at James and then added, "Almost!"

"I have a question." Morgan ventured out on a limb. "You mentioned Virginia earlier. Is that where you lived? I was there about a decade ago on a skiing trip in the Shenandoah Valley. I think I was more interested in drinking hot cocoa by the blazing fireplace than hurtling myself, like an unguided missile, down the steep mountainside." Amber held her stomach and laughed. "I'm serious. I felt like the entire skiing trip was a plan to kill me on the slopes."

"Well, you were probably with people who didn't take the time to teach you how to really snow ski. There is only one right way," Amber empathized.

"I was with people who were more like sharks in a feeding frenzy. I'm pretty much at home on the ocean, without the sharks of course, than on the snow-capped mountains. Just drinking hot cocoa satisfies any hunger for the high, snowy, slopes for me," Morgan explained to her, hoping she would not attempt to educate him in some new, kind of skiing instructions. He continued, "Tell us about your life in Virginia. We've all heard about me, this evening, so hearing a new point of view would be entertaining, wouldn't it, James?" He glared keenly at James, expecting him to get excited and join in, but James heaved a deep sigh of bored resignation.

Yawning, he replied, "Yep, I think I will get physically ill, if I have to listen to you tell that shark-eating-frenzy story one more time, Meredith."

"Well, I liked hearing about the shark-eating-frenzy, Morgan," Amber defended his mistreatment and sympathetically patted Morgan's hand. "Sometime, when we're alone, I'd love to hear more of your tales, Morgan." James dramatically rolled his eyes, as she playfully scowled at him and said, "Okay,

I will share about my life in Virginia and my most recent story with both of you, but only on one condition." They both smiled weakly, as she seemed to be laying down rules in a game. "First, James must describe his memorable visit to faraway Sweden." She cocked her sweet head to one side and appealed to him, as he sat comfortably in his cozy recliner. Then, she fluttered her black eyelashes and implored him with her pleading, green eyes.

"Sweden? What the heck are you talking about?" James sat up. Looking serious, he crossed his tan arms over the unbuttoned, blue-flowered shirt that he had slipped on after his shower. His expressive, black eyebrows furled over his chocolate-brown eyes. "Seriously, what in the heck are you talking about? I've never been to Sweden. Ever. Where the heck did you come up with that one?"

"Well, then, why is there a bunch of Swedish, postcards plastered all over the front of your refrigerator?"

"You mean those postcards in there?" He pointed in the direction of the kitchen, surprised at her concern and getting a kick out of her curiosity.

"Yes, of course, I mean those postcards in there. You must have twenty or thirty of them magnetized onto the refrigerator door. What are they doing? Just hiding the rust spots from the salt air?"

"Well, I wish I could tell you that's why I put them up and that's what they are being used for, but, the truth is . . . and Morgan can swear to this," he glanced over at Morgan's restrained laughter, "all those postcards were sent to me, anonymously, during this past year."

"You mean you don't know who sent them to you?" she gasped, holding her hand firmly up against her forehead in dismay.

"Nope!" replied James. "Not a clue. Whoever it is, knows

me and what I do and where I live. They just don't want me to know who they are, what they do or where they live." She slowly shook her head back and forth. Her delicate, pink mouth scrunched sideways, as she bit her bottom lip, puzzled and concerned by his troubling answer.

"That is very odd. I wonder who would do something like that. Maybe it is a fan that loves your music and understands English? Do they have your music in Sweden?" she asked, then, continued, not waiting for his answer. "I know you all have, no doubt, wondered the same things. Man, I would love to read them sometime? That is if they're in English. I love to solve mysteries." She wore a captivating smile, giving Morgan and James a subtle, but convincing wink.

"Well, maybe I might let you read them some day, that is, if you're brushed up on your Swedish!" he laughed mischievously. "But, that day is only possible, after you tell us all about your-self. Only then, will I let you read my stash of secret, Swedish, postcards. We both love mysteries, too." James fell back in his recliner and waited for her reaction.

"Okay, but it is a long story," Amber sighed, with a little reluctance. "I should have guessed it was bound to come to this. What I mean is . . . that . . . I would . . . I mean that I should tell you all what I'm doing here in Key West." At once, intuitively, James became uncertain about the pressure he was placing on her with his request. His brown eyes searched Morgan's blue eyes, seeking out support. Morgan kept silent.

James suddenly stood up, "Well, guess I'll go make another pot of espresso," as Amber and Morgan looked apprehensively at him. "It looks like it may be a long night."

"Better make mine a double," she suggested. "And can you bring a box of tissues, too?"

"Yep, I'll bring some out with the coffee," he answered.

Pausing thoughtfully, he walked toward the kitchen. *Maybe, it would be better for everybody, if she remained a mystery. My life is complicated enough. Why the tissues? I don't handle stress well.* He ran his fingers through his thick, mink-like, dark hair. Without thinking, he cracked opened the back, kitchen door for his meowing-cat, Pipster, who impatiently wanted out. He watched Pip's habitual, slow-as-molasses exit, as he rubbed and wound his way over the door sill and finally, out onto the porch. James, as usual, grazed his high, plume tail with the closing door and took no notice of Pip's customary jumpiness, but somberly considered, *"Ponder" is too simple of a word to describe how I'm feeling right now.* He thoughtfully scratched his head with his long fingers. Rubbing his nose with the back of his hand, he grabbed the tissue box from off the kitchen table.

Thirteen

Amber sat by the warm fire at sunset, intrigued by a passing sailboat. The fanciful reflection whimsically sailed upon the fluid, pink-mirrored sea. A fiery, orange sun trickled liquid-fire over the glassy surface, as the blazing ball melted beneath the ocean's horizon. Left behind in its wake, was a resplendent palette of lavender, pink and gold streaks floating throughout the still water. The sound of the gentle waves lapping against the soft, sandy shore lulled Amber's mind away into a dreamy fantasy land. She was sitting on Smathers Beach, leaning back against the smooth, hard trunk of a coconut palm. She gazed upward, seeing the first evening stars magically appear from nowhere. Flickering flames were fading in the burning, clay, chimney-stove, that Morgan brought over from his backyard on Caroline Street. He threw a piece of crumpled-up, brown, palm frond into the dwindling fire, delighting in watching it blaze up, but only too soon, to return to hot, golden embers, again. The festering coals heaved with a slow, lingering glow, as if breathing in their final breath of air. Amber picked up a stick and stirred the vanishing embers around, heartening them to breathe once more. *They really do seem to be gasping for their final, deep breath. The poor things, they're in anguish.* She looked around for some more dried leaves to cast on them. *They're slowly dying an agonizing death.* Her heart seemed to skip a beat, as an unexpected thought passed through her mind. Suddenly, she was overcome by a shocking awareness. *What about Peter's last moments on earth? What were they like? What was his final breath like for him? With no remains of his body found, his death couldn't have been prolonged. I pray not.* The low, heat from the remaining, smoldering embers felt warm against her flushed cheeks. Overhead, the long, palm fronds clattered and chattered, brushing against each other, as they played together in the balmy, sea breeze.

Amber narrowed her eyes to a slit, hoping to make out the ocean's vanishing horizon. She wondered in amazement, that only a few minutes earlier, she had glimpsed the cotton-candy-pink clouds billowing above the distant, blue line. The sun had quickly gone away from her sight, disappearing to the other side of the world, leaving the horizon to be swallowed up by the oncoming darkness. Amber whispered a prayer, thanking her Jesus that she would see the shining sea, again, tomorrow morning. Amber believed He was the faithful Master who designed the radiant sunsets every evening and a glorious sunrise, every dawn. Since, arriving in November, she had come to the realization that she only needed to take a moment to look up, for they were always there, right on time. Laying her trust in Him for the daily paths that she chose to walk, was exciting, as she stepped in harmony to the unfamiliar, but captivating rhythm, of the mysterious Key West rhapsody. It tempted her heart to beat with a fresh tempo. Each beat springing forth, throughout her spirit, as deep touching deep, accenting her new Island life with fresh meaning.

December had arrived, adorning her with welcomed, joyful changes and new celebrations. Holiday cantatas overflowed from the well of her heart, as Christmas knocked at the door with merry melodies, beckoning her to come and celebrate the Christmas season. However, this music, Amber discovered, was not the sound of the customary snowy, sleigh-bell carols and sugar-plum songs that she sang in old Virginia. She was discovering that sun-soaked skies and a spectrum of rainbows orchestrated her Christmas concertos. Mounting anticipation for the new blends, mixing with the old traditions, was pleasurably, turning out to be her present delight. Even her store-bought, traditional spruce pine would be garnished with colorful, Christmas ornaments made from delicate sea shells and painted sand dollars.

James returned panting and sweaty from his run on the beach. She gave him a thumbs-up, as he approached Morgan and her sitting together by the diminishing fire. The white foam danced on the edges of the rushing waves, as they eased in and kissed her toes. The tide was moving in much closer to the borders of their large beach towels, stretched out on the dry, bumpy sand. Amber gave him a pensive smile, as she reflectively, closed the doors to the gallery of her mind and the endless corridors that only she could enter. She brushed the sand off her slender, sun-tanned legs and stood up to stretch. James poured a cool drink of water into his red plastic cup. He opened the Igloo cooler and thrust his hand through the cold, slushy ice, retrieving a wet, yellow Key lime. Squeezing it hard with his strong thumb into his water, the peel instantly flattened with a burst, piercing the air with a shot of tart juice and hitting Morgan, smack in the eye.

"Man!" Morgan cried out, as he gripped his burning eye with his fingers and rubbed it profusely. "What are you doing to me?"

"Sorry, Captain. I guess my lime got a little bit out-of-control. These things don't grow with a warning printed on their peel." James held back his undetected smile, "Are you okay?"

"No, I'm not okay. My eye is on fire. Man, that thing stings." He winced in pain, as he rubbed his watery eye even more. "That's some potent stuff."

James's amusement was cut short, as he realized Morgan was in some unusual pain. He swished some paper napkins around in the cooler's icy water. Dripping wet, he handed them to Morgan to cool down the burning in his extremely red eye. James realized the poor guy had rubbed it doggedly, into a blood-shot state. He didn't comment, but being of no help in the situation, James surrendered to Amber, who gladly stepped in to assist, at this point. Morgan did not resist.

"Gosh, James! Look what I've missed these past few weeks, not hanging out with you guys!" She laughed and began giving careful and methodical first-aid treatment to Morgan's eye. He never put up a fight when she insisted that he rest with his head cradled in her lap. "Last time I saw you all, was at the little Spanish bollo stand, eating hot bollos together, the day of the last Old Town lobster festival." She dabbed at his eye tenderly. "We should have gotten together sooner than this. Christmas is practically around the corner and here I am, buying a sail boat. I guess that will be my Christmas present to me. It is hard to get use to this 'always mañana' place, but yet, I'm busy all the time with so many loose ends to tie up in this new move to Key West. The latest boat-quest almost seems like fun, when I think about the routine business that I've been attending to, lately."

"You're sure this is what you want to do?" Morgan tried not

to be negative, as he looked up at her pale, serious face illuminated by the glow of the dying fire. "I mean the boat deal, not
my eye! Please, don't stop! I'm enjoying all of your attention.
My eye is starting to feel much better, already." He gave James
a hard stare, then advised Amber, "The longer you wait, the
longer you'd be able to think your decision over and make sure
this is what you really want to do. It is a pretty bold move, may
I add, and little impulsive, moving onto a boat."

"I've prayed and even fasted for one day, Morgan, and I
know this is the right thing for me to do," her eyes filled with
tears. "I'm happy you both care so much and that we can be so
honest with one another. I do appreciate your sincere advice. I
know this does seem unreal, that a farm girl like me, would
purchase a cruising sailboat to live on. But, I feel it is time to
begin living out my dreams, even though, it will be lonely doing
it all by myself. Regretfully, I now, have no family at all, not a
living soul, so I've come to understand that is what will keep
my dreams alive and drive me on to dream more dreams. I own,
practically, nothing, except for a lot of money and my
new, olive-green Jeep." She paused, then flooded with recent
memories, she exclaimed, "I am proud to say, that when I went
car shopping, since I've seen you both, I accomplished that
transaction all by myself and happily, closed on the deal. I even
got the gold trim around the wheels that I wanted. That's a first
for me and it showed me, that if I'm going to learn to survive on
my own, that I need to practice making my own decisions, good
or bad. Not that I don't value your's and James's advice, too. I
do need to hear your opinions and I promise I will always listen,
although I may not always follow your suggestions. I know that
I'm in for some powerful lessons living alone on a big sailboat."

"Yeah, you'll learn some big lessons alright," James
fervently interjected. "You know nothing about the water or

boats. The most you can hope for, at this point, is that the owner is an honest guy and is telling the truth about the boat's history!" James dropped down on his knees, arranging his towel up next to Amber's beach towel. He had been imagining, intensely, what her strange venture would be like, in reality. He nudged Morgan's head with his hand, "You look like you've recovered, Captain. Amber is probably tired of holding your heavy head in her lap, by now!" Amber looked down and patted Morgan's sore eye with the cool compress, giving him license to stay and linger, as long as he wanted.

"Look, if she has any problems, she has us to call on," Morgan boasted sarcastically, watching James fall back with a thud on his outstretched towel.

James sighed and caught his breath, tired from his extended run on the beach. He reached out and grabbed Amber's wide-brimmed, straw sun-hat, pushing it over his face to block out the world. The perfume-fragrance of her hat smelled good to him. It smelled like the fragrant, frangipani flowers that he had sensed before, when he sniffed the paper towel that she wrote her cell number on. He deeply inhaled the sweet scent again.

"That's right," she giggled. "Why else would I be so confident?"

"Okay," Morgan caved in. "I think we should go along with you to the marina in the morning, for the final closing on the boat and give you some moral support. A twenty-seven foot, *Island Packet* is a good find and especially, at the price you're buying it for." He tossed his silky, sun-streaked hair back out of his glinting eyes, and grinned, "You said you didn't own much of anything, anyway, so this might be a good investment for you. Now, you'll have a home that we can all profit from!"

"That's right, Captain, you guys can teach me how to sail her," she giggled, "but, Morgan, I don't think I'll be calling you by your infamous title of 'Captain' when you are aboard my new sailing yacht."

James rolled his eyes under the straw hat and chuckled, waiting for the fuse to be ignited, as she cackled, "I will become the new Captain, right?" Morgan sat up quickly and picked up a fist full of sand. He pitched it lightly on her feet. She laughed and immediately got up, playfully, moving out of his range.

She kicked off the sand and shook off her beach towel, continuing with her conversation, "Just thinking about it, my worldly possessions are really very few. I own some original paintings and a handful of old, but valuable, family keepsakes, which I have stored in Williamsburg, Virginia. Most important-ly, I guess, are the papers that I have in my bank's safety deposit box, here in Key West." She hesitated. "Oops! Almost forgot my new Jeep and of course, the sailboat that's waiting for me to move on board! It's sure a difficult decision, choosing a name for a new boat, isn't it? I've got one I may like . . . mmmm . . . yes, maybe, it seems like I have thought of a good name . . . we'll see. And that brings me to the question that I've wanted to ask you, James? What is your last name? I know Morgan is called Captain Morgan Paul Meredith, and I'm Captain Amber Jean Albury, but who are you?"

"Let's not run this Captain thing into the ground, Amber," he admonished, annoyed by her little joke. "My name is James P. Shannahan. But in the music world, I just go by James, unless you read the fine print."

"Okay, J.P. Shannahan, now that I know that you're definitely an Irish musician and a lad who is not accustomed to lady captains, why don't we mosey over to that Irish pub, Finnegan's, and get a cup of Irish coffee?" Amber giggled. "Mine, of course, will be served with some of Bailey's chocolate mousse on the side."

"Okay! Sounds like a plan. Let's pack it up. Then, it's settled. Tomorrow morning, we'll come over to Seaside Marina for the closing and celebrate the deal onboard the *Island Packet*," James agreed. A bright smile spread across his sun-tanned face, as he added, "We'll take her out for a maiden voyage, with 'yours truly' at the wheel, and christen her with the new name that you've chosen, using the best, pink champagne that Morgan's mom has in her house."

"A brilliant idea! You're always surprising me, Shannahan," Morgan agreed, in his best Irish brogue. "Let's go." And they headed over to the Irish pub on James Street in Amber's new, olive-green Jeep, with Amber at the wheel.

Fourteen

"To *Lady Poetry*!" they cheered in unison the next morning, holding their bubbly, pink champagne high up above their smiling faces, in an official toast to Amber's new vessel. Clicking their plastic-stemmed glasses together, they christened The *Lady Poetry* with this new name and a salty salute. The seas were a bit rough and the wind brisk, but excitement was in the briny air, as they cast off from the marina dock for the first time. The diesel engine purred, as the graceful, pristine yacht idled out the deep, emerald-green channel into the open, blue sea. James stood on the wide, fore deck preparing to hoist the mainsail and unfurl the colorful, genoa above the pointed bow. Amber sat comfortably at the helm, in the cockpit, under the burgundy canvas, shade-top.

"This is a breeze," she called out over the spirited wind to James. "No pun intended," she laughed, as suddenly the big brim of her sailing hat blew back, flat against the top of her head. The strong, windy gust startled her, lighting up her almond-shaped eyes, wide with surprise.

Noticeably, the breeze was increasing, as the sleek craft

plowed through some bigger swells of blue water in the following sea. Making good headway and kicking up a vigorous, white, sun-sparkled wake behind the high stern, the billowing sails stretched, spreading upward, into the clear, powder-blue sky. Morgan's camcorder caught everything in full effect for the first couple hours, as the boat lifted and fell with a gentle swoosh, gracefully upon the lofty, blue waves. The crew steered her toward one of their favorite anchorages, Eastern Dry Rocks, near Sand Key Light.

Amber looked back and anxiously pondered. *Key West looks so small way out here from the distant shoreline.* The sturdy craft continued to plunge through the now, much darker, indigo-blue water. *I wonder when we're going to get there. We must be seven or eight miles off shore. This is far enough for me. These guys are really hard-core sailors.* She looked nervously at James, as he turned the steering wheel effortlessly, yelling elatedly for everyone to duck their heads. The long boom swung hard, over to the starboard side, making a swift alteration from their current course. Sails shifted and chattered, as he changed her tack and the vessel heaved over on her side. The rails cut through the surface and splashed salt-spray high in the air, while the craft raced in the direction of the lighter, green water ahead. Soon, it would be touch and go because of the spotty, coral reef and the extremely shallow places lying in her path. Touching would mean crunching a gaping hole into the seemingly, egg shell-thin hull and the going would send them sinking, straight to the bottom, if they ran upon the razor-sharp, coral heads.

James knew how unforgiving the brittle, coral fingers were that sprawled throughout the surrounding area of the Dry Rocks. He cautiously sailed up near the coral reef, observing the jagged, coral beds in the distance. The dangerous, serrated edges rose up, exposing themselves above the ocean's surface. Myriads of waves, continually, rolled in and heaved against the sharp, flat formations of spiky, elk-horn coral. Each of the crew was alert, keeping a close eye on the fathometer, aware of the keel's shallow draft.

James went below, where he again, bent over his frayed and worn navigational chart of the familiar area. Preferring to plot courses the old traditional way, he used a pair of elongated, metal dividers that looked liked overgrown tweezers and a set of extended, clear-plastic, parallel rules for measuring the latitudes and longitudes. He walked the parallel rules up the face of the old, spread-out, laminated, paper map, while twirling the dividers from point to point, with a precise, circular motion. After plotting a different course, he would call out the coordinates to Morgan up in the cockpit, who would quickly repeat them and punch them into the boat's GPS and autopilot. The altered course would cause the craft to fall off the wind and the sails to go slack, causing the sails to luff and make a shuddering noise, as if they were crying out for more breezes. This signaled the men to bring the boat in closer to the wind. Winching the ropes and cranking the windlass, the guys moved together, hastily from one task to another. Each attended every minute detail with clear-cut accuracy.

Amber heard James give the commands and watched Morgan carry them out, without question, finding their seamanship skills to be truly remarkable. She stared up at the tall, mainsail that was blocking out the sun, thankful for the cool shade it cast on the cockpit, where she sat, leaning back on a life cushion, against the guntle. Her mind was deep in thought. *Studying these two sailors is like watching a ballet at sea. I've so much to learn. What was I thinking when I bought this boat? I would be scared to death being out here without James and Morgan. The* Lady Poetry *draws two feet and eight inches, with her center board, in shallow water. Otherwise, a twenty-seven foot Island Packet without the centerboard would draw three feet and eight inches water. I'm glad I got the one with the centerboard. The previous owner assured me I have the best sailing yacht for shallow waters. He sounded like an experienced navigator to me.*

Amber kept a check on the fathometer to reassure herself they were still in navigable waters. It was more out of fear that she shouted warnings of the constant depth changes. Every time it got near fifteen feet of water or they approached depths less than this, she would panic. She learned quickly that any depth below five feet would mean impending disaster. James's previous experience in the Key West Coast Guard, as an experienced Quartermaster, bolstered her with a measure of confidence, but it still did not quell her jittery nerves. Amber's dreamy idea of being a boat captain had completely vanished, since they had gotten underway. Once they were far out in open water, her cheerful composure changed like the weather. Her inner-barometer reading rose from very relaxed to super stressed out and Morgan didn't help matters much. He kidded her about her gripping, white knuckles, which, of course, was often, for whenever the boat ran close to the wind and heeled over on its side, just a bit too much, she would let out a scream, scramble over to the opposite, higher side of the boat and hold on tightly to the railing and life lines for dear life. James reassured her that this tactic was the fun part of high-speed sailing. He tried to restore her withering confidence with explaining, by sailing extra close to the strong wind, added thrill to their adventure and with a super-equipped boat like The *Lady Poetry*, sailing was easy, safe and exciting. That all sounded very convincing and she politely considered everything he said, but she knew her best advantage was to trust the Man upstairs. She wanted Him at the helm of the gallant *Lady Poetry*, right next to James.

"Let's lower the sails and start the engine." James called up to Morgan from the teak-paneled cabin below, where he had returned to his navigational chart at the boat's small lazaret. Plotting a course leading away from the far-reaching fingers of the hard crunchy bottom, into deeper water was, presently, his main mission. "The 'nav' chart says we have plenty of room, but we can't be too careful with Captain Amber's new baby." James winked at Amber, who was not smiling and gazing down at him through the cabin opening, biting her lower lip. He knew she was afraid. "Prepare to lower both of the sails. I'll turn her into the wind and start the engine," he shouted, limberly jumping up the narrow steps to the cockpit. The sails started fluttering loudly in the stiff breeze, as James brought the boat about. Morgan scooted from tip to stern, tending the mainsail and genoa by securing them both, while the motor idled. Then James shifted the bow around and made headway to a safe anchorage north of the Eastern Dry Rock's sanctuary and preservation area in a tight, ten feet of water. The boat's anchor took a strong hold between the rocky, hard bottom and soft sand. The robust wind that had been at their back, had finally, laid down.

The two sailors caught their breath, calmly rocking at anchor. Visibly, they could make out the silver hook that had set itself fast in between some rocks below. James killed the diesel engine and the silence of the vast sea was intense. Concealed, but now uncovered, the stark quiet was a welcomed respite. Soft, lapping sounds of slushy waves against the fiberglass hull shaded the peaceful stillness with a salty lullaby for Morgan, as he went below and stretched out on the massive bed in the roomy, forward cabin. Songs from the placid sea lulled him into a well-earned slumber, while he gazed at the horizon, bobbing in and out of view, through the clear glass portholes above the bed.

Soon, the gentle swaying eased him into a sweet, serene sleep. Amber and James reclined on each of the long, cockpit seats, resting without a word, for about an hour.

"Want to help me write a song?" James asked, breaking the hush, sitting up and unzipping the black nylon case that held his small back-packing guitar. "I need some fresh ideas in my new song that I'm working on and you look like you're much calmer now."

"I guess I'm not the sailor that I hoped to be."

"You did really good for never sailing on a boat before. I grew up helping my dad on the water and Morgan was raised around boats, too. Joining the Coast Guard at seventeen and trained in Hawaii, as an authorized Quartermaster, gives me a slight advantage, too."

"What does a Quartermaster do?"

"He does what you saw me doing earlier. He navigates and charts courses for the cutters or boats going out to sea. I had to do other stuff, too. I transported boarding parties to inspect vessels coming into port and drove the rigid haul inflatable or RHI. I was what you call a Coxin."

"I'm impressed." She laughed. "I really am. You being a talented entertainer and song writer, so involved in your music, it doesn't seem likely that you were once, a Coast Guard man. I think that's great and I'm awed by it."

"Don't be! You don't know how good it is to hear you laugh again!"

"Don't be so modest! I am impressed. You were so young. Did you wear a gun or was that just for the older guys?"

"Are you kidding? Lots of seventeen year old Coasties are

trained to use nine millimeter guns. Mine was strapped to my waist at seventeen and I manned a fifty millimeter mounted on deck, too, if it was necessary. I gave them four, serious years of my youth and that was enough." James looked out at the horizon and remarked, "It seems to be getting rougher, since we anchored up. We need to keep a weather-eye out."

"Aye, Captain," she teased. "Now, about the song. I don't think I could help you write a song. I can hardly carry a tune, let alone put lyrics to music. I do write poetry though. I have written pages and pages of poems." She ran her graceful fingers across the strings of the small, compact guitar resting upon the cockpit's burgundy, contoured, seat-pad. "I would love to show them to you sometime and get your professional opinion."

"My opinions are just if I like 'em or not. That's about as professional as I get. But, I still would love to read your poetry. Can you recite any of your poems from memory?"

"Yes, I believe so. I wrote a poem about the autumn leaves in Virginia, just before leaving there in November. My name being Amber, like the color of the leaves, before they fall, inspired me to write the poem." She glanced down at her hand and strummed the strings softly. "They inspired my mom and dad, too. That's why they named me Amber, because I was born on October seventeenth, during the peak of the changing, fall color."

"That's interesting. Your name matches your hair, too. You say you've got that poem down in your memory? What's it called?" James studied her glistening, green eyes, as she removed her sunglasses, but, abruptly, became distracted by the darkening, overcast, grey sky, closing in high above them. "Guess we don't need these anymore!" He flipped his shades back on the top of his brown, wind-brushed hair, adapting his eyes to the sudden cloudiness. "Maybe we should listen to the marine weather update. The wind is blowing stronger and I noticed that lightning over there is getting closer. The computer update didn't say anything about an afternoon storm, before we left the dock this morning. Must be one they missed."

"Well, I'm not worried because you're experienced with that weather stuff and I'm not. It sounds like the thunder is still pretty far away to me. Anyway, the name of my poem is simply, *Flight*. Are you sure you want to hear it? I can recite it for you if you really want me to, but I'm a little shy." She joked and hid her blushing face behind her round, sun hat. "I feel kind of silly."

"Don't feel silly. I want you to recite it for me." He hopped up and stood on the boat seat, questioning the sky with his keen, brown eyes, but still, attempting to show interest in Amber's poem. "The sky sure is getting dark, isn't it? The wind's really picking up, too." At that moment, Morgan appeared in the doorway of the cabin, stretching and yawning. "Hey, about time you got up, Morgan. Amber's gettin' ready to recite a poem she made up and we wouldn't want you to miss it."

"Hold that thought, folks," Morgan said, switching on the NOAH weather, radio station. "Amber, can you wait just a minute? I think we better listen to the weather channel." James reached over and turned up the volume. Amber was concerned, but she hoped they would let it go. On the other hand, Morgan was increasingly becoming more uneasy. "James, where did this cloud-cover come from? It wasn't blowing like this ten minutes ago. I've got Key West's underground, weather channel downloaded on my cell phone. It should show us what's going on. I'll get the radar loop up on the screen and we'll check it out."

"We've been busy talking, and the weather change sort of snuck up on us, but I can tell you, the wind is definitely blowing harder then it was, ten minutes ago," James answered.

"I'd say. And the air feels cooler, too. Let's see what NOAH radio says for Key West," Morgan accessed, buttoning up his tropical, parrot-printed shirt that was flapping freely in the blustery breeze. They all listened closely to the marine advisory for the surrounding area.

"There's a violent high wind and electrical storm forming right where we sit, it sounds like," Amber whimpered, "just a few miles off Key West. And they're warning boats to take shelter and not venture from port in Key West. This sounds serious. They say radar discovered it an hour ago. What should we do? I mean they're saying deadly cloud to surface lightning strikes. What's that about?"

"Well, it does sound like it's forming right here, over us, by the way the wind is coming up so strong and swift from the north," James surmised. "I'd say it's about five miles off shore out on the Atlantic and at least ten miles away from us, here at Yellow Rocks, but regardless, it's moving a heck of a lot faster then forecasted and it'll be full force, upon us, in no time." James rubbed his chin and furled his brow. Raising his voice over the almost, twenty knot wind that was blowing against their boat, he exclaimed, "I suggest we batten down the hatches. It's starting to rain harder." A lightning bolt flashed in the near distance. Thunder boomed overhead. He looked at the fear in Amber's watery eyes, as she clutched the edge of the sail cover on the quivering, lashed-down boom and tenderly ordered, "Go below, Amber and watch out for flying objects down there!" James squeezed her clammy, cool hand, as he helped her down the steps. Leaving her alone, inside the dry cabin, he slid the overhead hatch shut and sealed the cabin door closed, behind him.

Fifteen

"Lash down the mainsail, Morgan!" James screamed above the howling wind. Sheets of rain drenched them both, as they cautiously edged their way over the slippery, fiberglass hull with their wet, bare feet. Together, they worked, trying to secure the loose and twisted lines flying about. Presently, forty knot, gale-force, wind-gusts were bearing down solidly against the vessel, attempting to break her hold and blow her onto the jagged coral, looming behind the stern.

"If the anchor doesn't stick fast, we're sunk. This is the storm from hell! Formed up right here ... and with no warning!" Morgan cried, over the howl. James strained his ears to hear what he said, as he hung on tight to the halliard. Towering dark waves bashed against the knife-blade-sharp coral, casting a spray fifteen feet high in the air above the treacherous formations.

"Hook this lifeline to your waist," James shouted, tripping on it, as he tried to swing it over to Morgan. Grabbing out at the jerking, swaying boom, to catch himself from falling, he swerved and hurled his body around into a wild spin that spit him out into the bottom of the cockpit. He smacked the deck hard, crashing flat on his back. Pelting bullets of stinging rain blasted against his water-streaked face. He winced in acute agony. The pain spread like wildfire throughout his aching body. Lying motionless, he held his breath, as if it might be his last. Finally, he exhaled hard, gritted his teeth and steeled his mind to push away the intense throbbing from deep within his side. Pulling with his hands on the boat's attached, padded cushions, he sat up and braced himself with his feet against the vessel's helm. James gasped for air, but it hurt to breathe in. The pain was sharp and severe. *I've gotta get up ....* The storm raged in defiance, as the bow perilously rose ten feet up into the air and pirouetted on the edge of a giant swell. Then, downward, she was dropped, against the steep, back-wall of the monstrous billow, plummeting into the bottom of a deep, watery trough, many feet below. Immediately, she began climbing up the wave's face once more, as she rose upward, on another furious surge.

James clutched the teakwood slats of the cockpit deck with raw knuckles, waiting for his chance to make his move again. *When will this torment stop?* He noticed the Bimini top that he had previously folded down was starting to go. *This top is going ... I gotta make it fast with a lanyard ... the seat pads are gonna go, too.* He leaned over from where he sat and frantically lashed ropes around the tattered, burgundy canvas top with its bent aluminum framework. He glanced toward the transom. *At least, the rudder is stationary ....*

"Are you okay?" Morgan hollered over the howling wind, which was escalating upward to forty knots on the wind indicator. "I can't get down to you. This sail's gonna go. We gotta lash it tighter. Forget the sail cover. I need to stash it in the seat locker or we're gonna loose it." The thunder boomed and rumbled on for countless seconds, echoing and reverberating all around the powerless sailboat, as the canvas, sail cover took to the air, out over the turbulent ocean, like a runaway kite. Intense crashes of electrifying fingers reached down from the black sky, close to the stern, lighting up the ripped-off, maroon seat pads, skyrocketing in flight and following the sail cover in hot pursuit. Flying away, they all disappeared high above the tall, towering Atlantic waves. James's shaggy hair stood up on end.

"That was a closes strike!" he yelled, still flinching, as he saw Morgan's blond hair doing the same thing his hair was doing. James's brown eyes widen in amazement, shocked to see how Morgan hair was standing straight up because of the electically-charged field surrounding them. Torrents of fierce rain beat inexhaustibly against Morgan's chapped hands, numb from gripping and trying to tame the wild, flapping sails. Escalating winds tugged ruthlessly on the anchor's hold and pushed hard at them. The anchor rope, secured with its fisherman's bend knots, was being stretched to its limit, as the jagged jaws of biting coral waited for their prey. James managed to crawl up from the cockpit, with some ropes that he had secured from the seat locker. While keeping pressure on his left ribs, he slid along, balancing himself amidships on the cabin roof. James clutched the quivering boom and sheet-rope tightly with a free hand. He made his way along, facing windward, to the aluminum mast. Loose ropes, like striking cobra snakes, whipped and stuck out dangerously in the mounting, bursts of wind.

"Feels like I cracked all my ribs," James sputtered, pressing the bunched ropes into his ribs with his pale, cold hand, as he whimpered aloud to the roaring wind. The bolts of lightning that slashed the dark sky and ripped it apart with shocking splinters of searing voltage, returned to him, a merciless reply. His pale face lit up in fright, as the golden rods injected illumination into ink-blue sea below. He threw the slack end of a sodden rope up the sheer of the vessel to Morgan, where he spontaneously caught it with one hand, while holding on to the handrail with the other. He then strategically fed the coils over to James, who was balancing at a pivotal point on the cabin roof. Handling the unruly mainsail under the most extreme adversity, he aptly utilized his Coast Guard knot-tying skills, lashing yards and yards of unfettered Dacron rope around it and binding the sail to the potential, battering ram of a boom.

"Look, Morgan!" James yelled, holding his hand on his broken ribs, under his life harness. "Over there, off Sand Key Light. A waterspout's forming down from that giant thunderhead. It's coming down fast. Look at that crazy tornado's tail waving around. That funnel is huge. It's trying to reach the water. Look at it! That's the biggest one I've ever seen in my life."

"Yeah, that's all we need! A twister on the water to suck up Amber and her new boat," Morgan bellowed. "And she thought heeling over was a scary way to sail! Wonder what she's thinking now? Keep your eye on that spout! I'm going below to check on her, after we tie down the jib."

"Okay," James shouted, "but don't mention anything about spotting the waterspout. If that anchor line breaks, we'll smash up sideways on the coral rocks. Let's just keep that one between us, too. Tell her to put on her life jacket and bring mine up top. Grab any fowl weather gear you can find, too. Watch out for our lifelines when you climb down."

Morgan nodded and slipped over the slick side of the cabin, like a wet lizard. Hurriedly, he shoved the teak hatch door open and crawled in, as fast, as he could, closing it behind him and the driving rain. Amber was lying in fetal position on the salon couch staring straight ahead and clutching her worn, wine-colored Bible. She appeared to be living out every pitch and dive the *Lady Poetry* took. A killer wave smashed violently against the lurching bow with an especially hard blow and threw Morgan off balance. He landed on his knees next to her, where she reclined. Her stone-cold gaze focused on the water-plastered port holes, as fear and shock etched her solemn face. The horizon of the reckless sea had disappeared from view, consumed by the tireless rocking and tumbling. *Lady Poetry* strained, rebelliously, against the force that was intent on breaking her taut anchor line. She wrenched feverishly, pulled by the fierce wind's screaming shears, as they cut into the fiberglass hull.

"How are you holding up?" Morgan asked, hesitating and waiting for her to speak. His saturated shorts and soaking shirt were dripping water all over on the smoky-blue carpet, while his teeth chattered from the chill that had settled on him.

"Are you warm enough? Can I help you with anything?" he offered.

"I've tried pulling scriptures out of my diverted mind and as hard as I try, I can't meditate on them, very easily. We need God's help! I'm trying to not be afraid." Amber removed her hand from under the plump, down-filled comforter, "But, it's really hard." She held it out to Morgan. "Down deep, I'm really scared." She bowed her head and closed her eyes tight, so as not to see Morgan's face lighting up again with gold light from the lightening flashes that radiated through the oblong portholes. The bright reflections and the exploding thunder filled her imagination with images of Peter's sudden death. She looked into Morgan's caring eyes. His teeth were still chattering, as he sat down in his soggy clothes, next to her on the sofa. Her warm skin felt comforting between his icy fingers. She pulled the comforter up over Morgan's quaking knees and pleaded, "Can you pray with me?"

James, up-top and alone, had come to the decision that the diesel engine was their last hope. He knew if the anchor line snapped and hurled them upon the slicing coral, they would all be killed. The wind whistled shrilly through the rigging, sending a chill down his drenched back. Driving rain pelted his tan face, causing his eyes to sting and burn. He turned the ignition key and the engine sputtered. Turning the key once more, he listened anxiously for the motor to start. Nothing happened, just plumes of white smoke puffed out from under the boat, behind the stern. He shrieked and held up his shivering hand to heaven, loudly crying out, "Help me! I need some help!" The water was blinding and the visibility was zero. Volatile bolts cracked relentlessly around them, resembling upside-down, sizzling, silver trees from a thunderhead's garden, piercing the angry sea with their fiery, leafless branches.

Sixteen

Heart-stopping explosions of booming thunder shocked the ocean's surface and sent tremors rattling through the rigging and cross stays, high above the wind-tossed sailboat. Wielding frenziedly, the halliard's metal fastenings clanged and clanked loudly with an endless, deafening banging, against the swaying mast above. Voltiable flashes of lightning mirrored against the tall, aluminum pole, reflecting brightly down upon the doused sailboat. The *Lady Poetry* appeared like a defenseless, bobbing cork on the spiraling surf of deranged waves, but still she fought to hold her ground. Enormous, soaring sprays dumped icy, saltwater down James's back, while he fought with the engine's choke, trying to start the unresponsive motor. The high-pitching bow maintained its steady, steep ascents and cascading nose-dives. Buried, once more, under another heavy deluge, James clasped his pulsating ribs, while wiping the brine from his burning eyes with the back of his other hand. "Morgan! Get up here!" he desperately shouted, over and over. The roaring wind and pounding rain drowned out his fading, hoarse voice. Repeatedly, there was no answer coming forth to his futile calls. The *Lady Poetry* raised again, high onto a lofty perch. On the plummet downward, she dropped with a tremendous jolt into a treacherous trench below, thudding hard upon impact. Once again, the tired crew braced themselves for another towering summit on the next cresting wave.

It seemed like an eternity had passed to James, when he finally beheld Morgan bolting through the cockpit door and back out on the slushy deck. Wearing a diving mask on his head to shield his eyes and block out the blinding rain, he was immediately assaulted, as the teeth of the storm wrenched it off his face with one fierce bite. James, feeling like he could take no more, flicked the stinging, salt spray from his long, black, eye lashes, and attempted to assimilate what had just taken place. Watching the strong gust, scrape the mask off of Morgan's bruised, red face and suck it out to sea, stunned him beyond wonder. He stared in awe at Morgan's look of surprise, illuminated by a cracking, lightning bolt.

Spitting the dripping water off his sputtering, chapped lips, James rasped, at the top of his voice, "We're in serious trouble." His eyes burned from the hammering raindrops, as he observed Morgan, heaving to and fro on the deck. He was wearing, what looked like, turquoise-colored, rain-gear. His bright, orange, life jacket bulged out around his neck and chest, while he held on tightly with his left hand to the teak handrail that was attached to the cabin roof, next to the hatch-cover. He reached into his rain jacket with his right hand and passed the lifeline through the snapped-up opening, clipping it to the life-harness that he wore beneath.

"You've always said 'one hand for yourself and one for the boat' and I've always remembered it," Morgan screamed over the shrieking wind.

James did not react to his proclamation, but noticed Morgan pointing valiantly at his foot. He had a small, zipped-up, duffle bag tied to his right ankle. James nodded approvingly and motioned it over. Morgan stretched out his long leg toward James, without letting go of the handle. Unthinking and exhausted, James released both of his hands from the large, steering wheel and eagerly snagged the bag. He quickly dug out his rain gear and life jacket, but suddenly, without any warning, he was violently thrust up high and slung over the helm. The stainless wheel compressed against his cracked ribs.

"Ahhhhgh, I'm loosing it!" he howled, as the boat took another mountain-high, nose-dive down into the watery abyss below. For the first time in his life, he felt seasick.

Morgan stared at him, alarmed and yelling "Hey! One hand for the boat! Remember?" Managing to slither over to James, Morgan hauled James's slumped body aloft, onto the remaining, battered, seat cushion and struggling to hold him steady, he accomplished outfitting him in his foul-weather suit and life jacket. Tightening the hood-strap under his chin, James's labored breathing began to ease up and he felt some welcoming relief.

"What took so blasted long down there? I've been screaming my head off for you to get up here," James bellowed over the shrill, whistling wind, as he bit on the ends of his cold, numb fingers. He paused, giving Morgan a very hard stare.

Morgan sheepishly replied back, "Been down below praying with Amber."

James screwed up his mouth and his dark eyes took on a strikingly, wild look. He raised his dripping eyebrows and retorted, "Yeah, right." He handed the boat keys to Morgan. "Hope you prayed for me . . . and this mindless engine that won't start. We're gonna need all the help we can get."

The gusting flurries whistled and wailed, pushing forcefully against their two bodies, huddled together in the bottom of the cockpit. "There's such a strain on the anchor line. It's gonna break any second if we don't get this motor started fast and make some forward headway," James anxiously shouted, trying to ignore his painful ribs. "We've got to overtake the oncoming wind and get the anchor up or we'll be blown sideways and smashed on those coral heads."

Frothy, salt water sluiced down the drenched, water-logged, teak decking. They both acknowledged that the immense downpour could not sink the self-bailing boat, but the fear of smashing on the distant coral reef would do more, than sink them to the bottom. Electrical energy glowed and raged in the racing, dark, cumulous clouds boiling overhead. Strafing rain riddled the rolling vessel, as the earsplitting thunder pierced and reverberated throughout the fiberglass hull. James winced at the closeness of it. Squinting his dripping eyelids, he managed to read the wind indicator's foggy glass. The needle jumped and quivered, responding to the echoing cracks of the lightning strikes and brutal wind. Loose flying, sail-corners, moderately knotted and roped down, flapped defenselessly in the powerful blow. Gripping the keys, Morgan instinctively nodded at James, stood up from where he was squatting and prepared to fire the engine.

"Morgan—duck!" James screeched. The boom swung over, like a giant pendulum, violently bashing Morgan square in the left side of his skull. His feet flew out from under him, throwing him halfway out of the craft. Morgan laid balanced, faceup, across the metal, lifeline cables, on the starboard side. His upper body dangled, hanging in suspension, out over the water from the gunwale edge. The raging sea blotted out his shoulders and head from James's sight, as the high, billowing, whitecaps snatched at him hungrily, salivating for his motionless body. His slender legs and bare feet stayed in the boat, while his hips hovered at a distressing angle, over the boat-seat. James dodged down low to avoid the swinging, out-of-control boom and crawled over to his injured friend. Clutching Morgan by his soggy, life jacket, he wrestled his limp body from off the lines using what strength he could muster, to situate him back onto the seat. Morgan's face was red with streaks of blood and he was completely knocked out cold. As the lightning flashed, James discovered that the floppy screws had worked their way loose from the stainless traveler-track. Experiencing shock from never hearing of such a thing happening before, he realized that the boom's main sheet had released from its fastening restraint.

Swiftly, he removed Morgan's nylon hood and pealed it off his wet, unconscious head. It fluttered and snapped in the wind defiantly. The menacing, black sky was no help in determining the seriousness of his gapping head injury, but he recognized the wound was bleeding profusely and he was worried. James tore off his own rain pants and tied them tightly around Morgan's hemorrhaging, split head. Checking the beating pulse on his exposed neck, James was ecstatic that he was alive. Nightfall was upon them and only the frequent, lightning flashes made anything visible, outside on the deck. By this bizarre light, after wrapping it up, James concluded Morgan's cut was, indeed, severe. Also, he realized, he could not allow the powerfully flailing boom to swing back and forth many more times without, possibly, capsizing the sailboat.

James cautiously climbed up on the glassy-slick cabin, waiting for his chance to catch a hold of the wildly, swinging boom, as it shot back in his direction. Swathed in a dangling, white mainsail, the free-flying boom looked eerily ghost-like and seemed to have a mind all of its own, as it swung crazily from one side to the other. James suddenly bounded on top of it, straddling it like a wild, bucking bronco, as it made another aggressive veer to port side. He clung to the swerving boom, with all of his might, then, as the monster passed back over amidships, James jumped off and pulled it down hard, using the remainder of any reserved strength that he might still have.

Adrenalin coursed throughout his exhausted body, as he successfully stabilized the free-wheeling tyrant over the center of the pitching yacht. Grabbing hold of the whipping halliard, he seized the hardware on the end and secured it around the rolled-up, shaking sails and boom. By loosening two of the repressing dacron lines, he nimbly tied the slack ends off to the port and starboard cleats and turn-wenches, providing more holding power. Inspecting closely with his sharp eyes, he made positively sure that the tension was bearable on the mast's downhaul. Carefully, he inched and groaned his way, along the secured boom, dropping down into the cockpit, next to where Morgan was restrained and spread out on the last, seat cushion.

"You're not dying on my watch, buddy," James proclaimed loudly, between tugs on the ropes, to make sure they would hold the boom in place. "God heard your prayers, Captain." James tilted his head back and looked up pleadingly toward the luminous heavens above, as the rain drops pelted his smarting eyes, "Just hold on! Help is coming!"

"Amber!" James cried, as he lowered himself into the disshelved cabin. "I need your help on deck. Morgan is down, unconscious and bleeding. Hurry! Gear up and bring up some dry towels!"

"What? Unconscious? Bleeding?"

"Yeah, all of that and much more. Morgan's in bad shape. I'm calling channel sixteen right now."

"Who's channel sixteen?"

"The Coast Guard."

"But you are the Coast Guard."

"Yeah, not lately . . . Amber, we're in trouble. The engine won't start and Morgan dropped the keys overboard when the boom smacked him. Do you have another set of keys to try and start the engine again?"

"No. The previous owner left only one set of keys with me. I was supposed to get some duplicates made."

"Okay . . . Don't worry about that now! You're gonna need a lifeline when you get up on top. Put this harness on over your gear. Hurry and get geared up, but wait for me to help you out there. We go out together. It's beyond dangerous on deck!" James lifted the VHF radio, handset. He held the microphone to his mouth and flipped the switch on. Clicking through the channels on the receiver, he quickly found the pre-set, Coast Guard, channel sixteen. "This is the *Lady Poetry* calling . . . May Day, May Day!" he bellowed.

"We read you *Lady Poetry*. What are your coordinates? Please, state your position." The man on the other end answered back.

"Twelve miles southwest of Key West. Anchored in ten feet of water . . . I'll activate emergency, transmit button for . . . " The radio squelched and went dead. James pushed the transmission button and snapped the switch frantically up and down. The radio crackled again, sparking with life.

"May Day," he shouted, "May Day! This is the . . . . the *Lady Poetry*. Come in. Over." The radio crackled one last time, with no reply and then went completely dead.

"Do they know where we are?" Amber cried with a trembling voice. Her stomach felt queasy and she had sweaty palms.

"Only God knows that!" James clunked the headset back on its hook. "Your VHF radio is equipped with emergency DSC and interfaced with your GPS plotter, but just as I depressed the button to transmit the positional-coordinates, the radio went dead. If I transmitted our NMEA in time, the Coast Guard will respond."

James clicked the GPS switch, changing the lighted screen's displays. "See here," he spoke hastily, "the SAT radar shows no current change in the weather where we are anchored." His voice dropped, as he regarded her confused face. "Forget about all this tech-stuff. Let's just get back up to Morgan, who may be bleeding to death. We need a miracle. If I don't do something fast, we may all die on the coral heads out there."

"If we can't get the motor going, what can we do? Will the Coast Guard come looking for us without coordinates?"

"Yep. They will fly Bar-Pat searches in helicopters off Key West trying to find us in this mess and it will be very dangerous for them." James took a deep breath and climbed up the cabin steps. He looked back at her and offered, "I'm sorry things turned out this way." He squeezed her chilled, soft hand and pushed open the hatch, "Hurry! Let's get up top! Morgan's head is cut bad."

Torrents of salt water greeted and battered him heartlessly, as he stepped back up on the storm-battered deck. He checked Morgan's gloomy condition and then, he weighed up their chances. *The tempest has yet to deal with my fury.*

Seventeen

Amber held onto any stable object she could find, as the traction on the slippery upper-deck was almost impossible. The wind rushed hard against her petite frame and its power surprised her. Fighting for a grip, she knelt down and bent over Morgan's head, pushing some compressed towels against his gapping wound. Amber directed the beam of the bright, LED headlamp that was strapped over her hooded head, onto Morgan's gash.

Her windbreaker whipped loudly in the gale, as she braced her feet and body, thinking ruefully that the endless rocking, reminded her of the last ride she took, on a wild horse she once owned named, Nightmare. He had gone off the deep-end and was sold at auction not long after that final ride. She hoped her boat venture would have a more positive outcome. Although, James requested her to move up, out onto the deck, in the midst of the storm, she felt, suddenly, confident and ready to help with Morgan, in spite of the violent wind and pelting rain. Bearing in mind that the lightning bolts did resemble blue fire-balls and the billowing waves looked like towers of water, they were diminutive when she compared them to saving Morgan's life. That meant more to her, than saving her own. Seeing him lying there so alarmingly quiet and unmoving, caused her to rebuke the fear and dread that filled her mind. She felt them flee, as she boldly replaced these cowardly demons with faith and fortitude.

She pointed her light toward James's sure hands, as he immobilize Morgan's shifting neck by wedging a rolled-up towel within the bulky, stuffed collar of his life jacket. The sailboat continuously dove, as the treacherous waves pushed it tumbling over the immense, cresting precipices, only to crash between the massive breakers and ascend their dreaded climb once more. Amber's hand jarred and twitched when she touched Morgan's soaking, white cheeks, but Morgan felt nothing. James squatted down next to them and held onto the teak floor slats of the water-logged decking. He greatly appreciated the LED head-lamps that Amber had found, squirreled away in the lazaret's storage compartment, just before coming up to the cockpit. Praising her for the good find and the gift of a new, light source, he wondered how he could have ever seen anything before, when he was forced to rely on the power surges that fluxed from the lightning. The undependable, doused, deck-lights continued to flicker on and off with the constant banging of the hull. Morgan was undisturbed and never moved a muscle in the raging uproar.

James bowed over him and tried to shield him from the hurtling raindrops. It was useless. He called loudly to Amber over the booming thunder, "If you're able to lift his feet, Amber, we'll try to carry him carefully below and get him out of this fiendish storm."

Storm? This is sure more than a storm. It's more like a hurricane. What's a hurricane like, if this is just a storm? She pondered, as a huge wave came over the side and slapped her down to the deck. She landed hard, on her rear end. Helplessly, she gripped the edge of the only surviving seat cushion and catching her breath, she laboriously fought to sit up.

"Amber, can you clasp his feet tight and guide him on down into the cabin with me?" He didn't hear her answer over the wind's howl. "I'll support his head and shoulders, then follow you down. We'll lay him on the sofa." He paused thoughtfully and asked, "Can you do it?"

"I don't think I can lift him. I can hardly stand on my own two feet," Amber whined over the shrill, wind gusts, as the increasing walls of water swamped the cockpit. The uninvited invaders crashed and exploded on top of them, mercilessly. "I keep falling down." She clung tightly to the teak handrail next to the door, bolstering herself against the next rise and fall.

James glanced out toward the bow, aiming the beam of his LED light. Anxiously he noted the ever present, severe strain on the anchor line. He knew his chance to heave to with the engine was gone and their window-of-time was running out. He couldn't hide the worry that creased his brow and etched his jaw line. The thought of the taut, anchor line breaking sent sudden panic through his mind.

"Look, Amber, between the smashing waves, driving rain and electrical bolts from hell, we've got to get Morgan below and throw out two storm anchors. It's our last chance." He brushed her stringy, wet hair away from her burning eyes. He tried to support her light weight against his firm body, while she moved herself amidships in the cockpit. Taking hold of the rails on the helm's edge, she braced for the next huge, thunderous wave. Nervously, she bit the inside of her cheek, as she glared out into the face of the frenzied storm.

James examined poor Morgan and checked his laceration, again, then, he spoke decidedly, "It will take both of us to move him with his severe bleeding."

"Let's go!" She spluttered driving rain from her lips. "Grab hold of him. I can do this." James was stunned, but relieved to see her rally up the courage. His rain-streaked eyes locked on her dripping-wet eyelashes and sputtering lips, as their faces illuminated in their lamp's glow. Suddenly, he reached out, impulsively, catching her when she staggered and she clung to him. Regaining her balance, she stumbled backwards once more and he quickly stopped her, restraining her and keeping her from falling back against the hatch door.

"Aye, Captain," James concurred. "We can defeat disaster if we hurry and that especially means, getting you down below, too, before you get seriously hurt up here. Come on, time to move!"

Torrents of rain slashed and whipped her billowy coat that stuck out from around her snug-fitting life jacket. The wind tugged to eradicate her fastened rain hood. The water streamed over her unfaltering shoulders. She shoved open the hatch to the cabin and without flinching, she lifted Morgan's feet. Together, they carefully lowered him down the tapered steps, leading into the cabin below. Jumbles of papers, cups, saucers, charts and anything that wasn't tied down littered the cabin floor. Amber quickly cleared the couch for Morgan, as James positioned him comfortably upon it, laying him quietly at rest. Morgan never uttered a groan of complaint.

"Can you get his dry shirt on him after I go back up top? He brought a change of clothes in his green, backpack. The bandages are in this first-aid box," he instructed, handing her a white metal box with a red cross on the lid. "Can you put a dry, life jacket on him? I can change his wet shorts when I come back down." James threw a blanket over his long, still body.

"Do you want to take this flare gun up there with you?" She pointed to the Coast Guard flares and flare gun in the net bag swinging wildly, to and fro, from the hook next to the door.

"I'll bang on the door and you can hand it out to me, if

I hear a chopper approaching. It may go overboard if I take it with me now." The corners of her mouth turned upward and she held up her fragile fist, extending two slender fingers and forming them into a v-shape.

"Peace-out," she sparkled faintly, "and may God be with you, James." Her green eyes filled with gratitude. He returned the peace sign and weakly grinned. Amber sniffed and fought back the urge to break down sobbing, as she watched James's feet fly up the steps and back out into the forceful gale.

He knew his latest plan was not going to be an easy one to execute alone, but now it turned out to be his only choice, for the tension on the single anchor line had held far longer, than he could ever dreamed possible. He hastened to tug the heavy anchors out of their storage lockers, as he struggled to keep his balance against bashing waves coming over the sides. Thrashing back and forth, he battled to keep his footing. The anchor line tangled and whipped about his legs and he tripped over the precarious, thick rope. He stared out at the mighty swells and muttered defiantly, *you'd like to get me, wouldn't you?* The angry sea made no reply, as he dropped the first anchor in a free fall up and over the stern. The weighty, hefty chain clinked and clattered, scraping the gunnels, as the heavy anchor plummeted through the raging water and stopped upon the turbulent bottom below.

Seizing the second storm anchor, James yanked it upward and cast the burden against his broad back. He felt the unforgiving wind gusting upward to nearly fifty knots, while he inched along the slick, narrow edge extending toward the bow of the boat. He held on stalwartly with one hand, to the boat's shuddering lifeline, that ran the length of the craft, from tip to stern. The powerful blasts shook his shivering, wet frame, pushing him too close to the edge. Abruptly, he felt a strong increase in the wind. The storm played a game of tug-of-war, placing the boat's hull in opposition making James the sacrifice in the middle.

Aware of the awkward weight shifting upon his shoulders, he suddenly lost his balance and released the heavy, steel anchor, as he felt himself falling overboard. It hit the deck with a reverberating thud. The wind was winning its risky game, waiting in anticipation for its prize, but James spontaneously grabbed a hold of the lifeline cable with his right hand, when he realized he was being propelled head-first over the side. He watched his burning, headlamp whirl out into the murky obscurity. Twisting his body around into a circular spin, he gravitated, and spun to the top of the narrow passageway, slamming brutally against the outer, cabin wall. He arched his spine and rolled his eyes in relief and marvel, feeling the solid cabin up against his aching back. He detected his hands trembling and his teeth chattering. *That's different,* he thought, amazed at his own unexpected vulnerability and he laughed aloud. *Is this fait or is this God?* Gulping in a huge breath, he didn't wait for his answer, but shoved the metal hulk ahead of him with both of his feet. Latching on to it with his one free hand, he bumped and banged it across the top of the fiberglass, walk-around deck. Slowly, he lugged it along, shoving it inch by inch and then, he finally reached the forward tip of the bow. *I sure wouldn't be here without this safety harness strapped on me. If I had gone overboard, Amber wouldn't have known anyway . . . Hope she's praying big-time prayers!*

James quaked, as he looked out from his lofty position, perched upon the rocketing, pointed bow, awash with enormous, pounding waves. Clinging to the stainless, bow rail, the perilous, pitching bow was like a roller coaster ride, gone mad. He nudged the anchor along slowly with one strong hand and clutched his chafed fingers around the trembling forestay, with the other. Then, maneuvering the shackling of the anchor line, he secured it tightly to the bow cleat. Drawing on all his reserve strength, he kicked the big anchor overboard, thrusting it powerfully with his bare feet, and sinking it into the violent, turbulent sea below. The line sprung taut, as the anchor buried itself into the ocean's patchy floor. He looked at his raw hands in the white refection of the blinking, bow light. *They're bleeding, alright.* He heaved an audible cry and carefully turned to crawl back on his hands and knees, the way he came. The steel tackle of the halliards clanged a deafening chorus above him, banging uncontrollably on the swaying mast. Hair-raising, lightning strikes lit up the thin pathway, while he cautiously crept along on his skinned knees. At last, he dropped solidly down into the slushy cockpit. Thankful to feel his feet hit the deck, he looked about to check if the three, deck lights were still, at least, intermittently flashing. He noticed the one light, up high on the mast, was completely off. *Faulty wires. I can't imagine why?* He mused, as he wiped the water out of his blurred eyes with a saturated towel that he had found slopping around on the sloshing deck-boards. He focused and fixed his burning eyes intensely on the wind indicator. *I'll bet your needle's never done this before.* Then, he saw that the red, hazard light, mounted on the top of the cabin seemed to be staying lit, for some mysterious reason and he determined the same thing for the red and green running lights on the port and starboard side. Satisfied, that they were all now working and that the storm anchors were holding tight, he shouted out a pent-up roar.

He started to open the hatch door, when suddenly, he heard a loud pop and felt a tremendous jerk. He lurched and staggered backwards, and hit with a ruthless bang, against the sturdy helm. He then, shot forward, striking the hatch door with a crashing thump. The vessel listed slightly at an angle, as the shallow-drafted keel dug itself into the sandy bottom, in a resting position. Amber promptly cracked open the door. She was holding the flare gun kit in her hand and was surprised to discover James, lying on his back in the sluicing storm-waters, looking up at her.

"What was that?" she gasped. "I thought you were banging on the door for the flares."

"No, the main anchor line just snapped! But, fortunately, the storm anchors snagged. We would all be dead just about now, smashed to bits on the coral reef, if they hadn't held." He studied her pensive face in the dim glow of the cabin's battery-driven light, behind her. James climbed inside, below and shut the door snug and tight, muffling out the raging wind and deafening thunder. He felt completely drained, after his completed mission.

"How is Morgan doing?" James asked, as he dried his face. He vigorously rubbed his bleeding hands with some paper towels while, trying to kindle some heat in his wrinkled, washed-out, wrinkled flesh. "Thank God, the running lights, stern light and bow light are miraculously lit again! The mast's light is dead, but that's okay."

"Jesus always answers prayer. Believe me, James, I've been in a state of begging and pleading down here, for you. I'm just so glad your task was done before that anchor line broke. I feel a little better or stronger, even though, we're still in this huge storm! Like faith and thankfulness all mixed together some-how." She gave him a grateful hug. "I think Morgan's head has stopped hemorrhaging for good. Everything is looking up and even the old Captain's appearance grows better with each passing minute. Although, he's still out, cold-as-a-cucumber, his color is slowly coming back to his pale face.

He looks kind of peaceful, doesn't he?"

"I'd say he's doing great, considering what I just experienced."

"We're finally all down here together. Can you believe it?" She poured James a cup of barely-hot coffee from her stainless thermos. "I saved this coffee just for you and Morgan, but you might as well drink his, too, since he's unconscious."

"This is the very best coffee I've ever tasted." He declared, swallowing it down, then pouring some more. The black coffee brimmed to the top of his enamel, blue cup. "Here's to you, Morgan and all your prayers that you prayed." He looked curiously sideways at Amber and polished off Morgan's share. She smiled a wide, knowing grin at him. "And here's to those blessed, storm anchors, too!" he added appreciatively.

"Hey! Listen! Do you here that?" Amber yelped, holding her hand over James's mouth. They listened closely over the shrill, roaring wind. "They found us! I think the Coast Guard has found us!"

"Sounds like a chopper getting closer, doesn't it?" His adrenaline started pumping, again. He grabbed the flares and bounded out onto the turbulent deck and fired the first blazing, red flare high up into the black, tumultuous thunderhead. Reflecting ominously, the golden, ruby-glow permeated the vaporous atmosphere above and illuminated the white sailboat below. James watched the helicopter's dim lights getting closer in the very near distance, as the hazy, shadowy blackness returned and covered the sailboat, seconds later.

"Hey, James!" Amber shouted out through the crack of the hatch door. "Morgan is coming to. He's okay, I think." She paused and tried to make a distinction between the whirl of the Coast Guard's helicopter and the constant booming of the thunder, as she fastened the door closed. Presently, Morgan groaned and opened his puzzled, blue eyes. "Welcome back to a brave, new world, Morgan. We really missed you," she whispered tenderly. He touched his throbbing head with his quaking fingers. Amber gently smiled at him. "You'll feel better, I promise."

"They'll be sending a basket down for him and whisking him off to emergency," James called into the cabin to Amber. "The hospital will be waiting for him in Key West." Exhilarated, James shot off two more burning, red flares. He then peeked inside through the small opening of the door again. "Hi Captain. Glad you woke up to experience the ride of your life. Not to say, the ride you're on right now isn't a close runner-up." He smiled brightly at Morgan, but he could only lethargically stare back at James through the crack. "I'm only hoping you'll remember it," James lamented, then, his smile changed to concern, adding, "Maybe not . . . . " Morgan attempted to respond with a blurry-eyed, courtesy grin. "That's what I'm looking for!" James snickered happily, as Morgan's eyes rolled back slightly and James drifted from his view.

"Well, I think I'll go up in the basket with you, Morgan." Amber teased and shut the door firmly in the storm's face. "I'm your official nurse."

James saw the flight crew's bright return signal soaring overhead. "I know the drill!" he shouted up to the three Coasties, who were hanging out the open side-door, waving their arms excitedly. They loudly circled in the rainy sky and never heard his exuberant greeting. Bottled-up tears flowed freely down James's salt-sprayed face. Turning his misty eyes toward the whistling and groaning wind, he shouted triumphantly, brandishing his fists to the raging sea, "You tried to break us on the rocks! But you failed!" He laughed and screamed at the wild tempest above him, "Fate? I don't believe in fate. Fate jumped-ship hours ago!" The lightning ripped, the sky tore apart and James knew he was absolutely right.

Eighteen

"Two more days and the stitches come out," James gasped, as he fluffed up the pillow and tucked it snuggly beneath Morgan's bandaged head. Then stooping down, he scooted a lengthy, body pillow under the back of his lower legs that were drooping over the rattan sofa's thick, padded arm. His large feet extended down, pointing toward the well-preserved, Dade-pine floor. James studied him closely, than determined, "Those couch cushions must be getting pretty uncomfortable after four days of just lying there. Wouldn't you like to sit up in my recliner for awhile?"

"Thanks James, but with the pain pills that I'm on, even a bed of nails would feel great to me." Morgan lifted his glass and took a huge gulp of water. "Yep, James, it's like my heroic conduct is being rewarded. Basking here at your quiet home, surrounded by the Island ambiance, has caused my recuperation to come along swimmingly. With the attention I'm getting from you and your sweet accommodations and the lovely Amber, as my beautiful, caring nurse, what better sickbay to be in and what more could I want?" He answered his own query. "Maybe,

I might want my shaved hair to grow in faster. That would be nice." He reached up and carefully felt underneath the taped-up bandage, on the side of his bristly head. Agonizing over the imaginary and scary sensation of the spiky prickles against his soft fingers, he whimpered, "I know I look like an idiot with this huge thing on my head." Then, he confessed, as if in deep reflection, "Probably I look too stupid to go to Louie's Backyard for dinner, tonight." He fell back on his pillow. "My mom is counting on me going, too."

"Louie's Backyard? What in the heck are you talking about? You believe you're feeling like you're in good enough shape to actually go out for dinner? What are you thinking? And drinking alcohol is definitely out of the picture for you, considering the powerful, drugs you're dropping." James looked into Morgan's partially dilated pupils. "Your mom hasn't seen your condition since the hospital. She might want to reconsider planning this celebration for another night, 'cause you don't look hardly lucid to me!" James glanced at his dive watch. "How's your mother doing at home by herself, anyway, without you around there to help her out?"

"By herself? That's an understatement! She's doing great. You'd be doing great, too, if you had Cates for your own private driver." He stared up at the stained, aged, Dade-County-pine ceiling through the slowly revolving, Bahama, fan blades. Holding up his thumb and fingers on one hand, he started counting off his mom's hired servants. "There's the culinary artist, Pristine, fom faraway Gloucester, *Señora* Yanni Ruiz, the maid and housekeeper, Province, the pool-girl and the new Cuban gardener, Willy. Rodger walks the dogs, and Donna is the bird-lady. Don't want to forget the landscaper . . . her name is . . . . What's her name? I unwillingly work with her in the yard on occasion." He wrinkled his brow, straining his drugged brain to remember, as he switched over to count on his other hand. "Barbara Clambarker!" he moaned. "The thorn stuck in my side," and he extended a single finger up in the air. "And most important, we have the jovial Yvette, her personal hairdresser that visits the estate, at least, twice a week. Wonder if I left anybody out? Wonder if Mom even misses me? I think I'm a heck of a good bargain for her, don't you? I bet she'll probably appreciate me, much more, now that I've been away awhile. She'll, no doubt, see how very indispensable I really am."

"No doubt!" James agreed, as a wide grin spread across his suntanned face. His straight, white teeth gleamed. "Or no doubt, how replaceable you really are!" James aimed the television, remote control toward the set. The screen went black. "What are you doing about tonight? Are you really up to going out? You don't look so good to me, but it's probably the drugs. I've got an old, Jimmy Buffet ball cap you might be able to cover the shaved half of your head with. We can just expand it to fit over your big honkin' bandage. Then you won't look completely stupid."

"Thanks for your thoughtful idea, James. I'd just look half stupid, right? For that, I'm not telling you that my mom wants to take you and Amber out, too. It's her way of thanking you guys for taking care of her little boy, these past few days. As disabled, as Mrs. Emma Meredith is, she always looks forward to our traditional Christmas dinner and celebration at Louie's Backyard. We've done it annually, for years, as you well know. Just me and mom. I've never known her to ever invite anybody else. The sky's the limit. But, then, that's right, I'm not telling you."

"Thanks, Morgan, for not telling me." James eyed the med-bottle on the coffee table. "That bottle of pills I picked up from Walgreen's sure is . . . shall I say . . . potently fresh?" James held up the brown, plastic bottle close to his long, black lashes. He read the small print, double checking the dosage and strength. "Ummm . . . It looks right, but unless you're really in great pain, I'm holding back on giving you any more of these, today. Your morning dose will have to last you for awhile, Cap." James ripped his Velcro pocket flap open on his khaki cargo-shorts. He slid the small bottle deep inside and tightly pressed the pocket closed, smirking at Morgan's bewildered expression. James patted his pocket with an "in charge" manner. "Taking all of us to Louie's for Christmas dinner? Is that what I heard you say, that you didn't want me to hear you say?" Morgan bit his lower lip and covered his budding smile, as James chuckled, "Okay, okay, on my latest observation, like right now, at this instant," he shot another peek at his watch, "you're lookin' better and better with every second that goes by. What time do we pick up your mom?"

"We don't. Cates will be here at five o'clock with a rented stretch-limo. So, I need to ease into the bath tub and start getting ready. I figured you'd want to try encountering Louie's again, so I told her we'd all be ready when she arrives. This will make your third attempt at eating there this month, won't it?"

"Yeah, it sure will! Twice, I go there, get settled at my table and twice, I get up and leave, before I order. First time, all I could say to the hostess, as I jetted out the door, was, 'I'm sick, but I'll be back,' and the second time, the next Sunday, when I do finally return, they had a boring, lunch menu full of break-fast delicacies, that in fact, were just pricey eggs and I wanted a fried grouper sandwich, really bad. I quickly swigged down my Beach Blizzard. They have the best fruit-blends in town. And might I add, once more, that I'll be drinking one tonight. But anyway, as I was saying, I got up from the table and cancelled my order with the waitress. I can still hear her shrieking, as she went speeding passed me, sprinting toward the front bar, 'Hold up on the Bloody Mary, Adam, he's not staying, again!' I laughed so hard when I was walking to my truck."

"Morgan, Key West's famous chickens are great and I don't want to take any credit away from any of them, especially the hens. I'm sure that their eggs are the best Key West has to offer. Scratching out a living on the streets of Key West isn't easy and I know that better, than any of these chickens around here. Fleeing the money-grubbing, chicken-catchers, every time the cock crows, can be unnerving to all of our feathered, fowl-friends. Their facade is always on the brink of cracking. I sympathize with the roosters and the hens, but choosing between a chicken egg and a fresh grouper fillet for lunch, I'd opt for the fresh grouper every time!" They both enjoyed the laughter, as James impersonated the server's shocked face again and repeated the funniest parts of the story over. "Hey!" he stopped abruptly. "We forgot to call Amber at the boat. She needs to get her boongie over here right away, if she's gonna go out with us. The boat-detailers were almost done when I drove by the marina earlier." He picked up his cell phone from the coffee table. "The boat looks great. They waxed and buffed it inside and out and oiled all the teak, too." He tossed his tiny phone impulsively in the air, seizing it excitedly with a sudden snatch. "Man! I've got the whole night off from the Green Parrot. This party is one I'm not gonna be walking out on and I don't have to entertain at it either, for that matter." He gingerly flipped opened his phone with gleeful anticipation, "Just pure relaxation is in store for me tonight, if I play my cards right and I couldn't be more game!"

Morgan pointed to the stack of postcards, situated a bit too close to the shiny puddle from his sweating water glass. "Speaking of cards . . . has Amber unlocked the Swedish, postcard mystery, yet?" he asked, scratching the side of his head that still had hair. "She sure spends a whole, long time looking at them, when she's over here . . . ." Morgan's voice trailed off when he realized James wasn't even listening to him, but was talking to Amber on his phone.

James snapped his cell shut and slipped it into his flowered shirt pocket. James scrutinized Morgan's expression inquisitively. Morgan felt a little annoyed that James wasn't paying attention to the seriousness of his questions, but he intently continued on, "Man, Amber is fanatical about your postcards from Sweden. Ever since, she found out that you were kidding about her needing to know Swedish to read them, and that the cards are written in English, she has been relentless. She has taken every written word apart, letter by letter. From the time, you gave them to her to study, she's transformed herself into some laborious code-cracker. The dates, times and places they were all mailed from are exhaustively important to her. Not to mention what she notices in each strange picture on the front of the card." Morgan slowly sat up, preparing to go get ready. "I never knew how obsessed a person could get over a few anonymous, foreign, postcards." Morgan picked one up off the top of the pile. "Look, she's circled all the misspelled, English words and even underlined all the wrong letters in each word, hoping that she's successfully deciphered some special message." He winced in pain, as he stood up and lost his balance. "She's become some sort of secret-code breaker." Baffled, he replaced the card upon the top of mysterious collection, as he glanced over at the DVD's digital clock. Morgan gasped, staring at James incredulously, "Why didn't you tell me what time it was? These pills seem to make time stand still . . . I hate that!"

James patiently shook his head, "Well, Cap, you know, there are those people, who may appreciate that effect!" Laughing, he handed him a clean, fluffy, bath towel and gently prodded him toward the bathroom. Shoving Morgan inside, he closed the door behind him. James felt an unusual peace fall upon the cottage. He inhaled a cleansing breath of air, while he picked up his guitar, sat down and began to strum a new song.

The stark-white, linen-covered tables were beckoning the small group to come and sit at their inviting, heartening places. Each table was soaking in the essence of a golden glow of sparkling, candlelight, accented with fluted vases of red roses. The concierge was standing at her place of duty. She was an alert, blonde woman, who stood straight and tall at her post. With the air of a palace guard, her personality was challenging, as she directed lingering patrons with her sharpened pencil, from the elevated, oak, reception desk, situated at the entrance of Louie's banqueting hall.

At once, she immediately recognized the arrival of the Meredith party. Greeting Mrs. Meredith warmly, she led them personally to their awaiting, dining table, giving James the once-over. The filled, crystal, water goblets reflected the candle's flickering flame, as myriads of shimmering prisms brilliantly twinkled upon the pristine table-covering. Like a tiny band of dancing fairies, dispersing their radiance over the warmly-lighted surface, the illuminations bounced merrily off the clear, contours of fiery crystal. Starched, folded, cloth napkins stood up like tiny, white canopies on each gleaming china plate. Morgan seated his mother first, then sat down next to her. James sat on the other side of his mom, next to Amber. Their server brought their finest bottle of pink champagne. After filling each stemmed glass, she returned the cold bottle to the tableside, ice bucket and left them alone to enjoy their drinks.

"I'd like to make a toast to the three of you," Morgan's mom laughed nervously. "I'm so pleased to toast your safe rescue and a future filled with smoother sailing. Here's to a very Merry Christmas." They raised their gleaming, bubbly drinks. "Here! Here!" They heartily agreed in unison.

"I'm so glad to see you again, Mrs. Meredith. You look great. Thank you for asking me to be your guest, tonight," Amber softly whispered.

"You're so welcome, dear Amber. You sound so sweetly Virginian when you speak. Please call me, Emma, after Emma Street, here in Key West, where I was born. The last time I visited with you was at our home on Caroline Street. You were new to salty, old Key West, then. And now, since your maiden voyage on your sailboat, you have become quite the old salt, have you not?" Amber blushed, smiling modestly. Emma motioned for their personal server, standing nearby at her station, to come fill their glasses again. "Morgan has told me about your strong faith in the Lord. I, for one, would not be alive today, if it were not for my faith and fervent prayers. You won't hear me saying Happy Holidays at Christmas time, like most people are doing left and right, nowadays! They wouldn't have a holiday to celebrate if it wasn't for Jesus having his birthday every year. Christmas is Christmas for me, just as it's been for many believers, for over two thousand years. Now, I might preface this with the fact, that it may not be the exact day the Virgin Mary gave divine birth to our Holy Savior, there in Bethlehem, but it's still a time set aside to celebrate his triumphant arrival and Blessed birth, don't you agree, Miss Amber?"

"Here! Here!" James saluted jubilantly, again, with his lifted, nearly-empty glass. The rosy, swirling champagne sparkled effervescently, fizzing and bubbling in the candle light, as the attentive server refilled his drink. "I know I believe in those fervent and faithful prayers. We wouldn't be here tonight, if I weren't for Morgan's and Amber's prayers."

"Morgan's prayers? Why you didn't mention your prayers, dear," she gently pried, turning her puzzled face toward her only son. "This is wonderful news, sweetheart." He smiled a sheepish grin and stared into his filled glass. She dabbed her eyes with her silk handkerchief. "You seem to appear quite affected, by just, the bubbles from your champagne, Morgan. Are you feeling alright? You have not touched your drink. Maybe the bubbly would be a bit too strong for you in your weakened condition, do you suppose? Perhaps, you need to eat something, instead." She glanced at the others decisively, and then suggested spiritedly, "Let's do order, if that's alright with everyone. I'm feeling quite famished, myself."

James rolled his big brown eyes at the ceiling, but only Amber took notice, as he revealed, "Well, truthfully, Morgan has been taking some pretty, strong, pain pills up through this morning, so that may be what is still affecting him." James, then, boldly reached over and picked up Morgan's brimming champagne glass, "Here's to your health, Captain," he saluted, holding it high in front of his cheery face, as he quickly removed the pink fluid from Morgan's reach and sipped it with gusto. His dark eyes glinted mischievously, when he thumped the glass down onto the table, declaring, "That's it for you, tonight, Morgan. You're riding high on the wagon this evening, Laddy. Sorry, but you're not permitted to drink even one glass of champagne. A first for you! Even so, we will, nevertheless, still count you in on all of our toasts!" He laughed rakishly and reached over, playfully nudging Morgan in the ribs, while the wise Emma Meredith nodded approvingly. She then, waved for their server to come take their orders. The delicious dinners soon followed. Every presentation fulfilled their highest of expectations and a king could not have eaten better fare, than they did. One course followed the next, bringing a smile to every face and satisfying their fondest desires. Decadent desserts rolled out to their table, placed on royally adorned carts and each decorative creation fought to out-do the other. With all the sumptuousness sweets appearing to be more exquisite, than the next elaborate delicacies being offered, it was difficult, for everyone at the party to choose, just which one, they wanted, off the four, lavished carts. So as it turned out, for the sake of argument, they were delightfully forced to indulge in several dainties, at a time. The elegant and scrumptious bounties were ravenously savored and devoured with extravagant pleasure. Christmas cheer spread abundantly around their table and it continued throughout the evening, down to the last, creamy cup of hot, steaming cappuccino.

"Well, it's getting late, my dears. James, would you see me out? Cates will be waiting for me." Amber swiftly got up out of her chair and assisted Emma to her feet, handing Emma her wrap. Mrs. Meredith leaned on her old, hand-carved Lignum Vitae, wooden cane. "This cane came from the tree grown in our back yard on Caroline Street. It's the hardest wood in the world, so it should hold me up for a long time, yet to come," Emma chuckled and winked at Amber. "Continue tonight, to celebrate the coming Christmas for me. This evening is my Christmas gift to all of you. You are my special guests, as long as you are here and anywhere else you should wander. Cates will return and be parked outside the restaurant, on standby, for you all, the rest of the night."

They extolled her generosity, as she received hugs, gratitude and goodbyes from each of her guests. James, then, carefully took Mrs. Meredith by the arm and escorted her slowly out to the front veranda, where old Cates was dutifully passing the time, sitting at the top of the steps, waiting to take Emma home.

Nineteen

"We're alone at last," Morgan reached over and touched Amber's smooth hand, whispering in a hushed tone to her. "I've been waiting all night for this moment to be alone, together. I have to ask you a very important question."

"Why Morgan, are you getting ready to propose to me?" she teased, shaking her long, sun-streaked, auburn hair from side to side. Morgan's blue eyes widened with amazement. She winked at him, bantering, "If this is the moment you've been waiting for, your timing is slightly off and you better hurry up! Hence, our dashing, dark-eyed friend is skirting the dining room, as I speak, and is drawing imminently closer to our table. Proceed, if you wish, but alone together, we will, soon, be not!" She tossed her head back like a lively filly, giggling with even greater hilarity, than before. "You better hurry! Your special moment is almost history!"

Morgan sneered at her surprising behavior, then, weakly, the corners of his mouth turned up sharply, into a bewildered grin. He averted his vision in James's direction, as he watched him rapidly closing in. Amber narrowed her mischievous gaze, enamoring Morgan with her sultry mystique. Gushing tenderly, she confided, "I, too, have been waiting for this special time, Morgan, but I must say, I think we may, or may not, be waiting for this matchless-moment for the same reason. For me, my being alone with only you, merely improves, if we include our companion, James."

She screwed up her moist, blushed mouth, trying to hide her titillating amusement, as her dark, outlined, green eyes twinkled in the glowing candlelight. Leaning over the table, she held up her rounded, peachy-polished fingernail to her pursed, rosy lips and then, whispered guardedly to him, "I have a secret to share with both of you."

Morgan sighed, as he closed his eyes and took in a deep breath of relief. He nodded in agreement, by bobbing his bulky head-dressing up and down. James, presently, slid lithely into his crimson-cushioned chair and joined the two of them, once more.

He pointed at Morgan's hand reaching out over the table, still resting on top of Amber's small, graceful fingers, "What'd I miss?"

Embarrassed, Morgan's cheeks reddened. He swiftly shrunk back his wilted hand and performed a bogus check of the puffy, gauze bandage that protruded conspicuously, out from under his borrowed, sun-faded, ball cap.

"Morgan was just getting ready to pop the question," Amber beamed, angling her head toward Morgan.

"I think he's popped too many pills," James retorted, signaling for the new server, who seemed to be sleeping on his feet.

"She's definitely had more, than enough, bubbly," Morgan rebuffed, as he dramatically lifted the wet, drained, champagne bottle high up out of the frosty ice-bucket, for all to see. Then, dropping it with a thud, it hit the slushy ice-water with a splash, splattering and spurting on the diners, sitting behind them.

Morgan never noticed the outbreak of their flourishing napkins.

"Actually, the truth is," Morgan went on, "I was just hoping to get her alone, to confront her about an issue that I've had on my mind, lately." He turned to Amber, "I want to ask you what's going on with those Swedish postcards you're so blasted obsessed with?" He looked back at James and said, "But now, unfortunately, her unexpected aspiration for yours truly has caused a powerful yearning, deep inside me, for some sort of tropical fruit, mixed with rum and blended into a concoction, such as, a Beach Blizzard. It will help bolster my nerves when I ask for her hand in marriage." His eyes shifted Amber's way, as he winked, "I don't want to dash her hopes!" She kicked him with her foot underneath the table.

"Okay, okay save it you two, for when you both are absolutely alone, 'cause I really don't want to see how disappointed you're gonna look, Morgan, when you hear her depressing answer!" James snapped, looking thoughtfully at Morgan, and his bulging head-garb, poking precariously out from under the stretched-out, ball cap. "You know, I'm thinking, maybe one glass of wine wouldn't hurt you, Captain, since that pain medication has most likely worn off, by now. I agree it might do you some good. It may help you to sort out your feelings for Amber, considering you're probably headed straight for Heartbreak Hotel." Amber mocked James's for his silly advice, then, looking down, she dug anxiously through the sparkly, black, evening bag lying in her lap. "What in the heck are you searching for?" James asked her entreatingly, "I sure need some help with this situation! It's getting out-of-hand!"

"Well, I've confessed already to Morgan that I've got a secret to share with both of you and it has to do exactly with what he wants to know about!"

James's face lit up with superficial anticipation, "Hold that

thought just a second, would you, Amber?" He waved again for
their dozing server, calling sympathetically to him to come over
to take their order, "I think I may need something to ease the
shock . . . maybe . . . a Beach Blizzard?"

Amber gave him a hard stare and shook her head, replying,
"No, James, the marriage-subject is closed," Amber groaned,
fluttering her long eyelashes at them both. Her green eyes
sparkled with shades of deep olive. "For the present time, anyway!" she giggled jokingly and blazed an impetuous smile at
Morgan. James finished ordering for all of them. "Oh, please,
make my Blendy-Blizzard or Beachy-Lizard or whatever these
guys call it, a non-alcoholic," she called to the yawning, departing server, "And, by the way, you look like . . . you may need
some serious sleep, sir." The young man ignored her, but
however, he did noticeably pick up his feet, as he zipped toward
the bar.

As the motivated waiter moved out of ear-shot, Amber lowered her head, scrunched over the table and leaned toward them,
resting on her bare, tan arms. "I know a secret about those
postcards that is more, than just scenic pictures of beautiful
Sweden," she murmured quietly. Attentive and curios, Morgan
glanced over at James, as the waiter punctually delivered two
very tall, golden-pineapple and coconut-cream, blended drinks
to their table. One with rum and one without rum, but both
were sporting Christmassy-red cherries that surfed merrily on
top, in the swirled-froth of the thick, foamy beverages.

"Amber, you're so different!" Morgan piped, reaching over
and plucking out the fat, juicy cherry from James's Blizzard and
propelling it into his mouth. "What's this all about?" he garbled,
as the plump cherry rolled around in his gapping mouth. "I was
waiting for my mom to leave, so I could finally ask you about
those dumb postcards and what you've found out." He deliber-

ately chomped down and squished the cherry with his front
teeth. The red juice turned his white teeth scarlet. James, who
appeared to be noticeably distracted by the swizzling, red juice
oozing down from Morgan's crimson lips and dripping from his
chin, waited patiently for his friend to regain some composure.
Momentarily, his eyes filled with a bit of mortification, but
turning his attention to his drink, James blissfully sucked up his
icy, fruity cocktail through a yellow, paper straw. Falling back
against the back of his padded chair with a thud, he exclaimed,
"I rest my case! This is definitely the best drink in Key West!
Oh! Morgan, I've totally concluded, you may not drink any
wine, whatsoever. Strong pills? I'd say!" James shot a linen napkin in Morgan's direction for him to wipe his mouth with and
ordered the server to take away his glass of untouched wine.

James promptly reached the bottom of his drink with a final,
noisy draw through the flattened straw, "Now, what's the secret,
Amber? I can't wait a second longer!" James asked, clunking his
empty, streaked glass on the table. "I'm all ears," he snickered.
"Do I look like ears to you all?"

"No, you don't. But you do look like a man who downed his
rum a way too fast," she sneered and pushed her drink toward
him, "Here, you can try my non-acholic and I know you'll be
surprised! Now pay attention! This one goes out to you, James!"
She laid her diminutive, glittery purse on the green and red
Christmas, cocktail napkin, lying in front of her. Cracking it
open, she pulled out a small, lavender note pad and ripped off
the top sheet. Snapping her purse closed, she cleared her throat
dramatically and fixed her intense eyes on her captive audience.

"I will now read to both of you from my paper, here," she

declared. James smiled a proud grin and his dark, eyebrows arched upward, in surprising anticipation. Morgan happily sipped his lemon-water, resembling a contented cow, while, James, nonchalantly cupped his hand casually on top of something that he had laid on the table.

With an audacious motion and a gleam in his eye, James slid Mrs. Meredith's American Express Black Card across the white, tablecloth over to Morgan. "Your Mom's parting gift that I forgot to give to you. And remember, lest we forget, old Cates is on call for our driver, the rest of the night, if we need him. Sorry, I interrupted you, Amber."

Morgan bit his cleaned-up, bottom lip and chirped cheerfully, "Read, Amber! Read on, my lady. Sky is the limit, guys!" He tossed the credit card and it landed in the middle of the table. She good-naturedly grinned, but squinting her elfin eyes, she jested, "Now, since you're both are feeling so much in the Christmas spirit, I've decided I will put this to Christmas music." The boys shot a double take at each other, not sure they were ready for this novel idea, but she didn't hesitate. Amber briskly sang forth to the tune of *God Rest Ye Merry Gentlemen*:

Your songs flood my soul,
Your words fill my mind.
You strum the strings of my heart.
Sing only to me, "You're My Rainbow."
Not for any other to hear or anyone else to know,
"Rainbow," I'm your pretty "Rainbow."
Play for me and only me,
Sing just for me to know, your special song,
That bares your heart,
"You're My Rainbow."

"Where'd you come up with that?" James quipped, whipping the paper from her hand and scrutinizing it. "That's about my song, *My Rainbow*. What's with that? How does that tie in to Swedish secrets?" He ran his long fingers through his thick, brown hair, creating a stubborn cowlick above his forehead. Baffled, he flipped his hands upright and raised his arms, asking, "Who-the-heck wrote that?" He laughed, "You, Amber?"

"I know that you're wishing that I had written it, but no, it was not me," she teased. "It was the invisible author of your mysterious postcards. I successfully broke the secret code that was inserted into each of the messages, written on the back of all of the cards that you received. You've both, just now, heard the real message. The postcards have stopped arriving and you have a grand total of twenty-seven cards. Therefore, the mystery lady, and, I'm sure it's a lady, by the lyrics of your popular song, is secretly telling you she's twenty-seven years old and head-over-heels in love with you." Amber pointed to her paper which was scrawled with several of her notes. James stared vacantly. Morgan looked stunned.

"I can't believe this! Why would a Swede, who obviously, lives in Sweden, listen to my music? It's all in English," James cocked his head back and pursued the beach-bar out by the Atlantic. "Let's go get a breezy table, out at yonder watering hole for some fresh, salty air. It's all free! The breeze, that is. I'm ready for a change. Changes are good . . . sounds like an interesting title for a song, doesn't it?"

Amber leaned over and smiled, "Yeah! That sounds like a great title and a good idea. But to answer your first question, I think this lady is well educated and probably speaks English, maybe, better than I do. Remember, the postcards are inscribed in English, as well, as in Swedish. And anyone can order your CD's on line, from any local pub or music store, up and down the Keys. As a matter of fact, she could have ordered them from your web-site, perhaps, but not likely, because you would have seen the invoices for any international orders."

Morgan looked extremely puzzled, "I thought they were all written just in English and not in Swedish . . . didn't someone say they were just only in English? I hate these stupid pain pills that I've been taking. I feel like a few days of my life evaporated somewhere up into cyber-space, and I can't retrieve them back. I feel like I didn't get to live any of them . . . ." His befuddled complaining faded and he flagged over the extra-over-alert server, requesting that his party be seated at an umbrella table, beyond, on the lower deck, out by the beach. Then, he put a ten dollar bill on his small silver tray and politely suggested, "Better get some sleep, buddy."

James pulled Amber's chair out and asked, "How do you know that?" Amber picked up her small purse and cover-up, stretching significantly, as she rose, from her seat.

"What? That the mystery woman is very smart and clever?"

"Well, yeah, that . . . and, I just find it a little hard to believe that you know how to crack codes from some scribbled, unintelligible messages, that don't make a flip-of-sense. Actually, a lot-hard to believe! Do you, by any chance, speak Swedish, on the side? And, about the code-breaking? What are you? A secret agent working under-cover? What gives with that? Were you operational with Peter in Iran or wherever-the-heck, he worked? I'll bet you even speak Farsi!"

"Calm thyself down, Lad! I'll tell you both everything when I return from my covert operation in the lady's room." She flashed a stealthy smile, enjoying holding them both in suspense. Turning to walk to the front of Louie's, she called over her shoulder to them, "Meet you out oceanside." She giggled, playfully. "Not to worry. Do I look like I'm sneaking off to perform some undercover mission?" Amber shrugged her shoulders and faded off into the hazy glow of the candle-lit, dining room.

Twenty

"Oh! Excuse me," Amber cried, hesitantly, pushing open the entry door to the lady's room. "I'm sorry. I didn't realize . . . ." Her startled voice trailed off.

"Come in. I'm just changing into something more comfortable," quipped a tall, youthful blond with a European accent, as she smoothly tugged a fuzzy, baby-pink cashmere sweater down over her slender, long torso. "I am almost finished." She reached around and unzipped her floor length, silky, taupe skirt. It dropped to the spotless tile below and ruffled around her bare feet, exposing her pale, willowy legs. An over-sized, cosmetic bag was sprawled open next to the porcelain sink. Tubes of lipsticks, hair brushes, combs, mascara, and eyeliner pencils were scattered indiscriminately, upon the surface, of the marbled vanity.

"So sorry for intruding," Amber blubbered, as she cautiously slid past the unembarrassed lady and into the bathroom stall. She pushed the bolt firmly into the lock position. *What am I doing apologizing? I feel like I'm invading the girl's private dressing room. She probably just stepped off the cruise ship in*

*Old Town and is going wide-open. She'd feel right at home
during Fantasy Fest.* Suddenly, above the woman's noisy
rustling, a cell, phone ring pierced the awkward silence. Amber
jumped with a start, as it played an obnoxious, bouncy tune. She
surprised herself by her own jitteriness and her far-off thoughts
disappeared.

"Hello." Amber heard her perky greeting on the other side
of the door. She listened closely, as the young woman spoke a
few responses in English, than switched to a foreign dialect.
Amber remained still and listened, finding the call
to be slightly entertaining. After a few moments, she heard the
snappy clack of the phone closing. Chaos commenced with a
commotion of snaps popping and zippers clicking, followed by
the deliberate swoosh of the heavy bathroom door opening
wide. The bang of the door, marked a grandiose exit, leaving the
bathroom remarkably quiet and Amber all alone in the silence.
She cautiously peaked through the crack of her door, then
unlocked it and stepped out.

Reaching over the marbled counter to dry her hands, she
discovered the intriguing visitor had left her small, cell phone,
on the vanity top, under a tossed-aside, wadded-up, cotton,
hand towel. "Oops! What's this?" she gasped aloud, picking up
the very minuscule phone. Amber looked keenly at the peculiar
display and detected it was a foreign phone with overseas
service. Hastily, she dashed out into the foyer, next to the
service bar and searched the immediate area for the blond
woman, but turned up with no results. Then, she looked across
the hardwood floors of the entrance hall, leading to the front
veranda, facing Waddell Avenue, but there was no sign of her
there or anywhere around. Unfortunately, the austere concierge
was absent from her lofty desk, therefore, offering no help.
Almost all of the comfy chairs were empty and most of the
diners had departed. She determined that the stranger was either

out by the oceanside bar or had left the building, by way of the beach. Louie's inside-restaurant was almost totally vacant, as she threaded her way through the dimly-lit room, but the lively voices and laughter coming from the bar was raucous. She spotted James and Morgan sitting over at a corner table, next to the wooden railing, overlooking the water's edge. The sight of the lapping waves beyond them, calmed her spirit with renewed tranquility, as she stepped down the broad steps, onto the timbered deck. Pausing, she tilted her face upward, wincing at the overpowering glory of the black, star-strewn sky. A tropical, balmy, breeze blew softly. Poignantly portraying the Island's persuasive personality, the light wind caressed her bare skin.

Amber closed her eyes to listen. She was inspired by the sounds of the coconut palm's dry, brown fronds brushing up against one another, making their music, in the breezy air. Opening her green eyes again, she looked up and beheld countless, transparent clouds that resembled sailing ships. Glowing and luminous, they flew hurriedly across the dark heavens. *Where are they going in such a rush? I wish I was sailing upon them and leaving the world behind.* The solitary ball of silvery moon, stationed itself, like a lonely, night watchman, slowly drifting across the twinkling sky, amidst his countless, fluffy charges. She closed her eyes and listened to the constant waves, above the din of party-people, relaxing under the canopy of stars and sky. Whishing leisurely upon the sandy beach, below the spacious deck, the peaceful tide beckoned her to draw closer.

"Hey! Open your eyes!" James yelled to her from his chair, shocking her back to her senses. She blinked her eyes a couple of times and grinned, reluctant to abandon her fantasies. Mechanically, she meandered over and joined the two of them at their candle-lit table.

"Okay, I know this evening has ranked just about ten so far, but I've got a slight problem to share with you two." Holding up her hand, high in the air, she dramatically dropped the petite, gold phone onto the middle of the square, washed-board table. It spun like a top. "I found this on the vanity table in the lady's room. I looked everywhere around Louie's for the owner, but I couldn't find her at all."

"Don't worry about it. I'll take care of it. I'll turn it in to the concierge's desk, later on. I thought you said you weren't going on any covert operations when you went to the lady's room. Yeah, right!" James sneered. "Hope you don't mind, but we went ahead and ordered a bottle of Zinfandel. You know, it's known for very high antioxidants and has the promise of being an extremely ancient vintage."

"Well, you can enjoy sipping it, James, while I finally explain to you all how I cracked the code on the postcards. Is the Captain imbibing this time?"

"Yes, he certainly is. That's one glass for me and one for the Irishman," Morgan beamed, as he poured the pink liquid into two, slender-stemmed goblets. The glasses brimmed with a sparkling, pink blush when they raised them aloft. "To my recovery!" Morgan chimed, lightly tapping their glasses together in exuberant agreement. Amber tried adding something to the toast, as the noise level suddenly increased from a large, nearby party. "I didn't hear you. Can you speak a little louder, Amber?" Morgan asked. "Lively group next to us, isn't it? It's the whole, dang Madina family from the Sapodilla Lounge. They've had their Christmas bash, here at Louie's, for nearly twenty years." He laughed heartily, "I've never seen the Madina clan enjoying one, like this one, before. Man! It looks like their ship has just come in, by the appearance of everything. That's a huge spread of food and drink, James." He waved amiably at the elder, Mrs.

Madina, who was seated at the head of her special banqueting table, then, returned his focus back onto James and Amber. "Maybe, a Spanish galleon, hauling the mother-load, made port at the Sapodilla Lounge! You know, I feel like actually crying, I'm so happy to be alive and on holiday with you two, tonight." James winked faintly at Amber. Morgan tipped his glass to his lips. He then picked up the wine carafe and held it close to his face. Squinting his eyes tightly, he peered at the dimly-lit label, wrapped around the bottle. "What's the alcohol content in this stuff, anyway? Is it supposed to make me cry, as well as make me healthy?"

"No, Morgan, you've just been dried out for several days and your body is more sensitive to little changes, so this being an older, stronger vintage makes it a bit more overpowering, then usual. Remember, you've been made comfortable with bed rest and pain pills, lately," Amber consoled him, while ignoring James, as he animatedly held back his laughter. His dark eyes glinted in the candle light and she purposely disregarded him, asking, "Do they ever play live music here at the bar, Morgan?"

"No, not when we've ever dropped in. And that covers a lot of dropping-in, over a lot of years, for me and my mother," he replied, seemingly, wiping some tears from his blue eyes. Amber put her hand over his and patted it tenderly. "Okay, okay . . . that's it for getting all emotional!" he sniffed, regaining his composure. "I think I'm all set for your CIA report, Agent Albury." He sniffed again, then, pushed upward on his reddened nose with the palm of his hand, and quickly saluted her in a silly, military bravado. "Let's hear the top-secret report." She returned a bold salute, followed by a broad smile.

"Here it is. The messages on the postcards were written in long hand script in the English and Swedish languages. No, I do not know any Swedish, except for the little bit I have picked up in translating each correspondence. I did, amazingly, discover that the texts were all excerpts from advertisements for cosmetic companies and beauty spas in Malmo, Sweden. That seemed a bit odd to me. Most of the postcards were postmarked from Malmo and showed photos from local, upper-end places in that city." She dug out the lavender, note-papers from her purse, once again. "See, it says here, on a few different lines, 'Malmo.'"

"The content makes sense, but the cognizance behind them, consequently, makes little since at all. So far, that is. And, as for the incredibly short time they arrived in, I have absolutely no explanation. I guess the writer wanted them to be delivered in multiples, with more than one or two arriving at a single time," she fluttered her long lashes at James. "Maybe, she did that just to keep your interest and grab your attention, James. Confuse you or entice you, one or the other. Who knows? Also, Morgan, you probably didn't ever pay any mind to the Swedish inscriptions, because of the predominantly English text, but that's understandable with the drugs you've been on and all you've been through. You just didn't notice, I guess. But, no, in answer to your query, earlier, James never told you or me that they were just written in English. You, no doubt, dreamed that one up, as you laid in a drugged-up stupor on the couch, at James's cottage." She tenderly patted his sturdy hand, again, then, sympathetically soothed, "But, please, don't cry in your wine over it, Morgan. It's just another one of those obscure moments that escaped along with all of those fuzzy days that you already recently lost! That's all!" Morgan grimaced at her explanation. *That's all? . . .* he wondered . . . . *That's all? . . . Does she really understand how I feel about my vanished days that will never to be found, again?* Morgan sighed and gazed intently at the flickering candle's flame.

"Well, where's the poem about my song?" James inquired,

"Let me see that once again." She, thoughtfully, gave him the paper with the love-sonnet written on it, from among her complex collection of notes. "What did you do to derive this poem from that vague, web of words?" he pointed to the pile of lined pages. "Given to the fact, that the information is useless and I don't get it, please explain your method." Smiling at her with a puzzled expression, he raised his black eyebrows and handed the paper back to her. "Hope I'm really not as dense, as I feel, right now, and that you're much more brilliant, than we could have dreamed possible."

"Thanks for that, James! I'm just not sure which way I'm supposed to take that . . . ." She paused, inhaling in a deep breath. "Okay, you see, guys, my late husband, Peter, at times, worked with some very special kind of espionage-type people, way over in the Far East, when he was doing his news-reporting job. Unlike Peter, they were the kind of people that did their job, but never questioned why they did it. These educated Americans worked within a complex of classified encounters. They were *brilliant* people, like me," peeking at James, she giggled, "who circulated around him. You did admit, James, that I might be surprisingly brilliant!" Amber continued on, "But seriously, Peter learned some very basic procedures for breaking word-codes and how to decipher different, secret messages. Foreign or not foreign. Important things like that was just part of a day's work, for Peter." She had gotten their full attention. "You both knew, who Peter was, by watching cable TV and reading correspondent's reports in newspapers and magazines. In the past years that he was abroad and alive, when . . . ." She glanced away, awkwardly blinking back her tears and stopped talking. Drawing in a breath, once more, she turned back and met their sympathetic stares. Their intrigued expressions had changed to a serious nature. Amber looked uncomfortable and embarrassed.

"Yes, we knew who he was by the nightly news." James spoke softly, trying to console her. "And we do understand how tender you are feeling, at this minute. We realize, coping with your suffering and the loss of Peter has been difficult, but, right now, I want you to concentrate, Amber. You can make it, if you try." He picked up her fleecy, crimson wrap. "Here, put this around your shoulders. This will make you feel cozy." He draped the downy covering about her tense shoulders. "Just relax and take it easy. Morgan and I will shore up your weaker moments, anytime that you need us. We'll always be here to support you and stand with you. Just know that, okay?" He gazed tenderly at Amber, convincing her with his warm, coffee bean-colored eyes, half-closed, looking out between his black, Bambi-like lashes. "Now, start again. We've got all night, if you need it."

"You're so right, James. You both have been my best friends, since I've arrived here, on the Island. I needed this special time, very much with you all, tonight. Can't Christmas be wonderfully beautiful for some, but so bleakly lonely for others? So much of my life, lately, I think about the past year and what it has taken for me, to be victoriously brave. From those thoughts, I seem to get stronger in my faith, but then, out of nowhere, just like, the impact of the storm that hit us, out on the *Lady Poetry*, I suddenly, get bonked with a wave of loneliness and grief. It's really been such a short time and I miss Peter so much." She stared away at the moon-lit waves, tossing on the breeze-swept shore. "I know you guys really do try to understand how I'm feeling. I just don't know how I would have made it, here in Key West, without you all." She studied their solemn faces, reflected in the golden light that twinkled from within the tall, glass globe on their table. "I'm relying on Jesus for all of my strength, while I'm leaning on you both to help me, too. A great combo, don't you think?" She visualized the two men in her imagination, as her faithful guides traveling through a strange land, but then, composing herself, she giggled, "I'll take all the help I can get, right now. Christmas is so special to me. Jesus was born and laid in a simple manger in Bethlehem, over two centuries ago. God sent His only Son to earth to save the people, who would believe in Him, from eternal destruction. Heavenly life, forever and ever, sounds like a wise choice to me and this Christmas season, I'm reminded of that more and more, each passing day. I'm so thankful, He sent you both, into my life." Her shy smile was effervescent and contagious. They soberly nodded in agreement, studying Amber's serene visage, as she glanced down at her necklace of polished, white pearls that gleamed in the moon-drenched ambiance.

"We're the lucky ones, wouldn't you say, Captain?" James broke in, shattering the silence of the awkward moment.

"Absolutely!" Morgan lifted his only glass of extremely languishing wine, "Here! Here! Much appreciation spills from our steadfast hearts for you, Amber Albury!"

"What a group!" She tossed her head back, feeling a release of freedom flowing from every fiber of her body. "I hope we will always be close friends. Let's have a glass of red wine to celebrate our unique Christmas-camaraderie. That certainly seems appropriate, don't you think?"

"Let's do it!" Morgan confirmed, and with a snappy wave, he signaled the barmaid and she hurried to their table, bringing with her, three bottles of port to choose from. "You may have the honors, Amber. Choose a special one, since you rarely imbibe in anything, but Coca-cola."

"Alright. I think I want red for Christmas." She sparked excitedly, while the chuckling barmaid showed her the colors by holding the bottles up close to the candle. "I'll pick this one,"

Amber smiled contently.

"An extremely excellent choice," she agreed, twisting the metal corkscrew down into the aged, brown cork. It popped out of the cold bottle with a gusty release of pent-up, misty vapor. "That's exactly how I feel, tonight," Amber gestured toward the mouth of the bottle, as the server placed the cork on the table, next to Amber's crystal glass. "My sad feelings that were all bottled up inside me, now, are gone. Loosened and liberated. You all have helped me escape from myself." She got up and kissed James and Morgan on the cheek. "Let's toast to us and a pressure-free holiday, okay?" And they did so, with many best wishes, lots of joking and merry hearts. Amber sipped her wine very slowly, drinking in the moment and esteeming the radiance of its rich, rosiness in the silvery moonlight.

"Well, it's hard to jump right back into reality," Morgan offered, as he carefully adjusted his ball cap on his bulging bandage. "So, if I may, good Lass, I'd like to quote the astute and knowledgeable James Shannahan with one of his most renound phrases." James held his breath for what might come next. Morgan bawled in his best pirate accent, "'No worries here shipmate'!" He winked at her with a squinted eye. "Aye, young Lass, we're waiting to hear about your expertise in espionage!"

"Your rendition of Black Beard is rather good, Morgan. I must try to remember your buried talent for impersonating the famous buccaneer, in case, I throw a party, or something, and I need some fresh entertainment. Remind me, please, if I happen to forget." Wittingly, not looking his way, she picked up her papers, again and continued. "Now, it's really a simple procedure, once you catch on know how to apply it," she said. "In each translated sentence, there were always a few words with misspellings. I used three very reliable resources for the Swedish to English translations. They covered verb tenses, word orders and the like." She enjoyed using her oval, French-manicured fingernail, as a pointer. "See, when I wrote down these misspelled words with the incorrect letters and replaced each wrong letter with the correct one, in the order in which the text was written, all the right letters eventually formed words. Voila! We triumphantly have the masked and mysteriously hidden, love-sonnet, revealed. James's lady of anonymity, no longer, conceals her scheming secrets from him and little, does she know, that her selfish, little tricks, are now, completely exposed."

"Wow! Good work, Amber!" I'm amazed at your resolve, not to mention you're more than, true brilliance, for determining that there was a message surfacing from within a message, in the first place. Especially, encoded in a foreign message and in a language you don't even know." James crowed. "Well done, Amber. You get the prize for this one."

"I'd say! Hey! Maybe, James is going to buy you some kind of prize, Amber! But, truthfully, I can't believe you pulled this off, either, Amber." Morgan gave her a combined look of disbelief and respect mixed together. "I can't believe I missed seeing the Swedish parts on the cards, but then . . . I haven't been myself, lately . . . I can see now why you were so obsessed with those strange cards, though. Your suspicions were right-on, about them, hiding a message. You really were a woman with a mission. Very good job! My hat's off to you!" He promptly removed his Jimmy Buffet, ball cap and laid it on the bench beside him. "Man that feels better! My head feels really hot. I think that cap's cutting off my blood's circulation, to my brain!"

"Well, we sure wouldn't want that. No telling, then, what part of your brain you would be thinking with," James teased. "Myself? I like to use both sides of my brain." He laughed and took a playful jab at Morgan, as he stood up and put the loose, ball cap on his own head. "Hey, man! I may need this to keep the moonlight out of my eyes." He scooted his chair out, threw the cap back at Morgan and chimed, "Who's down for a moonlight stroll on the beach?"

Twenty-one

"Amber, you might want to consider jogging with me, some-time, in the special coolness, of a Key West morning," James cheerfully suggested. "You gotta get in shape to be a squared-away sailor." She huffed and puffed, gasping for air and holding her small hand over her pounding chest, when they finally returned to their reserved table up, in the seaside bar. After, the exuberant jaunt on the calm, wave-splashed seashore, Amber was relieved to be back. Standing awash, in the floodlight of the brilliant moon, she steeled her gaze on the stress-free features of his illuminated face. She pushed him playfully, toward his wooden chair.

"Thanks, Hercules! Are you suggesting I'm pretty much out of shape?" she shot back, slinking down onto her slatted, sun-bleached bench. She placed her bent elbows on the table's edge and rested her head, upon her outspread-hands. Tilting her face toward James, she gave him a cool, green-eyed stare. "You said we were going to take a stroll on the beach, not a workout, as I recall. Even, barefooted, I still had to sprint, to keep up with you and poor Morgan's still down there on the beach. He might

make it back, before dawn, if he's lucky. His loose, unmanage-
able bandage was flying like a banner, in the breeze." Drained of
energy and parched with thirst, she alerted their new waiter,
standing by for service. He briskly reported, eagerly clutching
onto his order-book and radiating with hospitality. "Could you
please bring me a pitcher of filtered water and a glass of ice
cubes, with sliced Key limes on the side?" she requested, as she
gasp to catch her breath. He dashed off and headed for the
crowded bar, without hesitation. "Thanks!" She called after
him, not really caring if he heard her or not. "Look out there!"
she exclaimed. "There's poor Morgan. I see him coming up the
beach in the moonlight. The moon is much higher, now. Can you
believe how bright it is out there? Key's Energy could turn off
the city lights and save on their power, tonight, if they wanted to
really help conserve oil."

"Yes, they could, but they won't, because, almost daylight, is
not the same, as daylight. I know what you mean, though,"
James concurred. "I can actually see the moon's shadows shifting in the breeze on the beach, just as if it were shade, on a sunny
day." He pointed to their limping, disheveled friend. "See how
Morgan's shadow is stretched out on top of the sand?" He snickered, chiding her mischievously, "You did notice the moonlight's
shadows on the beach, tonight?" He grinned and challenged
her, "I thought you were supposed to be an actual artist. You
know, like the famous Claude Monet, master-painter, of light
reflections. Wasn't he the head-dog, Impressionist painter of all
time?" He widened his fiercely, expressive eyes, displaying more
fire, than any Monet masterpiece. Easing into a loose, jesting
sneer, he ran his pink tongue slowly from one corner of his
mouth to the other, between his white teeth, as he waited for her
rebuttal, with intense pleasure.

Without hesitation, she sat up abruptly, and peered out at the different shadows expanded on the sand, below the raised, plank deck that they were perched upon. "Listen, Monsieur Art Critic," she swiftly defended herself, "Impressionists happen to be my expertise. I've always thought Monet was the best of the group and Claude happens to be my very favorite artist, but I'm, also, a true admirer of all of the famous, early Impressionists. I adore their works of light and shadow. Van Gogh is my other favorite artist. An Impressionist with the same passion as Monet, but unlike Claude, Vincent's techniques went unappreciated in the late 1800's, when he was alive. After his sudden death, at such a young age, people were desperate to locate his misplaced works. They were finding his paintings in chicken pens and covering drafty holes in plaster walls." She looked thoughtfully up at the bright stars.

"But, allow me to get back to your original question about the shadows, when we were out on our, so-called, stroll. Yes, I did observe the moon's grey shadows on the brightly, lit beach. But, at the present moment, I've found myself a bit distracted from our topic of discussion." She felt his curious gaze, as she deliberately toyed with him. "Why, James?" she asked coyly, baiting him in further. Her oval, elfin eyes danced impishly in the glimmering candle's glow, while she spontaneously replied to her own question. "Because, unlike you, I can hardly catch my breath. Your walk was more like a marathon event." She panted and smugly complained, "I'm barely hanging on here, in case you haven't noticed." She took an exaggerated gulp of the cold water and squeezed a tart, yellow lime on her tongue. He mused at her pathetic logic, but enjoyed the teasing defiance in her terse voice, which then, trickled into a fickle plea, "You know, all joking aside, James, sometimes, I wish we could have the full moon longer, during the month, then we do. I think of it, as a giant light bulb, up in the heavens. But, then, on the other hand, if I got my wish, we wouldn't have those really dark, special nights, when the stars look like sparkling diamonds twinkling in a black-velvet sky." Her wistful tone dropped and her words lingered, like a sweet perfume, as though she was remembering a blissful night, from her past, long ago. Turning her head away from the candle's light, she lowered her eyelids. Her long, black fringe of lashes, cast a soft moon-shadow, down upon the boarder of her perfectly, sculptured, high, cheek bones. James became inquisitively daunted by her austere beauty, as she soothed her blustery spirit and sat tranquilly before him. Unexpectedly, he found himself enamored by her statuesque features, prominently defined by the romantic, subdued glow. Helplessly, he was entranced by Amber's surprising splendor. His awestruck mind drifted into deep reflection, imagining her in this whole, new light. *Amazing . . . her face looks like a Grecian Goddess etched by a master-sculptor. Not even real. Peacefully serene, yet in power. I can see why Peter was mesmerized. She is really a work of art in a sort of mysterious, strange way. Almost within my reach, but very untouchable, all at the same time.* She was unaware he was staring at her, as she gazed up heavenward. Spell bound by her majesty, he contentedly remained captivated by her enchanting beauty and discovered he was being overtaken for a fleeting, but unmoving instant, by a time that made no passage and possessed no beginning or end. *My brain must be broken! What's going on? These are the fairy tails I write about in my song lyrics. So odd, but yet, so real . . . .*

He shook his head, as if awakening from a fantasy and fixed his sight keenly on Morgan, as he approached. He blinked away the starry-eyed look from his dreamy eyes. Promptly, he secured the silver, stainless carafe, poured some icy, cold water into his

empty wine-goblet and swigged it down. Morgan looked wind-
ed and was hobbling on one foot, when he finally reached the
table. He slumped down hard into his deck-chair. James
promptly refilled the wine glass and handed it over to him.

"Here, you are, Captain. You look like you're gonna pass
out. Are you okay, old buddy?" Morgan threw his faded, ball
cap on the table and shoved his bulky, loosely-wrapped, head-
dressing in place. Frustrated, he attempted to cover his exposed
stitches. He gave James a hard stare and glanced at Amber, looking for her reaction. Inhaling a huge breath of air, he downed the
small glass of chilled water and promptly drank two more,
before scooting an empty bench over, under his twisted ankle.
Morgan visibly propped his foot up, for James to behold and
Amber oozed with pretentious mercy over him. But, without
warning, Morgan sadly discovered his pity-party being disrupt-
ed, by the shrill ringing of the petite, cell phone lying in the middle of their table. It generated a dazzling, neon-blue, display
screen, while playing an annoying jingle. Startled by the unexpected interference, the three of them paused momentarily and
just stared at it, as if the thing were alive.

"Who's gonna answer it?" James asked, looking straight at
Amber.

"I guess I will." She snatched up the phone and pushed the
only green button that she could see, hoping it meant "talk" to
anyone, anywhere in the world. "Hello," she said, holding the
tiny, strange phone to her ear.

"Yes. That's right. We have, I mean, I have your phone. I'm
the woman that interrupted you, when you were changing your
clothes, in the restroom at Louie's Backyard Restaurant. I found
your phone on the vanity table in the lady's bathroom, after you
left." She paused for a few moments, than continued speaking
in abbreviated responses. "Yes! Okay, Eva . . . I've got that.

Eva Svensson. Is that correct?" Long pause . . . "that's quite alright, you're more than welcome . . . I'm ever so glad, to be of assistance." Longer pause . . . "well, it's safe with me. My name is Amber Albury and I'm still at Louie's, out at the back bar, next to the seashore. I'll be sitting with two men, at the far, corner-table, overlooking the beach. I'll look for you." After a few seconds passed, she said good bye and thoughtfully, snapped the phone closed. The guys were inquisitively hanging onto her every word. "Eva, the cell phone's owner, will be here very soon. She's just down the beach, somewhere at a party. I could hardly hear what she was saying, the background music was so horribly loud, but her English was amazingly good and I could understand everything she said."

"We can see her plainly from this position, when she comes in. Amber, you know what she looks like and you'll recognize her," Morgan specified. "After we're done with her, why don't we go over and do the Duval Crawl, just for the old time's sake of it?"

"That sounds like a great idea, Captain, especially, since crawling would be less stressful on your twisted ankle. We'll get to see what's going on in Old Town and maybe catch some local sounds," James agreed, happily. "Would you enjoy a crawl, this time-around, Amber, as opposed to a stroll?" He chuckled and stood up. "I'm headed for the restroom. Be back in a few." James took off and left Morgan and Amber to wait for Eva's arrival.

Minutes passed by and out-of-the-blue, Amber exclaimed, in a hushed tone, "There she is, over by the end of the bar. She's looking this way." Amber eagerly motioned her hand to get her attention. Eva caught site of them at the table and waved back.

"Hello!" she greeted Amber, gushing in a broken-English accent, as she rushed up to their table to meet them. Amber, immediately, handed her the small, cell phone. Eva sighed heavily, in grateful relief. "I am so very happy you found my phone. I was frantic. All of my important numbers are stored in here. This phone is the lifeline of my business, here and anywhere, I travel." She grasped the tiny phone tightly, thrusting the device against her svelte torso. "You were so kind to keep it for me. Thank you so terribly much. How can I repay you and your acquaintance, who is sitting here with you?" Morgan and Amber laughed at the incredibly, unexpected proposition. They both notably shook their heads in refusal. "No, I'm serious," Eva insisted. "I want to do something in return for you helping me, Amber. If you had not been in the restroom, at that time, when I left, who knows what would have become of my cell phone. Please let me buy you each a drink or a bottle of wine to share between the two of you, perhaps."

"That's really sweet. Thank you, but Morgan and I are . . . " Amber, suddenly, stopped in mid-sentence, catching herself and realizing Eva was waiting for an introduction. "Oh! I'm so sorry that I've been so rude. Where did my manners go? I forgot to introduce you to my good friend, Morgan Meredith. Eva this is Morgan." He smiled shyly. Self-conscious, he began patting his head, hoping he didn't look too ridiculous with the large, lopsided bandage, drooping down the side of his half-shaved head. He was resigned, to the fact that it was, now, past the hiding under-the-ball cap stage. "We're waiting for a friend to join us and then we're planning to leave," Amber continued. "Thank you anyway for your generous offer. We're really glad you have your cell phone back." Amber raised her finger in front of a comical grin, "Can't be without that one!" Amber's lame humor left Eva wearing a courtesy smile on her bemused face, as she extended a friendly hand out to her. Amber gave it a limp bob, up and down, and proffered, "Hope your visit here in Key

West is a good one and it was nice meeting you." She fired a glance at Morgan, urging him to say some sort of farewell.

"Yeah," he sparked, "it was really great meeting you. Sorry you had problems with loosing your phone. You may have to tie it 'round your neck. At least, it wasn't your suitcase!" Morgan chuckled at his dim-witted joke. Eva only nodded, baffled and unsure, if his weak attempt at humor was funny or just stupid. Her light, flaxen hair blew over her face, hiding a small smirk. Morgan concluded, "I hope the rest of your stay here in Key West will be just great." She fluttered her hand at him, overlooking his chivalrous endeavors completely. Giggling and shaking her head, Eva waved good-bye and turned to leave.

"Oh!" she said, suddenly twirling back around to face them, again. She deposited her cell phone into her pocket and fished a sage-green, business card, out of her vivid, pink-flowered, slingbag. "If you ever come to visit Sweden, here is my own private card. Please call me and I'll personally show you around the countryside. It is a beautiful place. I would love to return your thoughtfulness. You both will love Sweden and I owe you a favor, now."

Eva stepped backwards in her exuberance, and awkwardly knocked into James, who had just approached the table. "Oops! Pardon me, please. I'm so very sorry. I didn't mean to step on your foot. I'm so clumsy." She stepped aside, considering the outcome of the mishap and instantly, her mouth dropped open, as she exclaimed, "Oh no! I can't really believe this is happening!" She touched his shoulders with her manicured, polished, finger nails and searched his expressive eyes with a piercing stare. "Don't you recognize me, James? Don't you remember me? I met you out on Mallory Square, last January. You told me your name was 'Dan'." James looked shocked and puzzled at the same time. He ran his fingers through the top of his thick, black hair, as he studied her eager face, quite intensely. Her luminous, steel-gray eyes riveted on his, searching for a hopeful connection, while his mind reeled. *How does she know my name is really James? 'Dan,' was just a name, I made up for one night. This is getting too weird.*

"Heck . . . yeah! I remember you!" he abruptly cut in. "You were the weirdo, foreign girl that followed me home that night in your rental car. I refused the ride that you had offered me, earlier, at Mallory Square, when I was headed to the Green Parrot. For some ridiculous reason, you met up with me and my friend, Morgan, in the front of my cottage, later on that night." He flashed his big, brown eyes over at Morgan, pressuring him, with an animated hand-gesture, to think hard. "Come on, you remember this lady, don't you, Morgan? She was the one that drove up on my driveway, right before, our old New Jersey buddies showed up. She was just there for a minute or two and then zoomed off, in a hurry. Remember her now?"

"Well, I can't say that I recollect what your face looked like, then, being it was so dark and all, that night. Not to mention, that we went on to survive a pretty lively adventure, after your quick departure. Too bad you couldn't have stuck around for the party that followed!" Befuddled somewhat, he pushed his gauze bandage up off of his eyebrows and took a closer look at her unusual, but charismatic features.

" 'Danielle' is it, or something like that, right?" James asked. He moved on around and stood in front of his bench-seat, so he could see her better in the candle light. "Yeah, I sure do remember you. You blew a kiss to me, as you left Higgs Lane and you wanted me to sing a song to you, out on the Square. It's all coming back, real clear to me, now."

"I feel a little embarrassed, because I made up the name, 'Danielle,' that night. I wish you didn't have such a good memory for names." She fanned her hand and pretended to hide behind it. "But, your name isn't really 'Dan' either, is it?" James pursed his lips and concealed a coy smile. "I've told, Amber, who so wonderfully retrieved my cell phone for me, my true name. It is really Eva Svensson. I'm not Danielle Stoddard, which is what I told you that evening. I'm sorry for lying to you. I hope you will, please, forgive me, James. I did have good reasons for lying to you." Morgan's blue eyes widened in awe, while he watched James growing more perplexed, with each passing second. Eva chattered on, "But, I want you to know that I did, later, buy all of your CD's. You told me that night that you were going to make a CD and I could buy it, after you copyrighted all of your songs. I looked for the works by title, several months, later and I found a number of different ones, recorded by the real James, and not, 'Dan,' of course. They were all available on the internet. So, recognizing your face on the CD covers, I bought all of them and I've been one of your best fans, ever since. I enjoy your music very much, back home, in my own country of Sweden."

"I'm sorry, this is so surreal. I guess I'm in shock," Amber remarked. "I can't believe you know each other." Amber flew at her, "Are you, by any chance, twenty-seven years old?"

"Why, yes I am," she stammered. "How do you know that?"

"Oh, nothing. Just a lucky guess."

"Well, you guessed right. Unfortunately, I must look my age. How old are you?"

"I'm, also, twenty seven."

"We are the same age!" she tittered weakly. "I am amazed. I could have never guessed that."

"Yep! I think we, now, know who sent the mystery post-cards," Amber quietly mumbled, her voice falling within ear shot of the two guys. Eva fixed her smoky-colored eyes directly on Amber.

"Pardon me. I didn't hear you. What did you say?" The charming visitor playfully cupped her hand, around her ear and giggled uneasily.

"I was just finding it so hard to believe we are the same age, that's all!" Amber gushed ostentatiously, hoping she was covering well. "I just turned twenty-seven this past fall."

"I suppose that makes me the slightly older and perhaps, wiser woman," Eva teased. "My birthday was March nineteenth," she laughed, winding the tension tighter than a guitar string, "but, I hope, I don't appear older, then my age, because I'm hoping to look young, forever!" she stated audaciously. Then, she turned to James and said in a serious tone, "Now, that I have seen you, once again, there is something I have always wanted to tell you, but I never had the chance to do it. I hope you will show me much mercy, after I explain my foolish behavior." Tears welled up in her flannel-gray eyes. Her golden, blond hair whipped lightly, like spun-silk in the breeze, framing her fascinating, Scandinavian facade.

James looked deep into Eva's misty eyes and remembered them well. *Umm! Here comes the true confession of the lover that penned the peculiar postcards.* He glanced over at Amber, as she, too, steeled herself for the messy confession.

Eva's voice grew timid. "It's about that January night, when Rod and Lloyd paid you a visit at your little home."

"How the heck, do you know about Rod and Lloyd?" James asked, astounded by her words.

"They hired me at the Square that evening to follow you. They wanted me to find out where you lived. When I got to your home, then, I was to call Rod and direct them to your place, by using my cell phone. So that's why I introduced myself to you, earlier, that evening, and later, trailed you home. I followed you from the Green Parrot bar, like I told you that I did, but I didn't tell you the real reason why. After, I saw them arrive at your place, I left and became curious. I ran back from the corner, stop sign to see what they were up to. I saw the gun they were holding on you and your friend, Morgan. Rod paid me fifty dollars, to source you out that night, but I had no idea why or what for. They are the ones that told me your name was 'Dan'. But my suspicions grew, earlier that evening, when they kept joking back and forth, about you being the 'yogurt boy' and the impending, dismal future that you were about to experience. You seemed like a really nice and extremely talented guy, to me. I started thinking over their dumb remarks and surmised that they were wrong. After, I enjoyed hearing you sing and play your music, I thought, you sounded like you had the promise of a great future. I became convinced, following your performance on the Square, at the Sunset Celebration. I knew I was right, but I had already, reluctantly agreed, to do the job for Rod. He paid me my filthy money in advance and I was scared to back out, even though, I began having second thoughts. I thought you were the sweetest guy that I had talked to that whole week, since, I had arrived at the Old Town dock, on the cruise liner." She giggled, "Even, though, I didn't impress you too much." Her face became acutely perplexed, as she spoke on, "I thought, seriously, about how sneaky and greasy, Rod and his toady partners looked, as I drove away, down Higgs Lane, to that stop sign. And stop, I did! I stopped my car and considered the names they had called you. 'Sucker' and 'Idiot' seemed to be their favorites. So, I pulled over on the side of the road, parked and got out. Sneaking back to your cottage, I witnessed the gunman forcing you both into the house and I, immediately, phoned the police, to report exactly what was happening. Actually, I called on the very same cell phone that Amber found this evening. I was amazed how fast the patrol cars, with their bright, blue lights, arrived at your *chalet*."

"Wow! That's not what I expected to hear." James took a nervous bite on his bottom lip and then, a swallow of water from his wineglass, peering at her intently, over the rim.

"I am sorry to tell you all of this, James, but I am glad I finally did it. This whole thing has been a burden on me for a long time, because I left very early, the next morning, on the ship and never knew how it turned out for you and Morgan. I hid in the shadows, until the police cars arrived and hauled the men out of the cottage, but that is all I knew. I still do not know why they wanted your address or what they could have wanted from you. But, I was foolish and I feel like I put both of you in perilous danger. I have been sorry, ever since, that fateful night." Her voice quavered and her chest heaved, trying to hold back an outburst of tears. Amber studied James closely and waited in suspense for his next response. Morgan held back any remarks, searching his good friend's puzzled expression very earnestly.

"I just don't know what to say," James commented.

"Please, don't say anything. Just think about it. Amber has my phone number and you can call me if you ever want to talk. I visit Key West very often." She hastily hugged him, and then, quickly, darted away into the night.

Soon, they saw Eva immersed in a flood of opalescent moonlight, walking down the white, sandy beach. Her silent moonshadow drifted gracefully along beside her, never wavering, but following her every move.

Twenty-two

Amber uncontrollably laughed aloud, recalling the New Years Eve gala event that she attended, at the Meredith's gated estate, on Caroline Street, the night before. She wistfully thought about what a wonderful evening it turned out to be, aside from the fact, that she barely knew any of the invited guests. Being the only new kid on a very Old Town block wasn't so intimidating, after all, she assuredly decided . . . . *Everyone ended up looking so ridiculously funny, after Morgan went into his over-the-top mode and cranked up the bubble machine, into high-speed. My hair was dripping wet and the women were all crying and rubbing their eyes, as the soap bubbles popped on their mascara-smeared faces. But, when he sped up the confetti blower into high-gear and aimed it like a cannon out over the balcony, everybody looked like a silly bunch of sprinkled, Christmas cookies caught in a snow storm of multi-colored polka-dots. What was the man thinking? No one seemed to even care, anyway. I loved every hilarious minute of it and we were all so deliriously happy, sliding about on the slippery, wooden floors, coated in sticky, paper speckles.* She sighed deeply in retrospect. *Glad Morgan, finally, got his awkward stitches out. He's been really going through it, lately. He may have drunk way too much, last night, but he's finally gotten back into his high spirits, again . . . Ummm . . . maybe a little too much. . . . . He was in such rare form, last night . . . celebrating his recovery, I guess. His mom and their "old family" friends enjoyed the party, as much as I did. What a party . . . lots of odd people . . . but, I really felt comfortable meeting everybody. Wonder what people may have thought of me? I didn't imbibe in the fancy punch and I probably laughed way too much, but then Emma doesn't drink anything alcoholic, at all. She's such a sweet mom to Morgan and as disabled, as she is, she does so much for him. She sure loves her son. What a mess the clean-up crew will have, today. Morgan will probably sleep for a week. I wonder if he'll even remember the storm of bubbles and confetti that he created.* She laughed again. Tears welled up in her green eyes, as she pictured the sticky and amazed guests. Picking up her sliver-of-a-cell phone, she hit speed-dial.

"James, it's me, Amber Albury. Did I wake you up? I would have phoned earlier, but I didn't want to disturb your torpid-dreams."

"My torpid-dreams? What the heck are . . . ? Do you mean stupid-dreams? Never mind! It's way too early to get philosophical or get whatever it would be that I don't want it to be. So, yes, moving right along, it's really good to hear your overly-cheery voice. Top of the morning, Lass." He glanced at his wrist watch. "I never sleep in this late. My espresso pot was late wakin' me up, but it's perkin' right now, as we speak. The rich aroma is wafting into my room. Give me my morning coffee and nobody gets hurt! That's what I always say."

"Well, I hope I'm never at your cottage when you run out of coffee beans. Thanks for that warning. By the way, without getting too philosophical, torpid means out-like-a-light-kind-of-dreams. I thought you'd know all about torpid-dreams. I did notice a dusty book on dreams at your cottage, in the kitchen," she chuckled, highly amused by his curt reaction, then quipped, "Happy New Years and top of the morning to you, too, Laddy. I'm busy making black-eyed, pea soup for good luck. In Virginia, the old-timers say, if you prepare the soup and eat it on New Years Day you will have always have good luck for the coming, new year."

"Well, Happy New Year, Amber and what you're doing sounds quite interesting. But good-tasting is not the same thing, as interesting. I'm not so sure about this special, lucky soup, you're making. I'd have to test it, first."

"Well, its best served when huddling in a cozy cabin, snowed-in, on a frosty, Virginia, New Years Day. I always liked it served in front of a roaring fireplace, with warm, lemon-silk pie for dessert. Why don't you and the Captain come by, later on, for a sample? I'd say he could really use the good luck that it is supposed to bring."

"Maybe, I'll get over there for a steamy bowl of it but, if it's all the same to you, I want mine served on the bow of your Florida Key's yacht. That would suit me fine, if not better, than off in some snow-covered cabin, defying the freezing-dog-winters of Virginia. But, please, don't count on Morgan. He's probably shot for the day, or should I say the week, so I know he won't be driving over to the boat, to eat soup. He's living up to all my expectations, lately!" He paused, then, thoughtfully tagged on, "But, about the luck-part, you're right-on about that. He could sure use a bit of that. Yeah, that's what he needs, alright. Maybe, I'll bring him a whole pot of the stuff to eat for dinner, tonight."

"No, I think not. It might affect him adversely. That would be like eating a whole pot of black, turtle-bean soup. We want to change his luck, not put him back in the hospital!"

"Okay, just a small bowl of soup for our reckless friend. That'll definitely work. That is, if I try it first and I like the taste of it. Believing in the luck it promises has a lot to do with how it tastes. That's a given. So, is around five o'clock good for you? I've got to go up to Big Pine Key and see my folks."

"Sounds good! But, don't you forget, James, you promised to take me up there to meet them and go to the Big Pine Flea Market, some week end, soon. I want to see the Key deer, too. I know you told me how much your mom loves the little deer. I've never seen small deer like that and I hear they are really endangered, by the traffic that moves around, up there on Big Pine. Our Virginia white-tail deer are like giants, in comparison, to those tiny deer." James smiled and silently nodded his head, while taking a sip of the fresh coffee that he had just finished pouring. Amber continued chattering, as if, she had already downed a triple, Cuban *buchi-espresso*" But, while you're on Big Pine, I'll be cruising about, out in my little dinghy this afternoon. The weather is so beautiful, I just feel like I want to be a part of it. I'm going on a voyage over the flats and up to that tiny island that's sits away, just beyond the marina. I thought I'd check it out and see if it's a possible bird-roosting sanctuary. I'm dying to try out my micro-digital camera you and Morgan got me for Christmas. I would like to do a water-color a painting of some flora and fauna, along with a bird or two from my pictures, one day."

"Any birds in particular you're looking for? Because the ivory bill woodpecker has already been rediscovered in Arkansas and taken off the extinct-list. You're a few years late on that one, Lass."

"I know that, James. They don't even live here. I want to take shots. Oops! I mean, I want to take snapshots of the pink roseate spoonbill, if I can find him roosting on the side of the island. I saw two flying over in that direction yesterday."

"There's that ol' Virginia huntin' mentality surfacing, again. Hard to keep a lid on it, isn't it? Now remember, that the mangrove islands are a state refuge that legally protects lots of aquatic birds, so sadly, you'll only be able to take your camera."

"You're real funny, James Shannahan. I'll show you my prize-photos when you get here, later. I better get going, if I'm meeting you back here, at five o'clock."

"Okay, I'm gonna look foreword to this dinner and a movie or should I say pea soup and a slide show. I'll bring a loaf of hot, Cuban bread to go with the soup. You know, just in case I don't like the stuff. Anyway, it doesn't matter if I eat the soup, 'cause I'll always have the luck of the Irish with me, with or without the soup, Lass. I don't really need to eat your pea soup for luck."

"I promise you'll love my soup. It's got smoked Virginia ham in it. I just need some of your Irish luck with me today, when I go searching for those elusive spoonbills, because I'm waiting to eat my first bowl of the lucky soup with you, later, when you get here with your bread and your appetite. See you then and you better arrive plenty hungry."

They signed off and she prepared, with high anticipation, to disembark in her sturdy, wooden-planked dingy. Dressed in a dark-olive, Columbia-style shirt and white, cotton, cargo shorts, Amber squared up the sailboat's galley and cabin. She switched the knob to 'off,' on the gas, under the large, stoneware pot of soup, snugged down the portholes and locked the cabin door, from the outside. Slipping her boat keys in her short's pocket with her small, cell phone, she carefully lowered her canvas, tote bag onto the seat of the blown-up boat, below. Amber descended the narrow, stainless steel ladder attached to the stern of the sailboat. Lowering herself down into the light-weight boat, she situated herself comfortably on the solid, slatted seat in front of the petite, outboard motor. Turning the key, the engine hummed and Amber cast off from the *Lady Poetry*, scooting off across the grassy, shallows. The water was like a sheet of glass. A foamy wake trailed out behind the craft, leaving the marina behind. Amber peered through the clear face of the bottle-green water. It magnified the sea urchins and sponges that lived in the lush, turtle grass, just inches below the light boat. Resembling a stretched out, water bug on a rain puddle, she glided lightly across the wide, sandy flat ahead. Looming before her was her destination. The impenetrable, round, mangrove island glistened in the golden sunlight. Her heart leaped with joy, as she saw the numerous sea birds circling the green, tree branches above and picking out a place to rest from their ongoing, fishing expeditions. Amber slowed her little boat down, as she neared the hard, rocky formations that snaked up next to the island's shore. Staying clear, she ventured only, as close as she dared, to keep from running aground, upon the sharp, rusty-colored iron shore and puncturing her supple dinghy. This seemed easy enough. She could easily make out the rocky bottom through the crystal, clear saltwater. Steering the boat with her knee resting against the hand tiller, she tugged her diminutive camera out of her bag and flipped its leather strap around her neck.

Idling across the front of the island, she cut the motor off and listened to the screeching of the disturbed, wading birds. A variety of them perched high on the branches above, blissfully sunning themselves, but suddenly, took to flight when they spotted Amber, and fled, at the last second. They looped around the island, keeping a fixed-eye upon her, hoping she would get the message and leave immediately. She was amazed at the assortment of sea birds that were roosting there. *This is better than a box of chocolates,* she mused. Little and great blue herons were thick, as thieves, but more profuse, yet, were the snowy egrets and great white egrets. There was even a tiny, cocky kingfisher, close by. He flitted and dipped by her little boat, watching her with a keen, black eye, as he darted over the backwater. Quickly, he screeched to a stop and hovered in mid-air, over his catch-of the-day. A distinct white belt of feathers fluffed out from around his neck and white underside, contrasting brightly against his small, blue-grey body, as he plunged head long into the water below him. When he popped up on the surface, he swiftly flapped his way up into the azure, blue sky. Amber giggled at his comical, whipped-back feathers that stiffly pointed flat-out, straight-backwards, from his cocky, dark head. His funny, swooshed-back, spiked-up plumage made him look, so much, less serious, than he took himself for. She scratched her own head, watching him flutter off again, and squawking with bossy articulations. *Gosh, he's noisy. The way he's showing off, he must be upset or mad. What a little character. Wish I'd gotten a picture of him. He's too fast for me. Where's James's Irish luck when I need it. Should have eaten some of my own lucky soup, before I left.*

She paddled and pushed along the shore with one of the aluminum paddles, scrutinizing how close she could safely get into the tree line, without becoming entangled in the low-lying, green, leafy branches. Silently, searching for the rare, pink roseate spoonbills, the shade under the tree branches made it easy for her to observe the small fishes and a lobster feeding in the still, transparent water. Amber squinted her eyes to see where the sun was. She snapped a few pictures of the birds roosting above her, with their out stretched wings, as they prepared to fly away from her intruding dinghy. The mangrove's brown, snarled, root system formed the entire foundation to the green island and their soft bark teamed with barnacles. A busy assortment of miniature crabs lurked and scrambled deep within the twisted, dank-smelling vegetation, fleeing the unexpected, daunting boat. The bent roots were so tightly entangled, Amber felt severely locked out, knowing only a crab could easily venture into the island's perimeter. She noticed that a few, old, plastic bottles and crushed, styrofoam cups were caught under the edges of the wet, curved roots. They bobbed up and down with the moving tide, trapped forever in a growing prison of amassed, tree roots. *Anything floating up against the island would soon be snagged and imprisoned in the roots forever, never to know freedom again . . . even a hurricane would have a hard time dislodging anything, from their twisted hold,* she thought, as she gingerly poled along, straining to look inside the dark, dense, leathery foliage. Ahead, she saw the mosquitoes swarming in a moving cloud, deep in the shade of the thick, over-hanging branches. They seem to be hovering above a red object, lying in the water. She paddled closer to check it out. Apprehensively, she pushed the branches aside with the end of her paddle and peered in under the glossy, green leaves.

"Oh my God! It's a body! I can't believe this!" she cried, jabbing at it lightly with her paddle. It swayed eerily, moving back and forth with the falling of the ebbing tide. "This person is dead. Who can I call?" She took the time and studied the bloating corpse very closely and, then, quickly pushed her dinghy out from the island's edge and out into deeper water. "I'll motor down to the end of the island and call 911 or the police department." She continued to talk to herself along the way, still feeling the pangs of shock from her discovery. Securing the thin, bow line up to a mangrove branch and cutting the engine off, she decided to phone the nearby, sheriff's department, on Stock Island.

"Hello. This is Amber Albury out of Seaside Marina on Stock Island. I'm in a dinghy, out at the end of the small mangrove island facing the shore off the marina's docks. I have found a floating body . . . you know . . . a dead person . . . a man, I think . . . he's snagged up inside the island's roots . . . you know, what I mean, right? Lodged in the roots . . . the body is caught directly within the mangrove roots. Could you send someone out here, right away? I'm out here by myself." A pause. "Okay, whoever it is, in whatever department it is, just, please, arrange for someone to head out here ASAP. Thanks." She flipped her phone shut. "Ummm . . . *bet* I forgot to give them my name," she mumbled reflectively.

She waited for their response, thinking they might call her back again, but then, she realized she had "bigger fish to fry". She put her cell phone down into her short's pocket. Positioning herself, where she could watch for an approaching vessel and still gaze down the island's border, where the body was floating, she pulled her phone mechanically out of her pocket, once more, to call James to cancel the soup-date. But, reconsidering this idea, she decided not to hassle him, by disturbing his visit with his parents and slid the phone into her canvas bag. Amber pulled the brim of her russet-colored, sun hat down, to shade her eyes, from the bright, fiery ball-of-sun blazed in the shimmering, western sky. Calmly, turning the unusual situation over in her mind, she untied her boat and started the motor. She decided to put her new digital camera to use. Returning to the place where she found the body, she edged up slowly and observed that it was definitely a man. He was floating on his back with his head and arms wedged into the thick, tree roots. His squatty legs, splayed out in front of him, as he rested on top of the clear, green water. He was dressed in khaki slacks and a red, tight, polo shirt. His metal-framed glasses, hung, dangling down from his ears and sat upon the chin, of his sanguine face. The man's head was balding and he looked about forty-five years old. He didn't appear to look like he was dead for very long. Maybe a day or so, she ascertained. Carefully, she squatted in the bottom of her sturdy boat and investigated the problem, lying before her. After some extensive inspection and deliberation, she finally took out her digital camera and snapped several photos of the lifeless man, from different angles. Amber, again, took a few moments more to assess the bizarre circumstances, then, inquisitively shot a couple of more photos. Once her womanly curiosity was satisfied and the task completed, she then, hurriedly, returned back to the appointed waiting spot. Soon, she saw a white motor boat with a vibrant, orange stripe, angled on its side, swiftly approaching. They idled up, as close as possible, to the island without running aground, but still remaining in the channel's edge. Four eager, young guys dressed in navy-blue uniforms and bill caps waved at her. They each had nine millimeter guns strapped to their leather belts and they appeared overly-anxious to help her out, as almost immediately, two energetic men proceeded to jump overboard into a rigged, hull, inflatable craft, being towed, behind their vessel. They both gave the impression of being cracked-up, over a hilarious joke, as they sped over the glassy shallow water toward her. *They're sure darn glad to get off the base.* Amber was entertained, while she watched their practiced approach. They left a foamy wake behind their orange craft. She chuckled to herself and brandished her wide-brimmed, sea grass hat high above her head, showing herself to be a friendly, typical boater. Idling up close, the two, very young Coasties smiled and introduced themselves. They motioned her aboard, and then, carefully helped her into their inflatable, seating her foreword. Tying off her dinghy to their stern, she assisted in showing them the location of the drifting victim trapped in the mangrove roots.

On the way, she noticed the keen, little kingfisher had returned and was flitting up and down above them. His sharp, shiny eyes peered directly at her. Then, he flew along, ahead of them, as if, leading the way. He instinctively knew where she was going. Amber did not hesitate. She took aim and shot his picture. *This is one smart kingfisher,* she surmised. *He's not as stupid as he looks. My fantasy-spoonbills will have to wait, until another day. I wonder how long all of this will take?*

Twenty-three

"James! I'm so glad it's you!" Amber gasped, breathlessly, flinging her flip-phone open with a brisk flick of her hand. The jumpy tune it had emitted from her short's pocket was an unexpected and welcomed disturbance. "I'm so thrilled to hear your voice!"

"Good! I'm so glad to hear you're so thrilled. I never knew my simple "hello," transmitted such a thrill. I wonder if I affect all my callers, that way? Remind me to call you, whenever, you're feeling down. It's the least, a good lad can do for a sweet Molly-dear. That's brandishing a bit of Irish banter about, in case, you were wondering, lass." He piped, in his best Irish brogue, but he didn't give her time to respond. Clearing his throat, he gallantly remarked, "Alrighty, then, let's be getting back to the real reason I was calling. I have a very important bird-sighting to report. A mated pair of black, white crowned pigeons are sitting and feasting upon the seasonal, plump berries of a poisonwood tree. They're perched just above my truck, right here, next to Key Deer Boulevard, as we speak! I just had to pull off the road and check 'em out, before I turned onto US One and headed for your boat."

"That's really great, James, but I'm not at my boat. . . . "

"Yeah, I'd give it a 'D' for decent, that's for sure. So, Miss Bird-watcher, I'm not believing that you're still out there, on the water? Man! You're a real addict, at this birding-thing. I should have given you more credit. So, what the heck was your big discovery of the day?"

"A dead body!"

"Sorry, Amber. Nature can be so blasted cruel sometimes. I hope it wasn't your rare, roseate spoonbill." He constrained his amusement, by barely composing himself, but managed to offer some consoling words. "Tell me, seriously, what kind of dead bird did you find, Amber?"

"A bald-headed, dead-man-kind of bird, floating in the mangroves roots. That's what kind of bird I found, today."

"I know you're joking, right?" he chuckled, as he continued down Key Deer Boulevard and rolled to a stop at the traffic light. "Where are you anyway? I hear a bunch of people talking in the background."

"Just a minute, James. Hold on a second, okay?"

"What's going on?"

"I've gotta go. There's a bunch of stuff going on, all around, me here. I've already answered a ton of questions for the *Citizen* and the local TV station has, even, interviewed me. Once, they heard I was the late, Mr. Peter Albury's widow, I evolved into the most fascinating human-interest story, of the day. I guess they're a bit starved for exciting news around here. Heather wants to take more pictures of me and I look a total mess."

"Who the heck is Heather? And why does she need to take more pictures of you? You weren't joking about this, were you?" His black eyebrows knitted close together upon his furled forehead, as he glared down the incredulously lengthy, US One, stretching out before him, toward Key West. Extending beyond his Ford truck and coming into view, was the high span of Niles Channel Bridge, connecting to Summerland Key. "I'm on my way to get you, as fast as, this irritating forty-five miles an hour, will get me there. Where are you?"

"Come down to the Key West Police station. The officers are still keeping me busy, filling out reports. I've been with the Sheriff's detectives, too, from the Special Investigations Division, for the last hour. Not to mention, *Key's Radio* and the *Key Noter*, are here to get a piece of the action. My story wouldn't be half so intriguing to anyone, if I wasn't the famous Albury-widow. I can't believe this. There's a *Miami Herald* reporter, standing, way-too-close, to me, disgustingly slurping his hot coffee and intensely booming into his cell phone. I know he's looming about for an interview with me. This place is a zany zoo. If maybe, the dead man that I found, was important, I could understand the pandemonium, but no one has really clued me in. All the convo seems extremely hushy, between the officers and detectives. But, James, I did overhear . . . or I guess, I should confess that . . . well . . . I admit, that I did listen in and snoop around some closed doors, just a little. My girlish inquisitiveness, kind of got the best of me, but now, I happen to know a few facts that are surfacing about a prominent, missing, laboratory researcher. The authorities are, hypothetically, hoping that this floating body could be the renowned super-scientist that has been missing, for a few days. Wouldn't that be a find? Hope nobody is tapping my cell phone. You never know who's listening in, nowadays, on your phone, but anyway, that's the buzz. Guess he would need to be identified with a coroner's examination, to find out a positive ID on him, right?"

"I don't know anything about it, Amber. I don't ever worry about someone tapping my phone and, truthfully, you shouldn't stress over it either. I just like to play my music and use the 'pop-top-blowing-out-my-flip-flop' benchmark, in my life, as much, as possible."

She was silent, as she strained to figure out what on earth he was talking about. He could hear her rapid, tense breathing. "You know," he continued, "that's about as much stress, as I'd like to experience in a day, but after listening to you, and doing some real reflection on my part, I'd say, maybe, you should have eaten a bowl of your lucky, pea soup, before you went off bird-hunting, this afternoon." Lightly chortling, he qualified his concern, "Be careful what you tell these prying reporters. They're so out-of-control, with probing for any exclusive information that they can worm, out of a person. They don't accept the words, "no comment" and that's why I don't ever give private interviews, to any press reporters that I don't know, personally. Guess I get a little paranoid, too, but I can't help it, that's just how I feel. So, I'll get there, as soon, as I can, if I'm able to maneuver around these sight-seeing snow-birds. The traffic is a killer this time of year. I don't want to become some fatality number, posted up on the road sign, like a poor, helpless key deer."

James seized the chance and passed a string of cars, after breezing his way, onto Cudjoe Key, and zipping toward the Sugarloaf Key stoplight. "You know, you'll probably be on the local, evening news, tonight. Not to mention, you'll be the headline story of the *Citizen*, tomorrow, at dawn. Morgan can enjoy beholding your puzzled face and dismal story, while sipping his morning coffee, right along with all the rest of Key West. Then, watch out! You'll be so famous, you won't even be able to shop at Sears, without somebody detecting your charismatic charm and asking you for your autograph!" James laughed with pleasure. "It's all over for you, now, Mrs. Albury!"

"I know, I know. You might be closer to the truth, in that

case, than you realize, James. And I can tell you why. It's because, I already, signed press releases and now, I'm like putty in their hands. I've answered all their countless, nosey questions. I only hope that there was no harm in that. The reporters appear to be mostly interested in Peter's last days, alive and the top secret story that he was working on, just before he was killed. As if, that story about Peter's untold report and its sealed results, wasn't in every news release, in the nation, shortly, after his death. Not even, I, know what he was working on or what was in the contents, of his latest operations. Only close personnel, like Peter's good friend, Colonel Benson, would even have any knowledge or information about his modus operandi. . . . " Her voice trailed off and she spaced out into oblivion for a few moments. "And by the way," she chirped spiritedly, dropping back into the discussion and changing the subject, "I was bird-watching, today, not bird-hunting, James. Just want to set the record straight. I might, possibly, be popular for my important discovery this afternoon, but it won't be for spotting an uncommon bald eagle. It will be for finding a floating, fat, bald-headed sapsucker. Gotta go! They're calling me over for pictures, again."

"Okay. Glad to see you've kept your weird, twisted sense of humor. Watch your back."

"What's that suppose to mean?"

"Nada! Nothing! Just thought I'd throw a little humor into the mix! Lighten up! See you in a few." Click.

Amber stared, thoughtfully, into the ceiling fans, whirling above her head, as she tapped her phone shut and slipped it back into her pocket. Feeling a bit uneasy that she had been, perhaps, too approachable, concerning her private life, with the TV and news reporters, she reflected solemnly on the past few hours. *Wish I'd stayed on the* Lady Poetry, *today and finished my watercolor painting. Sure would've avoided all these dumb complications. Guess I'll call, Colonel Benson, in Williamsburg and tell him about my adventure. He would love hearing this one. No, on second thought, I'd better not. He'll start freaking out about me, living here, in so-called, 'Paradise,' on a sailboat and try to get me to move back to a farm, somewhere, in hot Virginia, again. His only idea of Paradise! How much more, he might understand, that I've improved, since I landed here, last fall, if he would just venture down here and confirm it for himself. He could witness the changes I've experienced, first hand. No matter, how hard I try to explain what I'm doing with my new life, here, in Key West, he doesn't seem to respond with approval. He is such an ol' buzzard, sometimes! And lately, he seems too preoccupied, to even hear what I'm saying when we're talking on our weekly phone calls. He'd love Key West and so would Marsha, if just, he knew, how laid-back it is down here and how much the atmosphere and my new friends have increased my inner-healing, since Peter's passing. Colonel, used to always want to hear about the positive steps that I've taken and seemed, to almost, walk on that path beside me, but lately . . . I'd love to tell him that my heart and mind are completely healed, but they're not . . . and in most recent conversations, he has been acting so strange, when I do want to discuss my progress . . . like he isn't listening, anymore.*

She sighed deeply, feeling exasperated, as she glanced over at Heather, the *Key West Citizen* photographer, gearing up for another picture of her. *Hope James gets here fast. Heather, whoever she is, sure is a nosey neighbor. She claims she lives a dock over from me and has been moored there, on a houseboat,*

*for over three years. I've never seen her at the marina, before.
She seems to be all over this case. I'm so done with this chaos.
I sure don't know anything about a missing, prominent scientist.
And even if I did, how would it be of any help to the detectives.
If it is the famous scientist, they've been searching for and keep,
clandestinely, whispering about, they should be giving me a
reward for ending their search and finding their missing man,
for them. And if, they did consider that it might be him, I sure
saved the tax payers a bundle, today. Instead, my reward will
be seeing my bewildered face, on the evening news tonight, and
published, flagrantly, in tomorrow morning's newspaper. Think
I'm going to ask the detectives if I can leave now. I'll wait outside. Wish I never told them where I lived. Great! Okay, now,
I'm getting paranoid! Like, where I live, isn't public knowledge
on any library computer in the world. Come on, James. Please
get here soon. Wish, whoever, I found, was still alive . . .*

Amber rested her graceful back along the sun-baked,
cement-block wall, outside the police station. She closed her
eyes behind, her sunglasses and soaked in its soothing warmth.
Waiting for James to roll up in his pickup truck, seemed almost
therapeutic to her, after enduring the surreal encounters inside.
Before long, she heard the beeping of a friendly horn. James
cruised to a stop, under a shady Jamaican dogwood tree, across
the street. Lowering his window, he enthusiastically beckoned
to her, as she immediately bolted over to the passenger's side of
his Caribbean-blue, colored truck.

"I wish the man was still alive! That's all I can say!" Amber
huffed, as she jumped up onto the leather seat and slammed the
truck door, much harder, than necessary. "I can't wait to get

back to the boat, James. They insisted on escorting me down here, thinking I was too shook-up to drive, by myself." She giggled and threw her auburn, sun-streaked tresses, behind her shoulders. Pushing back the shorter wisps of hair above her eyebrows, the tension lifted from her frazzled countenance. Granting James a coy, sideways glance, she whispered, "We can still have soup and a movie at my boat, if you want, but I decided I don't want to look at my digital photographs, tonight."

"Why not? Your pictures might relax you and I'd love to see them. What could be more peaceful, than viewing sea-bird photos on a cozy sailboat?"

"Because my new digital camera has more on it, than just a few pelicans, James."

"What do you mean?"

"I mean, that I took a bunch of snaps of that corpse, floating in the mangroves roots."

"That's really strange. Why did you do that?"

"Call it curiosity. And fortunately, it didn't kill the cat this time! Or call it female intuition or just plain stupidity. Take your pick. But I felt like it was my womanly-prerogative to take them, since I found him. And besides, a cat is supposed to have, at least, nine lives . . . but, in recent times, I've lost count. Oh well, this is a New Year's Day, I won't forget, for a long time. Thanks for coming down to rescue me, from all of this, James. I loved my new, little camera you guys gave me. It worked beautifully. The small, preview-pictures were really sharp and clear that I saw on the camera, earlier this afternoon. Sometime, I'll print the good ones out on my picture-maker for you, but not this evening. I can't look at that eerie corpse again, with his waterlogged clothes and his wrinkled toes, pointing up to the sky. Not today, anyway," she sniffed back a few tears. "I got a great shot of a lively kingfisher. The pointy feathers on his head were all sprigged back. Alas, I didn't see the elusive spoon-bill, at all." She pouted her pink, glossy lips and heaved a bleak sigh.

"Okay, okay! I believe you need a break from all of this. I can see it's been way too much for you. Don't worry about the photos, please. I'll see the photos some other time. I got a great idea! Let's go rent *Gone with the Wind*. Ever see it?"

"I love that movie, James!"

"How did I know that? A southern girl from Virginia, like you! I'll bet you love to eat popcorn, too? Am I right?" His smooth grin melted her, like warm butter.

"Yes, especially if it's served with something, chocolaty . . . like home-made fudge . . . that sounds so good, doesn't it?"

Craftily, James moved through the seasonal, congested cars, scooters and bicycles on Truman Boulevard. *I feel like I've promised her the moon.* They better have *Gone with the Wind* and the *popcorn, too!* He determined, as a flinty fire sparked from his dark, brown eyes. He pulled into the parking lot of the movie-rental store. Turning the truck off, he looked over at Amber's glowing face and rendered a hopeful thumb's up. "'It's an ill-wind that blows no good,' Missy," he grinned, "and I sure, as heck, hope, it isn't whipping up any trouble for me in the classic's section of the movie store. They better still carry *Gone with the Wind* or I'm gonna be really disappointed."

She rolled her almond-shaped eyes at him, as he lightened up and teased, "Scarlet O'Hara, no doubt, knew that ancient adage, very well. Poor lass! She didn't have much Irish luck with her, when she, finally, returned to her beloved Tara plantation, as I remember. Obviously, your over-ripened, southern custom, of cooking black-eyed pea soup, on New Year's Day, was unwittingly overlooked by Miss Scarlet, too. Poor girl! Perhaps, she plum-run-out, of those cotton-pickin' field peas."

"To think, how amazing it is, that I have taught you so

much, in so little time, James Shannahan." Amber's eyes mischievously twinkled, as she turned her head to conceal her proud pleasure. Casting open the door, she leaped out of the truck and slammed the door shut.

"Frankly, my dear, I don't give a dang!" James smugly smirked, as he called after her, "Hang around me and you'll see that I'm an extremely, fast learner!"

Amber made a tight spin and lithely darted away. He could hear her heartening giggles, reminiscent of leprechauns bells, lilting back, drifting on the balmy air, like musical notes rising upon a hale and hearty wind.

Twenty-four

Faint tones tinkled gently from a weathered wind chime, suspended under an overhanging eve. Echoing through the open, louvered, bedroom window, it slowly played in a swaying, southerly breeze. The soft, high and low pitches of the hollow, steel tubes lulled, James, deeper into a peaceful slumber, unaware that dawn had broken. Just outside, an early, rising rooster, glorying in the day break, proudly stretched and flapped his iridescent, black wings, in all of his chicken-grandeur. Gallantly, he flew down from the lower limb of a hovering gumbo limbo tree and perched on the worn, wood railing, bordering the back porch of James's sun-bleached, yellow cottage. Greeting the warm, golden glow of another Key West sunrise, he cranked up with a binge of crowing, that would convince anyone within range, that he was the very first, to welcome Key West's new day, like it or not. With the brilliant, keenness of a chicken's eye, one of James's bright, brown eyes popped open and peered over the plump, white hill of pillow, propped under his head. He squeezed the other eye, tightly shut, in hopes that he could drift back asleep, again, but soon, resigned that it was useless. Aware of his present defeat, James conceded that the rooster had won, again, and the night was over.

Surrendering to the inevitable, James lay still and studied the swinging, wind chime. Catching the sun's brilliant light, it sent myriads of darting, silver flickers inside his window and bathed his room, in splashes of sparkling radiance. The cackling, gold-mantled rooster, cautiously shuffled his way, foot by foot, down the banister until he squarely came into James's view. Peering intently through the screenless window, as if he had poor eye-sight, the bantering bandy, gingerly flipped his fiery-red comb, from side to side. Cocking his head, his black eyes glistened, while he eagerly anticipated James's familiar reaction. It wasn't a long wait.

James stretched out, extending his broad shoulder, as, far as, he could reach, without sliding off the bed. Grabbing a beaded-line, he yanked down on it hard. The wooden blind crashed and clacked to the window sill, with a bang. The ruffled fowl brandished his fine feathers, affronted by such rudeness, and then fluttered to the ground. His cranky complaints could be heard, all the way down, Higg's Lane, as he stridently sauntered, into the volcano-red smolder of a breaking, new dawn. James knew he'd be back in the morning, if the shadowy chicken-slayers didn't get to him, first.

Man! Why can't I remember to shut those stupid blinds at night? Oh well, I'll leave 'em closed, for now and get ready to go over to the Fantasy and deal with Lonnie-the-Looser. He probably slept at his club, last night. His bar is his bed . . . . I guess I can't leave this man, hangin' forever. Wonder if I can get out of this contract without my lawyer.

The small print, on his contract, is, as murky, as the Gulf of Mexico, on a windy day. Strangely enough, it's not even show-ing up on my copy. If I can't freelance, at other pubs in Key West, then, I'm not playing at all for him. Let him try and sue me. The snake doesn't own me. I'm nobody's property. I may need Prescott to bail me out of this one, again. Best lawyer in the Keys. Man, he is good. I probably won't get, anywhere, talkin' to Lonnie Foreman. It'll probably be useless. I just want another agreement. Maybe he'll come around, today. If not, I'm headin' back to Green Parrot or Sloppy's or whoever wants me and my music, on my terms. I better give, Prescott, a call, after my meeting with Foreman and get his advice, on the matter. Think I'll stop and get a Citizen, *on the way to the club and see how Heather handled Amber's big story.*

After brewing some strong, shade-grown, mountain-coffee that his landlord, Lionel, had brought back to him, from Costa Rica, he dressed in a pair of light, tan shorts and a tangerine-orange, T-shirt. Grasping a steaming, thermal cup, filled with creamy café con leche, he snapped the lid on tightly and was out the door and into his truck. Driving over to the old Turtle Kraals,he noticed the local traffic was amazingly light, but then, it was still very early. Winter tourists were still recovering from partying the night before, while the Island locals were just more practiced up, at making quicker recoveries. There was no trouble finding a parking space and the quiet streets were pleasant. Winter's cool air was like air-conditioning for free, as he strolled over, dropped in some coins and removed a daily *Key West Citizen* from the corner, newspaper stand. James laughed incredulously. There was Amber's serious face on the front page. After, glancing through the story, he then, folded the paper and placed it under his arm. He'd read more about it later, when his current problem wasn't so much, of a problem. He walked toward Fantasy's, while remembering, how he had played, on the outer deck, at the Schooner Wharf, on the Key West Historic Seaport, not too long, ago. He recalled, what a positive experience it turned out to be for him, when he had filled in for an ailing musician. It all worked out pretty good. So good, that the Wharf had been bugging him to return and play afternoons, starting in a couple weeks. The engagement sounded hopeful, but the owner and manager of Fantasy Flight was standing in his way and James knew, Lonnie was not going to go down, without a fight. Foreman was rich and powerful. He had nothing to loose. Exposing him, for the crooked sleaze that he was, could be an option, James considered, as he curiously, entertained the fleeting thought, of exposing him, to Amber's new and nosy acquaintance, Heather. *She's got a lofty position at the* Citizen.

Soon, he walked through the double, entry doors of the smelly saloon. His nostrils filled with the reeking stink of stale tobacco and the stench of sour beer, left over, from the long night, before. Closing out the salty-sea air, that smacked with the scent of rotting fish, the heavy door slowly latched shut. James paused, adjusting his sensitive eyes to the dimly-lit room. He spied, white-haired, Lonnie Foreman, hunkered over, at the end of the long, granite bar, sipping a whisky-smoothie and sucking a smoldering cigarette. James primed himself, for the argument that was guaranteed to follow. Realizing, that the dull man cared nothing about the exclusive music that he performed, James was convinced, more than ever, that Lonnie was only interested in head counts and lots of money. Of course, the notoriety of being an owner of an Old Town club was just an extra perk, for Lonnie to collect, along with his cash.

James believed, that for himself, his two strongest elements had always been his own songs, mixed together, with his performances. He, alone had composed this successful chemistry and formulated their powerful results, right there, on the streets of Key West. "What does Lonnie know about the heart of my music? Absolutely nada! So, here goes nothin' ," James muttered under his breath, as he boldly hopped up onto the bar stool, elbow-to-elbow, with Mr. Foreman. He caught Lonnie's eyes in the mirrored wall, facing the bar. James gave him a friendly nod. Lonnie lowered his droopy, blood-shot eyes and grunted. He reminded, James, of a planted, unmovable, stone statue, as he sat, balanced on his bar stool, covered with clouds of smoke. He didn't appear to James, that he was sober enough, to reason rationally, or haggle over, any new deals. Lonnie was nursing a hangover—Island-style. Pushing on his aching-head, with his fist, balled-up, he rubbed against his inflamed forehead, trying to alleviate the throbbing pain that he was enduring. His dry mouth drooped slightly open and the hard lines that receded from the corners of his lips were set like concrete on his weathered face. Sprigs of his wiry, white hair stood up on his head like ghosts in flight. James leaned back, musing, *it don't get much better, than this!* He checked out his own face in the mirror opposite the bar. He hoped he was, as confident, as the guy, looking back at him in his reflection. Expecting a little pain from their conflict of interests, he now figured, it would be, a whole lot more, than just a little. He rubbed his hand nervously through the thick, cowlick of hair, positioned above his apprehensive, dark-brown eyes. James braced himself, gripping the edge of the bar with both hands. Sizing up his opponent with a final once-over, the game was afoot.

Amber sat straight up in her wide, cozy bed, situated in the forward cabin. Awakened abruptly from a fascinating dream, she caught her breath and listened, again, for the disturbing noise. Who was knocking on her cabin door, so early in the morning? *I just can't catch up on my sleep, lately.* She pulled the covers up over her tousled head and buried her face in her feathered pillow. *This really can't be happening. Now, what was that dream about? Such a nice dream. Please come back sweet,*

comforting dream. I want to see how you end up. How will I know how it was all going to turn out?

"Amber," the piercing voice called. "Amber Albury, are you aboard? This is Heather, your neighbor, from the newspaper office. Are you up? I brought you the morning paper and some hot coffee?"

"I'm up now!" Amber grumbled, as she hurled the comforter off her body. She lay rigid and still for a few seconds, and breathed a big sigh. "Just a minute and I'll open the hatch-door." She scooted off of the wide, comfy bed, making her way to the stern of her sailboat, quickly raising the salon's window shades and unlatching the lock. Smiling weakly, she motioned Heather down into her spacious, snug cabin. Heather's long, blond hair was pulled, severely, back against her head, into a tight ponytail. "Good to see you again. I guess I was only trying to sleep in, if it were possible." Heather hobbled down the steps, as Amber pointed at the cozy, breakfast nook, beneath the sun-filled portholes.

"Have a seat at the table. Here are some clay mugs for the brew. They'll be much earthier than, those paper cups and plastic lids. There's cream in the fridge and the sugar is in the green, stoneware bowl, sitting on the counter. I'm going to throw on a robe, if you don't mind."

"Yep! It's one of those, sort of, imaginative, nippy and fresh crisp-blue-sky days in Key West. We wait for this weather all summer long, down here, don't we? Breezy and cloudy, clear and sunny. I love it down here."

"How long have you lived down here?" Amber called from the bathroom, amused by Heather's weather report.

"About fifteen years. I came down here with my parents, when I was sixteen. Later, they sold out cheap, after a huge hurricane hit their home and moved back to Pennsylvania. I go see them every Christmas. Me and Baily, the beagle. No husband. Just my old doggy and me."

"Oh, the coffee smells great," Amber gushed, tightening her silk robe-sash, around her slender waist. She slid over and eased comfortably onto the cushioned, padded bench, behind the teak-wood table. Picking up her tan, glazed mug, she savored the spicy aroma, wafting into the air. After one sip, her green eyes sparkled with life. "I love this. What is it?"

"It's a tamarind tree, fruit and spice blend, mixed with ground, organic Peruvian coffee beans. It's taste so good with cream and sugar, too, but I can't have it that way. My New Year's resolution is to loose fifty-five pounds by next New Year's Eve, so I drink it, fashionably, black, now. I think, Chef Boyardee and I have been hanging out, too much, with each other, for too long."

"Guess you should try some of my soup for luck. It's not fattening and you sure look, like you could use, all the luck, you can get."

"What soup? What do you mean about luck and soup? I don't get it. Do you have a special miracle-diet soup?"

"No. Never mind, I think it's too late for you, anyway." Heather's eyes widened. "No, I mean, it's not too late for you to loose the weight, but the soup has to be eaten right on New Years Day, in order to work. Just forget about it! Let's not even go there." Amber bit her bottom lip, but then, gave way, and yawned unreservedly, while inquiring, "What brings you over to pay me a visit, so early this morning?"

"This!" She seized a rolled up *Key West Citizen* from the large pocket of her purple windbreaker and slapped it down on the slick, oiled, wood surface, next to Amber's cup. "Hope you like your story that I did. Good picture of you, don't you think. You made the front page!"

I guess," she worriedly replied, scrunching up her mouth. "Well, like it or not, anyone who reads this paper, today, will know, exactly, who I am and where I live."

"Yeah, and maybe where you work, too!"

"What do you mean? Where I work? I don't work. I haven't had a job, since I arrived in Key West."

"I know. That's why I'm here. To offer you a job."

"A job? At the newspaper office?"

"No. I have an important message for you from an eccentric millionaire and businessman, who owns a local cable TV station here in, Old Town. I don't know him very well, but in my line of journalism, I run into his news reporters, quite frequently. They seem to like working for Mr. Dominique Sardis and to experience all the razzle-dazzle that follows him and his devoted entourage, wherever he goes. He's a very powerful man in Key West, and elsewhere too, is what I hear. He called me this morning, after he read my account about you and ask me, if I would contact you."

"Why on earth, would he contact you, to come see me?"

"He read the news story about you finding the body. Your discovery certainly grabbed his attention and from my article, he discovered you! He thought, you would be an interesting subject, for a viewing audience, because of your fascinating background."

"You mean the part about me, being the widow, of the famous journalist and reporter, Mr. Peter Albury?"

"Yep! You catch on fast, Amber. You would be a real bonus, for the local Key West viewing audience to gaze at."

"Well, that's not too hard to figure out." Amber quipped, lacing her graceful fingers, of one hand, into her silky hair, and lifting the coffee mug to her puckered mouth, with the other. Slightly, glowering, across her cup rim, at Heather, she asked,

"What kind of television job is he thinking about hiring me to do?"

"Don't ask me. He gave me his private, cell phone number to give to you and requested I come over to your boat and talk about all of this, personally."

"Maybe, he thinks I'll help raise his ratings!" She chuckled and drained the last, sweet drop from the stout, squatty mug.

"Well, maybe. You'll have a chance to ask him very soon. He wants you to meet him, today, at Louie's Back Yard, for lunch. Just phone him, and say, if you can be there, at twelve o'clock, noon. He's already made reservations for the two of you, in the dining room."

"Oh, he has, has he? Very assuming, isn't he?" Her blushed lips pouted, than turned. into a spiteful smirk. "I may just surprise him and take him up on his invitation. But, I'll go over early, so I can do a preliminary check-up! I might be sorry, if I don't! Prior to eating lunch with a rich, arrogant man, like he is, and one that I've never laid my eyes on, before, makes me want to see what in tarnation, he looks like, first."

"Yeah, I've heard he does come across as a privileged, pompous ass, at times. You sure sound like you know your players, that's for sure! Hey! Has anyone ever told you that your southern accent sounds a lot, like the lady that starred in the old movie, 'Gone with the Wind' a long time ago?" Amber giggled and nodded her head, knowingly. "Here's the mystery man's phone number," Heather said, as she inched out of her seat. She placed the paper on the counter, next to Amber's phone, and then, she wobbled up the tapered, entry-way steps. Amber's fiery-green eyes, suddenly, looked wildly distracted. Her mind was reeling in different directions and spinning around in summersaults, as she thought about the whole proposition.

"Hey, hand me my phone. Time is a'wasting, Heather! Louie's serves the best blue crab in Key West!" Heather heaved an exaggerated sigh and slowly, backed down, the smooth, teak steps, making sure that her feet made contact with each step, before proceeding to the next. Retrieving Amber's cell from the counter, she grinned politely and handed it, over the table, to where, Amber sat. "Thanks! I'm totally overwhelmed, right now." Amber's voice quavered a little, and she nervously took the phone, from her hand.

"Well, good luck. Maybe, next time, I see you, it'll be on television!" Heather gestured a friendly goodbye, then awkwardly, climbed back up the steps and out onto the deck. She balanced herself on the narrow gangway that was connected to the planked dock and the side of the boat. Perched precariously on the miniature bridge, she placed, one sneaker, in front, of the other, taking each step with care. Amber held her breath, watching her disembark.

She felt the boat rock underneath her, as Heather jumped off and landed squarely, on the sturdy dock, "Hope your new diet is a success. Next time, I see you, you'll be, as skinny, as a string bean." Heather signaled in agreement, with a confident thumb's up and Amber waved goodbye.

She eagerly banged the hatch closed and descended the steps. Leaning back against the galley's stainless refrigerator door, she pushed the numbers on the cell's key pad. It rang only once and an amiable voice answered the phone. The conversation was limited and brief, as Amber agreed to dine with him, at noon. Mr. Sardis acknowledged that he would enjoy the pleasure of her company. Amber ended the exchange, with a short-goodbye, and then, snapped her phone shut. If nothing else came from the *rendezvous*, she mused, the savory blue crabs would taste delicious. Served very "Virginia" style and making it all, worthwhile.

Twenty-five

"It's really happening! I start filming Monday morning. Can you believe it? I've got my own local TV show. The interview went, as smooth and fast, as a water bug, scootin' over a glassy millpond. Oops! Sorry. I forgot that you two Conchs aren't familiar with water bugs or millponds. How about, a dolphin rollin' in a boat wake? Now, there's a local description, I know, you all can grasp. But, anyway, the strangeness of Dominique Sardis has certainly become overshadowed, by the exciting job opportunity that he's given to me. Being able to experience the media world that was, once, so familiar, to Peter, does intrigue me. I know, Peter would approve of me taking this job, if he were here, today. This unexpected change has given me wind-beneath-my-wings. Me! Mrs. Peter Albury, broadcasting live, to whoever, is watching, over the balmy airwaves, of charming Cayo Hueso! Peter would be so proud of me!"

"Whoa! Hold on, wait a second! Before you soar out of sight with your invisible wings, I have a comment to make!" James cut her off at the pass. "It's not like you're out on location, deep in the heart of the Middle East, thwarting the devious plans of evil terrorists. I mean, are we talkin' about car bombs and hostages, here?" He chuckled. "I'm not saying your new job at Key West's most popular, cable TV station, isn't commendable, but you probably won't be dodging suicide bombers, IED's and enemy snipers, on a daily basis, while trying to stand on your feet and still report, the second-by-second news."

"I know all that, Mr. Shannahan. Are you, by any chance, jealous, because you aren't on TV, with your own music-show? Am I seeing a green monster, rising out of the blue and sitting in the truck, next to me?" She held her small hand over her chest and laughed, "So, is this how it really is? Has not, the thought, crossed your mind that I might be able to put in a good word for you and your musical genius, to Dominique, now, that I'm his new '*Jargon Bargain*' hostess and his morning, news reporter?"

"Oh, so it's Dominique now, is it?" Morgan's voice inflected, as he curiously sneered and slapping his bare knee, he snickered defiantly. "I can't wait to meet this operator. Who, in good conscience, would hire a totally unproven person to perform on a specialty show, like you'll be doing, without insisting on credentials, knowledge, or at least, some experience, to back them up? Doesn't that seem a little odd to anyone or am I just stupid?"

"Can I be the one to answer that question?" she laughed, freely tossing her head back. Resting it against the back of the truck seat, she glanced over at James, looking for his response. She lightheartedly, winked at him, but noticed how intense he was getting, as he began tailgating the van that had just passed them. She then, turned her eyes back onto Morgan and thoughtfully, countered, "Morgan, it took me less, than two hours, to complete my program training, so, I'm confident that Mr. Sardis believes, I can handle the job."

She thought, Morgan, looked unusually handsome, as the soft, early, morning light silhouetted his lustrous, blond hair. She felt extra comfortable, sitting between the two men, in James's roomy pickup. Shifting her eyes back and forth and watching Morgan's good-natured expressions, she was arrested by his spirited manner. The Coke-bottle-green sea, formed a peaceful backdrop, behind him, as she looked past his brawny, bronzed features and through the passenger window that he was sitting, next to. She detected, with her artist's eye, for detail, how the varied, aquamarine hues, made a perfect milieu, for framing his sweet face. Endless shades of vast, turquoise water, spilled around the outlying, tiny, mangrove islands, sited on each side of the highway, as they passed by. The deep-rooted isles, lay aimlessly strewn throughout the inshore waters, dotting the clear, backcountry water of the Gulf of Mexico, on the gulf side, of the bridge, while other rounded mounds of mangroves, nuzzled together or sprawled, like slinky felines, outstretched over the Atlantic Ocean, on the other side, of the bridge. The puffs of islands, glistened in the sun, like gleaming emeralds floating on a tranquil, turquoise bay. Soon, the trio passed over the Niles Channel Bridge, leaving Summerland Key, behind and closing in on Big Pine Key.

"No, Morgan, seriously," Amber broke the silence, not wanting to let go of the subject, "I'm sure there may be a fragment of truth to what you're saying, about me, not being experienced, but you're, perhaps, not aware of the fact, that I could have latent talents that have never been tapped, before. Since, I discovered the dead scientist, floating up in the mangroves, for instance! I certainly have achieved some local fame and notoriety for that astounding deed." She giggled and waited for his obvious rebuttal. "Simply put, Captain Morgan and Sir James, it is, what it is. I will ride out, on the very famous coattails, of my renowned, journalist-husband and then, presto! I will, successfully, establish my own mark of distinction. I plan to enjoy the legacy he left me and find gratifying pleasure in it. But, make no mistake, my friends, amidst my flamboyant self-assurance, I will constantly be throwing lots of prayers up to Jesus!"

"Sounds like a good plan to me. You're gonna need 'em!" James joked. He angled his suntanned face her way, as he burst into a wide smile, showing his white, straight teeth. Their early ride to Big Pine Key developed into an exceptionally breathtaking trip. The sunny, winter's day felt inspiring to them all, as if they were beginning the path, an unplanned adventure, together.

"Doesn't the water look greener, than ever, this morning?" James blurted out, caught up in the moment. The bright sun glimmered and sparkled, like millions of diamonds, on the ocean's reflective surface. "I love the drive up here. It is so peaceful out in the pines. Wait 'til you see my folk's house. You'll love it. It's like a tropical jungle. I just wish they weren't in Central America on vacation, so you could finally meet them, Amber. One day, in the near future, we'll get up here, after they get home. But, at least, you'll finally get to go to Big Pine's, famous, flea market. No matter, how hard, they try, to sell it or close it down, it just always keeps thriving, in one way or another. For years and years, Big Pine Key has always been known for their flea market. This new one is just a larger version of the original one, that was here. Saint Peter's Catholic Church started the whole thing with a weekly, flea market, years and years ago. They held the first one." He paused, as he started turning off US One and exclaimed, "Yep! And here we are! Can you all smell the bacon frying? Best breakfast plate served on the island, dished up, right here. Best kept secret, too. Looks like people decided to shop, instead of going out fishin' in their boats. Man, it's packed. Hope we can find a parking spot up close to the vendors. There's someone up near the concession, pulling out now. If I can still manage this annoying five-miles-per-hour, speed limit, we'll make it, before, one of these other snow-birds gets to it. I don't think my Ford, even knows, where five miles is on the truck's speedometer."

The sun was much higher in the cloudless, blue sky, than when they first arrived at the market a few hours, earlier. Amber never tired of shopping and she examined every booth like a detective, on-a-case. Begging, to go back, to the first isle that they had walked down, three hours ago, she had her eye, on one thing that she swore, she could not leave the flea market, without. And, the one thing was an Eagles Nest hammock, just like the one, James had, slung up between the two mango trees in his back yard. His hammock was a single size, in kaki and olive. She had already determined that she was ready to break out of her earth-tone rut. The tropical, banana-leaf green and lemon-yellow-trimmed, double hammock had struck her fancy, when they past by the hammock booth, earlier that morning. A light hammock that bunched into a small, attached bag! How utterly convenient! She had seen how compact they were for traveling and just to hook it up with the special "slap straps" between the mast and forestay of her sailboat was, unbelievably, an answer to prayer. Amber had always wanted to relax topside, up on her forward deck, in a hammock, but she could never figure out, how to suspend one, above such tight quarters. Now, she would have no problem. Hanging up the Eagles Nest hammock was a breeze. Being made of breathable, rip-stop nylon, and allowing the air to pass right through the tiny micro-fiber holes, she could sleep out on her deck on a sultry, summer's night, comfortably. She would be cooler in the hammock, then out of it! And, if it rained, it would dry out in minutes, in a light wind.

She was at a mild run, with Morgan and James trailing after, but, as they approached the hammock booth, suddenly, she became distracted. All morning, she had wondered what the sound was that she was hearing, echoing throughout the market and, now, she knew. Here, sat a diminutive, mysterious woman, dressed in a long-sleeved, pale-yellow, faded-cotton blouse. Over-sized sunglasses were balanced, on the bridge, of her sunburned nose and a ridiculously, giant, exaggeratedly-wide-brimmed, straw hat was scrunched down, over her ears. She had a huge hand-grabber, square, blue topaz on her index finger and she sat poised on a white, Coleman cooler, behind a wee, wooden, table top, that resembled a pizza box. It was draped in purple, as well as, lime-colored, beach towels and was positioned just a couple of feet, from the hammock-display. Spread on the table, in front of the unembarrassed, eccentric lady, were several green, brown and black, carved, wooden frogs. Meticulously, the cheerful woman would stroke each frog with a short, wooden stick. Amber knew the vendor wasn't there earlier, when they first arrived or they would have heard the distinct croaking and noticed the frogs, not to mention the peculiar peddler. The odd lady smiled, curiously, at the three of them, as they stopped to look at her unusual gathering of frogs on the table. There were super-large, bright, green frogs that emitted deep, bullfrog sounds, when the lady ran, what she called, a "striker" stick, up the high ridges of their hard backs. The jumbo ones were big and produced the loudest croaks. The medium and little "croakers," made higher calls, like tree frogs, calling for rain. Amber thought about how the frogs could fit comfortably in her purse. The woman held out the sticks to Morgan and Amber to try out the different sounds. The bigger the frog, the deeper the sound, Amber discovered, as she tried each one. She was enthralled and she decided that playing the various, colorful frogs, was more fun than trying on different shoes in a shoe store! She bought the biggest and noisiest green frog that the laughing-lady had on her table. Amber handed her an easy fifty dollars. The jolly merchant was delighted to let her big frog go, although she feigned regret, but, only, for Amber's sake. The older, yet, wiser woman's animations portrayed a sad loss for her almost, nearly-last, huge frog. Succumbing to the sad sacrifice that she had made, in relinquishing it over, to a new owner, she carried on with, previously-rehearsed sentiments. Elaborating dramatically, the crafty woman, pretended to have only Amber's best interest, in mind. She coyly, emphasized Amber's victory, over seizing and capturing, her favorite frog. She praised Amber for her talent and her ability to strike such excellent bargains.

After a bit, the frog-lady, wittingly showed a sense of satisfaction in the knowledge that Amber would be giving the giant frog a good home. Amber thanked the lady profusely, over and over, for allowing her to buy the special frog and take it with her. The gleeful vendor, relieved that it was a done-deal, smiled and shoved the fifty dollar bill down into the bodice of the gold, strapy top that she was wearing, beneath her bleached-out blouse. She, then, went on significantly, telling Amber how happy the frog would be living on a sailboat and that she and her husband, of fifty years, the Hammock Man, sailed often, on their own, twenty-three-foot-long, Compact. The salt-and-pepper-haired gentleman looked their direction, while overhearing the merry conversation and the mention of his name. He gave James, Morgan and Amber, a jovial hand-salute and invited them to try out the demonstration-hammocks that were swinging in the gentle, playful breeze. He happily suggested that they could stay in the hammocks, all day, if they wanted to, and hang out. His salty, friendly manner was convincing and inviting. The confident man proudly explained that the hammocks were designed and manufactured by his two, older sons up in the North Carolina mountains, in Asheville. He said those green mountains had sucked up, all four of his sons, right out of the Florida Keys, just like, the sucking-up of a waterspout, on a black, stormy night.

James patted him on the back and told him not to worry. He went on to kindly add, that they'd all come to their senses and be back, one day. Amber paid little attention to the conversation. She took out the frog and studied his expressive, cute face, then tucked her huge, new frog-friend away for safekeeping in the recycled Winn Dixie grocery bag that the strange "Frog Lady" had wrapped him up in.

Without hesitation, all three companions took a "load off their feet" and fell back into the empty, welcoming hammocks. The ten foot by ten foot, heavy, wood-beamed, suspension system easily supported their combined weight, as they relaxed in the colorful, parachute-style hammocks. A different hammock dropped down, from each of the two sides and there was a beautiful orange and fuchsia, sunset-colored, double hammock hanging in the front of the canopied booth, next to the crowded isle. Amber enveloped herself in it, as if it were a silk cocoon and the nice gentleman slipped a famous Eagles Nest, Pillow-In-A-Bag or Pack-Pillow under her silky, long, auburn hair. It was so comfortable, that she closed her eyes and relaxed and listened. The proud father went on and explained that his son conceived the "Pack-Pillow" brainchild, while flying in a Chinese airplane, off of the border of China, on the far-side, of the world. Amber opened her green eyes and looked over, hardly seeing, James, through the dark, mosquito netting that sheltered his Caribbean blue and green hammock. The remarkable, brilliant colors definitely reminded her of the Caribbean Sea, south of Cuba. She observed how the zipped-up, bug net, that enclosed the hammock, never touched his face or body. The fleecy pillow, under his head, matched the Dry Fly stretched out above the entire length of the hammock. Amber recalled how the pesky no-see-ums or biting gnats, sometimes, attacked her with such loathing fierceness in the still evenings at the dock. She wanted that Bug Net. She wanted it all. The whole "One Link" bonus package! A complete sleep-system, that weighed only four pounds. The old-timer said she'd look like a rock star slinging up her hammock, using his boys' special "Slap-Straps" and people watching her, would be amazed, at how fast, she could sling up her hammock. Everything could be stowed in one roomy, colorful, drawstring bag, which the nice man was throwing in for free. She realized her dream was becoming a reality. *He can stop braggin' on his boy's hammocks. I'm already there!* Now, she determined, after a stressed out morning on live television, she could return to her boat and stretch out in her very own Eagles Nest hammock. Of course, she planned on having the loud, croaking frog, in the hammock, with her, to needle near-by-neighbors that needed needling.

After, the exhausting tour of the flea market and exploring the rambling, waterfront compound, belonging to James's mom and dad, the three friends strolled the storm-torn landscape, over to the front hedge, where they observed, three, small key deer, eating some lower, hanging, red hibiscus flowers that drooped lazily over the fence, along the white, coral-powder road. James pointed out to Morgan and Amber, that the names of the deer were Kimberly, her son, Bucky and poor Princess. Princess was in obvious pain, from her ripped-open leg and twisted hoof. She was attacked by a free-roaming dog, but managed to escape and now, it was very difficult for her to feed and hobble around. Her mother was usually with her, James explained, but today, she was hanging out with her friends, who were probably relatives, anyway. Kimberly, "number one" doe, had birthed, at least, one buck a year, for the last, four years, according to James's mom and dad. She never had any does, or twins. Kimberly, "number two" doe, had delivered two sons every year, for the last, four years, and never produced any does either. For, as long, as the two deer had been mothers, they had always birthed sons and no daughters. Since, the previous destruction, of the last, hard-hitting hurricane, the low growing shrubs were scarce and slow to flourish because of the salty ground and lack of rain. The very sluggish growth seemed hardly enough to support the dwindling, deer herd and many key deer had starved to death. Some herd members, possibly, had perished in the high, storm-surge that covered most of Big Pine Key. The salt water came over the island quickly and rose over four feet and higher, in some places. But, even, before that violent hurricane, the key deer's fatality-rate, increased from automobile-related deaths, and had far-surpassed those of previous years. The annual number of road-kills were always tallied and counted and they were mounting with each passing year, because of the influx of vacationing tourists and countless drivers, traveling too fast, about the island. Key deer advocates fought for their peaceful, furry friends to insure they would have a brighter future and James's claimed his parents were no exception. Furtively, they defended the rights of these rare, small deer. Explaining the current situation to Amber and Morgan, he made his case for all of the helpless deer, who could not open their mouths, to protest, possible, unfair building and zoning laws and violated speed limits. These things would remain a constant threat to the future of the Florida Key's protected key deer, James clarified, making it alarmingly clear, how desperately the miniature, brown-eyed wonders, needed an impartial jury on their side. The deer required active defenders that could guarantee that their home on Big Pine Key would always be safe from exploitation and a shaky future, and with that said, James, then, asked Amber and Morgan, if either of them knew of anywhere else in the vast universe, that the linage of the unique key deer could be found. Where was there another island in the world, other then Big Pine Key, that the rare key deer, could call their natural home? The three agreed that there was, nowhere, else on earth.

"I'm starving!" Morgan sighed. "These deer are making me hungry! I mean, watching them eating all these flowers. We can go over the bridge to No Name Key and see if there are any raccoons, for Amber to see, at the end of the road. After that, I'm treating everyone to the No Name Pub. They have the best home-fried potatoes and fried grouper sandwich on No Name Key."

"Well, maybe, that's because there is no place that serves a fish or potato on No Name Key, unless you want to catch your lunch from the bridge," James grinned, rolling his dark, chocolate-brown eyes at Amber. "The Pub, Amber, was an old brothel and general store in the early 1900's. It's located on Big Pine, just before the bridge, leading over to No Name Key." He glanced at Morgan, who looked like he might pass out from hunger, adding, "And, Morgan, I know why you want to treat this time. It's because your resolution to stop drinking for three months has kicked in and you know you won't be running up a bar bill. Right, Mate?" James kidded sarcastically, and then quipped, "Today, El Capitan will be a little disappointed that he extended such generosity, when he sees, how thirsty, I am." He sneered, mockingly, at Morgan, who was, now, giving James, a sizzling glare. "And, about those raccoons," James, continued, on with his history account, ignoring Morgan's reaction. "They all have extremely light, sun-bleached fur, down here. Some new Keys residents have put a hurtin' on our coon population the last few years, claimin' the coons are robbing their garbage cans. I've heard tell that they secretly bait the poor animals into traps and then, they drown 'em. I've heard, too, some trappers proudly keep a tally on their kills. It's really sad. When I was a little kid, we'd drive out to the end of No Name Key and there would be about twenty raccoons, waitin' in the evening, before sunset, at the end of the road, next to the water. You could drive close down to the water's edge back then. No signs or engraved-boulders, to keep you out. There, families of masked, little critters, would be, all stretched-up, tall, standing on their hind legs, and reaching out, as high, as they could reach, with their little soft hands, claspin' the handouts comin' through the car windows. A bag of whole-wheat bread went fast. There was never enough to feed the hungry crowd and we ran out of food quick. Back then, out on the roadside, we never saw a deer appearing hungry or friendly, either one. Nowadays, you rarely even see coons in the broad daylight. My mom would paint their fur really gold-colored, on her driftwood plank-paintings, because they were so bleached-out, back in those days. That's when she and Dad operated their 'World of Driftwood' shop, next to the extinct glassworks, on Big Pine."

"Rumor had it, that the owner, way back in the day, didn't live to see the sun rise, after he ran smack into a tree, chasing down strange deer-poachers, in the middle of the night. He was drivin' around with his car lights turned off. But, anyway, as I was saying, my dad and mom loved to go out, old, bottle huntin' or 'boon docking' on the outer mangrove islands. They found some really old, rare bottles, too. Sold most of 'em, but they still got a few nice ones that they hung on to. My dad, as a kid, used to dive around the broken-off, wooden pilings of The Old Wooden Bridge that once led over to No Name Key. He'd spear fish there all day."

"In the real, old days, before, he was born, a ferry use to dock, at the end of No Name, bringing folks over from Marathon. Then, there was the Big Pine Inn, up on the highway. It was an old railway stopover that entertained and served a lot of early passengers, before the monstrous killer-hurricane of 1935, wiped out a lot of the train and most of the train's tracks. Later, the old, wooden building burned down from a grease-fire that got out of control. They showed me the pictures of it, from the early days, before the fire destroyed it. It was once, the only rockin' place on Big Pine Key! Hey, Amber, remember those endangered, white crowned pigeons that I spotted, here on Big Pine? Well, I read in a book that those migrating birds were actually hunted in Cuba, years ago, by a famous Key West writer, named Ernest, for high stakes."

"Too bad, so sad," Amber moaned sorrowfully, "I hope the book is wrong, but a least, the birds are still thriving and he didn't shoot all of them." Her mouth turned down at the corners. "Times, people and hurricanes have changed the face of this whole island. But, today, thankfully, we still have the ol' pub, still standing, so let us take our leave of these precious, little deer and go over to the infamous place and allow Morgan, here, to treat us all to cracked stone crab, conch fritters, fresh-caught, fried grouper-fingers and hush puppies, dipped in mangrove honey. And James can drink all the beer, he desires, right,

Captain?" She asked flippantly, fluttering her long, black eye-lashes. "Also, I will have to sample their very famous key lime pie. Then it's, back into Key West for me, boys! I'll have to see the manatee and alligators, another day. That expedition will have to wait. I need to get my rest this weekend and get ready for my Monday morning television *début*." She sighed slightly and then, looked up at the gray, puffy clouds gathered overhead, crying out, "Hey! It's starting to rain! It's a sun-shower! Look! Look, up there, at the size of that rainbow! The colors go all the way across the sky and down into the woods!" She stood stone-still in the soft rain and dreamily, stared off across the key deer refuge. The showered pine trees and sprinkled silver palms glistened, beneath the vibrant, pastel mists of the sprawling rainbow.

"Think I'll sleep out under the stars, in my new Eagles Nest hammock, tonight," Amber purred, dazed by the splendor of the moment. Morgan motioned impatiently for her to get into the truck, so that she wouldn't get soaked and he could go eat. "Okay! Okay!" she spurted, pleasantly licking the fresh rain-drops off of her lips, "Let's get going!"

"Come on! Let's go watch, James, down his one beer," Morgan sighed. "I'm sure he'll make it just one, or none, since he'll feel awkward drinking, alone."

"Yeah, right," James snapped sarcastically, starting up his truck. "And for you, Mate? What will be your pleasure? Will you be drinkin' expresso?"

"Yea, I guesso!"

Twenty-six

Amber frantically pitched another blouse-reject onto the pile that mushroomed above her wide, disheveled bed and grabbed another garment out of the cedar-lined closet. Gliding smoothly into an emerald-green slip-over top, she tugged it down snuggly about her shapely torso. Then, snatching a pink, flowered, silk scarf from her jumbled, dresser drawer, she quickly encircled the hibiscus-patterned, cream sash about her neck and secured it with a loose knot, tossing the fringed ends over her shoulder. Hastily, she pulled a pair of fuchsia, linen slacks up over her rounded hips. She sucked her flat tummy in, while she tied the draw-strings tightly against her slender waist, then, she seized a clear, plastic, makeup bag from the bathroom counter and unzipped it, exposing what looked like a cosmetic store inside. After, fishing out silver tubes of glossy pastels, buried deep within a pile of paraphernalia, she puckered her lips into a rose-bud pout and ran a tube of pink, luminous, lip color over them, enhancing the naturally, turned-up corners of her full mouth. Glimpsing her artistry in a petite, compact mirror, she then, smiled a spicy grin at her reflection and twirled in a tight pirouette. "Lookin' good!" she declared, confidently, when she, at last, took in the whole colorful package, that faced her, in the full-length mirror, mounted on the quietly, swaying bedroom door.

"I'm ready to make my splash! Please bless me, Lord Jesus," she prayed aloud, tilting her face toward heaven. With a self-assured nod of her head, she dashed up onto the cockpit deck, locked up *Lady Poetry*'s front hatch and leaped off the edge of the sailboat's gunnels. Her bulky purse and heavy, tote bag, flew off-beam, as she landed squarely onto the marina's dock with both feet, almost loosing her jewel-studded sandals in the process. Bouncing to her green Jeep, with keys in hand, Amber jumped into the car, slammed the door and cooed, "Life is good." She was five minutes ahead of her schedule. *God is good.* She started her car, flipped on a lively, Brazilian, instrumental CD and sped away.

The heavy, entry door of Paradise Television Studio gave way under the pressure of Amber's two hands. The door suddenly jerked out of her grip from a strong wind that gusted up behind her. A sizeable, tall individual, quickly ran over to help her, inside the building. Pulling the massive door closed, the stranger shut it, with-a-bang.

"Hi there! Get use to it! That happens a lot! I'm Miss Molly Greene, queen of this beauty-scene, and your personal makeup artist, while you're working here. I hope you'll like being my masterpiece-model, because I can see already where I'm going with this one!"

"Happy to meet you, my name is . . . "

"I know," the queen quickly cut her off, roughly interrupting. Molly glared at Amber's somber face with overly-outlined, zealous eyes. "Your name is Amber Albury. I've been acquainted with the reports of your correspondent-husband and there's been plenty of talk, around here, among the crew, about you, being the famous journalist's wife. I'm sorry for the loss. We all miss him."

"Thank you for your kind words," Amber replied, feeling a little confused and silently wondering, if her own makeup job was making a favorable impression on the robust, styling-queen.

"Well, let's get going. You're on in twenty and it looks like I have my work, cut out for me!" Amber didn't expect such a quick answer to her query.

She followed Miss Molly to a cozy, segregated area, in a back corner of the large, entrance room. There, she was seated, in a firm, over-stuffed, black, swivel chair. Molly's powdered cheeks raged with reddened intensity, as she furtively pumped the foot peddle of the big chair, up and down, with her massive sneakered-foot. Adjusting it with either, a hit-or-miss-jolt, to the exact height that Miss Molly, aimed for, Amber bumped and jostled, erratically. Enduring, repetitive jarring, she continued ricocheting back and forth, until the plunge and lift process was punctuated, with a final thud. Cautiously, Amber loosened her white-knuckled grip from the chair arms, only to see, the billow of a huge, plastic apron, parachuting, down on top of her. It enveloped her tense body, as she closed her eyes and sucked in some deep breaths of air. Parting her thick lashes, she ever-so-slowly, peeked out and regarded her captured reflection in the large, lighted mirror, in front of the stiff chair. She felt like a sheep positioned before the shearer. A streak of stress shot through the base of her rigid neck.

"Is Mr. Sardis here?" Amber asked, attempting to converse, while Molly brusquely brushed her long, brown hair up and twisted it tightly into a big, unsightly top-knot, that sat, smack-on-top of her stinging head. She abruptly turned Amber's chin, digging her exaggerated, pointy fingernails, into her soft skin and faced her toward an approaching figure.

"Yep! He's here, alright! You can see, as well, as I, that he's coming this way. Don't dare speak or breathe!" Amber looked back, observing her own worried reflection that stared at her, from the mirror. "He practically lives at the studio, lately." Molly greeted their boss with a hardy handshake and shared a brisk hug with him.

"I see you've met our legendary New York makeup-queen," he laughed, as he waved his hefty arms and loomed above Amber, studying her in the illuminated mirror. His strong scent of sickening-sweet cologne suffocated her and she muffled her cough. Mr. Sardis gave the chair, a slight spin-around, so he could view his new employee, straight on. "I hate talking to people that look out at me, from a mirror, don't you?" She slowly nodded, recalling, how, she happily spoke to herself in her very own mirror, not less, than an hour, ago.

"Yes, I've had the pleasure of meeting Molly. I'm really pumped up, so to speak!" Amber glanced down at Molly's giant sneakers, as Molly blobbed a glob of red-rouge onto Amber's face. "I'm excited and ready to take Key West by storm, figuratively speaking." He grinned at her approvingly. His exceptionally white teeth gleamed in the artificial light. "I can hardly believe, I'm doing something similar, to what my husband, Peter, did when he was alive . . . " Her voice trailed off wistfully.

"Yes, well, I can tell you're geared up for the show and believe me, it's worth every dollar we've invested, to have you on board with us. I'm betting the financial returns will come back in spades, plus interest gains, accrued, on top of that!" Sardis beamed over his innovative speculation. Amber's eyes widened, in surprise, when she heard his frank prediction.

"I hope, I'm a winner, too, now, that I'm going on the air in five minutes," she retorted, laughing nervously, "and the pressure that I'm feeling, at this second, is probably, only my imagination!"

"I'm sure I've picked the right person for the job," he replied. "Just relax, girl!" he sparred, poking his finger at her ridiculous top-knot. "Oh, there is one thing I want to ask you, before you go on the air."

"Sure, what is it?"

"Well, when you found the body of the, now, declared, missing scientist, Doctor Harold Vickers, while drifting out, by the, nearby, mangroves, was he completely dead?"

"Of course! Why, what do you mean? Is there another way to be dead, other, than completely?" She hid her irritation. "Why would you ask me a thing, like that? If you watched your own news's broadcast or read the *Citizen*, like you told me that you did, during our interview at Louie's, then you already know the answer to your question."

"Oh, I know, what you told the news's reporters, but I'm still curious, if there was, well . . . more to it, than they reported. You get my point . . . beyond any doubt, confirmed dead, like when you first came upon him and discovered his body. You were, allegedly, out there, totally alone, in your boat. What did you say, again, that you were doing out there, all by yourself?"

"Bird watching, Mr. Sardis. I was out there to watch birds. I paint watercolors of sea birds, so I puttered out to a nearby island, where flocks of them enjoying roosting. There, I did what I planned on doing. I took photos of the different, aquatic birds."

"I'll bet you also took pictures of the dead man's body, right? Being the good reporter that I know, you are, I'll wager that I'm right!" He chuckled maniacally. "Did you photograph him, Miss Albury?" He smirked at her.

"I'm not much of a gambler, like you, Mr. Sardis. Gambling is a risk, I do not take, but I do take investigative photos of birds, Mr. Sardis. That is my specialty. I was out in my skiff, that day, by that particular island, to photograph birds—and birds are what I photographed." She skirted around his snoopy question, thinking. . . . *I won't blatantly lie to my new and enormously nosy boss, but what does he think? I shared a cup of tea and crumpets with this guy, before he took his final breath? And why would it matter to him, if I did or not? This has nothing to do with my job criteria. What does he care about me and my personal business? And what gives with his acute interest in a dead, blotted corpse? Man, this guy is morbid, besides being bizarre!*

"Well, I suppose I'm just being meddlesome. I'm an extremely curious, newspaper reporter, myself. Sorry, that I pried into your private affairs. I should've stopped myself. Hey, please, call me Dominique, will you? I'd like that . . . oh! Look at the time! We better get you over to your anchor-desk. Times up! She looks absolutely gorgeous, Molly. Good work, sweetheart! You never fail to impress me. Here's a twenty dollar tip for doing such an excellent job. Treat yourself to the café, where we went, together, last week. You deserve it! Molly has transformed you into star-quality!"

Amber openly grimaced, believing that the man needed glasses. She climbed awkwardly out of the over-stuffed chair. Amber detested what the New York, beautician "Queen" had done to her. With hair spray, almost dripping down her foundation-caked face, the rouge-dollops, blotted on her cheeks, raged, fiery-red, from the lacquer fumes that oozed from her damp, stiff hair. She silently pondered . . . *it is way too late, now! But, I'll be on top of this person's stupid game, tomorrow. I'll just arrive late. How much more can I take? Looking like a cartoon from a comic book, on the first day of my talk program, isn't exactly what I had visualized. From now on, I will do my own hair and makeup or else! Queen Molly's style sure isn't my style and Sardis needs his eyes examined. What a kickoff they have both given me, this morning. A painful kick that I'll definitely dodge, tomorrow!*

"Good morning, Key West. Welcome to the new '*Bargain Jargon Show*'!" She looked straight into the camera, as if she had done it a thousand times. "I'm your hostess, Amber Albury, the wife of that special, international journalist, the late, but still living in our hearts, Peter Albury. I know many of our viewers remember him well. I may not be able to fill his shoes or, even, dream of trying them on, for that matter, but I'll give Key West a good run for their money, if I can! And, here's my first phone call ringing in, already. Remember folks, to prevent confusion, please, turn your sets down, when you're talking to me, on the phone and watching your screen during your television, phone call. Why, do we ask you to do that? We don't want you to get confused, when you watch your call being answered, because, we have a one minute delay on every call that comes into our show. That's so I can edit and delete any phone-convos that might be a bit too *risqué* for our daytime show. Just in case, one of you, gets too outlandish with the description of your wares, I can erase or control your dialogue, with a flip-of-my-finger. If you're thinking, of making a sneaky try at selling yourself to a lonely listener, you better think again! I'll be onto your tricks, quicker, than a snapper on a live shrimp! Any articles that you want to put up for sale on '*Bargain Jargon*' must go through a little screening by me, first. Can't be too careful, nowadays, with all of this free advertising, we're giving away."

She stared at Dominique Sardis, through the illuminated, glass wall that separated him, from her. He keenly acknowledged her gaze. He gave her a big toothy grin, spiked with an unnecessary wink and a thumbs-up gesture. She felt like his new trophy, inside the clear-glass, recording, studio enclosure. Amber returned the friendly sign and sneered, ever-so-slightly, conveying a weak, mutual enthusiasium. She noticed he was wearing ear phones and intently listening in on her and the callers that were phoning in. She wondered about the one minute delay, as she sorted among the jumble of new questions that were tumbling, endlessly throughout her brain. Realizing, that he was clearly on target with each call, as long, as he had on the earphones, she couldn't help, but inwardly question, why he was so focused on her performance.

He scanned her like an x-ray machine, as he stood with his hands on his hips, watching her closely. She doubted if he would be cutting off any of her callers, himself, but, then he certainly was intensely studying her and she discerned he was unpredictable. He was observing her every move, as if he was holding her under a powerful, magnifying glass. Sardis stood there a long time and continued to listen to her conversations through his over-sized earphones. After, the conclusion of the first hour's segment, he slowly removed them from his large head and disappeared into his private office, located back by the makeup-booth.

Amber felt relieved to see him go. She snuck the opportunity, to play some background music that she knew James would recognize, while she took a five minute break for commercials and several local announcements. She laughed quietly to herself, as she listened to her favorite song, from his latest CD. The

steamy island-tune, colorfully enhanced the station's stuffy, identification commercial. *Sardis will love the flamboyant,
sultry tone, of James's music, when he hears it playing. Just hope
he and the Captain are watching. They know I'll be checking on
them to find out, later . . . . Okay, it's back to the phones and a
little news-update.*

"News! Live! At fifty-five! Coming-up-soon, five minutes of
the most current info, circulating around the Island, straight
from your news, anchor-lady, me, Amber Albury! And perhaps,
one morning, I'll tell you all a tale or two about some anchoring
spots that I've survived, way back, in my glory-days, out sailing
the briny waters of Key West! It's a balmy eighty, Paradise-
degrees, at home on Duval Street. And that's where we call
home, here, at Key West. We're Old Town's only cable-broad-
casting network. Located, precisely where we can overlook a
peculiar parade in Paradise or watch a shimmering sunset trans-
verse, across the turquoise Atlantic. It all blends together, on
steamy Duval. Alright, next caller, what did you bring us? It's a
muggy morning in Old Town and maybe you're already thinkin'
about something cool to help you chill! Good deals are everywhere up and down the Keys, today! Selling your treasures on
'*Bargain Jargon*' is a breeze. It's not the sale, it's the art of the
deal, we're talkin'about, here on the '*Bargain Jargon*' show. The
rip-off sharks are hungry this morning and they're cruisin'
about, Margaret Rita's Village, to be sure. Tell us about your
stuff, caller. These bargain-hunters are ready to strike!"

"I am Doctor Carlos Balderas. I know you have a slight
video-delay, so I will talk fast. I want no one to hear this
message, but you, Mrs. Albury. I read in the newspaper, you
would be the new hostess, on Sardis's television program. You

must listen to my warning. Sardis is using you to get to me. You may be in grave danger. Meet me at the Rusty Anchor Restaurant, after your show, around one o'clock. I will find you and explain everything to you. Please erase this call." Click went the phone and the line went dead.

Amber, hurriedly, erased the less, than one minute, my sterious communication. Pausing, she bit the inside of her cheek. She caught her breath, regained her senses and quickly snapped on the live-feed switch, once more. "Holy cow-fish! I guess that caller fell overboard! We lost 'em down into Davy Jones's locker. Possibly, next time we hear from that visitor, he'll be playing in the Liquid Jones Theory Band! And that reminds me, rumor has it, that the Liquid Jones Theory Band has returned to Cayo Hueso and is playing in Old Town, today. Folks, don't miss hearing their tunes, at Sloppy's, this afternoon, at two o'clock! Look for you there!"

Amber glanced up, just in time, to see Sardis striding toward her, at a galloping pace and she was, squarely, in his sites. He looked really agitated, as he opened the heavy door of the sound room, extending his turned-up palms, in question, "What just took place?" he mouthed in a hoarse voice. Amber shifted to commercial. She tried hard to hide any guilt that might show, on her, already, rouged-red face. Smiling broadly, on purpose, she whispered back, "What's wrong?" Am I doing alright?"

"What was that all about? You have forty-five seconds missing, from the recorded dialogue, on the last phone call!" He folded his elongated arms across his expansive chest, as he continued to rebuke her sharply. "Why did you erase it? I want nothing erased, without my permission. Is that understood, Mrs. Albury?"

"Of course, Mr. Sardis, I understand completely, but I thought you instructed me to use my best judgment and screen all the calls that I felt were not appropriate." Furiously, he interjected, "My mistake!" Amber spat back, "This is my first day, working with all of these assorted gadgets, on the sound board. I probably hit the erase-switch, too quick, without realizing it and over-reacted, to the prankster on the other end of the line. I certainly didn't know your directives concerning the tapes. We overlooked that point in my training. I thought I was just doing my job and you had gone to your office, trusting me to do it. Thank you for informing me. I'm, ever so-sorry, I upset you. I would just die, Dominique, if I thought you were unhappy with my first day's performance. Please forgive me, Dominique. I'll be more careful in the future and allow you, to do all of the erasing, of the calls, when necessary." Placated and pampered by Amber's syrupy apologies, he managed to calm, himself, down.

"Thank you. Please do not tamper with the dialogue-tape and we'll work just fine, together. I know you've got first-day-jitters and you're nervous, but I keep all call-records, for future references, if needed, so don't worry about it. I'll trace the caller's history on my caller-data search." Sardis groaned and walked slowly back to his office. She noticed he left his door partly ajar, so he could watch her in the sound booth.

"What's so important about missing a caller, trying to sell a rusty anchor or two?" she remarked aloud, as if he was still standing there. "Oops! Glad he didn't hear me say that. I shouldn't have mentioned rusty anchor. . . . ." she quipped, uneasily. "Ridiculous rules with ridiculous reasoning. Why would he even care who called in and hung up, anyway? And what would he gain from tracking a seller down? A good-deal, for himself on someone's stuff, because he owns the station? What is he thinking, anyway? He is so strange. Hope Doctor Carlos doesn't make the mistake and answer his phone when Sardis calls him back, at the number, where he phoned from."

She sighed, stroking her rosy-red cheeks with her polished, oval fingernails. She decided to go to a commercial-break.

The obnoxious advertisement, for the annual Nautical Flea Market was finishing up. Amber sounded chipper and looked, as if, she was keeping it together, when she came back on the air, for the conclusion of her program. She hoped she could get out of the studio speedily and without Sardis getting in her way. After, signing off the air, Amber packed up her canvas, tote bag, to leave. She was glad to see a distraction appear. A tall, vogue-looking blond, walked into Sardis's office. Amber observed her *élan* hair-style and striking manner, through the partially-opened door. Her slender back was turned toward Amber and her long, shapely legs were crossed. She sat very poised, behind a flat, computer monitor that glowed from atop Sardis's wooden, inlaid desk.

Amber could not see her face, although she certainly tried. At that precise moment, Sardis leaned out and closed the door. Amber shot him a glance. Their eyes met briefly, before the door clicked shut.

She made a quick exit from Sardis and his building. While, on her sudden escape, she pondered, *I've got to get busy, with my own personal plans and pretend, that my day, is just getting started. Pure fantasy, I'm ready! Let my day begin!*

Twenty-seven

Amber decided to drive straight home from the studio, to the boat and change, into a pair of comfortable shorts and top. Thinking over the events of the morning and sifting through the results of her first day, on the job, she couldn't get her mind off of the mysterious warning, from the anonymous caller. Over-shadowed by apprehension, she tried sorting out her thoughts while she headed for her Jeep, but still she was puzzled.

Pearly, white-rimmed sunglasses shaded her troubled eyes. She studied the sun-baked pathway that she walked. Buried deep in confusion, she struggled with her inner reasoning and she began to pray . . . *Lord, Do I respond and meet this strange man, at the Rusty Anchor? What if he's some pervert, trying to get me have lunch with him? I would be really dumb to be baited in, by a plate of conch fritters. Maybe I'm just being stupid, but stupid or not, I feel like I should go meet this man, at the Rusty Anchor, on Stock Island. This is an opportunity to*

help somebody else, if it's a legitimate, plea, for help. The island of, Key West, harbors a lot of trustworthy people, as well, as many freaky-people. Key Weirdest! You love all geeks and any-body else, on the Island, but . . . of course, I know, I can't be, too, careful! That's what Colonel Benson warned me about on the phone, last night. He was really pleased that I landed the TV spot and I liked it, when he said, that it would've made my dear husband proud, too. I wonder if Colonel Benson was able to tune into the show, over the internet, this morning . . . he said he was going to try. He thinks I'm becoming famous, after seeing my picture on the front page of the Citizen, *on his computer. My very own local, cable-show, being broadcasted, world wide, online, doesn't seem possible, but with You, God, all things are possible.*

Morgan promised he would watch the show and I wonder if James caught it. I don't think he has cable TV hooked up at his cottage, right now, but maybe he saw it on his cell phone. . . . I'm sure the Colonel and Marsha would love coming to Key West. I can't wait, until, they come down to visit. Maybe, in the near future, is what he told me, last night. They'll love James and Morgan, I know. Seemed like he was holding back, telling me some secret, he had going on in his life. Perhaps, they're get-ting married, soon and he wants to surprise me with the news, when he gets down here. At times, Lord, he acted so mysteri-ously quiet and preoccupied, during our conversation, I wasn't sure what to say. You know it all, when I don't. Maybe, he thinks someone is tapping his phone line and he's being careful with what he says, but that might be a stretch, since he's retired now, or supposed to be retired. Well, it's possible, but not likely. Nowadays, who knows? Ummmm. . . . scary thought, to be sure, but, thankfully, You know all things, Lord, and You are in control. Whenever, they both do finally get down here, and

I hope it's soon. They'll love experiencing the Caribbean, blue-green water and all the tropical flowers blooming, on the island. Taking them sailing on the Lady Poetry *will really impress them, too, I hope. So much to think about, so many ideas, so little time.* Amber's car came into her view. She pointed her keys at it and the lock triggered open.

The wind had picked up and she could hear the high-pitched whispers passing through the long, dark-green needles of the Australian, whispering-pine trees, suspended above her car. They had dropped several, small pokey-berries, onto the hood, but she didn't mind. It was worth the nuisance, just to have a few of the tall, wispy trees, left standing on the Island. She thought, about, how stupid it was that the county had practically removed all of them and they continued to destroy the few remaining ones. Just because, someone decided, years ago, that they were not native to the Florida Keys, they must be eliminated. James explained this problem to her a short time back, but that seemed so long, ago, to her, as she deliberated. . . .

Where has the time gone? I thought time was supposed to slow down here in Paradise. The "always manana" myth that, Key West, is known for, doesn't really exist, for some of us Islanders . . . it all reminds me of the rusty, metal, green frog that is stuck in the middle of Morgan's flower garden. "Welcome to Paradise" it says, on the frog's little sign, but somehow, the glory-frog has a drooping smile, a cracked, broken head and leans over crooked, hanging on by a thread, to his green-corroded, copper post. Like Morgan's frog-friend, this aging Island is, nowhere, near perfect. My trust is in the true Rock of my Salvation. That's what I gotta stand on. Jesus is my Rock and my Deliverer. He will never fail me! Even if this frail Island-

Paradise, gets harder and rockier to live on, I need to tell myself, more, each day, that Jesus is the real Rock, even, if nobody else wants to hear me talk about it.

She slipped her sun glasses up onto the top of her head and opened the car door on the driver's side. The lofty pines had kept the car's leather seats cool with their bountiful shade. Amber was glad to arrive at her Jeep. She heaved her bags over onto the passenger's side. Standing there, all alone, silently by the open door, she extended her lean arms, up over her head and reached high, toward the trees. Her exaggerated yawn, amplified throughout the tiny parking lot and she felt her tight, back muscles release some of their stress. Amber basked in the savory stretch.

"Hey!" Morgan called gently, while he lowered his car window. "Where you headed? To a celebrity luncheon?" Amber jumped. Morgan startled her, from a most luxurious repose. Feeling some ease from the tension, she regained her composure and managed a welcoming grin. The tight, studio parking space that was reserved for her car, hardly had room enough, for her to park in. But, Morgan managed to squeeze in, right next to her, with his mom's BMW.

"You shocked me! Where did you guys come from?" she cried, observing James's silly expression, as he laughed and pointed at her slicked-up hair. Childishly, he doggedly teased her about her distressed appearance. She glared at him over the rim of her sunglasses, displaying genuine irritation. Squinting, her black eyelashes, closed-down and her jade-green eyes, fiercely narrowed, she shot, James, with a fiery, wordless dart.

"We came to take you to lunch, if you want to go," Morgan

freely offered. "You know, to celebrate your first day on the job and all. We watched your program. You did a great job, even, if you didn't really look like you were wearing your own hair." Amber gasped! She was horrified that he would bring up the subject again. The two men played it off, as they stared over at her, from Mrs. Meredith's car. Both were amazed, to witness Amber furiously pulling down her knotted hair, from off the top, of her head. It tumbled loosely upon her shoulders. Running her dexterous fingers frantically through her sprayed tresses, she smirked at her fascinated audience.

Morgan continued, not missing a beat, "My mother even had all the house-hold-help, lined up and sitting with her, in front of the television, eating brownies and drinking espresso. They unanimously decided that you were the best thing, since chocolate. I had to agree, since I ate most of the cook's brownies. Your new fans chattered, incessantly, in, at least, three different languages, while they watched your *début*. My mom will be hard-pressed to get them to do their work, every morning, if she's got, you, tuned in on the wide-screen."

She turned, and sank down on the leather seat. It felt good against her weary body. Observing the two of them, joking around and acting so lighthearted, Amber found they, actually, soothed her jangled nerves. A pleasant smile peacefully turned up at the corners of her crimson mouth and spread across her cameo-shaped face. Suddenly, a red rooster with dark, green tail feathers hurriedly ran over and hopped up onto the hood of her car. He crowed a proud, shrill crow, showing off nobly, for the three, homely hens, below and an additional bitty, scattered here and there. They were busily pecking at the sandy, loamy soil, where tiny fire-ants skirmished around the chicken's fast, flat, bare feet.

"Well, I'm glad that you all liked my first show. Sounds like the chicken liked it, too!" The pompous rooster flapped his wide wings. They beat in a striking rhythm that was, definitely, his very own, accented by a noteworthy, swooshing sound. "Hope I can always live up to his and everybody's expectations," she remarked shyly, but glowing with appreciation. "Even though my headache is still throbbing, you both look mighty good to me, right at the moment." Morgan flashed a concurring grin of at James, who nodded back, in agreement. "I'm serious, even though, you made fun of my stupid hair style, you look like a couple of sunbeams that have broken through the clouds, after a stressful storm. And, we all know what that is like!"

"Well, we couldn't agree with you more," James replied superficially. "Would you care to have lunch with us two sun-beams? Your choice, any restaurant, any time!"

"Rusty Anchor at 1:00!" Amber blurted.

"She makes up her mind fast, doesn't she? Either that or she must be starving," Morgan joked, blinking his eyes with a hasty double-take.

"Both!" she snapped. "But I need to go to the boat and change clothes first. I'm feeling suffocated in these long pants!"

"Well, we wouldn't want to see that happen! But, get this . . . James has reason to celebrate, today, too." Morgan quipped, pointing in James's direction. "He's celebrating his court victory!"

"You're kidding? Is it really true?" she asked.

"Yep, it is true and it is, now, history. The judge dismissed my case and my lawyer, Prescott, prevailed again. We were in court, early this morning, for less than thirty minutes. The judge finished with the hearing, while you were just getting warmed up, on your show! After that, I headed over to Morgan's house and caught most of your program and might, I add, you were really great." James gave her a small applause, then continued,

"Prescott is the most honest lawyer that I know and he's really very good, at what he does. I'm getting pretty familiar with this legal diligence-stuff. Especially, after all the garbage, I went through, to put, Rod and Lloyd, behind bars, with my copyright case."

"Squire Prescott is first-rate. He's very skillful and he's won another case for me! To top it off, he wants to hire me, to play at his fancy home, out on Shark Key. He's giving a benefit-bash, next weekend and he said, if I would perform for his important guests, he would write off, all my attorney fees that I've racked up. Prescott has triumphed, again. He's my hero! I'm free to play any place and anytime, I please. Lonnie and I are history. I'm not even going back to court to hear his sentencing, tomorrow. The judge based the ruling on Lonnie's fraudulence and Prescott's solid proof that Lonnie altered the heck-out-of-my contract, *after* I had already signed it. That, sure, as heck, sealed the suck-er-dog's fate! It was beautiful!" James's mouth broke into a winning grin, which radiated contagious elation, "Let go! We got to get to the part, where the celebrating kicks-in!"

"Well, I'm game for that and I'm glad it's over, James. You never, even revealed to me that your court hearing was this morning. I know you didn't tell me, because you didn't want me looking worried on live TV! I'm so happy for you. You always seem to come out of these things, smelling like a rose," Amber teased, winking one green eye at him. "You're the golden boy, but all that glitters, is not gold, so you've just found out! You've got to be more cautious and try not getting involved, with these slimy characters, anymore. That's what I say, anyway."

"Yeah, well, it's not like I plan these things, Amber."

Morgan slugged James in the arm to get his attention.

"Hey, what are you doing?" James reacted to the sharp pain, pressing his aching arm. "There are other ways to get my attention, Meredith. I've got permanent bruises on my upper arms, from you!"

"Look! See, over there! Speaking of slimy characters!" he pointed across the street. "There are those same sneaky-looking guys that I saw over at Cecilia's Sapodilla Lounge, a few months, ago. They just pulled in, across the street, in that Mercedes sedan that I saw 'em driving in, that morning. Remember, I was waiting there for you, James, so, we could take Amber diving? It's definitely them. They remind me of those copyright thieves that held us up at your cottage. Look! One of 'em is pointing over at us. Now, tell me, this ain't odd?"

"Maybe, it is and maybe, it isn't." Amber interjected. "They might work for Sardis and they may be spying on me! They could be watching, to see what I'm doing and where I'm going."

"Okay, yeah, right. I get it. You stole some of your boss's hair-styling gel from off his desk, just before, you left your first day at work," Morgan joked, tossing his yellow, silky bangs out of his eyes. "And now, he's sent his henchmen out to get you! Whoa! You better watch out, Miss Bargain-Jargon, they're watchin' your every move! You're the one they're after!" Morgan teased, giving Amber, a perturbed-roll, of his china-blue eyes. She patiently considered his comical animations, as he went on to conclude, "You know, I was observing, how this gooey Sardis-creep, was wearing his hair on his TV commercial, this morning. James's new song *Atmosphere* was playing in the background, quite fittingly." He good-humoredly snickered, then added, "Sardis glistened like a greased-up pig, with that sticky-looking gunk that was slathered, all over his hair. Obviously, he dyes his jet-black hair to look younger. That blue-black color that he sports, reminds me of, Veronica, in my great grandmother's, old Archie comic books."

"Veronica? Now, there's an old fashioned name from the

long-lost past!" she giggled, before presenting Morgan with a sizzling rebuttal, "I didn't steal any hair pomade from creepy Sardis! All joking aside, I haven't told either of you about my anonymous caller that phoned me, on the show, this morning and wants me to meet him, at one o'clock, at the Rusty Anchor Restaurant."

Carefully, she explained everything that happened, from the time she arrived, at the studio, to leaving the building, just a few minutes, ago. "Sardis was acting very suspicious of me and being nosey, as ever, most of the morning, but I didn't know why, until much later, in the morning. After, the unknown caller phoned in, I began putting the puzzle pieces together."

"Yeah, I recall you saying some casual statement, about a disconnected caller. You said the person fell overboard, which I found very amusing," Morgan laughed. His lilted mirth resounded. It was reminiscent to, Amber, of the wide ripples of water that circled, out and beyond, a small pebble being plunked into a pond. She smiled softly at him, as he voiced his assumption, "Well, Amber, after hearing the account of what you experienced, today, we know why you knew exactly when and where you wanted to eat lunch."

"That's right," she replied. "Sardis was furious about the tape being erased and even, before I went on the air, he badgered me to reveal information on the scientist I found. He wanted to know, if he was dead, when I discovered him floating, up in the mangroves."

"Well, was he?" James asked.

"What a dumb question, James! Of course, he was!" He got that funny, inferring grin on his tan face. His dark-chocolate brown eyes twinkled. Amber, smirked at him, quite annoyed,

"He also, stupidly, asked me if I took pictures of the body."

"And did you take pictures of the body?" Morgan inquired.

"That's nobody's business!" she rolled her green eyes.

"She did!" Morgan chimed out, looking slightly shocked.

"Okay, so I did! I admitted it to James, in confidence, the day that I discovered the scientist. He knew, I had snapped a few shots of the guy. Don't look so surprised! It may sound like strange behavior, but what's stranger? Me, taking pictures of a dead guy that I've never met, before, or some guy, calling me, out-of-the-blue, on a live-televised, phone call and warning me about my new boss and his devious plans for placing my life in imminent danger? Only you guys, know my secret, about photographing Mr. Herald Vickers."

"Oh . . . I forgot to tell you, in case, you were not aware, that's his name . . . thought you'd want to know . . . if you all hadn't heard. And there is one other thing that I failed to mention to you both, but . . . just forget it, I won't need to! I can already see my suspicions were right. Do you recognize the lady, who is walking over to that Mercedes, right now? When I left the studio, a tall, blond was sitting at Sardis's computer. I thought that she resembled Eva, or Eve, or whoever she is. You remember her . . . the Swedish, postcard-chick, that we met at Louie's Backyard? And look, gentlemen! There she is, right now, big as life! She must work for Sardis." The three of them silently stared at her and then, at each other, amazed by Amber's surprising discovery.

"That's it! Let's go!" James exclaimed. "Let's get out of here, now, before, she spots us sitting over here. Amber, follow Morgan and me, around the building and out the other way, so she won't see us leaving. Come on, hurry, start your Jeep! I'm just not ready, for another Eve-or-Eva-encounter. Or whatever-kind-of-encounter, she is! We'll meet you over at the marina."

Twenty-eight

James, Amber and Morgan drove across the hot, narrow roads of Stock Island in the BMW and arrived at the restaurant, in short order. Morgan parked in a safe spot, far from other banging car doors and bored kids with rusty keys. Morgan was getting use to paying for touch-up paint jobs on his mom's blue car. It had been "keyed" three times, already, since she purchased the car, a year ago.

He locked the car and they walked into the Rusty Anchor at exactly one o'clock. Looking around the dining hall, they saw no evidence of a man sitting alone, at any of the dining tables. The early bar-crowd was scanty, with only a few, unmistakable regulars. James and Amber were elated to find the colorful, salt-water fish, swimming in the massive, crystal-clear aquarium, positioned at the end of the dining room, near the entrance.

Morgan returned to his two distracted partners and the tank, after, searching the entire place. Cheerfully, he reported to Amber, "Well, your one o'clock is late!" Without hesitation, the brightly lit-up tank caught his attention, too. He drew closer to the aquarium, and focused on the alert, pink shrimp, pattering gently about on the gravel and remarked casually, "Man! Those fat shrimp, looking up at me, with their black, beady eyes, sure make my mouth water. Ummmm . . . Amber, have you observed the behavior of the brilliant, tropical fish, darting and flashing through the water? Did you know that they are each directed, by an instinctive signal that is transmitted and collected in their small, soggy, fish-brains? They don't possess the aptitude for decision-making or cleverly choose what tasty morsel, they shall have for lunch, today, like you and I do. Nor, are these slippery creatures just sitting around, kicking back and reading a menu about the catch-of-the-day. Only, after, receiving the command signal, they automatically, counter with a behavioral response, establishing what they must do next. Their limited comprehension does not broaden, by experiences and they do not process learned procedures, but rather they follow their own instinctive reasoning. I, myself, have branded their oily kind, as having reasoning that is illogical or even invalid, because of the difficulty, I have encountered, when attempting to get into the mind of a fish. I've been absorbed, by a string of these slimy problems, far-too-long and I have decided, the whole supposition seems spongy and is full of holes. I discovered that its substantiations are a bit squishy and clearly, the theory doesn't hold water, conclusively, leaving the facts smelling pungently fishy, to me."

Amber's almond-shaped eyes widened with surprise, as she listened intently to Morgan's senseless dissertation, on the subject of marine biology. "With that said, and in wrapping-up," he continued on, while noting his effect on her, "my highly, developed, human brain has just made a logical decision for me and has determined that I'm practically starving. So, guess what I'm planning to do?"

"Eat the indecisive, stupid shrimp in the aquarium?" Amber mocked. Morgan thoughtfully glanced down at the jumbo shrimp, as they tapped on the side of the glass, with their touchy-feely legs and waving their whiskery-antennas. He playfully rubbed his growling stomach.

"Okay, I got the picture, Captain," she declared. James had ignored his mindless-drivel, making his own study of the beautiful fish, while Amber grabbed Morgan by the arms, declaring, "Let's go order three pounds of steamed shrimp and some conch fritters all 'round. I want conch fritters, more, than I want a challenge, with a strange, creepy character, right now. But, you know, guys, I think we can relax, because my "no-show" probably fabricated the scare, to make me suspicious of my eccentric boss. People do odd things, when they know their message might be publicized by a media-magnet, like me!" she giggled and blushed, but then added, "I think a grouper-fillet sandwich would definitely set-me-right and relieve my rotten mood. I'm so famished. We need extra tartar sauce, on the side, please, and plenty of sliced key limes. Who knows? This Carlos-man might even be a stalker. Wouldn't that be a great? I don't like the idea of fooling around with a warped, frequent-caller, everyday." Amber sighed and gave the dining room the once-over. "Hey! Can we sit over there by the window? We'll still be in view of the tank and we can unwind, while we watch the tropical fish!"

The men, knowingly, smiled at one another and agreed that was a wonderful suggestion, surmising that Amber would be much better company, if she did put some food in her stomach. They ambled over to a round table, under the sunny window. Amber elected a few more delicacies to munch on, for *hors d'oeuvres* and then, left the men at the table, to order the food.

She strolled back over to the long, lighted aquarium, to study the colorful fish, once more.

A bright blue and yellow, immature angelfish swam up and looked straight-on at Amber, through the glass. The tiny thing seemed to be mouthing a fishy message to her. Amber noticed that the vibrant fish, intelligently, decided for herself, much to Morgan's displeasure, to stay away from the stationary, lavender, stinging anemone that was slowly bobbing his deadly, fluid-filled tentacles, at her. Amber looked beyond the bleached, staghorn coral, lying on the white, gravel bottom, past the angelfish. On the backside of the aquarium, she saw a human hand, through the clear glass, moving, up and down and beckoning her. Pressing her forehead, against the glass tank, she squinted her eyes and made out the face of a short, balding man, who looked like he was inside the aquarium. *That wasn't there before.* He was smiling and fluttering his fingers at her. He, suddenly, stretched up and peeked over the wooden, aquarium lid. Amber conveniently, moved up, onto a child's step-up stool, that was sitting on the floor, beside her. Rising onto her tip-toes, she encountered a friendly face, gazing across the top of the tank, at her.

"Hola, Mrs. Albury" he said, "I am Doctor Carlos Balderas, the man who called you this morning, on your program. My friends call me Carlos, which means Charles, in English, and is my christening name from birth. You may call me either name that you like. That will be fine with me." Amber gave him a curious stare. Self-consciously, he cleared his throat and respectfully continued. "Thank you for meeting me here. I recognized your pretty face. I saw your picture on the front of the *Key West Citizen* newspaper. Regrettably, I had to sneak and hide, this morning, in the Sears store's, electronics department. This was the only way I could secretly watch your show on their many television sets. I read that your TV show would be debuting, today, and I wanted to check it out. When I saw, positively, it was you, who appeared on their television screens, it confirmed that you were the same sweet lady that I had read, all about, in the newspaper. Immediately, I wanted to get to a public phone to call you. So, I did. I know, well, the bad person, who owns the cable network that you are working for. He is a dreadful man named, Dominique Sardis, but before, I tell you my awful plight, I just wanted to say, that many folks, besides me, were gathered around the giant televisions in Sears, watching your new show. We all enjoyed it very much. I thought that you might appreciate hearing that." Amber gave a gracious, but troubling nod, unsure, of where the man was going, with all of this. Carlos turned his head and suspiciously glimpsed Morgan and James, as they happily perused their diverse menus. "Please, excuse me for not being, how do you say? Ummm . . . detectable . . . when you arrived at the restaurant, but, at that moment, I was hiding behind here, until I might be able, to speak to you privately," he continued. "I was aware of the perilous chance I was taking, coming here to meet you. I did overhear you and your companions speaking about my questionable motives for this clandestine meeting, but let me make it clear, my reasons are truly upright. I must be very careful, not to let any of the Domique Sardis-mob, see me. If they find me, I will be killed, also. I am on the run and they will certainly end my life, too, if I should run into them!"

Amber shuddered. She extended her lean torso upward and her tummy became fully illuminated by the glowing, aquarium lights. Stretching as tall, as she could, she got a better peek at this strange-looking character, who was straining to peer back at her over the top-edge of the tank-cover. Amber shot a fleeting look over at Morgan and James. Carlos's eyes followed her glance and he discerned her worry.

Considering the two men and her relationship, with them, he

cautiously asked, "Are those your good friends at the table?" Carlos studied them inquisitively. "I saw you bring the two men into the restaurant with you, when you came in. Can I trust them? Do you trust them?"

"Absolutely, I trust them with my life and you can trust them with your life, too. Of course, that is, if you are really telling me the truth, about you and me being in some sort of impending danger. They would both be very angry with you, if they found out that you were lying to me. We are best friends and our loyalties, to one another, run very deep. I don't want to even imagine how they would react, if you were lying to me."

"Please, believe me; I am not lying to you, Mrs. Albury! Nobody followed you her in another car, I hope. Did you see anyone who could be doing that, hanging around?" he asked guardedly, as Amber noticed that his English was delicately sprinkled, with a spicy, Spanish accent.

"No. We were careful, but there was a black Mercedes sedan, with about three or four big guys in it, parked across from the studio, when I left from work, at noon. They pointed at me, as if, I may have been their topic of conversation. But then, my two friends, that you see seated over there, under the window, suggested that we should leave immediately, so we got out of there really quick. I don't think they took note of my friend's car, but I would venture to say, that the men only watched me, leave in my green Jeep."

"*Bueno, bueno*, you did well. I call them the 'Big Suits' and I call them other names, too, besides that!" he chuckled. "Of course, I know they have a devious plan. They always do."

"Well, I can't figure out why you believe I'm part of the plan. And what did you mean when you said 'killed also'? What is your implication of this 'also' part of that statement? You must be completely up-front and explain everything to me and my two faithful amigos, or we cannot help you. You *comprehendo,* right?" Carlos nodded politely. "Wait here a few minutes, while I go discuss this situation with them, por favor. Did I hear you call yourself, 'Doctor'? I don't understand that."

"Yes, Mrs. Albury. I am the other missing scientist, Doctor Carlos Balderas. People just don't realize, yet, that I am missing. The bad guys have reported me, as going back to Costa Rica, my homeland. That is the story Sardis wants everyone to believe, until they can find me and kill me, too." He paused. "Okay, you must leave. I will be right here sitting, on the floor, in back of the aquarium. You go and I wait for you to bring them over to me. Take your time, I do not mind waiting. What other things are there for me to do?" He sadly ducked down and disappeared behind the tank. Amber mechanically walked over to the men at the table, dazed by Carlo's serious words. The restaurant had suddenly become extremely busy, with tourists and locals, pouring in the doors. Finally, the electrified, bustling waitress was approaching the group to take their lunch order.

"Okay, boys what would you like to order. We've got some yummy specials-of the-day. Umm, let's go over them, shall we?" the flaming, redhead glowered, while zinging out a rapid-fire discourse from her orange lips, and smacking and cracking her blue gum between her snapping teeth like a ravenous baracuda. "We have the catch-of-the-day, which is . . . "

Amber, surprisingly, cut her off, "Look, would you do me a big favor? We need this order to go A.S.A.P.! Can you get it together, really pronto? And double everything, I'm really starving! I'll throw an extra big tip, your way, if you oblige me on the express-request!" Morgan's eyes got big. Perplexed and bewildered, James ran his long fingers through the front of his thick, brown hair. His expression was that familiar, puzzled look, that Amber had learned to interpret, as the, "count on me, but what-in-the-heck, are you doing?" look. She sort of smiled and did an animated, motioning-movement with her head, in the direction of Carlos, who was cowering, patiently, behind the fish tank.

"Anything you want, Missy," the server retorted. "I'm here to make sure you get good, fast service. We want you all to come back, the next time, you visit in Key West. Now what'll it be?"

"First off, we're local and not visiting," Amber asserted herself, with a proud smile. "And I, guaran-darn-tee you, we'll be back! I live here on Stock Island, so that's a given, but for right now, we need to quickly get our order to-go. Thanks for your help. Maybe, we can stay longer and linger, next time we come in."

Amber's smile faded, as the annoyed waitress smirked at her. The redhead's gold, eye-tooth, caught the reflection of sunlight that streamed in through the sparkling, window pane, above the table. Throwing Amber a little off-balance, momentarily, she boldly waved her away. Without hesitation the waitress, hurriedly, rushed off to the kitchen with their orders. Amber commenced to brief the guys, on what took place, behind the aquarium. After, a diminutive discussion and answering all of their legitimate questions, she left the two of them at the table. She did not forget to leave them with some extra cash, too, for the fiery waitress, when she came back with the packaged-up, food order. Amber returned back, behind the tank, where Carlos was concealed, to tell him of their new plan and what they could do to help him.

The guys procured the bulging bags of conch fritters, grouper sandwiches, steamed shrimp, and the rest of the massive order, and joined Carlos and Amber behind the tank. After making awkward introductions, Amber grabbed Dr. Carlos by the hand and led him along, following close behind the two guys, as they raced out of the restaurant and across the breezy parking lot. Swiftly, they all leaped into Morgan's car and headed back to Amber's sailboat. Carlos rode huddled in the back, slumped down, below the rear window, just in case Sardis's men might be about. When they arrived at the marina, Morgan retrieved his mom's hooded, rain-poncho from the trunk. He threw it around Carlos for a disguise. Amber's poked Mrs. Meredith's big, old sunglasses, down snuggly, over his eyes, giving him a new look. They briskly, scurried him along, the long, wooden docks and soon, Carlos was safely aboard the *Lady Poetry* with his three, new friends.

"I can't believe we ate all that food!" Carlos exclaimed. "I thank you all so much for the wonderful meal. I'm not use to such fine fair! Lately, I have been sneaking in and out of convenience stores, buying fast-food. You all should see my disguises that I have worn for these tasks. They are very funny, some of them. I am afraid to go into the fast-food restaurants, here, on the Island, for fear, one of the 'Big Suits', will be in the place, gobbling down hamburgers."

"Well," Amber began, "speaking of these 'Suits' you referred to, earlier, it's time for you to explain some facts to us. We want to help you, if we can. We appreciate that you called me, on the phone, to help protect me, from these so-called bad men, but we're unclear, as to why, I am in need of protection. I hardly know Dominique Sardis."

There was a fond sentiment for Carlos in her soothing voice. James and Morgan rested, contentedly, against the back of the soft, cushioned sofa, with their feet up, while digesting their huge lunch. They propped their bare, tanned feet on two small, padded, collapsible foot-stools and looked ever-so-comfy. Carlos and Amber remained at the galley table, sipping their strong, Cuban *café-con-leche* that Dr. Carlos had prepared for everyone. Amber hoped the gentle lapping of the water, against the hull of the boat, wouldn't lull James and Morgan into an afternoon *siesta*, after consuming such an enormous lunch. She gingerly hopped up from the cozy nook and refilled their empty coffee mugs, to the brim. Nudging both men, gently, to pay close attention, she firmly squeezed in and sat down between the two of them. Together, they listened as Carlos began his tale.

"Amber, fortunately, found my friend, Dr. Harald Vickers, floating in the mangroves, somewhere off of Stock Island. He was happy, and well—most of the time—when he was alive and he was my best friend. We had worked with one another in the world of exploratory science for five years in California, and then, later, we worked together here, in Key West. You may ask, why would Sardis want to end his life? Why would he want to take mine? I will tell you, but the three of you, must promise me that you will not ever tell, a living soul about the information I am going to share with you. It is top-secret and cannot leave this boat cabin. There are others who may be very seriously hurt or killed, besides me and, possibly, Amber, if this information should leak out. So, I must be assured that I am able to trust you three to make this honorable agreement with me." He scanned their pensive faces. "Will you make this promise to me and can I trust you to keep it?"

The three friends swore an oath of secrecy to Carlos. He

looked relieved, as he gladly nodded his head and shook hands, with each person. The strange, secular pack was curiously sealed.

"Now, I will try to explain everything, as best, as I can. You may stop me, at any time, if you have questions, but I think my story will answer most of them for you."

Before, beginning the account, Dr. Carlos made the sacred sign of the cross, over his chest, after mumbling a short prayer in Latin. Amber whispered a grateful "Amen" in concurrence, as if she fully understood the language. James screwed his mouth up and his face paralyzed with doubt, as he saw her, join in agreement with Carlos, knowing, she had no idea, on earth, what she had prayed for or agreed with. Morgan slightly turned his shaggy, blond head, sideways, to catch James's take on the whole matter. Silently, James sat like a stone statue, staring straight ahead, at the surreal Doctor Balderas; therefore, not giving Morgan much to go on, except for the fact, that James's was gripping his chin, with his thumb and forefinger, quite contemplatively. Morgan didn't let it go and *zoomed* in on him with a bit closer examination. Unmistakably, he detected a secret smile on James's pursed lips.

Twenty-nine

"I wish I didn't know now what I didn't know then," Carlos murmured, gazing far off into the distant clouds through, the open portholes, above the sailboat's sofa. "Focusing on the regrets, of the past could paralyze my future, if I'm not careful. I must not do that."

Morgan, James and Amber sat on the sofa. He was seated across from them, at the cozy, dining nook. Studying his pensive face, Amber noticed his facial features mirrored a familiar image, one, of poignant pain. Buried deep, within the premature creases that streaked his worried, middle-aged face, were dim reflections of anxiety and heartache.

"Lately, I've closed my eyes to what I know . . . and thankfully, it's best . . . " he reasoned allowed, as his voice softened to a whisper. Amber looked baffled and sighed. She reached up and firmly pulled the port lights down. Turning the brass locks securely, she locked out the rank, putrid smell, of a dead, decaying fish, floating under the dock. The vile stench had hung in the still air and carried on the wind, for a few days, now. Wafting about, it had entered through the open portholes. Amber's memories, of the buoyant scientist were triggered by the rotten smell of the fish. She cringed and cranked the locks down tighter.

"Carlos, you know what Sardis asked me, today? He wanted to know, if Vickers was still alive, when I spotted him, lodged in the mangroves roots," Amber paused, weighing the matter, further, "and I thought that was an unusual question. Don't you think so?"

"No, that is not unusual, at all, for Sardis to pry into the sordid details of your discovery. His direct question only proves his intentions, even more, emphasizing why the threat to your life, may be a part, of his pact with the evil one. He needs to be in absolute control of the mounting circumstances, or should I say, simply put, he needs to be sure, Vickers was not, possibly, alive when you found him, because he knows that Harold could have revealed concealed data, in his last dying words. Also, he is worried that in his final breaths, he may have told you, the identity of the people, who tortured him, for the vital information, they were seeking. He is concerned, perhaps, that the scientist could have given you the secret data that Sardis coveted for himself. Let us not overlook, the glaring fact, that Sardis, is wondering if Vickers, in his last, discernible declaration, may have gasped the name, 'Dominique Sardis' to you. If he were to believe that he did say, something incriminating, his only choice, then, would be to get rid of you. So far, he knows you have not released any information like that to the authorities, but he is a calculating creature and may believe you scheming, and, wisely, capable of playing some sort, of ambiguous mind-game with him. You did agree, to go to work for his studio after finding Harold dead and in his devious mind, he may think you're looking for more clues, before you breakout with a legendary, news story. I put nothing past him; he has been in the news business for years and lately, other seriously, dissimilar schemes. He's cunning, this one!"

Doctor Carlos feverishly brandished his hands in the air. "Don't limit this monster's imagination! He is able to make a decision based on any provocation, he might conjure up. He does not forget why your lamented husband was so notorious. Sardis is devilishly-gifted. From his dark legacy, spawns a sinister and suspicious mind. He could simply believe that you are shrewd enough to withhold the identity of Harold's killers, until you're ready, to overtly spill the inside-scoop." The three of them expressed amusement at Carlos's mixed-up English. His colloquial humor sounded, as a light note, upon the dark tone, of the moment.

"Sorry, but not, even, I, am smart enough to pull off an act like that!" Amber shuddered. *He's right! Sardis really is deceived by the devil.* She caught her breath, and rolled her green eyes toward the teak ceiling. "So, aside from all of these likely, strange scenarios, what kind of particular, secret information would Sardis desire, from Dr. Harold Vickers?" Amber asked, running her graceful hands, through the snipped, sun-streaked wisps of hair, resting on her forehead. "As, you said, he is the media-mogul, right? But, how would something like that, mean danger, for you or me?"

"Well . . . yes, he works in that field, but no . . . it has nothing to do with his media productions. He needed Harold and me, to help him accomplish the other nasty schemes that he's mixed up with." Carlos cleared his throat, stopped a moment to think and slowly sipped his coffee, then continued. "Harold Vickers and I have successfully withheld a valuable secret from the world. Only, Doctor Harold Laurence Vickers and I knew the composition of the classified secret, he was after. Not even the henchmen, that tortured and killed my best friend and personnel colleague, would recognize the value, of what they were demanding from the good doctor. That is, if they were successful, in forcimg the information from Harold, before they threw him in the ocean. But Sardis? That is another story. He would recognize the information immediately, and could try to process Harold's data. The treacherous man knows fragments and shreds of truths, about the core of the secret matter, but he does not possess the full essence, of how to make it all work. That is what he is thirsting for and that is why he is after me. He is hoping that I will contact you and warn you, of your dangerous involvement with him, hence, using you to lead him directly to me, Mrs. Albury, to extract the secrets that only, I know. If nothing else, he has set you up for this purpose, right now and is watching you, closely. It is very important to him that he capture me, Mrs. Albury, weather he obtained information, from Harold or not, before eradicating him."

"Call her Amber. That's what we both call her!" James interrupted, winking his eye at Amber, and then, returning his attentive gaze to the doctor. "And you intend to clue us in on your important finds and highly-secret, scientific data?" James earnestly inquired. His gentle voice was significantly laced with gripping doubt. "You're gonna trust three strangers with this kind of info? People you just met, practically, off the streets of Key West?"

"Yes, Señior, you have vowed to me your faithful friendship and trust. I am, as committed to you, as you three are to me and I need to tell you everything."

James shifted uneasily on the couch. He nudged Morgan's dark-tanned arm, purposely, and with force. With questioning eyes and without uttering a word, he asked him, "How committed are we, anyway?"

"Well, yeah," James said, "I agreed to be your confidant and friend. I'd be foolish not to be, considering that you have just scared-the-crap, out of all of us, with describing the peril that's on the horizon for you, Amber and, possibly, other innocent people. I'd say, I can handle a different sort of friendship, like that." He looked over at Morgan's serious face and then, at Amber's watery eyes and smeared mascara. "Yeah, I'm committed for the long haul . . . I'm beginning to really hate this Sardass guy!"

"Thank you, for your understanding, James. May I call you James?" James held out his hand and shook the doctor's hand for the third time that day, nodding his head, with a willing smile.

The doctor grinned affirmatively and continued. "You are, indeed, correct, my friend," Carlos accentuated, in a thought-provoking manner. "Now, let me explain everything and I may repeat myself, but better you hear it more, than once."

He crossed his chest, again, with the sign of the cross, folded his pale hands briefly, while gazing upward and murmured a tiny prayer, before resuming. "For several years, up until two years ago, Harold and I have been abroad in Sweden, France, Denmark and Germany, for extensive periods of time, experimenting, along side, with other VIP scientists, collaborating with different theories and revealing some remarkable findings. But, later, after returning to America and investigating our own personal theories, together, just the two of us, we climbed to new plateaus. By that, I mean, that our newest discovery was more dramatic, than we could have, ever dreamed, possible."

Doctor Vickers and I detected a breakthrough discovery. It was a youth serum that would change the world, as we know it, today. All human beings, using this serum could be changed ad infinitum. In layman's terms, that denotes *indefinitely*. We finally derived a working formula, after many attempts and failures that evolved into a startling success. It was unbelievably affective on the older, dying rats that we treated with the serum, reversing them back, to an adolescent state, again. We were faint of heart, at many times, to see how the rats performed. They were so youthfully agile. Time seemed to stand still as we tirelessly worked, in great anticipation, within our anonymous laboratory. Harold and I witnessed daily miracles that, in a sense, would make the legend of the 'Fountain of Youth,' as valid, as the conqueror, who envisioned finding it. We had made the monumental discovery and sometimes, we were actually frightened by our findings. We asked each other, what might it do to the world, as we know it, today, if we released our results and set it all into motion? Would it extend life-spans and serve, as a good purpose for mankind, as well?"

"Our unheard answers echoed around, inside vacant, biotech-vaults. The radical changes that we observed, occurring in our private lab were something, that not even a great Nobel laureate physicist, like Dr. Vickers, could imagine how to truly control. And I, a Princeton graduate and far beyond MIT professorship, educated in the extraordinary fields of chemistry and biology, did not come close, to harnessing the knowledge and management, of a breakthrough of this magnitude. So, we closely examined our only alternatives and options and resolved that we were the major puzzle pieces in a life-changing enigma."

"Well, you've grabbed my attention, *Señior* Carlos! James suddenly exclaimed, bouncing a glance over at Morgan, who was leaning foreword and gnawing on his thumbnail. "Where-the-heck, is your secret laboratory located, now, if I might ask? Is it here, on the sunny isle of Key West?"

"Yes, it is, somewhat in Key West. I don't think you will be surprised, when I tell you, who is the founder, capitalist and CEO of D.S. Pharmaceuticals. This risk-taker, spearheaded and financially supported our delicate research, while Harold and I worked silently in the obscure background."

"Wait! Let me guess!" blurted out Amber, evoking some sort

of warped humor. "I'll bet you worked for the same jerk, I happen to work for, just this morning, the powerful, paradox, posing in Paradise, as the money-mogul, Mr. Dominique Sardis! D.S. Pharma, himself!"

James's chocolate-brown eyes widened, "I know your guess was a good one, but you're, surprisingly, good with words, too, Amber. You just might make it as a *poetess*, yet. But, I'll reserve my judgment, until, after I hear your poem that you were going to recite for me, before we were so rudely interrupted, by a winter squall, anchored out on Yellow Rocks," he winked flirtatiously at her. She was embarrassed and the noticeable, hot blush, she felt on her reddened cheeks, proved so. She mused; *Ummm . . . the fact, that he remembered, that I never recited my poem for him, is amazing.* She inwardly proclaimed . . . . *One day, I'll bore him with it, regardless, of how childish it might seem to him.*

"Well, she's not only good with words, she's very good at her PI work, too," Carlos remarked, appearing quite impressed. "You're precisely correct. Sardis is our man and not only was he my deplorable boss, he owns an exclusive, fully, equipped laboratory, right here, on the waterfront of Stock Island, just a couple of miles from here. In fact, that is where Vickers and I finalized our experiments on the youth serum. While, Sardis, previously, employed us to study enzyme and molecular activations, added to controls and remedies, for rare congenital conditions, he was hoping, with my specialty in pathology and genetic research, that we would establish astonishing break-throughs, in gene-cloning and create immunities and anti-virus-es. These rights, would belong to him, and he could sell them to other giant pharmaceutical companies for millions of dollars, throughout, the world. His relationship with grandioso-pharma, left Harold and I asking, one another, about how drug-licensing rights would work with our secret formula, especially with the entanglement of politics and bureaucracy. Sardis wanting to take over the drug rights for himself, prematurely, before we assessed the entire value of the compounds, as to the added value they might show later, was another problem we were facing, not to leave out, the importance of FDA's approval, for anti-aging drugs in this country, before other less-strict countries jumped on the bandwagon. But, with Sardis's biotech-imprint solidly on our youth serum and our heads, we, the two, highest pedigreed-scientists, in the world, came to a screeching halt."

"Sardis was a master at surveillance. Our stall perplexed him and made him nervous. We worked under-wraps for him and factoring any kind of our own economic deal was completely out of our hands. We wondered how our pharmaceutical partners, would be able to put a price tag, on our anti-aging drugs and then, going-public, was another concern we had. Sardis knows, if he welds the international supremacy of these proven vaccines against powerful, super-dangerous viruses and incurable aging-related diseases, he could possibly, change society, as we know it, today and become the wealthiest and most influential man in the universe. Protection and survival are the main keys that mankind is looking for, to unlock the door, to longevity and transform immortality. With those keys being at our fingertips, inside Sardis's laboratory, our unlocking of the door, to anti-aging was now, assessable."

"I am sure, you all must understand how releasing this formula to Sardis, would give him all the power, he would need, to strong-arm all of the nations of the world. Corruption and greed, is all about money and lots of it! Vickers and I were achieving pharmaceutical history, as never before! Age-related illness and diseases would be *passé*. We knew clearly, this formula could not fall into the wrong hands. We knew D.S.

Pharmaceuticals would push and bribe their way through for FDA approval, the stock market would soar, sky-rocketing off of the map, for Sardis's company and we, the two "rocket" scientists, would still be left, questioning our own personnel motives. Who would be the right hands? And furthermore, how would Harold and I be guaranteed by any one, human being, that their hands were the right hands? As, I stated earlier, all licensing rights were out of our hands. Besides, we were thinking, at that point, perhaps, the entire discovery should be secretly shelved, until some unsolved questions, surfaced with ethical answers." Carlos looked mystified. "It is an anomaly. An anomaly like none other." Then reaching for an egg-white, meringue, Cuban cookie, he snapped off a bite with his front teeth and chewed it up meticulously. "By the way," he added, "the laboratory is not far from this marina at all. For that matter, neither is the derelict shrimp boat that I've been holing up in these last days. Trying to stay out of sight has been a full time job. I am able to stand the old, half-sunk barge, just so long, before I feel like I'm going to contract a weird stain of virus, just breathing in the musty, damp air that's trapped inside." He feigned a cough, then chuckled and continued, "We could be at Sardis's lab in three minutes by car, and five minutes by the small, skiff that you have tied up outside, next to your sailboat."

"Oh. That's James's sweet, little Boston Whaler. He lets me use it, whenever I want. That's the idea, so they won't have to be bothered taking me out diving! James gladly turns me loose with his boat and let's me go motoring about. I'm usually out plying the waters, all by myself, nowadays."

"Yeah, right! You are such an over-exaggerator, Amber Albury," Morgan broke in. "How many times have you taken her out by yourself to 'ply the waters' and motor about?"

"I'm not telling. A girl has to have some secrets, too,

you know." She defensively retorted, lowering her gaze and began nervously fingering, the bottom edge of her peachy-colored, strappy top. "Let's get back to the doctor's secrets, Captain. Shall we?"

James studied Amber closely. Her odd, sharp-toned rebuke was a red flag to him. "Is this too overwhelming for you, Amber?" he said, sensing her mood-swing. "We can continue tomorrow. I'm not playing any gigs until this weekend, when I play for Prescott's private party, at his home on Shark Key." He clocked her closely, trying to read her body language. She appeared uneasy, but after, a distinct sigh of relief, she was quite ready to proceed.

"I'm doing great!" she forced a smile. "I've got a million questions, that's all, that's on my mind. Please, do continue, Doctor Carlos," she faintly smiled, reassuring the concerned doctor and his serious expression. She flashed her impish grin at James and Morgan. They were not convinced that she was actually doing that "great" because, of the fact, that she was nibbling at her polished fingernails. They both heard plenty about the *mucho dinero* that she spent on her nails, every week. Morgan gave James a concealed thumbs-down and James acquiesced, by lowering his eyelashes, and staring at down at his watch.

"I need to clearly explain, how, the Dominique Sardis and youth-serum-quandary operates, because that is why Amber is in such danger at this time." He fumbled for the right words. "You see," Carlos addressed each person, and then, he looked only at Amber. His saddened, hazel-green eyes penetrated her curious ones, with deep concern. "As I explained before, and I don't want to sound repetitious, but just so you understand,

Sardis is using you, Amber, for his fishing bait. I'm the big catch-
of-the-day that he is trolling for. He knows that I will try to warn
you, of any peril that you have put, yourself, into, by accepting
his job offer and working for him, at the studio. When you
bought into his lie, that you, being the widow, of the famous
Peter Albury, made you the perfect candidate, for his popular
television show, Amber Albury fell into a stretched-out net. The
hunter had set it, purposely, just for you, the probable prey.
Sardis played upon your sorrow, from your loss, of Peter.
Drawing on false-flattery to snare your feet, he, then captured
you and made you his show-anchor, thus in turn, he will use you
for his bait to attract me in, for your rescue. He knew I would
see you on his television show and realize that you should not be
working for a dreadful man like him. Hoping I would notify you
of his evil intentions, he wants to catch me trying to warn you
and then, nab me and try to extract the secret formula from me,
just as he did to poor Harold. But, after failing to do so, I would
become nothing but rotten fish chum, when he was finished,
with me. That's why he was so angry when you erased the phone
call this morning from me. He was hoping that it was me, calling in, so he could trace me down, through you, and send out his
thugs to catch me."

Morgan regarded Amber's extremely glum face. He started
to feel guilty, for the negative statements he had made to her,
riding on the way, to Big Pine Key, in James's truck. He wished
now, he had not joked so much, about her light-weight qualifi-
cations, for the TV position. He could tell she was feeling very
insecure and he felt sorry for her. He reached for her hand and
held it gently.

The doctor continued on, "After, Sardis realized that we,

doctors, had discovered positive proof of the formula and its success, it was at that time that we became aware of his evil intentions. His hired associates did anything he asked. Harold and I had determined that money was never the issue for us. God filled our simple, everyday needs and we would, by no means, sell our findings to Sardis, nor any person or company we could not trust. When, Sardis, soon realized that we would not comply with his threats and strong-arm demands for the formula, he decided to take drastic measures. After searching through volumes of our computer files and all of our hard-copies, he found *nada* and zero results that would help him."

"He made a fatal error! He assumed Doctor Vickers had the secret formula memorized in his head. So, he and his buddies hunted the pitiful man down and tortured him to get it, but they probably failed. I have confidence Harold would die, before betraying me. Futility was all Sardis got when he tried to force it from Doctor Vickers, I'm sure."

"Snuffing out his life, he now comes after me, thinking that I have it programmed into my brain. So, now, he is suddenly bearing down on me. He will search every place in Key West, until he can find me, just as, he has been searching, ever since, Vickers's kidnapping, when I swiftly, disappeared into the Key West sunset. After they capture me, they will torture me for the formula, too, hoping to satisfy Sardis's greed, but, in the end, the only satisfaction he will receive, is the termination of my life. Why? Because, God be praised, I, too, never, ever committed the formula to my memory. We never put it on computer files, paper or on any discs. We divided it in two halves and placed them onto tiny, micro-films contained and concealed in miniscule micro-chips, where Sardis would never locate them." Carlos, proudly grinned, a huge toothy smile at his amazed friends.

"I'll bet you anything, no one would be able to locate them, from everything, you've described," James stretched, feeling anxious. He nervously yawned, wishing Carlos would cut-to-the-chase. Ready to speed things up and having drunk way too much Cuban coffee, he was ready, for Carlos, to move on with his story, a bit faster. He took in an edgy sigh and agitatedly asked, "Are you going to tell us where these two very sought-after, micro-chips are now?"

"You're asking the right questions, James. No one knows, but Harold and I, where the secret hiding place is for the treasured, dark secrets and, now, I'm going to, finally, share this information with all of you," Carlos heaved a big, releasing sigh, with James's sigh of relief, following behind.

"My half is transfused into the back of my eighteen-karat, gold Catholic Saint Christopher medal and Doctor Vickers's half is inside his gold Saint Francis medal. He was wearing it when he was kidnapped by Sardis. He always wore his medal. He never took it off. Ever! But, here in, lies the problem . . . I never saw Harold, again, after, he disappeared. I was in hiding."

"Amber, you don't happen to have, off-chance, a few digital photos of Doctor Vickers, lying dead in the Mangroves, among the bird photos you so skillfully took that memorable, winter afternoon, do you?" James rolled his teasing brown eyes, continuing, "You know, just a picture or two that the good doctor might check to see if Harold is wearing his medal, when he died. By the way, I never got to see those promising pictures, either, after that unforgettable day. Remember you were going to show them to me that evening, but we decided to watch an old, classic movie, instead?"

Amber eagerly jumped up from the couch, "Yes, I made them into photos on my picture-maker. They came out pretty good. Sorry, I failed to show them to you, James. All the fuss about getting hired for my new job and everything, I simply forgot about them. Just a second, there're back in my little, sea chest, next to my bed. I lock-up all of my special treasures, in it, for safe keeping. Mementoes only, no gold! I hide that elsewhere!" She giggled quietly and slipped through the doorway to the foxcel, and unlocked the wooden chest with a petite, gold key. She parted her rosy mouth slightly, then thoughtfully, decided, not to bring out her colorful, bird pictures, that she was so proud of.

"Doctor Vickers! So, there you are!" James exclaimed, after, Amber handed all of the pictures, to James. Glancing at the top photo lying, on the stack, he, thoughtfully, thumbed through the rest of them. "So, that's what the doctor, looked like, the day that you found him. Ummm . . . he looks dead, alright," James paused and inquisitively stared at the top photo, once again. Then, he glanced through the colored prints, a little more slowly, for a second time, with Morgan looking on. "Where are your wonderful, bird images?" He asked mischievously, portraying feigned regret.

"I don't think Carlos would be interested in my kingfisher prints, right now, James," Amber quipped, waving her hand at him, to back off, and ignoring his irritating jab.

"No, I will just study these," Carlos suggested. Lifting them, carefully, from James's long fingers, he closely observed each one. Wiping the tears from his wet eyes, as he did so, he sniffed, "I see, by examining each of these photos, that Harold is definitely not wearing his gold medal. His special Catholic medal is gone, from around his neck. It was probably ripped off his chest and is now lost or stolen. How sad! It is missing, but, as far as, the hidden formula goes, it is worthless to anyone, without the other medal, to match it up with. I hope that Vickers, did not sell us out and tell Sardis or his thugs, that the formula was hidden in his medal. If they stole it from off of his neck and murdered him, it was for nothing, but that would be another reason, for him to grab me. If, Harold was forced to tell him, I had the other half of the formula, in my medal, well, then he would be in quest, of my medal, too, as well as, for me. I just don't know all of the answers, but I do know, either way, medal or no medal, he's out to get me, one way or the other. I guess, my job is all about theories and that's all I can come up with, presently."

Amber got up and methodically, started wiping off the dining table. Embarrassed for Carlos, she reached for the coffee pot and politely offered more coffee to each of her guests. Attempting, to disregard Carlos's sad, uninhibited tears, the distress of the moment was beginning to overwhelm her.

Morgan reached over to the galley's marble counter. Tearing off a soft, paper towel, he offered it sympathetically to Carlos. The doctor dabbed at his damp eyes and snuffled loudly. "We are sorry you are going through all of this crap, Carlos, and we want to help you as much as we can," Morgan consoled him. "Amber, can you fix us some of your fresh, blackberry tea, please?"

She nodded and filled the copper teapot with filtered water, placing it on the propane burner. Taking down four, sandstone cups and matching saucers from the hinged cabinet, above her head, she began the familiar tea-brewing ceremony that Morgan and James loved watching.

Her graceful hands artfully toiled with the squatty, clay cups. James reflected upon their many, warm tea-times, together, in the past fall and winter months. The cozy cabin grew quiet and the smooth sound of a whistling teapot and clinking teaspoons could be heard. Sweet aromas of wild blackberries and mangrove honey, filled the air.

"Hey! What a pleasant surprise, Amber," Carlos cried. "Did you bake all of these little cakes?" She proudly nodded, placing a gold-trimmed, lavender, porcelain platter in the middle of the table. Amber tipped her teapot over each cup, filling them, with comforting, steaming, brewed tea. "This afternoon tea-time hits the spot. Those English colleagues of mine, certainly know what they're doing with a tea bag, don't they?" Carlos snapped, as he tasted the chocolate tea bread. A dreamy expression moved across his face.

"There's a not-so-sweet one, on the side and the yellow breads, with the poppy seeds have a more buttery-taste. I like them with warm cocoa at night." She paused, "We haven't told you, Doctor, but we have a pleasant surprise that we have saved for you. A special treat, even more pleasurable, than these tasty, tea breads," she picked up the nearly-empty platter and offered him another one, as she said, "I'm being a good neighbor and caretaking a friend's boat, down the dock, until fall. It's a live-aboard and it's a fifty-two-foot-long trawler. I have the only key to the door and I'm the only one, who can go aboard, without a security guard and clearance from the owners, who, by the way, happen to be living in their villa on the Mediterranean Sea, as we speak. That's the only place *she* seriously shops. So, if you can be really clever, we can sneak you aboard, today. I especial-ly don't want to alert my nosey, news-reporter, neighbor, Heather, who lives on her motor-yacht, not many spaces from their yacht. The trawler you'll be staying aboard is outfitted and arranged with deluxe, guest quarters, so you will be staying in the plush lap-of-luxury, for quite awhile. There are new, fluffy, monogrammed, terry-cloth bathrobes, in each private, luxurious salon. Sorry, it's not a C.B. monogram! You can kiss your old, derelict shrimp boat, goodbye, forever! How does that all sound, Doctor Carlos? It was our secret surprise, just for you. You may find out, we keep shocking secrets, too!"

"I am indebted to all of you. I am so grateful. I never expected such a wonderful thing and I promise, I will be, as quiet as, a mouse, while I'm staying on board. I can be just like a ship's mouse, but even more silent. I do not want to get you in any sort of trouble, Amber. Thank you for your splendid news. Thank you everyone."

"I must ask something, Carlos, while we are talking about my safety. You said there was someone else who might be in danger. Who else would be at risk?" Amber said, pouring him another cup of hot tea.

"Yes! She is my other top-secret! I only have three, that I can account for and she happens to be one of them! She would be at a terrible risk, if Sardis knew about our intimate relationship. She is the amazing love of my life! No one else knows. Only now, will anyone else know!" He laughed. "Harold did not even know we had a secret liaison. She was employed by Sardis when I was employed by him. And, unfortunately, she still works for Sardis. For a couple of years, we have kept are fraternization a dark secret. We all signed, a sort of Sardis-style contract, and it states, it is illegal, among his most valued employees, to fraternize with one another, as well, as keeping covert information secret from other co-workers, who are not privy."

"Operations were quite similar to the military's rules. Our clandestine affair, weathered the harsh, strange regulations, for almost two years. She and I are still in love, but we cannot be together, ever again, because I am hiding, from Sardis and she knows not, where I am. I do not want him to ever know of our romantic affiliations or he would threaten or hurt her for information on my whereabouts. She has no idea why I left to go back to Costa Rica. She thinks I have gone on a high-stress, science project for the company and she, wisely, does not question, Sardis."

"What is her name?" Amber asked, guardedly.

"Her name is the most beautiful name on God's earth. Her name is Eva Svensson, but sometimes people call her Eve. Eva or Eve, it matters not, for she is my Swedish doll and I love her, with all of my heart. I cannot wait to see her, again and I hope, one day, you all shall see Eva, too."

Amber's teacup fell from her hand and clanked into her saucer. James choked on his chocolate tea bread, spraying it into the air, while Morgan coolly smiled and leaned back, against the plump, sofa cushions. Taking a guzzling swig of his tea and popping a small, chocolate cake into his mouth, Morgan sighed and cackled, "Getting together with Eva would be fun, right, James? I know, I speak,, for all of us, Carlos. We would all love to see Eva."

Thirty

"May I use your bathroom, Amber?" Carlos asked, very politely, scooting out, from behind the dining table, standing up, and stretching. "I think my legs are asleep from sitting back there, so long!"

"Sure, the 'head' is just in the bow, port side. Help yourself." He assumed her boating terminology meant, *bathroom*, so he made his way toward the forepeak and disappeared behind the thick, teak door, latching it, behind him.

"Time is of the essence. Concern for Eva's safety should be our highest priority and she needs to know the truth, about what's going on with Doctor Carlos Balderas," Amber whispered, just loud enough, for James and Morgan to hear.

She seized this window-of-opportunity, with Carlos absent, to stress the fact that since, they had, already, met Eva at Louie's Backyard Restaurant, they needed to be totally up-front, with him and tell him. James and Morgan agreed, but they emphasized that they were still puzzled about the relationship, that Eva had with Sardis.

When Carlos, finally, returned to join them in the main salon and was seated at the galley table, Amber carefully enlightened Carlos about their accidental meeting with Eva, earlier, at Christmastime. He was surprised, but excited, upon hearing their amazing story. Morgan added, that the three of them had seen Eva, at noon, just that day, outside the television studio, too. James described how they saw her approaching some men in a black Mercedes, before they started over, to the Rusty Anchor, to meet up with him. That is all they told the doctor. The subjects, of the anonymous love-sonnet and mysterious postcards were not raised, nor, was the fact, that Eva had tracked James down at his cottage, going by the name of, Danielle Stoddard, a year ago. The peculiar details, became more, cloudy secrets, to add to their growing collection.

"We don't quite understand exactly what Eva's connection is with Sardis, but we're convinced, she must be contacted. I'm sure that I'm the only one that is providentially, able to get to her," Amber decided. "I'll try to spot a chance-meeting with Eva, tomorrow, when she is alone and warn her of the danger she's in. If she's still here, in Key West, and visits the studio, I may be able to talk to her. I will tell her where you are staying and you all, won't have to be apart, ever, again. We can make arrangements, so she can come here to the marina and safely *rendezvous* with you on the trawler."

"That sounds like a feasible plan and I hope that it works," Carlos encouraged her. "I hope that you are, as positive, in the morning, as you are, right now, because going back to that studio and performing live, on cable network, will be a difficult task for you to pull off. Now, that I have told my entire tale to you, this afternoon," Carlos smiled, "you will have be an award-winning actress, to conceal your true feelings for Sardis, next time, you see him, not to mention, how difficult it will be, to carry on, doing live television, before an eager audience."

Carlos removed his spectacles and nervously, ran his index fingers, over the filmy lenses, like tiny windshield wipers. His baldhead suited him and his astute appearance blossomed with wisdom and humility. "So, let me, explain," Carlos said, "Why you saw Eva at the studio and her connection to Sardis. I know, you three, must be very curious, but let me say to you, Amber, if you do make contact with Eva tomorrow, I will need her to come see me, immediately. It is urgent. The peril, she will be facing, coming here, to reunite with me will be nothing, in comparison, to the dangerous and final mission that I must ask her, to execute, for me. It is necessary, for her to do this, before she can be released completely from Sardis's tightening tentacles."

He looked, straight into Amber's eyes, "I have a strong hunch that Eva is still here, in Key West and has not returned to her own research headquarters, in Sweden." The reactions, were deafening, although no one said anything. "Yes, that is where she works. She is the top, Swedish biologist, over many constituents, in the cosmetic-field in Sweden and calls all of her own shots. She is the head of many laboratories, throughout Sweden and works closely with Sardis's American scientists. They maintain an international, communication pipeline that is continuously open from Key West to her private offices, in Sweden, at all times. That means, she spends, as much time, as necessary, in Key West to accomplish her critical business. In the past few months, I think, she has been over here, more, than she has been in Stockholm."

"I believe that Sardis is scheming like a busy spider, spinning a sticky web and trying to draw Eva, into his trap, unknowingly, to her. I have never told her anything, about the discovery of the formula for our youth serum and it would have been unwise to do so, for the sake of her safety. Sardis controls her life, much more than, she is willing to admit. That is another reason, why I always handled Eva with kid gloves and on a 'need to know' basis, only. But, make no mistake; Eva causes serious worry to Dominique. He fears the contents of our studies and experiments could leak out, and he certainly would not want Eva, ever, to learn of it. Her loyal hounds in Sweden, would steal his secret venture, right out from under his nose, with Eva leading the pack. If there was a betrayal, the reality is clear. Her consortium, would have immediately contacted Harold and me, if he were alive, to persuade us to sell our formula, to her prominent pharmaceutical laboratory. Then, Sardis, would loose out on becoming the biggest player, in the biggest deal, in *Big Parma*'s history."

"Undoubtedly, his fear blends, with suspicion and respect, for her and it formulates a deadly cocktail. A concoction nobody is willing to drink."

"This brings me, to why, Harold and I were always, under constant scrutiny, by his dutiful watchdogs. Sardis forced us and even, threatened us, to never divulge our findings, to anyone, so his sentinel, guarded us closely. But, now, Eva will have to be told everything that I have related, to all, of you, if she is join me permanently and help me with my move. I desperately need her help, without delay."

Carlos noticed how puzzled the three faces, looked, that were staring back at him and it caused him, to make some solemn declarations. "I know, I know, you're asking yourselves, why would I need Eva's help, now, that I'm in hiding? Isn't she possibly in enough danger?" He raised his graying eyebrows over the gold, wire frame of his glasses and he blinked back his salty tears. "I can see you are all, also, wondering what I am talking about, with Eva in such a precarious and risky position, at this time, still being held by Sardis, as an international power-player and me, hanging out, in total, obscure oblivion."

"Yeah, I understand what you're sensing," James sympathized. "You must feel like a wandering boat, broken-away and drifting, from its mooring. But messing around, and dodging these jack-legs is one thing, compared to working, every day, with them, like Eva does . . . ," James halted briefly and his voice trailed off, then he winced, and pointed over at Amber, giving her a hard stare. "Okay, okay . . . Amber, now what about you? Eva, the doctor, isn't the only employee we're talkin' about here. You're on D.S.'s payroll. What are you gonna do? You're not thinkin' of really going back to work, tomorrow, are you? Now, that we know, for sure, he's havin' you tailed, that would not be a real good idea. Sardis is stalking you! I mean, come on, Amber. . . . Think about it! You've signed on with a first-rate doctor, here, that you hardly know, but who changed your life, today, before the sun set in the west."

"He's hiding on board your freakin' sailboat," James continued, "and soon, you're taking on the responsibility, of personally, stowing him away on a nearby trawler, that doesn't even belong to you. And, keeping him out of sight, from Sardis and his friends? Do you think your life will just go on, as usual? What the heck are you thinkin' anyway? I'm just curious. Have you given the situation any thought beyond, serving us all tea and sweet cakes? These are some bizarre barbarians, you're mixed up with after, today. If this group, is gonna be spying on you, on a daily basis and testing your driving skills, by tailing your Jeep, every time you go off somewhere, I'd say, you're playing a risky game, with a dealer, that's got a short deck. I'm referring to your boss, of course, and your choice, to keep working at the TV station for him. You're placing yourself in more jeopardy with each passing hour that you stay there. The minute you enter Sardis's compound, you've lost control of whatever you had, before you arrived. They probably have some aficionado, parked out there, in the marina parking lot, right now, waiting to see, where you're goin' next. They'll follow you and see, if you contact Carlos, reporting, back, to their boss of bosses, regularly. After, this morning, with your erased phone call, still on his brain, Sardis will have more, than one mindless guard, watching your every move. Since, hearing all of this stuff that Carlos has just conveyed, we were just dog-lucky, to pull off the quick hookup with him, a few hours ago. His 'Big Suits' just didn't have their *ducks-in-a-row*, this time, to catch you or Carlos. I think that black Mercedes was probably gonna tail you, Amber, but fortunately, Eva, unaware of her diversion, distracted them, and helped us give them the slip, before they had a chance to realize it. After that, thankfully, we became fleeting memories for the creeps!"

"Yep, it's very possible they were ordered to follow her," Morgan agreed, "and it sounds to me, that Amber, with her . . . somewhat . . . stubborn attitude, is firm about going into work, tomorrow and trying to link up with Eva, no matter what you have to say, James! But you know, James, if she were to quit her job, suddenly, wouldn't that be like waving a red flag at Sardis? He would suspect that the doctor may have already contacted her, no matter what excuse she gave him for quitting. Remember, D.S. is not the brightest *bulb-in-the-pack* and obviously, Amber and Eva, are presently, in a lot of danger, regardless of, how we all figure it."

"Your anomaly, is certainly, snowballing, Doctor Balderas! Two innocent girls are about to be hurled into an arena of fiends that feed on a concoction of confusion and destruction. Amber, has bravely taken a chance and thrown you the trawler for a life-ring, Carlos, but Eva and Amber are not even close, to being out of harm's way, especially, if Amber insists on warning Eva. What can we expect from this 'Eva encounter' anyway?" Morgan's proverbial gaze shifted to James's intrigued expression, as he ranted on. "What more do the girls need to do, to help you, Carlos? The peril of Amber contacting Eva and then, Eva coming, here, to see you, isn't enough? Sounds pretty scary to me!" Morgan was agitated by the reality of their plight and he shifted uncomfortably on the sofa, putting the doctor, squarely, on the spot.

"I know you will understand better when I explain what I have been thinking, ever since, I saw the pictures of the late Doctor Vickers and the medal missing from Harold's neck," Carlos winced with grief, thinking about it again. Amber, politely, offered him a fresh tissue and poured him a tall glass of filtered water to drink. He became very pensive and hurriedly, removed his flexible glasses. Momentarily, he dabbed at his tears streaming down his cheeks.

"Where is your medal, Carlos?" Amber asked, as the doctor pushed his spectacles, back on and bent them over his nose. He marveled at her inquisitive air. "Can you show it to me? Are you wearing your medal?" Amber continued to inquire. A pixie-like smile nipped at the corners of her pink, pouting mouth.

"I was waiting for at least, one of you to ask me that! So many questions, so little time, Amber, my dear," Carlos teased playfully, trying to lighten up the mood a little. "That is a very important questions, Amber," answered the doctor. "I hope, I can make myself clear. It's a little hazy, at this point, because I am still formulating my perfect plan, for Eva to aid me and it does involve my Catholic medal. My plan for her at the Stock Island Key lab will finalize everything for both of us, forever, once and for good, if it goes well. It will remove the two of us, from later, becoming one of Sardis's deadly targets. You all can help me, too, by just understanding that I promise, I am implementing a safe plan for her and I am confident she can do it."

"Yeah, okay, I know, we do understand. You're confident in your plan for Eva assisting you. We got that down. But, what about your medal? We would love to help you, Doc, in whatever way we can, but it is only fair that you first show us your Saint Christopher's medal that conceals your formula. We want to see solid proof that we're not hopping down some friggin' rabbit trail with you," Morgan quipped. "Amber does have a thing for gold necklaces and I can tell she can't wait to lay her eyes on your medal. She's become a real gold-hound, lately. Right, Amber? She has certainly bought her share of Cuban, eighteen-karat gold trinkets, since she hit Key West, last fall. Amber calls it, 'seriously hedging for the future' and she's addicted. A real hedge-hog! We watch her study the daily prices of gold bullion like a fanatic. She claims their going up and never coming down, ever again!"

"Gold-hound? Hedge-hog? Thanks Captain! But, I really don't want the whole world to know about all the gold jewelry, I have stashed on board," she protested. "My boat isn't exactly sailing with a Spanish Armada, you know! You would think I was living on some treasure galleon, the way you describe it. I am just 'hedging for my future' and that's it!" she snapped. "My secrets are not respected on this ship, I can see that!"

"Hey, there's no secrets barred here, today, Missy, the way I see it," James chided, "the good doctor, has topped any secret you could, ever, imagine keepin'!"

"Think so, Mr. Shannahan?" Amber shot back sarcastically,

flashing a teasing sneer, laced with a phony Irish brogue. She flippantly tossed her long, silky tresses back over her shoulders. "Now, people, can we get on with the medal?" She rounded her graceful back, lowering her shoulders and hung her head into her hands, heaving a heavy sigh. "Can we, please, just see Carlos's Catholic medal, already? Never mind about my gold addictions. They are my problem!"

"Well Amber, that is the big problem that I am facing, right now," Carlos moaned. "I can't show it to you. I'm not wearing it and I don't have my medal with me. It's over at Sardis's laboratory, here on Stock Island. So close, but so far, from here. I took it off when I got very frightened of Sardis. His eccentric behavior caused me to become fearful, so I hid it in Eva's lab-frog."

All three of his listeners looked suddenly sickened, by the thought of his deed. "No! Not one that she uses for testing purposes!" They still appeared disgusted with the idea, as if it mattered, what the frog was being used for. "No, you must understand . . . it is not a real frog, *mis amigos*, but a green, carved, wooden bullfrog. I bought it at an open-air market, from an eccentric, jolly lady, up on Big Pine Key. I gave it to Eva, for an amusing gift that I knew, she would want to take back with her and put in her office, at the laboratory, in Sweden. With her, being a biologist, the green frog was a natural present for her and I can tell you, it was love-at-first-sight, between the frog and Eva, when she opened the box and saw it. But, Eva wanted me to keep it safe for her, secure within my lab, until, she was ready to go back home, to Sweden and take it, along with her. I certainly didn't hesitate, because this frog was so special and I really loved him, too. If I ran a wooden stick over his ridged-back, a croaking noise resonated from his slightly, cracked-open mouth and he sounded, just like a living and breathing bullfrog." Amber smiled a sly smile at the boys, knowing that her own green, croaking frog, was only a few steps away, next to her bedside, in the sea chest. Carlos continued on with his *exposé*. "When I realized things were going from horrible to horrific, working with Sardis, I disappeared and I was never able to go back to my lab, again, and get the frog for Eva . . . that meant leaving my medal behind, too." His demeanor changed and his mouth turned down at the corners with remorse. "I, unfortunately, removed the medal from my neck, one day, and hid my precious treasure, deep inside the wooden frog's hollowed-out body, making it undetectable to Sardis. I needed to protect it the best way I could, at the time." Carlos took a long drink from his refilled teacup. "Then, after my great escape from my enemy's sharp claws, I was tormented day and night, wondering if the brute would find the frog, sitting in my lab and discover my treasure rattling, inside the cavity. That is why, I must have Eva slide into the facility and somehow, slip into my private quarters, obtain the gold medal and frog, without being caught and bring it to here to me, before it, ever, is found and perhaps, the microchip discovered by the enemy. I must have faith this will work out and may I say, I find myself, praying to God about all of this, more each day."

"I can't believe this," cried Morgan, as he beheld James and Amber, with their jaws dropped open, in shock. "You left your most, prized possession in the dragon's dungeon? Treasure hidden, right under, the dragon's nose?" He walled his eyes, showing his skepticism. "How could you have forgotten something so doggone important and left it for Sardis to find?"

"Because, Morgan, he was running for his life!" Amber retorted, in the doctor's defense.

"Yeah, I know, but now, Carlos has planned that Eva will be, with any luck, snatching it back?" Morgan moaned. "And you'll be the star of the drama, tomorrow, when you drop the bomb on Eva. She is really gonna be shocked, when she finds out the lost-love, of her life, is not in Costa Rica, on some trumped-up, mission-impossible tryst." Morgan glanced over at James, who had grown quietly somber. He took in a deep breath and added, "Now, I can see why Amber wants to go into the studio, tomorrow morning. She is anxious to hook up and warn Eva and get her over here to reunite, with Carlos. The plot thickens, and with added romance!" He paused, thoughtfully, "I guess I see no other way around it but to let the brave, little cupid fly, into the heart of her work and get them back, together."

"Carlos, I have a question," Amber asked, puzzled over Eva's position of authority. "Once, I am able to speak with her and she agrees to come here to the boat, to be with you, how will it be? I mean, after, she knows everything that has happened to you, since your so-called departure and she grasps the dilemma, about the missing medal, or medals, in this case, why, then, can't she just walk into the laboratory and bring your medal back to you? Why is there a problem with that? Doesn't she have a key to the building or something, to obtain access, since she has *carte blanche*, to come and go? Her position at the Stockholm pharmaceutical company should be her ticket into the place, right?"

"That is not how it operates at Sardis's place, Amber. Each employ is assigned to a particular level of control, in this well-guarded facility and they have their own personal, armed security guard with them, at all times, where they work, standing outside their office doors. The patrolmen are not aloud in the workplace, themselves, but each guard is wired and knows who is who and where each person is suppose to be, at all times.

The whole place is bugged and video taped, twenty-four seven. Everyone is watched and every room is monitored and wired for sound. One better, never be, where one, hasn't got, special permission, to be! That's all I can say about that! The guards have nine millimeter guns, strapped to their waists and they're trained, very well, to use them. The unusually strong, hurricane-resistant building is fortified with insulated concrete and reinforced bars. It can easily withstand a category six hurricane, if one existed. The entrances and exits use iris-scanners and fingerprint-impression boxes. Each high-priority section functions on a permission-only basis, to gain entry into the prominent, smaller areas, which are laced with infra-red rays, when they are on close-down. The business of the day, operates on an official, need-to-know basis. So, yes, she can always enter the building and she doesn't own a key. Just, by possessing, the correct identity, Eva gets through the door. But, even if she can enter and pass with no trouble, in and out of the facility, she would never have a reason, to go into my private office or lab, where I perform my top secret experiments. These places are off-limits for her and she should never be caught in there, or else, it would go very badly for my sweet and innocent Doctor Eva Svensson. All of the high-profile power that she possesses, wouldn't help her, then. And, so therein, my friends lay the problematic situation. She requires an open egress into my work area, to complete my unique plan, successfully."

"Yep, I've got a much clearer picture now. So, how is it, then? Does your ingenious plan give her this open egress . . . or whatever you called it . . . an open door . . . to your personal office or lab? Can she safely snag your gold necklace?" James asked, in a sort of slow-mo-tone, deducing for himself, that the whole mess was nothing, short of a knotted-up ball of tangled, fishing line, anyway.

"Well, I do have a fool-proof plan that I believe will work and I would never ask Amber or Eva to do anything that they don't believe in. Amber is willing and I know my beloved will be a believer, too, after Amber's *rendezvous* with Eva, tomorrow. If Amber can make contact with Eva, there is much to be gained and nothing will be lost. I'm positively confident of Eva's stealthy skills. She is still in Key West, I know. I can feel it in my heart. She is that close to me. She will, no doubt, be at the studio tomorrow, conferring over company matters, with Sardis. That is where he always meets with her to discuss important, private business. He trusts her explicitly and the facility-goons know that she is '*numero uno*' in all of his viable transactions and personal affairs. At least, I have that on my side. She will be able to pull this off. Eva must be savvy and smart to get away with this quest, but God-be-praised, she is gifted with these traits, by Him."

"Okay, I don't mean to break up the party, but it's time to get Carlos on board the trawler and settled in for the night. Amber will advise you on all of the particulars aboard the boat, when she sneaks you over. Carlos. If you need anything, here's my cell phone. We're not using Amber's land phone or her cell, just in case, she's bugged. Only, call Morgan's cell. His number is programmed in as, number two. We decided we're gonna bunk here, tonight."

"You are?" Amber remarked, smiling curiously at James. "That's news. I didn't know, I was inviting you to have a pajama party on my boat!"

"Yeah, I think your *Island Packet 27* can accommodate the two of us, with the fold-out bunks, unless, James wants to sleep over on the trawler, with Carlos," Morgan chuckled, knowing Amber would take noticeable offence. "We secretly planned this, on the way over here, earlier this afternoon. Man! There's another doggone secret. Can you believe it?" He grinned and winked at Amber. "That black Mercedes is probably parked out there, nearby, right now, with plenty of back-up grunges on-call, so we thought it better, for tonight, anyway, not stirring things up and drawing attention to ourselves, plus, leaving you, alone wouldn't be smart, with the complex Carlos-Eva-thing, going down and all."

"Hey, I think you'll find my boat is right-comfortable and she's very cozy, too." Amber giggled, relieved they were staying. "Yep, I'd love the company and I will feel more secure with you both staying here with me. Not, that I'm afraid, of Sardis and his stupid buddies." Amber took a sponge, wiped down the table and tossed it into the galley sink. Her mind was whirling with a myriad of thoughts, of the next day's events. James yawned and turned out the deck lights, from below. Seemingly contagious, Morgan and Carlos responded to James's yawn with their own sleepy yawns.

"I'll show you where I stow the sheets and blankets. I'll even be a good hostess and help make up your bunks, but the morning coffee will be 'every-man-for himself' and notice, 'woman' wasn't mentioned in that old adage?"

She laughed, releasing some of her pent up tension. Throwing a plump, goose-down pillow at James, she giggled and teased, "Who is *numero uno* on your cell phone, James Shanahan?" She tossed a pillow to Morgan, hitting him squarely in the chest, and then motioned for Carlos to follow her up to the darkened cockpit. Carlos stood up and stretched, saying good night to his new friends. He had longed of sleeping on a real bed and laying his head on a soft pillow, night after night, while, on board the abandoned, shrimp boat. His feather-sound sleep, was now, only a dream away.

Thirty-one

Rising very early the next sunny morning, after a sound night's sleep, Amber sat propped up against a pile of plump pillows, nestled in the middle of her snug, warm bed.

She had positioned her laptop computer, up on a couple of cushions and was very busy composing a letter, before leaving for work at the studio. Onboard the trawler, the night, before and prior, to Amber abandoning the doctor, on his first night, curled up, in the lap-of-luxury, she and Carlos discussed realistically, what they thought, would be the best way to contact Eva, the next day. The two of them, decided that a small note describing the news of, Carlos, being there, in Key West and his special instructions, for their covert reunion would be the best way to communicate a warning to her. Amber would include a few details, but she would deliberately avoid any mention, about the formula or medal in the letter. Amber determined, as dangerous, as it might be, she would watch for an opportunity to meet Eva off the studio property, either before going into work, at lunch or during her brief, mid-morning break-time. Then, if she was fortunate enough to catch her unaware, she could, with a bit of providential help, pass her the letter, undetected by anybody that would hope to catch her.

Carlos had explained, it was virtually impossible to e-mail or call Eva on her cell phone, because both services were tapped and secure lines did not exist in Eva's world. He went on to say, that by now, Amber's cell was probably tapped, too, and, as James, alluded to the fact, it was not worth taking a chance on using it for their covert business. Anyone employed by Dominique Sardis, working in or out of the laboratory compound, was privy to Sardis's practices. Sophisticated bugging devices were routine. Carlos elaborated, that they were, as common as, fish beneath the sea, when it came to Sardis's undercover operatives. He explained that the people who carried out his missions would be shocked, if they knew just how advanced his spying capabilities really were.

Amber resolved that her best strategy to outsmart Sardis would be to incorporate action with absolutely no hesitations, as she ventured to approach Eva. She spoke softly to herself, voicing positive declarations, bravely preparing herself, for the day ahead. Shutting her cabin door gently, she blocked out the printer's hissing, from waking the boys, out in the main salon. Finished, she removed the paper, proof-read it and was satisfied with the letter. Then, adding, a final spurt of cinnamon-scented spray to the paper, she stowed the message in her handbag. Next, she hastily glossed a peachy-colored lipstick over her mouth and brushed a thin layer of dark mascara, onto her wispy eyelashes. She felt sad and even, reluctant to leave Morgan and James, alone on the boat. They were sleeping so peacefully from the gentle rocking of the swaying hull. She wished longingly that she could linger and fix them a homey breakfast, before departing for work, but, alas, reality was tugging relentlessly at her and had tightened its fierce grip. Surrendering to the pull, she rebelliously stopped and stole a small moment, to appreciate their docile expressions, as they both rested tranquilly in their bunks. A light, whimsical smile spread over her lips.

She quietly lifted the porthole covers, and checked to see if the smelly, rotten fish was still floating around under the docks. It wasn't. Gratefully relieved, she allowed the cool, briny, ocean-air to freely blow in. The salty breeze swept across her tender cheeks, calming some of the apprehension that she was feeling, deep within her spirit. Silently, Amber climbed the steps and pulled the hatch door shut, leaving the men to dream their dreams.

Making her way, down the dock, to the parked Jeep, she prayed for Jesus to watch over James and Morgan. Her leather sandals hit against the washed, slatted boards, causing them to creak, under each step that she took. She happily pictured both of her friends, sleeping like babies, as the swooping sea gulls cried out their raucous, morning lullabies, sending their laughing song out on the air and echoing through the open portholes. Suddenly, she giggled with uncontrollable hilarity, as if she released the jingle of tiny, tinkling, brass bells, spilling forth from down-deep inside her heart. A mirror-image flashed, fancifully, through the little-girl part of her mind. She pictured a whirling hurricane startling the boys awake and becoming, surprised by finding themselves, aboard her boat, in such a perilous situation, but she suddenly, discovered herself and her silly reverie, giving way, to some serious contemplation. She reflected upon the reality, that next summer would be her very first hurricane season, living in the Florida Keys. She had not only her own safety to regard, but a big sailboat would have to be shel-

tered from hurricane winds, as well. Amber sensed her gleeful-
ness fade, while butterflies fluttered inside her tummy. Her
whimsical smile disappeared and she pondered the huge responsibility that she would be facing. She plunked her wide-
brimmed, straw Panama, down over her sun-streaked hair and
buried the dreaded thought between the layers of frightful fore-
boding. Tilting her chin high, Amber peeked out from beneath
the hat's protruding border and to herself, she determined. . . .
*In the words of another southern belle, "I'll think about that
tomorrow"* . . . *and* . . . *Miss Scarlet O'Hara wasn't just
whistling Dixie!*

The pesky, black Mercedes tailed her into the small, studio
parking lot, pulling into a spot in the far away corner, out of
view from the front of the building. They obviously planned on
keeping her Jeep under constant surveillance. Ignoring their
vexation, to her spirit, she grabbed her leather briefcase and
canvas handbag from off the passenger seat, threw her Panama
hat, into the back of her car, shoved open the Jeep door and
defiantly, emerged from her car. Never giving them a second
glance, she slammed the door shut. Briskly, she walked around
to the entrance of the studio and out of their sight, but not, a second, too soon, for she caught a blurred-glimpse of Eva entering
the Star Fish Smoothie Saloon, just a half, of a long block, up
Duval Street. Immediately, she fished a shapeless, sea grass hat
from her bag. Plopping it, on top of her head, she tugged it
close down over her ears, so as to partly conceal her face, then,
she darted, like a chased cat, across Duval and over toward the
saloon that sat catty-cornered to the studio building. Managing
to dodge the sleepy, morning traffic, she slinked into the lime-

green smoothie shop. Panting to catch her breath, she spotted Eva, sitting alone, in a hot-pink-upholstered booth, at the rear of the island-decorated café and was looking down, at the *carte du jour*. Her golden, blond hair draped about her pale face, while she considered the menu held in her very fair hands. *Eva evidently doesn't get out in the Key West sun very much,* Amber surmised, as she made a quick-study of her, calmly sitting there.

She could see that Eva was certainly concentrating on her choices, for she never, once, looked up. Amber snatched the opportunity and limberly made a dash, in the direction of the lady's room, directly behind Eva's high-backed booth. Upon approaching the table, Amber promptly placed the folded, warning-message, just behind, the front of the menu that Eva was holding before her. The paper lay explicitly within her view and it boldly said on the front, in dark, red letters, "Carlos is in Key West! Do not speak to me."

Startled, Eva's mouth dropped open and she did exactly the opposite! "Where did you come from?" she cried. Caught off-guard, Amber gasped and looked instantly horrified. At once, Eva put it together, that Amber knew about the relationship she and Carlos were hiding from the world. Quickly, Amber surprised Eva, again, by deliberately shushing her, as she pressed a long, apricot-polished fingernail over her pursed, shimmering lips. Prepared for such a reaction, she bravely took a chance and directed Eva's gun-powder-grey eyes to a printed, index card that she discreetly pressed against the front of her torso. It clearly rendered, "DON'T SAY A WORD". The block letters went on to say, "YOU ARE WIRED. SARDIS IS LISTENING. SARDIS IS YOUR ENEMY! SARDIS IS CARLOS'S ENEMY! READ AND DESTROY OUR MESSAGE, ASAP! DO NOT FOLLOW ME!" Amber silently held the card, giving Eva adequate time to puruse its imminent warning.

Curiously, Eva acknowledged, by nodding her flaxen tresses

and Amber magically whisked the note away, sliding it down into the bodice of her v-neck top. Amber, then, flitted back and moved stealthily into the lady's bathroom. She hoped Eva would not tag along behind her. She waited ample time, and then, expeditiously, bolted out the door and sped past Eva, out of the smoothie shop, across and down Duval and into the studio, just in time, to go on the air for her *'Bargain Jargon'* show.

Sardis and the make-up queen were waiting impatiently by the sound room, for her late arrival. They both looked frantic, when she saw them looking at her, but Amber firmly waved them off, by saying, "No time for make-up, today! Sorry, I got no time for any renovating, this morning. I'm sick! I'm really sick and the show must go on! Gotta go!" She shot into her broadcasting booth and started, right on time, with her opening intros. Sardis and the Queen just stood there surprised and speechless.

They glared at her contemptuously through the clear, glass partition. Amber ignored them and remained cool, knowing that she did appear really strange, to them, but it was all she could do, to get through and "muster up" for the moment. Gladly, the "sick" part seemed to throw them off. Her job was complete, for the sake of Carlos contacting, Eva. And, now, hopefully, he would have a tryst with her at the trawler, later, that afternoon.

Carlos had reiterated to Amber the night, before, that if the *rendezvous* with Eva and the sequestering, of his Catholic medal, went off without a hitch, the entire mission should be completed, a few hours, after sunset.

After that, Carlos and Eva would celebrate on their flight-of-escape together, when the doctor would make the connection with his Key-West-ally, Katherine Grace. She was his private, on-call pilot and she would fly, both of them, in her private jet, to a safe haven, out of Marathon Key, later on, that night. Finally, Carlos would be returning to his home-place in Costa Rica and leaving harm's way, before the next sunrise. Katherine Grace, was a retired attorney in Key West and resided over on Fleming Street. She had generously given Carlos legal counseling, free of charge, at her insistence, for the past two decades. She remained his honest, dependable and compassionate friend of many years. Katherine Grace had stood, in the gap, many times, for him, always sheltering his private life and shielding Carlos's business endeavors, as well.

Again, the doctor was confident that Katharine Grace could be counted upon, once more, but, first, before the airplane trip, some important pieces were necessary, to finish Carlos's puzzle. Eva was one of those pieces. She was his *center piece* and he knew he would be asking her to take a great risk. He found himself wondering throughout the morning . . . *did Eva believe Amber's warning letter? Could she sense my plea and understand Amber's brief explanation of why she must take flight and break away from being discovered by Sardis? Was Eva's letter destroyed, before being found by the wrong person?*

He would patiently wait, hour by long hour and hopefully, before long, Carlos would know the answers to these desperate questions. He tried indulging his aching heart with faith . . . *if Eva wisely agrees and she follows my simple instructions, then she will arrive at the boat, sometime during the day. I hope she is successful and careful.* . . . Anxiously, he counted the minutes.

About, three o'clock, there was a faint knock on the front door of the quiet trawler. Carlos cautiously opened the entry a small crack. Eva beheld a bewildered face staring out at her. They both extolled the moment, as if it was frozen in time, and he flung open the door. They fell into each other's arms. When she was finally able to stop giggling, amid all the many kisses and hugs, she, all of a sudden, noticed James and Morgan and Amber smiling and taking it all in, sitting at ring-side seats, upon elegant, over-stuffed sofas, on the borrowed yacht.

She was overcome, by surprise, when her eyes locked on James's approving gaze and bemused expression. A slight questioning sneer filled his fiery, brown eyes, undetected by anyone, but Eva. Her laughter melted into muteness, as she went over and hugged each of them and thanked the three friends, for all they had done to hide Carlos and reunite them, together, again.

When she got to James, she took advantage of the circumstances and the closeness of the moment. She snagged the long-awaited chance to whisper a well-kept secret into his listening ear. Her confession sounded, as one, that she had rehearsed a million times, before this eventful day. She was prepared for this long-awaited moment and he caught every word, she hastily whispered, hiding her message, behind a friendly, zealous squeeze.

"I'm sorry for the many anonymous postcards I sent to you and for all the mushy stuff I wrote. I know you recognized that it was me. Please, forgive me for my sneakiness. Carlos doesn't know about my girlish-crush on you. I've been a love-sick groupie, but I finally grew up and I'm over you, now. You must admit I did get your attention, for a little while." She held her pale, cameo-shaped head, close to his face and mockingly, she shamelessly, cooed, "I thought I was a bit too clever. I realize now, my postcards were all a childish trick and my sonnet-of-passion, was boorish and silly, but I'll always enjoy being a fan of your great music. Thank you, James. I'll never forget you."

She sealed the ending, of her solitary, secret romance, by placing a kiss on James's soft, tanned cheek. He blinked his long, black eye lashes, smiled at her with admiration and his hushed reply, guaranteed that her secret would be safeguarded by his compassion and forgiveness.

"No worries, lassie. Your secret is safe with me, as well, as with, Amber and Morgan, too. They've been onto your postcard mystery-game, for quite awhile. Amber guessed it was you, as soon, as, we met you for the first time, at Louie's. No one else, not even, Carlos, knows a thing about it. This is just another secret, to add to my growing list of secrets. No problem. We'll always be friends and I'll make sure you get my latest, autographed CD, sent by me, personally, at no charge!"

She hastily whirled around and hugged Amber, saying, "You sure took a very dangerous chance this morning, following me into that smoothie shop, my sweet friend. Because of your early delivery, I have a brand new wardrobe for my move to Costa Rica. How do you like my new skirt and matching top?" She twirled in a circle to show them off. "No *eves*-dropping bugs, either, clinging to any of my garments. No pun, intended!" she chuckled. "I'm bug-free, at this moment, that is, unless I go into the Sardis's lab or studio, again!"

Carlos's expression turned serious and his brow furled, as he embraced her. He thought about the mission he would be asking her to complete for him. Eva chattered on in her dizzy exhilaration. "They've lost me for a short time and trust me, my friends, they'll be wondering where I disappeared." She sighed contentedly, but studied Carlos's face, asking, "Where am I going on this Key West assignment? I'm very curious, so let's get it over with!" She laughed and feverishly imagined, "Sardis will be very concerned about me and he will be wildly confused." Eva glanced over at Carlos and added, "I'm dying to hear your plan, for whatever, it is that I need to get for you, before we fly out of Key West. Tell me! I can't wait to leave here." She embraced Carlos tightly. "The secret letter just explained it was a life threatening mission, but what is it we're retrieving and why?"

"Carlos will tell you all about it and I promise you, it probably won't be the short version," James chortled and playfully rolled his sparkling eyes. "So, while he works on that, Morgan and I are going to go fix a Cuban dinner, for everyone to eat and celebrate your reunion with Carlos. We're glad you are here with us, safe and sound." With that, James and Morgan headed toward the galley, to prepare the food.

"That sounds really wonderful. Thank you so much. Amber will need to stay here with us and listen to the plans," Carlos called, after them.

He directed his attention, back to Amber, "You remember how I said that I needed you to help carry out my recovery plan? Well, I know the guys and you are thinking that your great risk, this morning, with contacting Eva and, now, another risk, with hiding us both out on this beautiful boat, is plenty and that I should not ask, you, for more. It would seem to be enough, I know, but I am sure that after, you and the boys hear how small your part will be, they will understand and be fine with it and so will you. Eva needs your help with the extraction, tonight. I can tell she feels very comfortable with you and I know her well." Eva nodded her head, thoughtfully. Amber grinned soulfully. "For that reason, I believe she would not put you in peril. It will not be that dangerous for you, Amber, I promise. Eva will be in high hazard-zones, the whole time that she is in Sardis's facility." Amber looked amazed and reached over and squeezed, somber

Eva, on her small hand, as Carlos continued to reassure the two of them.

"Doctor," Amber interrupted, "Eva and I are ready to go forth with this. Describe to us exactly what you want us to do and let's get started," Amber insisted. She then, looked in the direction of pots and pans, banging and clanging in the kitchen. "I don't want to disappoint the guys, but I don't think I'll be eating their delicious dinner. My appetite just is not in the celebrating-mood."

"Don't worry, my dear, there will be plenty of time for you to celebrate, later," the doctor poignantly pondered, her past history, and patted her arm, "and I'm praying that God will turn all of your mourning into dancing, one day, Amber." She gave him a promising smile.

Thirty-two

Amber's small, borrowed skiff came to an abrupt halt, stopping short of crashing into the white, coral-rock seawall, lying dead-ahead, of the boat's bow. Leaving the engine running at an idle, she promptly lifted the anchor from the forward storage seat and threw the gaff hook, overboard. It snagged the hard bottom, as the slack of the rope fed rapidly over the edge of the bow and disappeared into the dark water, below. The dive-boat drifted backwards on the light current, away from the facing seawall and halted with a jerk, as the hook stuck-fast in the shadowy bottom. Amber tugged the rope, so that the boat would come forward and shortening the anchor line, she secured it fast, around the bow cleat. After, checking the drag on the anchor to make sure that she was truly holding fast, Amber was satisfied, the little boat would drift no further, from its mooring. Confidently, she turned off the motor key. The red port and green starboard running lights went off, with a flip-of-a-switch and instantly, she was aware of the silent, black night surrounding her. She looked about, trying to make out the shadows, beyond the high seawall, opposite her. Bobbing up and down, like a cork and feeling very alone in the dark-hush, she plopped down, on a couple of dry, boat cushions that were lying in the bottom of the fiberglass hull. A cold chill ran down her spine, while whipping her head around, to catch the wet splash of a large fish, next to the skiff. Amber breathed a sigh of relief and she decided to make the most of her time by being patient and praying. Waiting for Eva to meet her there, at the vacated canal, on Stock Island, seemed like a good idea to her and she knew, she was way ahead of schedule. She pictured Sardis's kiss-up thugs, parked back in the lot, at the marina, doing their surveillance on her. . . . *Those goons have no idea that I've been out plying the dark waters in James's Whaler, this evening! Thankfully, he left it tied up, next to my sailboat, for these past weeks. Never did we realize, how important this little boat's mission would be, this particular night.*

Although tempted, Amber controlled herself from lighting up her cell phone to check the time. Imagining, Sardis's complex might trace her location, she powered it off, before departing from the marina. She sensed she had time on her hands, so, she tolerantly settled in, waiting until Eva completed her capture of Carlos's forsaken, gold medal and delivering it to her.

Amber mused over the minuscule part that she was playing in the doctor's dangerous extraction plan and presently, she, amazingly, began to experience a valiant calm. Feeling at ease in the familiar craft, she sat comfortably, rocking gently at anchor, listening to the playful waves lapping hungrily at the sides of the little vessel. Except, for the few biting, no-see-ums, gnawing at her exposed ankles, she stretched out contentedly, deciding that her *rendezvous*-job was actually a very easy task.

The immense, red moon was on the rise on the eastern horizon and the glimmering stars looked like bright, tiny, fairy-lanterns, hanging above, in the pitch-black sky. She hummed lightly, while turning over on her side, crossing her arms over her chest and staring out at the twinkling stars. But, suddenly, a creepy worry began worming its loathing presence into her peaceful reflections. *What if Sardis's guards catch on to Eva's scheme and follow her back over to our secret meeting spot, here on the canal.* She tried to dismiss the depressing idea and gazed hard at the rising, fat moon, resolving, that again, she should pray for Eva's safety, believing in faith, she would see her drive up completely alone, in her company-car, as planned. Amber reassured herself. . . . *Carlos and Morgan are, at this very moment, together, organizing their tactics, onboard the trawler and making flying arrangements with Katherine Grace. The thought of them, working with each other is comforting and their anticipated take-off is just a few hours away, if the whole plan goes, without a hitch.* Amber sat up and prayed that they would be off the ground, soon, and in the air. *Please, Lord let there would be no unforeseen complications.*

She tugged her purple, wool watch-cap down over her shapely, arched eyebrows. After, methodically, shoving her long, auburn locks, up inside the snug, fitting cap, with her slender fingers, she then, fell back, once more, against the square, canvas cushions, lying on the boat's deck. Adjusting them comfortably under her small frame, she pulled herself up and rested the back of her head, on the edge of the narrow, wooden seat. Consequently, her sweeping, long eyelashes closed down over her strained eyes and she began feeling very sleepy.

The soothing song, of the slapping waves on the side of the hull gently lulled her into a wistful dream, of James, restlessly standing on the faintly-lit deck, of the *Lady Poetry* and stead-

fastly, protecting her craft. There, he remained, anxiously awaiting her expected return, as it was agreed, that he should be the
one, watching for her, until she got back. She imagined him listening for the sound of his Whaler's engine, under the heavy
cover of darkness and watching fervently for her anticipated
appearance. She imagined him, in her dreamy thoughts, looking
fretfully for her, then spotting her, finally, motoring up, out of
the blackness of night and beholding her obscure, forlorn figure,
sitting stoically at the soaked helm. Tightly, she clutched the
valuable medal, in her delicate hand. Their reunion was exciting
and amorous and she envisioned James, powerfully lifting her
up, into his strong arms. Placing her tenderly into the sailboat's
cockpit, he praised her passionately, for a perilous job, well
done. Her sweet dream created a warm blush on her cool
cheeks, while a secret smile faded from her upturned mouth.
Amber savored the fleeting fantasy and fell into a tranquil sleep.

Eva had slipped into her baggy trench coat, donned a straw
sombrero and dark sunglasses, before she exited the trawler. The
disguise worked well when she arrived at the marina and it
worked again, when she departed. Sardis's alert watchdogs were
sitting in their black Mercedes, parked in their diffuse alcove,
but they never recognized her, at all, as she nudged her sunset-
red Vespa off of its stand and started the scooter's engine.

Speeding down, Roosevelt Boulevard, as fast, as she could
go, without being pulled over by a cop, she darted in and out,
between the steady streams of flowing cars. She knew Amber
would be anchored in the canal and waiting on her, so she,
promptly, arrived back, at the Eden House on Fleming Street,
in short order. The Eden House was a familiar oasis for Eva and

she was considered, as one of the long-term, permanent renters or "locals" around the place. The inherent staff respected and liked her very much. They joked about her being "Eva in Eden" and she always received the treatment of a distinguished guest.

She had made it back, before the customary, early closing of the front desk, leaving her scooter key with Carol, the clerk, for the return, of her bike the next day. Little, did the hotel help know that it was her very last visit, at the Eden House. Eva sadly pondered that thought, as she entered her upper suite and shut the door, behind her. . . . *I will probably not be returning again . . . for a very long time . . . or perhaps, never at all. Have not my frequent stays, during the last two years, been enjoyable and, at times, a bit lively and unpredictable?* Eva knew the answer was an undeniable "yes" to her question.

She felt a cozy warmth, come over her, as she remembered the previous summer's category "three" hurricane party. Some of the braver, hotel residents decided not to evacuate, but to stay there, in Key West for the very wet and windy storm that would pass, off shore. She recalled how many believers, counted big, on the ancient prayers, of a deceased nun that once resided in Key West and how she had prayed that Key West, would never receive a direct hit, by a hurricane. The famous, nun's, answered prayers had triggered the local Catholic church, to create a miniature grotto, in her name, several years back. Eva had seen other believers, urgently coming to plead their additional hurricane-prayers. Eva remembered, when she visited, the rock grotto, mostly out of curiosity, that it was a witness to her, seeing the yearly, candle vigils that took place, continually, with earnest prayers being lifted up to God, for Key West's abiding protection. The Catholic sister's hurricane-prayer had lived on, for decades and held true, for the island-town of Key West, but some inhabitants of the Lower Keys, Middle Keys and Upper

Keys, at times, looked at the violent weather, rolling in upon them and wished that she had included those islands, in her petition of faith. Each temperate, hot summer would narrate a new and different story, to the coral-rock isles, but those who stayed back with Eva at the hotel, that last hurricane season, had their own exciting tale to tell.

Smiling softly, she stepped to the window and pulled the heavy drapes closed, recollecting those meaningful hours, during the raging hurricane that whirled, nearby, over the sea. Fondly, she thought about, how each benefactor, helped the Key West Animal Shelter take care of their countless dogs and cats, during the huge, storm-surge. The loyal, hotel lodgers and staffers made an amazing impression, on all of the terrified strays that were left behind, bringing each of them to a safe refuge. The few SPCA workers appreciated the help of Eva and her neighbors, as they tended the needs of the different animals and soothed their desperate cries for help. Residents had been ordered to evacuate and it was mandatory, for them, to leave their homes and escape to the mainland. Fortunately, Eva did not go, but chose to stay back, along with a small few and help recover many of their ill-fated, abandoned animals, left behind in their deserted residences.

She wiped droplets, of salty tears from her eyes with a tissue and pondered. . . . *This old place has become my second home. I'll really miss the laid-back times, around the hotel pool, relaxing and drinking mango-smoothies, and visiting with my associates. But, my loyal, cat friends, I will really miss! Returning here, after a grim day, spent with Dominique Sardis and petting them and listening to their purring . . . the kitties always took away my tension and stress. I'll recall each smiling, whiskered-face, forever!* Whispering a touching good bye, she blew a kiss into the air, as if they were all, still within her reach.

Life had been good to her in Key West, but now, beginning
her new life, with her sweet Carlos, was more, than she had ever
dreamed, possible. Caught in the enchantment, of the alluring
Key West, they were both captured, by a lover's song that
played, only for them, to hear, but within a matter of a few
hours, they would be released together, to rise up on eagle's
wings and openly, sing , for the first time, their rhapsody of love.

Eva busied herself getting ready to make a speedy departure.
She wanted to change into something more suitable for traveling. From among her spanking new, bug-free wardrobe that she
had previously purchased, on a spur-of-the-moment shopping
trip, earlier that afternoon, she held up a pair of flowing, fawn-
colored linen slacks and a cornflower-blue, sleeveless top. . . .
These will be perfect for the flight. She pulled a pale-yellow,
knitted cover-up from her large, shopping bags and a soft
Chesterfield jacket . . . *I'll carry these onboard, just-in-case, the
late, night air turns cooler.* She tied a filmy, peach and turquoise
flowered, silk scarf on the strap of her new, taupe purse, for
backup. Considering, the quick decision, for leaving the country,
she thoughtfully, determined that her earlier idea of just taking
newly purchased essentials was the best and most sensible plan.
She settled on packing only two, brand-new, suitcases with the
rest of her fresh, unmarked and device-free clothes. She deliberated . . . *I will take only a scant amount of de-bugged jewelry.*
She wisely and expertly, cleaned the selected pieces, in addition
to, her identification documents and passport, so as, to avoid
any detection by Sardis's spies. She would load both bags in the
trunk of the company's car and drop them off at Hickory Street
on Stock Island, in the mangrove bushes, near the marina. *This
way,* she contemplated, *I will be able to arrive at the lab, off Old*

Shrimp Road, in a totally, empty car, when I go through the guarded entrance. She concentrated on other details. . . . *Apparel and jewelry are not very important to me, at this moment.* She knew she needed her priceless, American visa, her Swedish identification papers and her current pass port. *These items are tremendously important to me, but everything else?* Eva gave a breath of release, as she saw her material possessions, strangely growing quite dim to her.

She meticulously measured her steps, on this unusual evening. Solemnly, she wiped away another flood of unexpected tears from her storm-cloud-grey eyes. Reaching for one more tissue, she sobbed uncontrollably. . . . *Let the maids have my clothes! All the time, that it took me to fly around the world and shop for myself, I now count it all vanity. I would rather leave them in the closet and chests, for my old friends to find, then, to haul them away and only hoard the stuff, again, in another closet, in another place. I, sadly, have too many trunks and drawers, brimming with frivolous things and unnecessary items. What would I do, with all of that stuff, in Costa Rica, anyway? They would only remind me of my old, empty life, without Carlos, and my past sickness, to shop, to fill the void, of my loneliness. How I struggled, living a double-life, without Carlos at my side. . . . My outfits and countless other items will bless the girls, who work so hard, cleaning up, after me, every day. Let the clothes go! And all of my trinkets and collectables? Yes, I'll let them go, too! And every treasure that I have brought into this wonderful room, I will, also, leave them, behind, for I have everything that I will ever want, in my caring aficionado. Money cannot make lonely people happy. His presence, possesses more worth, than, all of the gold in God's universe! With that thought, I must depart, if I am to, ever, go away, with my love, tonight.*

She strolled out onto her private balcony, where she had spent many evenings, drinking her frosty concoctions of red papayas, bananas and orange mangos. *I will miss the early, song-bird mornings, out here, that were so anticipated, along with sipping sweet, hot coffee-con-leches . . . and lazy times of reading or visiting with the locals.* With one closing and meaningful glimpse, upon the pleasant grounds, below her lofty lanai, she resolved. . . . *Oh, my sweet portico-friend, I am finished . . . Finally, my soulful goodbyes are done.*

Moving, out into the hall, Eva eased the door shut and locked it for the very last time. She bent down and softly slid the brass key under the door. She knew she would miss the polished key, hanging from her silver key ring. She had always carried it with her, everywhere she went. Eva listened very intently, as it gently clinked, against the burnished, terracotta, tile squares. She, then, stood up straight and tall.

Throwing her shoulders back, she took a deep breath, walked slowly down to the lobby and out onto the welcoming, front veranda, where the white, wicker chairs, with their comfy, colorful cushions, seemed to be bidding her to stay and dawdle, for awhile longer. The elder Eden House conferred certain cheerfulness and it beckoned her to linger. Disregarding the invitation, she waved a small farewell to her favorite, cozy, porch swing that was suspended, at the far-end of the portico, framed by a milieu of overhanging, green, passion-flower vines.

With her bags, in tow, she blinked away the salty tears that were stinging her misty eyes and stepped out, onto the walkway that led to her car. She gave one last peek back, at the edifice of her earthly Eden House. The glowing street lights bathed the old hotel with glorious radiance.

Fearlessly and tearfully, Eva got into the car and drove out onto the narrow road. The illuminated street would lead her to Sardis's fortified laboratory, for the very last time. Whimpering, still, at the parting from her welcoming inn, she harkened with a spirited assurance of awesome anticipation. Eva envisioned this last night, in Key West and her final mission, involving Dominique Sardis, as the ending and the closing of an old, tired book.

Apropos, for this moment, she saw a fresh manuscript being laid into her humble hands. The pages were bound with a new strength. Fruitful chapters were created in abundance, promising her enlightenment for her future. The book was ready to be opened and Eva trusted it would read of love, hope, and faith. Her pounding heart knew, full well, that the greatest of these, was love.

Thirty-three

Eva hurriedly completed each identity-scan and quickly gained entry into the Sardis compound. She was not a stranger to these strict profile-procedures, but was accustomed to their stringent requirements. These vital details went with the territory, thus creating protection for all of Eva's ongoing operations, as well as, for herself. She used her professional expertise to function boldly, within an arena of extreme seclusion and critical concern, wherever she was doing her research work. Upon this unique quest, she had proven to be a devoted partner to Dominique Sardis. He considered Eva to be his closest ally, in the field of scientific investigation. And although, he cleverly managed to keep her completely ignorant of his darker, maniacal side, she accepted his alliance, as he entrusted all of his chief decisions to her. Eva was the hub that turned Sardis's wheel, producing pharmaceutical progress for his escalating company.

He never suspected her of any breech of confidence, the entire time she had worked with him and consequently, he executed an excellent job, at hiding his deceptive character, from her. They both achieved the same results, when it came to concealing their own private lives, from each other. She was incredibly good, at safeguarding all of the company's classified credentials, meant for Sardis's eyes only, but concerning her own private affairs, Sardis was craftily left in the dark.

The secret, for keeping her romance with Carlos, successfully hidden, from Sardis, stemmed from her ingenious skills to outfox the old fox, himself. Sardis and his facility-minded family, routinely relied on her and, providentially, not one, ever discerned that she and the good Doctor Balderas, were deeply in love with each another. She was respected by all of Sardis's friends and business associates, and especially by those, who were completely sold-out to his twisted ways and crooked establishment. His great faith, in Eva, had tipped the scales, to a falling point, that gave her license to judge, any of Dominique's liaisons, who might be, a worthless parasite feeding on his growing realm. Upon her recommendation, Sardis would accept her wise counsel and without dispute, the leeching, business associate was banished from the firm, no questions asked and no answers given. Any prior affiliations existed only in some lonely, memory-data, a mouse-click away, on Sardis's complex computer systems.

The exaggerated greeting of the friendly, front desk officer certainly represented the make-up, of a man, sold-out to the Sardis Empire. He fondly beckoned to Eva, as she entered the fortified building. She studied the gentleman's jovial expression. She was familiar with his more-than-friendly manner and, she attentively responded, placating him with a very sociable wave. *"Let the games begin!"* she mumbled under her apprehensive breath.

Feigning an exuberant smile, Eva gestured to the robust,

Roman guard with an extra bubbly hand-salute. His two, gold-capped, front teeth glinted, as a grin split, across his round, red face. He was sitting inside a cramped, glass, cubicle, upon a hard, steel-framed chair, leaning on a metal desk, with a magazine spread out, before him. Old pieces of hardened, glazed doughnuts, sprinkled the stained, Formica surface of his desktop. He promptly tried covering the mess, with a wadded-up napkin, but clumsily, dumped over his coffee. Embarrassed, he deposited his empty coffee cup, among other accumulated, empty containers, lined up on the desk. Shooting up from his revolving chair, he waddled out the narrow door to welcome Eva, as she stood watching him, from the green, tiled foyer.

"Good evening, Doctor Svensson," he schmoozed, taking hold of her delicate fingers and vigorously thrusting her hand up and down, like a pump handle. "We don't usually see you around here, at this late hour. What can I do for you? Would you like me to call someone to escort you to your office?"

"Hello, Marcello, I know it is late for me to come back over here, isn't it?" He nodded in agreement and she chattered on. "It is so good to see you, tonight. Always working so faithfully for our company! That's you, Marcello. We can always depend on you to do a good job, protecting our interests here at the Sardis compound. I have high hopes that by next year, here, everything will be different for you. It will be your last year and those retirement checks that you have worked so hard for, will be yours, at last." His face lit up and he nodded enthusiastically, as Eva overstated his performance and lathered on a few more compliments. "It is the leaders of D.S. Enterprises that should be rewarding you, Marcello, for all of your years of loyal services."

Then, she weakly cooed, as she warmly beamed at him, "Do you think you can help me with a problem tonight, Marcello? I could really use your know-how!" Marcello raised his thick, black eye brows. Puzzled, he measured Eva's words, listening closely, as she explained, "I have a slight dilemma where, I know, you could be of great assistance to me . . . and . . . if you can . . . possibly, lend me a hand . . . I'll be finished completely and out of your hair, so you can get right back to your magazine." His jolly features brightened to a cherry-red, with embarrassment, once more, knowing that she had caught him, breaking an important rule of the security-guard-code. She showed vague interest in his bumbling reaction, as he ruffled the stalk of black hair, sprigging up from the middle of his glossy scalp. She, then, lightly rubbing his arm, persisted, "I forgot something here that is very important to me. It is a special gift that was given to me and I must take it back to my lab, in Sweden. With all joking aside, I have left my large, green, wooden, laboratory-frog, here, on the premises and I just had to return, this evening and retrieve him. I am leaving tomorrow to depart for Sweden and I cannot go home without my dear, wooden frog." She lightly giggled, as if she was letting him in on her little plan and entrusting him, with her silly dilemma. "Our Swedish researchers have never seen anything like it, before and I am planning on bringing the frog back, to surprise them. It will be our special lab-mascot. They certainly will all want to come to the shores, of tropical Key West, after they hear my giant, green frog croaking away with his Island song in chilly Sweden." He laughed along with her childish joke and she squeezed his arm tenderly.

"Well, you are a good person to want to make your fellow-lab assistants so happy," he gushed, stepping forward and positioning his stout body closer, than necessary, to her. Feeling his hot breath on her face, she pretended not to notice it. "Allow me, personally, to take you back to your office, so you can retrieve your important, green friend, to carry along on, your trip. We must be quick and I will not need to call for an escort for you. I can do it myself, Doctor Svensson. You know, I will miss you, when you fly back to your homeland, but, before, too long, you will return to be with all of us, again. You love it here at the facility, too much, to stay away from your Key West. Now, please follow me, Doctor Svensson, I will personally escort you to your office."

"That is kind of you, dear Marcello. You are my favorite officer in the whole complex!" Marcello wiped his broad hands on his chubby belly, chuckling heartily. His puffy cheeks flushed with boyish glee. He, at once, glanced down bashfully, at his polished, brown shoes, and then frantically, he fished a wrinkled, used handkerchief out from his pant's pocket. He mopped his sweaty brow with his thick, sturdy fingers, and then stuffed the damp cloth, back into his over-sized pocket. He gestured for Eva to follow and started down the long hall toward her office. She swiftly closed in beside, Marcello and locked-stepped, with him.

Upon, nearing the entrance of her office, the iris scanner matched Eva's eyes and her hand imprint was read, as usual, by the x-ray machine, resulting in the unlocking, of the metal door and the bright overhead lights, coming on. Marcello waited for her to go inside, but as she bent forward, through the doorway and looked around the large, sterile room, she suddenly pulled back out. Pretending, to be innocently dumbfounded, she covered her gapping mouth with her cupped hand and gasped. He promptly startled and alarm engulfed his big, cow-like eyes, as he watched her frantically run her manicured fingernails, nervously through her straight, flaxen hair. Forcing the bulky door closed, Eva pulled it shut, with a clunk. She noticed that her loyal bodyguard was reacting, just as she had hoped he would. Happily, she witnessed his mouth hanging open, as he analyzed her with dread.

"What is it, Doctor Svensson?" he cried. "What did you see

in there? A ghost?" The big man shuddered.

"It's what I did not see, Marcello!" She hung her head, resting her forehead, in despair, in the palm of her hand. "My frog is not there!" Marcello looked mystified. "Mr. Sardis was supposed to bring my frog, to me, from out of the locked-down lab, of the missing Doctor Carlos Balderas and his deceased associate, Doctor Herald Vickers. He was to do this, today, and leave it on my desk, in my private office, for my flight back to Sweden, tomorrow. He must have forgotten all about our important agreement. I'm so disappointed." She put on an exaggerated, heartbreaking face, stirring Marcello's emotions. Her dramatic performance brought quick results.

"Why would they have your frog? They both have been gone, for a good while, now. What would they want with your personal, toy frog?"

"It was on loan, for a German humanitarian to use, while he studied here. The good doctor, borrowed, it for him to copy, during his exchange-visit, in our laboratory. You see, he was a foreign-art researcher and a world-famous, wood-carver, too," she lamentably, lied. "He wanted to use the frog for a model and carve one for himself, to take back to his lab, in Germany. Who knows, his sculpture may have ended up in a museum, thanks to my frog! But, I don't think he ever got around to using it for a replica . . . because, thankfully, my special frog is still sitting . . . sadly alone, in the poor doctor's lab." Eva pretended to wipe tears, from her smokey-grey eyes. "May I borrow your hanky, please, Marcello?" He hurriedly yanked it out of his pocket, once more, along with a few, loose pennies that bounced down, onto the hard, tile floor. Marcello told her to keep the hanky for a gift. She offered a fake smile and softly, blew her nose on the cotton cloth, while he repeatedly patted Eva upon the shoulder. She, in turn, reached up and gave his gripping hand, a grateful squeeze, providing him with a positive response. Then, with no hesitation, she lithely, stooped down and scooped up all the coins that were scattered about, on the slick floor. She stood up and pressed them firmly into the palm of Marcello's burly hand. He wrapped his strong fingers around her slim hand, compressing it tightly and she tried hard not to show her intense dislike.

"Please, Doctor Svensson, do not be crying over such a little thing, as a toy frog. You know, there are no security-scans on their vacant offices, any more and I have the only key to unlock the scientist's door. Would you like your friend, Marcello, to go down to their office and get the poor, lost frog for my lonely Eva?" Eva coughed, as she heard his syrupy words . . . *He called me Eva . . . I think, possibly, I may have gone a little too far with him . . . let's just get the frog, Marcello!* He released her hand and bolstered her arm, offering, "I can't see a bit of harm in me doing that, since Mr. Sardis forgot to recover it for you, today. He always has so much on his mind, with all those different irons, he's got burning in the fire. I can imagine, that he could have easily forgotten to pick up your dear, wooden frog." He put his strong arm about her narrow, sagging shoulders and hugged her tightly. "Buck up, now, my good doctor and I'll be, right back, with your green, frog-friend." Marcello gave her a reassuring smile and a redundant wink. Immediately, he streaked away, towards the currently, shut-down laboratory. A couple of minutes, later, he strutted back, toward her, clucking like a proud rooster and clutching the large, green frog, in his expansive hand.

"Oh! My wonderful Marcello! You retrieved my frog! Sweden's research laboratory will never be the same! Thank you so much!" She wrapped her long arms around him and gave him a courtesy-hug. "My colleagues will all thank you, too!" She laughed candidly, pinching his fatty cheek.

"Yep! There he is!" Marcello held him up to the light. "He's a pretty one. Sounds like he rattles, though. Like, maybe, he might have something inside him." He shook him extra hard, wanting Eva to detect the rattle. "Hear that noise?" She nodded her head up and down and granting him, a slight moaning sound, she concurred with his annoying discovery. Snatching the frog with a lightning pass, she snagged the frog from his hand, thus preventing the gold medal, from dropping out of the hollow frog and onto the tile floor.

"Oh, that noise?" Eva raised her delicately arched eyebrows, while shaking the frog lightly. "That is probably just wood shavenings from the wood-carver's shaping tool. He's all hand carved, you know. Who knows? Maybe the frog swallowed the carver!" Eva laughed nervously at her absurd joke, but, at that same moment, she heard the telephone ringing, at the front desk, in the distance cubicle, down the long hall.

"What's that fat stick for, that he holds, in his mouth?" Marcello asked, ignoring the ringing, for an instant and going for another, friendly embrace. Eva pointed politely toward the front office and he, reluctantly, responded to the sound of the phone. "Oops! I better get my lazy butt, back up, to my post or I'll have the devil to pay! It's probably Mr. Sardis. No one else would be calling me, at this time of night." Eva looked shocked and they each shot a serious glance, at one another, before jogging down the lengthy corridor, toward Marcello's station.

"Marcello, I'll explain the frog's stick to you, next time, when I'm in Key West," Eva huffed, stressfully, arriving at the reception area. She was breathless and was beginning to feel very on-edge. "You're about to get really busy and I've got some extremely last-minute, loose ends to tie up. Thank you again for all of your help. You will never know, how glad, you have made me and my colleagues." She hastily waved farewell, as Marcello sputtered something, about her, possibly, wanting to talk to Mr. Sardis, on the phone. "No, I can't talk now," she answered. "I'll probably chat with him, tomorrow, sometime." Fluttering her hand at him, she said, "Marcello, I'll be seeing you. Thanks for your help." He caught his breath and signaled, a goodbye to her, as he mashed, his sturdy finger down, onto the speaker-button. Finally, the phone stopped its ceaseless ringing and she opened the entry door. Stepping outside onto the covered entrance and holding the door ajar, she overheard Marcello, gasp a breathless "hello" into the speaker, followed by a shaky reply.

"Yes, Mr. Sardis . . . Doctor Svensson? She is here. I do not see her, at this moment, but . . . she was just . . . uh . . . uh . . . you will be so glad Mr. Sardis, to know, that you do not need to worry about Doctor Svensson's, green frog, anymore!" These were the last words that she heard Marcello say, before she and the frog vanished under the cloak of darkness.

Eva sped the car over in the direction of the old, defunct Hickory House Restaurant, on the shores of Stock Island. Once, the place basked in the glory, of old Key West, but now all that was left, of her anniversary celebrations, was the sureness of the sun, rising to her east and the moonlight, on this precarious night, beaming down, from the skies of Key West.

Eva flashed her car lights out over the water, as she drove up and stopped, at the edge of the seawall. Amber picked up her LED headlamp that was hanging around her neck and returned a bright signal, in response, ready for the anticipated, "frog drop" that she had been patiently waiting for. Eva cut off the lights, flung her door open, in a panic, left the engine running and jumped out, with the wooden frog in her hand.

"Amber, listen! You're in danger! I have to go! I'm really in trouble," Eva called out, over the calm water. Amber lit, Eva up with her head-light, as she stood standing on the seawall, holding the valuable frog. Amber let out a quiet cheer of victory. "Save the hurrahs until later! You're blinding me with your light, Amber!" Eva put her hand over her sensitive eyes. "Sardis knows I'm up to something. I've got to get out of here fast! They are tracing my car, as we speak. I'll leave the frog, here, on the top of the seawall. Can you reach it?"

"Yeah, I can net it with James's bully net. It's got a long pole on it. He doesn't go anywhere, in the boat, without the thing." She dimmed her headlamp and started the boat engine. Then pulling up the dripping anchor, she began idling up closer, to the high, coral-rock wall.

"Good girl!" Eva chirped. "I have to go. Sardis's hounds are on my tracks. Get the frog, back to, Carlos, pronto. I'll meet you at the trawler. I've got to dump the car, right away, but I'm going to drive it in, as close, to the marina, as I can, before I ditch it. After that, I'll be on-foot, lugging my bags." Eva turned to leave, but whipping back around, she retrieved her small, cell phone from her pants pocket. She held her slender arm up, above her head and flung the cellular phone far out, into the middle of the deep canal, with a noisy splash.

"What was that?" Amber cried.

"That was my bugged, cell phone and I suggest that you throw your cell, in the water, too!"

"Okay. You don't have to convince me. If I get in trouble, I've got my little VHF radio, with me." With that said, Amber tossed her cell phone overboard, too. "Well, I guess that's that!" she supposed, staring up at Eva's moonlit-silhouette, balanced on the seawall. Mumbling nervously, she rambled, "I have a landline on my boat, now, anyway. Besides, my closest friends don't call me on that phone, anyhow, since I've been working for Sardis. Next, cell phone, will be a phone that can't be traced."

"Amber, stop talking and get this thing into your boat! They are tailing me, right now, and . . . here they come! Hurry! Get the frog and don't let Carlos fly out, without me!" Eva dove into the car, without another word. Keeping her headlights turned off, she circled around and sped off, away from the approaching, distant car.

Amber, faintly made out her car's obscure image, disappearing into the shadowy night, as she idled her boat, very close and right next, to the seawall. She shifted the motor into neutral gear. Carefully, lifting up the long pole-net, Amber snagged the bulky frog. It fell with a thump, into the deep pocket of James's bully net. *Just, like plucking a plump lobster. . . .* She popped the frog, out of the net and stowed it, safely, down inside the seat's storage compartment, then she sat down behind the wheel and zipped down the canal, in high gear, putting the boat, on an even plane. Out of audible range, she looked back and observed the trackers, stopping their car and shining their high beams out over the canal, where she had just been anchored up. She uttered softly, "Thank you, Jesus. Just minutes ago, my place of resting, could have become, my final resting place. Thank you so much for watching over me and Eva. Please, God, keep her safe from our enemies. I pray you will lead her back to the boat."

Amber paused and narrowed her eyes, straining to make out the moonlit path, ahead of her boat. The silvery brilliance of the bright moon, shining down on the sea, blazed a trail that was challenging to navigate. Maneuvering the dark water, beyond the canal's narrow passageway, was the hard part. Amber knew the open water that awaited her small vessel would be tricky to navigate, once she left the security of the canal system. She glanced back and saw the dull, red glow of the culprit's tail lights, fading away in the distance, as they, at last, retreated from the trysting spot. Feeling confident, she flipped the switch on, for the running lights, slowed the boat down and started to make-way, into the open channel. She hoped she would not hit any floating objects or permanent markers, as she continued, moving at half-throttle, over the choppy water. *Wish I had James's bully light hooked up under the bow of the boat, then I could really see where I was heading. . . .* The reassuring, bright shore lights, twinkled, off her port side. Amber watched alertly, with tense pain mounting between her shoulder blades. The little boat moved along and Amber could see the motor, kicking up, a foamy-white wake, following the stern and glistening like sparkling snow, in the moonlight, behind her. Filling her lungs deeply with the clean, salty air, she forcefully exhaled and whispered, "Please, dear Jesus, navigate and chart my course, back to my sailboat. I've got a special delivery, of a green passenger and I could sure use Your help, at the helm."

Thirty-four

"After cruising alone, out on the high seas, being back here at the marina, reminds me, of how much I love concrete pilings and wooden docks!" Amber sighed, while she plopped down on the comfy, bench seat, behind the galley, dining table and settled in, from her nautical venture. "And stationary things . . . things that don't move! Like land!" she added, as she observed James, sitting across from her, positioned and ready, to hear the details of her and Eva's, earlier escapade. Demonstrating, a pleasant sort of patience, he remained quiet, and intrigued, as she declared, "Thank God, I won't be doing that little expedition, ever again." She cocked her head and peered over at him, musingly, "You definitely were a welcomed sight, standing out there, in the cockpit, waiting for me to show up. But, I know you were worried, as much, about your boat, as you were about me!" She jokingly shook her finger at him, as he nodded, good-naturedly. He chuckled and tried to hide the inquisitive side, of his humor. "When I arrived, I guess, I was hoping, I would get a little more attention, than you gave the skiff." James encouraged her, with a trifling wink of his brown eye and coaxed her on, to continue her weak defense. He became, even, more, intrigued by her surprising frankness. Fretting, she added, "I'm sorry, I deserted you, James. I should have helped you with the cleats, bumpers and ropes, but I just wanted off the bloomin' boat. It's your good Coast Guard training . . . you know . . . proper seamanship skills and all . . . that spurs you on, to always square up the boat and I do realize, that all of that squaring, must come, first. But, I'm not the practical sailor, you are, James. My dexterity for docking, gets a little hazy, at times, and I've a lot, to learn and . . . uh . . . I'm not saying that I'm more important, than your Boston Whaler, but. . . . I thought, when I arrived and caught sight of you and you caught sight of me . . . " Amber's voice dropped and she rolled her wistful, green eyes, at James, surrendering any idealistic dreams that were, possibly, still lingering in her mind.

He fought the urge to interrupt, finding it a little difficult, to catch the drift of her incongruent chitchat. She persisted, "Being out there, running the boat, in the dark, all alone, made me really nervous. I was glad to finally see your welcoming-face, watching me, slide in, close, within reach, of the sailboat and even if, you can't understand . . . " her words dropped hard, like a lead anchor. "Well, I really don't know, where I'm going with all of this, so, let me completely change directions and take another tack. That would be best, I think. So, okay, when I've taken your Whaler out in the daytime, by myself, I can clearly navigate where I'm traveling, but tonight, out there, in the dark, I found it rather creepy and strange. The moon's reflection looked like silver-glass, upon the water and I found that a great comfort. Can you imagine me, out there on a moonless-night?" She reached out across the table and purposely, ran her graceful fingers lightly over his hand, as if, shyly asking permission, to remove the cup from his grasp and polish off the remainder of his sweetened coffee.

"Yes, I'm feeling a bit over-caffeinated, but for-the-life-of-me, James, I just can't see, what you get out of running, all around, in your boat, during the blackness of night, with just one little, underwater light to see by."

"Lobsters, my dear. Nice, fat keeper-lobsters! That's what I get out of it!" James's fiery eyes twinkled at Amber, as he topped off her coffee mug, with a hot refill. The aroma of the fresh-ground, Columbian brew, wafted over the cozy, sailboat cabin. James, had tenaciously maintained, a steaming pot that waited on stand by, while he passed the time, looking for Amber's anticipated arrival. "I'm sure, if you had a light illuminating your course, you would have felt better. Hey! Maybe, if you're lucky," he piped, "I'll take you to some of my dad's hot spots, where the spiny crawfish party, one "moonless" night, next summer. That is, if we don't get blasted with a string of hurricanes, to run them all out of here, again, like they did the past two lobster seasons. The poor key deer, never got to evacuate, but the lobsters sure, as heck, did. . . . " James voice trailed off. He faintly sneered and his dark eyes turned stone-still, as he gazed off, above Amber's head. She expected that he was reliving, one of the horrific hurricanes, in his mind, but abruptly, he broke the absorbing silence, "Some of those monsters can put a man in a state of shock."

Before, dropping his glance, to stare through the cloudy steam, curling up from his hot coffee, he caught her staring at him compassionately. He gently breathed in the soft mist, as he divulged thoughtfully, "Yep, my dad has had some really looser-kind of crawfish seasons, in the past few summers and it's been a tough-go for the lobster fishermen! With each despairing blow, more and more lobster, just turned-tail and headed out of the Keys. The murked-up waters, force those bugs to pack up their bags and high-tail it, for clearer, Caribbean waters."

He reached over, tilted the glass pot and poured some fresh coffee, clear up to the brim of his white, porcelain mug. James glimpsed her oval, cameo-shaped face and curiously considered her concerned expression. "Okay, okay! I can see where this is headed. Thanks for ending the agony for me. Don't let me get stalled, like a friggin' hurricane, on that one, again!" He smiled, and then held out his open palm, "Let me look at that frog you caught, tonight!"

"Here he is, Mr. Shannahan," She opened her canvas tote-bag and lifted out her precious bounty, carefully placing the big, green, wooden frog in James's eager hand. He grasped it tightly and shook it hard. Upon hearing the distinctive rattle, Amber asked, "How are we going to slip the gold medal out through the crack of his mouth? It's just a narrow, thin slit. Maybe, it will fit through the two, round holes on his cheeks, but they don't look wide enough for the medal to actually squeeze through."

"I don't know. Isn't that Doctor Balderas's problem? It's his medal and Eva's frog. Why, the heck, should we worry about getting it out?" He rubbed his tense shoulders and propped his feet up under the dining table, on the facing seat, and, then added, "Oh, by the way, some calls rang in, tonight, on your landline. From what I could tell, they're from your mysterious Colonel Benson and I noticed "urgent" was blinking above his name on the caller ID! So, maybe you better check his messages, ASAP, 'cause he's phoned three different times, calling from three different phone numbers. Is his phone bugged or something, or does the man have some good connections with the phone company? I don't even need a landline! Why would he need three?"

"I doubt if he has any connections and three phones does seem excessive for a recouping, retired Colonel. But, I have noticed, lately, he's been acting really odd when we have talked on the phone. I rarely e-mail him, because I love to hear his reassuring voice, advising me in his fatherly fashion. Maybe, he wants to tell me more about Marsha!" Amber stretched and yawned. "I'm too tired to call him, tonight and after all that we've been through, today . . . that's enough drama for me and we're still not done. Isn't that enough stress for you?"

"Yes, it is and I know how you feel. I wonder where poor Eva is, at this very minute." James checked his watch, and then gave a sleepy yawn. "Run Eva, run!" he joked, hoping to lightening up the strained moment.

"That's not funny, James."

"I wasn't tryin' to be funny," he flashed his gleaming eyes at her, as he stretched his arms high above his head and worked his tight back muscles. Yawning again, he retorted, "Man, this whole thing is putting knots in my back. The best plan is to wait until we hear something from Eva, before I go over to the trawler, to tell them, you're back. It will just make Carlos worry, if he knows that you've returned and she's still out there, being hunted down by her adversary, on the dicey streets of Stock Island."

"You mean, our adversary," she quipped. He nodded his head amiably, in agreement, detecting her touchy correction. "Yep," she said. "I absolutely agree. Morgan knows how to keep Doctor Balderas preoccupied with the details of the flight plans and other important tasks, as well. They'll be plenty-busy over there on the trawler, talking things over. Morgan is an expert at distractions. He'll keep Carlos's mind off of Eva's perilous undertaking, I'm sure and this way, it will be easier on everybody, for the next couple of more hours. I'd rather we wait here, as long as we can, on my boat and hopefully, she'll arrive soon."

"Yeah, Morgan knows the deal. So, why do you want to see the medal so bad? Curiosity got the cat, you know? It almost got my cat, Pip, eight times, in the last four years, but I know, that doesn't mean anything to you, 'cause you're woman on a mission! I can see that in your cat-green eyes. It's gonna be hard, as heck, to get that thing out of this stupid frog, without scratching the gold." James studied the mouth of the frog. "It sounds like it would shake right out of the blasted thing, but it doesn't seem to want to fall out . . . I don't want to ruin Eva's frog, by prying his mouth open."

"I know! You can get it out with your red, white-cross knife. You're always looking for an excuse to use it and now, you have your work cut out for you, so-to-speak!"

"You're witty, aren't you, lass? Okay, Amber, let's give it a go." He fished his knife out of his pants pocket and unfolded the blade. "This red knife, that you see here, with the white-cross emblem, by-the-way, is called a Swiss Army knife. And, again, by-the-way, I do enjoy using my knife. Thank you, very much!"

"Hey! Do you think Eva can buy those knives cheaper in Sweden? I'd like to get the really fancy ones with all the useful gadgets inside it."

"Eva will not be going back to Sweden, probably, ever again, in her life. I think you better forget that little business deal."

"Yeah, you're right, James! Her life is completely changed, forever, now. No more laboratory research or circumventing the globe. Shopping in the expensive boutiques in Europe and most fashionable malls in America are history, for poor Eva, now. Skiing excursions in the Alps and diving trips to the islands will become only fleeting memories, for the lady-scientist, too." James gave her a hard stare. Somewhat confused by Amber's ethereal image of Eva, he had to laugh.

"Yep!" he interjected, "Her actual, new life with Carlos will be slapping mosquitoes, entertaining howler monkeys, at breakfast and keepin' up with the elusive sloths who will love hanging around her." He snickered, knowing he wasn't convincing Amber, adding, "Carlos and Eva will probably process their very own coffee beans, along with a few black beans, too."

"That sounds like fun to me! It's not such a bad idea to drop out of the rat race, to relax on some beautiful beach, on either the blue Pacific or green Caribbean. They can have a different choice of coast, every day of the week. Life in a bikini! Eva's new life will be, just that. She'll probably want to spend a lot of her time just being lazy and hanging out in a hammock!"

"So, why don't you give Eva your Eaglesnest hammock and mosquito net for Costa Rica? Believe me, she's gonna need it!"

"That's a great idea, James. I will plan to do just that! Outstanding idea, lad! She'll love my hammock. I'm going to give her all my gear, for a going away present and I have something special for Doctor Carlos, too."

"What? A butterfly net or a moth light? Maybe, a repellent, for the deadly fer-de lance?""

"You'll see, Mr. Curiosity, it's a surprise."

"So, now, I'm the curious one? You're right! I can hardly wait to see it! I liken myself to Pip, now!" he snorted, retorting sarcastically, as he withdrew the knife blade from the frog. "Get ready for your impressively-implanted, micro-chipped, Catholic medal."

The medal, instantly, fell out of the frog's wide, grinning mouth. Bouncing and clinking along, on the tabletop, it shimmered, as it stopped and leaned up against James's coffee cup. They watched, in awe, while the alluring trinket glimmered, bathed in the boat's soft lighting.

"You know," James said, "you were right about removing the medal. I think, we did a favor, for our new friend, Carlos, and he will be very glad that we got it out of the frog, for him. Remember, he said, before they fly out, tonight, he and Eva, plan to just throw it out into the ocean, together, to dispose of it, anyway. I think he just wants to be rid of it and get the quirky obsession, out of his life, so he won't be drawn-in by the powerful temptation to mess with universal laws, again."

"I know, James, it's all kind of surreal, but yet, tempting in anther way, isn't it? Although, I think you're right and that's probably how Doctor Balderas does feel about it, too. But, on the other hand, what if you were the actual person, who secretly possessed the two secret medals, all to yourself? Wouldn't you be tempted to revolutionize the world, as we know it, James?"

"No, I wouldn't, Amber." He looked intensely into her green, jade-colored eyes and asked, "Would you?" She smiled and hesitated before answering. Reaching behind her, she brought out the wooden Captain's box that held her photos and set it in the center of the table, between them. She, then, opened the hinged lid and inserted her slender fingers, inside.

"Well, it's possible," she cooed, opening her small hand, "for here is the second missing medal! I discovered it, dangling on this gold chain, from the pants pocket of Doctor Herald Vickers, when I found him, floating in the mangroves."

"Are you serious?"

"Yes. Quite. I've had it hidden in that box, since New Years Day." She sighed sullenly, then smirked with a slight smugness. "I didn't want to tell anyone that I had taken the medal, off of a dead man."

"I guess not!" he exclaimed. "You are so weird!" James nervously cleared his throat and carefully picked up the burnished, engraved piece, from off the palm of her yielding hand.

Holding it, close to the light, he then, scooped up the other medal and held the two medals, with their concealed ciphers, up next to each other. They bore a stunning magnificence. Appearing to resemble one another, but yet, exemplifying a striking difference in character, they both equally emitted a hypnotic splendor, as they swung back and forth, suspended on their linked chains. James stared at them. Spellbound, he whispered quietly, as if someone, other then Amber, may be listening, "Imagine, Amber Albury, with just these two, small, infused medals, we could flip the world, upside-down."

"Yes, James, we most certainly could." Her green eyes flashed with dancing flickers of light. "Probably, you and I, would become the wealthiest and most influential people in the whole universe, if we kept them and exploited their contents." The Saint Christopher and Saint Francis medals cascaded from their golden chains, twirling, then entwining, as one. Casting dazzling sparkles of light on the cabin wall, Amber stared at the pair of medals, mesmerized by their beauty and awed by their mystery.

"What are you thinking, Amber?"

"I'm thinking these two lost treasures have turned out to be quite the anomaly for me. And now, you, James, and I, are the only people living that know about them, being hidden, here, on my boat, together." Amber took in a deep breath, and then blew it out, forcefully, causing her fluffy bangs to flutter up and down on her smooth forehead. James held the swinging, gold medals up very close to her delicate features, entranced by their powerful promise. She pushed them aside, as her steely-eyes penetrated his flinty gaze, replying emphatically, "I don't really want to turn the world up-side down or inside out, nor, do I want to be the richest and most famous woman alive. I just want to be, simply, Amber Albury, and get on with my life."

"Great! I'm so glad you said that," He tossed the two price-less ornaments up into the air and grabbed both of the medals within the clench, of his tight fist. "You had me really worried there, for a minute." He reached over and squeezed her hand with his. "You never cease to amaze me. But, I do have a question or two or even three."

"Shoot!" He released her hand, but continued to gently hold it lightly. "I'm not counting. Ask away!"

"Well, first off, why did you take Vickers's personal property? You know, what I mean is . . . did you take it because you knew no one was watching and obviously, he would never know? Or was it a pirate-thing . . . a salvaging the spoils, kind-of-thing? What the heck, was going on? Which side of your brain were you using?"

"Well, I took it, not just because I am partial to gold neck-laces and slightly addicted to gold jewelry, but because. . . . " She stopped talking and thought deeply, before giving James his answer. "You're right, I won't deny that, actually, a bit of the old pirate might have come out of me, but, even I, have a problem in that particular area of my life, James Shannahan! I saw the abandoned treasure and I took it for my own! Plain and sim-ple!" He listened closely, as he heard her affectionately say his name, followed by an effervescent giggle, causing his imagina-tion to take flight.

James fantasized, misty rainbows, captured within moist, clear bubbles, he saw them in his mind's eye, freely streaming across hot dessert sands, on a bright-blue, cloudless day. Lowering his head, he startled at how much she, suddenly, was stirring his soulful senses. He began twisting the front lock of his thick, brown hair, in a circular pattern, above his black, expressive eyebrows. He watched her closely, while he shuddered, to get it together and regain his composure.

Unaware, of this unanticipated awakening, he paid attention, as she went on saying, "I knew he wouldn't miss it and I figured someone else would take it and claim it for themselves, when the authorities came to the island to get him. And I thought, it might, somehow, drop completely out of his pocket and get totally lost, under the water. After, going back, a second time to where he was floating, I decided to save it or I guess, *salvage* it, like Black Beard, the pirate, would've done . . . or the treasure hunters, here in ol' Key West, would do!" Abruptly, James gripped the table's edge, when it occurred to him, how serious the impact of her newly obtained possession, could be upon her life.

"Okay, I understand, now, the emotional roller coaster you were riding on, at the time," James said, signifying with his hands, for her to be still and listen to him. Showing his concern, he asked passionately, "But, what do you plan to do with it, presently, Amber? Now, that you know how dangerously valuable it is? It has already cost one person his very life. Not to mention, that over on the trawler, that you are currently, the caretaker for, there is a man hiding from his worse nightmare. And, have I forgotten to mention, that at this very minute, his fiancé is out there, somewhere, in the night, literally running for her life? And what about you? You're not exactly sippin' a snifter, relaxing, on the upper deck! We know what Carlos will do with his medal. He's chosen to cast it over into Davy Jones's locker. Who better to give it to! But, seriously, do you see what I'm trying to say?"

"I know, I know." Amber cried. Tears gushed from the corners of her eyes and spilt down her face. "I do feel so guilty, sometimes, for taking Doctor Vickers's medal. The whole time, Carlos was explaining everything and looking at the photos and asking me questions, about when I found his friend, I came so close, to telling him, I had Vickers's medal hidden away. But, I was embarrassed and ashamed for what I did and some odd feeling . . . I can't explain . . . came over me, restraining me, from telling him. I've repented a million times and I am sorrowfully sick about my behavior . . . more, than, you'll ever know. But, tonight, I have planned to give my medal to him, for a special gift . . . a token of my appreciation, in hopes, that he will forgive me for keeping it, from him." James heaved a big sigh, got up from his bench seat, at the table and sat down next to her, putting his strong arms around her. She buried her face, into his broad chest and wept uncontrollably. He hugged her and held her tightly, trying to tenderly console her with some hard-to-find, gentle words.

"Look, Amber, if it helps, let me say, that it's possible, if you had given Carlos, the missing medal, earlier, today or even if you hand it over to him, tonight, things may eventually get really twisted in a bad way. Sardis could, somehow, find out the truth, about the youth serum formulas, being infused inside, the two Catholic medals. If that happened, Sardis wouldn't delay, in getting really busy, trying to track both medals down and fatally, eliminating some possible leads. Look what happened to Vickers. You don't know the potential these bad guys have. It might be good that you took Vickers's medal and kept it hidden."

"What if, you, in your self-condemnation, gave Carlos the missing medal, earlier, because you felt guilty or you thought, you owed it to him, or because he was partners with Herald Vickers, at one time? Things and ideas can change. Things don't always seem the way they appear. He might have gratefully received your recovered gift, and then, suddenly, for some reason, had a change of mind, and decided he would not get rid of the medal Eva retrieved from the lab, tonight. He might render it senseless, to dispose of either one, now, that he had possession of them both, once again. He'd possibly alter the course of the whole world, for generations to come."

"If Carlos, all of a sudden, decided to control the power that the two medals contain, then how would you feel, about the error, that you made, relinquishing Vickers's medal to him? Amber, you may have made a terrible mistake, if you had given Vickers's medal to Carlos. You've possibly protected him, from unknowingly, becoming lured in and caught by some malignant bait and succumbing to the powerful pull that the two medals possess. Your intervention may have kept him from plummeting and landing into the ensnaring net of a wicked enemy." James held her close to him, hoping she understood. "I would think twice about giving him your medal. A moth light would make a much better gift!" Reluctant to let go of her, she raised her head, smiled at him and patted his worried face. He gently released her and stood up. Dampening a soft paper towel, he dried her eyes and wiped the tears from her tear-streaked cheeks. Amber's face glowed, as if it had just been cleansed by a spring shower.

"I feel a whole lot better, now. Just the way you described it all, makes perfect sense, especially, when you used your fisherman's metaphors to explain it." Amber sniffed and smiled. "My decision to take the medal off of Vickers may have helped the whole world! Who knows, James?"

"Well, we don't know," he said, pouring another cup of coffee for each of them. "So, again, I ask, what are you going to do with your infamous, secret treasure?"

"I've had this idea pop into my head out in the boat, while

waiting there in the canal for Eva." He sat back on the couch and gazed at the golden objects, lying clandestinely on the table, before them. He tilted his inquisitive face, waiting to hear about her enlightening revelation.

"I'm still astounded, when I think about it all. Do you realize, James?" She leaned over and hovered above the two shiny medals. "We are, presently, all alone, with a pair of very important relics, in our mists? No one else, but us, in the whole, wide world, have ever, seen these two, secret, treasures, together, except for, of course, the two doctors, who invented the formulas. Isn't that amazing?"

"You're right, Amber." James stopped speaking. They both froze! A knock resounded, upon the other side, of their cabin door.

Thirty-five

"**M**organ! My man! It's you!" James cried, as his trifling words tumbled from his lips, muddling one with the other.

Peering intently, at Morgan, through the crack, of the slightly open door, James covered up his feigned astonishment, "We weren't so sure who would be banging so blasted loud on the door. Been out here long?" James skillfully pried, yet attempting to appear casual. He flung the door open and heartily gestured, Morgan into the cabin, below. "Enter, my friend! So glad it's you! Can't be too careful, Captain," he punned, putting on a contrived smile. Morgan scoffed and with narrowed eyes, scrutinized James's suspicious behavior, as he jumped lithely down into the main salon of the sailboat, landing squarely on both feet. "You did that well," James applauded. "Have a seat!"

Morgan sat down upon the sofa, but quickly caught sight of Eva's captured frog, leering at him, from the table. The incessantly fixed stare and riveting, red, painted eyes, beamed, while squatting comically, next to the solitary, gold Saint Christopher medal. Morgan instantly recognized the cohort of the grinning, green frog. His cornflower-blue eyes locked, in a straight line,

onto the coveted, gold treasure. Reaching out, he delicately lifted the infamous ornament, as if it were made of mist. The solid,
eighteen-karat, gold treasure, swung gently from the sturdy,
linked chain that curled loosely around his fingers. He attentively held it up to the ship's lantern and examined it much closer in the light. A pensive expression spread over his bronze-col-
ored face, as the medal shimmered beneath the illuminating
glow. Morgan finally broke the silence, "So, this is the sinister,
little trinket that's been making our lives so difficult lately!"
Sneering, he plunked it down hard upon the table, next to the
continuously smiling frog. The loud clunk convinced James that
Morgan, was not exactly daunted with Carlos's secret cache and
he eyed Morgan, closely, giving him a smirk. James picked up
the chain and carefully arranged it over the pointy ridges of the
happy frog's back. Morgan loudly cleared his throat and slowly
shook his head in mild disgust.

Directing his attention toward Amber, Morgan grumbled,
"Well, up until arriving, here, at your boat, I didn't know you
had already gotten back from your undercover-mission."
Morgan glanced at James for his reaction and asked, "And why
would that be? Ah, don't answer, let me guess! Because, no one
bothered to come over to tell us that you were back? And, could
it be? Not only, are you back safely on board your sailboat, but
you're looking, actually, quite rested . . . and, as snug, as a bug,
in a rug. I'd say! But, not to worry, about Carlos and I and the
fact that we have been worried sick. We thought you would jet
over to the trawler, with the medal, as soon, as you, tied up the
skiff. I was concerned about your safety and Carlos was vexed,
as heck, about his stupid medal." Surrendering a sudden sigh of
relief, he resigned himself and offered a well-meaning grin, "I'm
just glad you made it back alive!"

Morgan glanced over at the "on" light button, glowing

neon-green, from the base of the coffee maker. Considering, the glass pot was totally empty and sizzling upon the burner, he then discovered the two, drained mugs sitting close together, upon the table, of the cozy nook. He began smiling like a skinny cat, gripping a fat rat. He was all too familiar with James's old, Coast Guard custom, of brewing a brimming pot, full of piping-hot coffee, right up, to the high-water mark of the glass beaker, whether there was someone around, to help him drink it or not. This was James's area of expertise. His concoctions were famously, well known, among his acquaintances. Well liked? That was another matter, but despite attempting to fulfill all manner-of-tastes, varied coffee beans, slung in the grinder and ground haphazardly, together, had become his specialty.

Observing Amber's conspicuous guilt, Morgan playfully toyed with James, "Knowing you, James, you've nervously downed, a whole pot of coffee, all by yourself, while waiting anxiously, to hear the sound, of Amber motoring in, from her trip." Morgan leaned over and inspected the coffee stains in the bottom of the two mugs. He continued, "I bet he didn't even save one drop for you, did he, Amber? And I'm sure, that after experiencing your harrowing, extraction-ordeal, savoring a cup of James's unique brew, would have been, just what the doctor ordered . . . no pun intended!" Morgan gave her a mischievous wink and taunted, "Come on, I know what's going on here!"

Amber shot a startled glance at James, then, rendered a tolerant glare, Morgan's way. Morgan's mouth dropped open, as he proclaimed in delight, "This much-too-comfortable, coffee-break is, right now, terminated for you two!" With that, he pulled a watch-cap, down, from off of a brass hook and tugged it down over his shaggy, blond head. "It's time to get that impossible medal, over to the trawler and back into Carlos's hands, because Eva has returned, from her Stock Island caper. Carlos is eager and chomping at the bit, to wrap things up. He's ready to dispose of the Saint Christopher medal and disappear from Key West! Immediately!"

James scooped up the medal and gave it to Amber to put into the side pocket of her slacks. Morgan uttered with relief, "I thought you all might be interested in knowing, Eva managed to ditch the bugged, company car, nearby and absconded, on foot the rest of the way back, to the trawler. She arrived, not only with her few bags, but with a few, bloody, blisters on her feet, as well. She, definitely, gave her pursuers the slip and she said that Sardis's spies were not parked out in the marina parking lot, anymore. I guess they're done dogging Amber, for a spell and using her for their live bait. Doctor Eva is a much bigger fish for Sardis to fry, now! But first . . . he'll have to catch her!" Morgan's lame joke was a tough one for Amber to laugh at. "Okay! Okay!" he lamented, "It was a poor attempt to ease the stress level around here! At least, I'm trying!"

James rolled his eyes and pleaded, "Please stop trying. It's not working!" Amber, giggled at James's comment, but James went on to hound him, "So, what's the hold-up, Captain? Let's get over there. What are you waiting for? Coffee? Um, I don't think you'll be getting any of that for awhile! Not from me, anyway!"

Morgan coolly nodded and sarcastically responded, "Obviously not! There isn't a drop left in the pot for me to drink! You guys happily hogged it all." Scaling the steps, he unlocked the door and said, "I'll see you both over at the trawler! Pronto! The plane is standing by at Summerland Key air strip, waiting for them, right now. Hurry it up! After, they take off, you two can get back to some really serious, coffee drinking."

Amber and James dismissively shook their heads at his speculative jab, while he fled from their sight. Turning, Amber silently slipped up into the forward stateroom, to collect a few things.

What seemed like an eternal era, turned out to be, only a succinct farewell. Amber and James, were strolling back from the trawler, to the *Lady Poetry*. Lulling peacefully at the docks, the different crafts that they passed, appeared to be sleeping, calmly at their moorings, but they did not sway Amber's mood, from the emotional turmoil that she was struggling against.

With the undertaking, of proclaiming their goodbyes to Carlos and Eva are really gone for good! Amber sadly cried, "James, I can't believe it's over . . . as quickly, as it all began. Carlos and Eva are really gone for good! Their departure from us went by so quick! It was sweet of Morgan to escort them to the plane, on Summerland, so we could get some much-needed rest."

She swung back the sun-bleached strands of her hair that blew across her eyes. "I sure hope Morgan didn't hear us talking about the two medals, when he came over, to see if I was back from my boating trip. Maybe he was standing outside, in the cockpit, listening to our conversation, before he knocked on the cabin door. Is that possible? Wonder if he overheard us discussing our secret?" Amber fretted, nervously, chewing on her polished fingernail.

James slowed his pace, hoping to draw out the moment. He pleasantly welcomed the walk, close by her side, down the moonlit, wooden dock. Returning from their completed mission at the trawler, she halted her step, turned and looked up at James. The luminous, blue moonlight, softly filtered over his handsome face. Arresting her momentarily, she felt, as if, she had found some fresh direction in her life. Pausing, she pondered, and, then thoughtfully, she gathered her words, continuing to stress her added concern, "I mean, Doctor Vickers's medal is our little secret, just between you and me, forever and ever, right, James? I sure wouldn't want anyone else, to know, about me taking the missing medal."

"Who would I tell?" James whispered devotedly. "No one should ever hear about these scientific, Catholic medals! We might all end up in Davy Jones's locker, if any word, leaks out about them. Then, we would have to worry about Jones!" He snickered. "Your secret will always be safe with me, lass. And, stop worrying about the Captain. He didn't hear a word of our private convo. I'm positive! And, furthermore, he'll never know our special secret, I promise." They continued their leisurely walk on down the planked dock, once more. Amber sighed and took heart in his words of encouragement.

"Didn't you notice? When Morgan came to your boat, to tell us, Eva had returned to the trawler, he wasn't really interested in Carlos's anomalous medal. That's the way it is with Morgan. It takes a lot to get him excited, about almost anything, except, if he's going out, diving lobster or drinking a cold one, on a porch, under a "gingerbread" overhang, somewhere in Old Town."

James started whistling one of his latest tunes, then added, "Our friends have probably boarded, Katherine Grace's little jet and flown out of Summerland Key airstrip, already. I bet, by now, Key West's rhapsody, is already drifting back into the remote corners of their minds. Tomorrow evening, Eva and Carlos will be discovering a new song, curled under a pastel rainbow, arched over a bright, new horizon. And, may I suggest that its time to put all of this stuff behind us, too? I've become concerned about you . . . what I really mean to say is . . . we both could use some new sunsets in our lives, don't you think?" James wrapped his arm around her straight shoulders and gave her a tender squeeze to bolster her spirit, then added, "It's late and Morgan should be back to your boat, shortly. Don't worry about a thing. Everything will look different when the sun rises at dawn. In the meantime, we need to get some sleep. Morgan and I, will be ready to crash on the trawler, by the time he returns."

"Yep! You're so right. You've always seemed to know just the right thing to say to me, James. You have a way of making me feel better, every time." She stretched and yawned, saying, "It is way past my bedtime, too. I'm looking forward to some very wonderful, inner-healing sleep. Today, has been a most unusual day. I'll need a week to recover from this one."

Amber yawned, again and politely covered her mouth with the back of her delicate hand. Gazing up to the vast heavens, a shooting star caught their attention, as it spilled out from the sprawling net, of brilliant stars, spread above them. She asked in a soft voice laced with drowsiness, "Do you suppose Eva liked the hammock? I mean, she didn't have time to study it, but she'll figure out how to hang it up and I know she'll love the color, too. I guess you were really surprised that I gave my special, personal wooden frog, to Carlos, as a going-away gift, weren't you?" James nodded his head, as he climbed aboard the sail-boat. She added, "I wanted them both to have their own big frog, as a memento of the Keys." He held out his firm hand to steady her, as she stepped down into the cockpit. "Thanks," she gasped, grabbing James's arm, catching her balance, on the slated teak deck, below.

Amber deeply sighed, remarking thoughtfully, "Carlos had his mind, on one thing and that was throwing his medal, out into the ocean, boarding the plane and making their great escape. Carlos took only one final look at his medal, and that was when, I pulled it out of my pocket and placed it in his hand. He hesitated, only a moment, to examine it, but, I must say, that seemed a little strange, I thought. I mean, since, it had been, always so precious to him. As, I watched him study his prized treasure, turning it over and rubbing it between his fingers, a notion occurred to me. While he closed his eyes and felt the raised embossment, with his fingers pressed, onto the etched adornment, it seemed almost like he was . . . well, praying. Then, without a word, he walked to the stern of the trawler and hurled it out, into the dark ocean. I saw a flash of gold, in the moonlight, as it soared through the air and I think it was, actually, saying goodbye, to him. I have never witnessed such a look of relief, as I saw, tonight, in the face of Doctor Carlos Balderas, when he turned from completing his arduous task, of casting his medal, into the depths of the sea. The heavy weight of his burden was finally lifted, from his shoulders and he was suddenly set free. When I saw him break down and weep, falling into Eva's arms, I cried, too. It was a glorious celebration, enjoyed by all of the onlooking Angels. And, Eva and I, shared the most wonderful goodbye." Amber reflected back and the salty tears soaked her thick, black eyelashes.

"*Onlooking Angels . . . onlooking Angels*? I did see you give Eva a small Bible with her hammock gear and frog, besides your frog, that you gave Carlos. What was that all about?" He unlocked the cabin door and they went down, below. He shut it behind him and he hastily bolted the lock.

"Oh, before you go into your explanation, I need to tell you something extremely important and I can't believe I forgot to mention this to you earlier, when you first got back to the sailboat, with the Whaler."

James tossed his head back, tired and drained; he ran his

hand through his thick hair, asking, "Where is my mind, lately?" Amber playfully shrugged her shoulders. "I called my attorney, Prescott, tonight on your, hopefully, *secure* land-line and I'm meeting with him early, tomorrow morning. He will compile all of our anonymous tips and supply them to Detective Barlow. That way, with the info being totally anonymous, Carlos, Eva and, of course, Morgan, you and I won't be tied in, at all. His criminal case against Sardis, will solve itself, without any of our help. Can you use the marina phone in the morning to call into work? Since your cell phone is now in the hands of Davy Jones's and your land-line number would show up on the studio ID, it might be best to use another phone. You should still, at least, try to protect the only private line that you have. Nevertheless, I want you to call the television studio and tell them you're not gonna make it in, okay? Being Friday, it will work out perfect, because, after tomorrow, you will be finished with your job, anyhow. Past affiliations that you had with Dominique Sardis will be history and going into the weekend, it'll take any heat, off of you and give Prescott and Barlow, time to accomplish some important things, before the surprise arrest, of Sardis and his buddies, on Saturday.

They are convinced that a couple of Sardis's men will easily agree, to enter into a Witness Protection Program and turn State's Evidence, against Sardis and completely expose his *modes operandi*. Your newspaper, reporter friend, Heather, may even get a phone call from Prescott, later, tomorrow afternoon, giving her the exclusive story, for the *Sunday Citizen*. They'll absolutely reverence the woman, over there, at the paper, after, her scoop, hits the newsstands on Sunday. Heather will make their sales, soar, up and down, the Florida Keys. This things gettin' ready to bust wide open!"

James whooped gleefully and broke into a bouncy, mini-

Irish jig. Rollicking in his Blarney merriment, he noticed Amber wasn't celebrating or smiling. He promptly got a sober grip, on himself, saying, "Okay, okay, I'll stop. I entertain for a living. Remember that, young lass? But let's get back to being serious, again. What was I thinking, anyway?" She grinned, with an admission of guilt and confessed that she loved seeing him elated. He good-naturedly winked at her and continued with his plan, "Sardis's attention will be completely off of you, for now, and on Saturday, any thought of you being the future contact and a connection to Carlos, will be just a bad memory for him. So, you can relax, because he and his goons will be behind bars, by sunset, Saturday evening. You know, Sardis has to be seething, when he recalls Eva's pretense, of a tight relation-ship.....and boom! Surprise! It blew up, right in his face. His little hen "flew the coop"! He's still, no doubt, puzzled and try-ing to figure out, what was so vital, about that green frog, that Eva snagged from the lab, tonight." James laughed, giving Amber a tiny pinch upon her sullen chin. "Come on and lighten up a little. Didn't you like my Key West "chicken" joke?" Amber smiled weakly, but then bit her lower lip. "What's wrong? Was it that corny?" he asked, snickering gleefully. "I'm sorry! Thought you'd appreciate it. The way you exchange ideas, with all the chickens, running loose, outside my cottage, I figured, you'd probably enjoy some funny, chicken-comedy. Guess I'll have to scratch, telling you any more fowl humor . . . it's just my cluck . . . I mean, luck . . . not gettin' you to cackle, at my jokes!"

"Well, your chicken jokes are extremely corny, James. The truth is . . . and I'm telling you the truth, in all seriousness." His jovial brown eyes widened, turning somber, as he displayed a baffled expression . . . *Is she that defensive about the chickens around here?* James rubbed his head and gave her a hard stare.

She solemnly gazed back at him, and continued, "What I'm trying to explain is . . . you know . . . if you hadn't ever made the "plummeting and landing into the ensnaring net" speech about Carlos, I was planning, on putting a little surprise, into my big, green frog's belly, before, I gave it to him for his going-away present."

"And what was that going to be?"

"My Saint Francis medal that I found on Herald Vickers!"

"But, you didn't"

"I know . . . but, I wanted him to find it, after he got to his new hideaway, in Costa Rica and rejoice that he, miraculously, owned, his old friend's lost medal. He and I would never see each other, again, so there would be no questions, being asked, by him or any answers, given by me. Of course, this idea was also based, on the fact, that, I knew, that he never had his or Vickers's formula, committed to memory, therefore, he'd never cause a world-shaking problem, if he had the Vickers's medal . . . and, I, definitely would have made sure that he had disposed, of his medal first. After that, he would have received my frog, containing Harold Vickers's medal, discover it later, and live happily, ever, after! But, then, I considered the wise counsel that you gave to me earlier, and I changed my mind and did what I thought, was the right thing."

"You would have made a grave mistake," he affirmed, with conviction, as he pushed both of his hands through the front of his thick, burnished hair. "You did a wise thing, Amber. You did a very wise thing." He blew out a deep breath, expressing his obvious relief. "I'm just glad, you didn't pull the wrong medal, out of the wrong pocket! I held my breath until I saw you holding up, the Balderas, Saint Christopher's medal instead of the Vickers, Saint Francis medal, that you safely hid in your other pocket! And upon that note, I have a special gift for you in one of my pockets! In special memory, of this auspicious occasion, it is one that I believe will turn the tide, at this point."

He dug down, deep, into his pocket, and fished out, his red knife and laid it on the table.

"A Swiss Army Knife?" she asked, in exhultant surprise.
He did not answer, but kept his focus and reached down deep into the bottom of his pocket, again. This time, he brought out a thin, gold chain that was wrapped around, an antique-looking locket. He carefully untangled the chain, from the lovely ornament. Holding it, in his open hand, the polished jewel, sparkled regally, as Amber gaped at it, in awe.

"Here, please, try it on. I want you to have it. It was my great grandmother's necklace. She wore it proudly and treasured it, when she was alive."

Amber was speechless and amazed, as James, fastened the hammered-gold, chain, around her graceful neck. "You are wearing a genuine, conch pearl that my great grandfather found in a broad lip, queen conch. He dove the shell up, off of the shores, of Key West, many, many years ago, then had the rare pearl, fashioned into a locket, for my great grandma, his fiancée. It looks like it's all one, solid pearl, but it's not! It cleverly opens up. Amber, you will make it appear, even more beautiful, than it is, just as my grandmother did. I can show you an old black and white picture, of her wearing it, when she was eighteen years old. But, there's one string attached to this jeweled legacy." He thoughtfully paused, then whispered sweetly, in a hushed tone, "I can't let you open it and look inside, 'til tomorrow night, after, the party. There is an old, family secret, buried deep, within and you must patiently wait to find out, what it is."

Amber was thrilled, but seemingly puzzled and very curious, all at the same time. "You see this tiny, gold key?" James asked, as he removed a shiny, splinter of a key, from inside of his wallet. "The locket is actually locked and this infinitesimal key is the only way, to open it up! I promise to give you the key, to keep for your own, tomorrow night, after the closure, of the Sardis case and the party is over. Then, before midnight, when we're finally alone, I will enjoy sharing with you, the incredible secret that is concealed, inside!" She lovingly smiled at him. Drawing the curtain on this scene, there are no words, in existence to express the bliss of the sweet moments that followed.

After, some time, Amber regained her senses and she sat, serenely, fidgeting with her new necklace. She glanced at James, admiring his sparkling, brown eyes, as she traced her fingers, over the smooth, glossy pearl that dangled from her neck. She spoke with sensitivity, "Yes, it's hard to believe that Carlos and Eva are gone, for good. I hope that they will find what they are looking for."

"You asked me, about the New Testament Bible that I gave to Eva."

James sat down and put his feet up and his head back, against a plump, sofa pillow. Admiring her beauty and his grandmother's lovely locket, he thought. . . . *She's so tired and so am I! Four more hours and it'll be morning . . . I'm heading to the trawler, for some shut-eye. I gotta be on top of my game, today. I'll be playing at Shark Key tonight and meeting with Prescott and Barlow, in just a few hours.* He laid his head back and closed his brown eyes.

"Well," Amber said, not missing a beat. "I'll explain to you what took place. In the space, of about five minutes, after Carlos heaved the medal, overboard, I gave Eva, the hammock gear and enlighten her about why I wanted to give her the Bible, too. I told her, I was a Christian and how simple it would be, for her to invite the Lord Jesus Christ, into her heart. Like chicken soup! Jesus is so good for you, I went on to say. He created us just for His pleasure and that she could make Him, Lord of her life, tonight, before she flew to Costa Rica. I explained, how Jesus can save her from hell's fire, for past sins, because He died, on the Cross, to pay for them. I described to her that He was miraculously resurrected, into Heaven, to be with God, His Father, again, and afterwards, He sent us his Holy Spirit to comfort us, upon our earthly journey. She easily could ask for His forgiveness and be given the assurance, of an eternal home, with Him forever, if she so desired!" Amber's countenance lit up. "What more could Eva desire?" She clapped her hands joyfully together. "God knows, Eva, better than Carlos ever will." She squeezed James's arm, checking to see if he was still awake. As he adjusted the pillow under the back of his head, he looked at her very curiously.

He opened his twinkling eyes, wide, inspired by her inquisitive face. He was listening intently, but he held up his hand, for pause. Lowering it slowly downward, he asked, "Hold it, a second! What about the *Onlooking Angels* part, that you referred to before?"

Amber nodded her cameo-shaped face and answered, "Well, I'm coming to that," She hesitated for an instant, gathering her thoughts. "Those Heavenly Beings are the countless-guardian Angels, that God sends throughout the Earth, to protect us and catch us, when we fall. And sometimes, we do make wrong choices and fall. You know, kind-of-like, when you were talking about Carlos and his possible-plummet into the evil net. When I mess up, I sure want God's Angels there, to catch me, if I should fall."

James gazed at her smooth, pink mouth. Glancing at his watch, he realized how late it was. Amber leaned back and propped a pillow up under her head, next to his and whimsically smiled, over at him, adding, "Then, Eva, asked me to pray, a simple prayer of repentance, with her and I did. She gave her life to Jesus and, now, she's a child of the King! We both hugged. I gave her a goodbye-kiss and then, Eva vanished from my life. And, what do you suppose all of the *Onlooking Angels* did at that precise moment, in time, James?"

"I'm gonna hope they shouted, 'Hallelujah,'" and he leaned over and kissed Amber tenderly, on her yielding cheek.

Thirty-six

T he wind was blowing, a good twenty knots and light rain was drizzling down upon the glistening, white, fiberglass sailboat. Moored securely at dock, the *Lady Poetry* bobbed and curtsied, like a wine cork, on top of the choppy water.

Quietly, James gazed out, through the port light, toward the hazy horizon. He thoughtfully studied the jagged lightning rods that impaled the dark, shadowy thunderheads, building in the faraway distance. Every volatile strike transformed the massive, pregnant cloud-shapes, into towering, glowing infernos. Miles from Key West's peaceful shores, out over the western Dry Tortugas Islands, the illuminated sky blazed with countless surges of voltage. The deadly, electrical bolts popped and zapped, as their fiery fingers reached down through the heavy, swollen clouds, to fondle the newborn storm. Billowing blankets of steel-grey shrouds wrapped the sprawling torrents of rain and swaddled, the sizzling hands that rocked the tempest's cradle with undreamed of power. Deep, rumbling groans and thunder-ous birth pangs, heaved and boomed over the western waters.

James gloated, knowing the turbulent Atlantic would weather the pain, as it always did, with no problem. His mind thoughtfully drifted back, as he silently reflected on the violent storm that he and his friends were trapped in, out at Yellow Rocks, not, so long, ago. He was relieved that the unpredictable disturbance, he was currently observing, had chosen another spot to rage, for the time being. Recalling the past memories, James decided, that it might not be a bad idea to "batten down the hatches" of the sailboat. . . . *"Just in case"* . . . he smiled to himself.

The refreshing fragrance, of new, falling rain blew through the open portholes, escorted by eagerly splashing raindrops. The airy wind, gusted a blasting, wet whoosh, against the side of the boat, as the rain pelted down harder. James started to pull the open port light down, but hesitated. He tilted his face up toward the incoming, light wind and drank in the intoxicating bouquet that saturated the breeze. It filled his senses, and overflowed into the very core of his being. Tenderly, the soft raindrops sprinkled and patted his drowsy face, momentarily, awakening slumbering inspirations, sleeping secretly, within his soul. Stirring dreams, suddenly, scattered across his mind, like dancing lights, over a sunlit bay. Struck, by the awe, of the odd, tranquil moment that he was experiencing, he hoped that the feeling would linger.

Calmly, James drew in a deep, cleansing breath. Peaceful inspiration, flowed freely, like a crystal-clear river, running through the channels of his mind.

Abruptly, the revelations faded. . . he exhaled. Bleakly, the vacating visions flew out the window and evaporated into the mist, as a repeated, vexing rap, struck sharply, upon the cabin door. Amber felt a chill go down the back of her neck and she opened her closed eyes. She nervously looked straight over, at James, with a penetrating stare. James, reluctantly, pulled the port light closed and fastened it shut.

"James!" she startled. "Who's that?" She sat upright, on the sofa's edge, wishing that the banging would stop. "That sure isn't thunder!" she joked, under her breath. Then a booming voice, sliced the stillness, echoing throughout the silent cabin.

"Hey! Are you guys in there? It's me! Morgan! Remember me? Let me in! I'm getting soaked out here!" he cried and pounded the cabin door with his fist, again. "Open the blasted hatch!" Amber grinned deviously, knowing that he was so desperate, to get inside the dry cabin. James ignored her impish behavior, but shook his finger, at her for misbehaving and finding humor, in Morgan's stressful plight.

James stretched up and placing his foot, on the bottom step, he unbolted the teak, entry panels and pushed them, apart. Amber was wild-eyed, as she witnessed Morgan sprint down the boat steps and into her main salon, dripping wet with rain water.

"Do you think you could have banged on the door any louder?" James snapped, at Morgan. "You're, no doubt, makin' this banging-noise-thing into some sort of twisted habit! And, it's sure gettin' to be an irritating one." Morgan took a dry towel, from Amber's hands and scowled at James. He patted his glistening, suntanned arms and shiny, damp face, sopping up, most of the water from his cool skin. He, then, reached out and slung the large, bath towel, over the stair railing.

"James, give me a break, will you? I never, even, thought twice, about how I should knock or not knock, on the cabin door! I think you're stressed out, with a rarer form, of cabin fever! On the other hand, my body is flat-out aching from the

359

humidity and I feel like crap! I've got a blasted head-cold coming on!" Morgan moaned, followed by an over-dramatized sneeze. "I've been driving through heavy, torrential downpours, ever since I left Summerland Key." He paused, but no one offered any comment. "I know you're finding it difficult to live with my interruptions, tonight, but, as much, as you don't want to encounter, a few of life's little intrusions, we must, even, at this late hour, realize, that we're all caught up, right in the middle, of our very own reality show and it's not over, yet. It never occurred to you, I guess, that I could've been out there, on US 1, in a high speed chase, with a strange enemy that's, actually, to begin with, not, even, my enemy! Not to mention, that I, myself, have never, ever, met, before. In fact, when it comes right down to it, I don't even have an enemy. Not one that I could call, my very own, anyway! But, here, I am, dodging the head-master-dragon and we've never, even, personally been introduced." Grabbing the towel again, he wiped his dripping nose on a dry corner and pushed the bulk of it, through his sopping, wet hair. "Thankfully I got back, here, to the marina, by being smart enough. . . and I mean, really smart enough, to avoid any of these likely events. Now, I ask, you two, is this welcome, the warm welcome that I deserve?" Morgan winked at Amber, as he sat down on a retractable, wooden bench, resting his clammy, sodden back, against the sturdy bulkhead of the sailboat, hopelessly, trying to dry out a bit. Next, he glanced up at her and suggested sheepishly, "Amber, if you're a prayer warrior. . . and we all know that it's no secret that you fit this description." He chuckled, but his expression changed and he very earnestly suggested, "This is, probably, as good, as time, as any, for you to do, what decent, prayer warriors, do best, because our new friends, who we will probably never, ever, see, again, are flying into the face, of a lightning storm, from hell."

"What do you mean?" Amber shrieked. "We will never see them, again? Why do you say that? Because you think their plane is going to crash? Or, do you mean, we're never going to see them, again, because they'll be living in another part of the world?"

"There's a slight bit of difference in these two scenarios. Which 'never, ever, see, them again,' scenario are you implying, Morgan? Either one, doesn't sound good to me, but, at least, the second one, doesn't sound so final." She frowned at Morgan and got up from the couch, retrieved the towel from the railing and headed into the bathroom, to hang it up.

"Well, with the weather, the way it looked, at take-off and the direction, the plane was pointing in, when it flew out, both scenarios are possible." He caught James, scrutinizing, him with a hard stare and he swiftly changed the subject, by asking, "Is it possible, Amber, for this drenched and shivering, young barer-of-bad-news, to get a cup of your special, hot coco? You mentioned how rich, it tastes, in passing, a couple of days ago, and the thought of it, has stuck in my brain. Ever since, I've been craving dark chocolate, like some fickle female, lately. And those little, party cakes you baked, weren't too bad, either. They were pretty good, I thought, party or no party. Are there any more of those fancy cakes, around?"

Morgan held up his finger, in pause, as he stood up, moved to the dining nook and scooted in, behind the table and onto the padded bench. Still holding up his long finger, poised in the air, he continued, "Speaking of parties, tomorrow night, or I guess, I should say, tonight, we know Prescott's big bash, is taking place, out at his palace, on Shark Key. Now, this important Key West gala will be the party, of all parties and we don't want to miss it! This event will be newspaper-quality-stuff! Amber, you can ride with me, if you want, because James will be busy, all day long, with legalities and then, going up to Shark Key, early in the evening, for set-up.

He's hired a very talented girl, who plays a mean fiddle, to perform along with his songs. Also, the rent-a-drummer, "Drummin' Biggs Digs Gigs" is performing back-up for him, too. James, will no doubt, need to practice, before the party actually starts, since the three of them have only played together, at a few Key West weddings."

James had dozed off, listening to Morgan drone on about the party, by leaning his chin, on his fist. Nodding his head, he caught himself, as his chin slipped off of his hand. Morgan laughed, leaned out, from the nook and shoved James, over on the couch. His head hit a soft pillow. Morgan continued, "It's gonna be a whole lot different for James, to share the attention with two other musicians, who like seeking the limelight, too. He'll put them both through their paces, I'm sure, before the night is over. Patience, the piccolo player, performs only solo, since past wedding ensembles. Amber, have you ever seen a singer reprimand his backup-musicians, while he's entertaining? You'll see why our leading man generally performs, alone, by the end of the party. I've heard that fiddle player is known for elbowing her way, right up, to the front, while still twanging her fiddle, so it may be sort of amusing watching her try to upstage James at the party or beat him up with her bow. Fortunately, he won't have that problem with Drummin' Biggs! It's all part of the show, right, Shannahan?" Morgan reached over and pulled James back up, by the hand, to sitting position. James smirked at him, ignoring his inept remarks. Leaning his head back on a cushion, he closed his eyes and he shook his head back and forth. Morgan chuckled and nodded at Amber, then he withdrew the BMW car keys from his cargo short's pocket. Slapping them down with a clatter, onto the galley table, Morgan snickered, as James opened his brown eyes and looked wide awake. "Okay, I think I've got your attention!" Morgan quipped cheerfully and he began to lay out the approaching day's plan, "Here are my mom's car keys, James. Please, drive her car when you go over to finalize all the official business, in the morning. Just leave it parked at your cottage and put the keys under the wicker, chair cushion on your front porch. I'll grab a cab, later in the day to your place, after I get up. Why? It' simple! I'm planning on sleeping late, in the morning and taking advantage of the cozy trawler."

"This is morning! Amber mocked. "The sun just doesn't know it, yet, Morgan." She was yawning exuberantly and rubbing her tired eyes, as she agreed, "That's sounds like a good idea and a great plan. Thanks, Morgan, I'd love to go with you to the party. I can be ready to be picked up any time, after four o'clock. I can't wait for all of us to celebrate together. Sardis will be locked up by then, thanks to our very own representative, Mr. Shannahan, who will not, be sleeping in late, but will be, faithfully, taking care of very important, big business, in the morning." Amber presented a heavy sigh, then cautiously uttered, "With that said, no matter what we all plan to do tomorrow, let's just take a moment, right now, and pray for Eva and Carlos for a safe journey. We don't want them to have a *Titanic* experience. Okay?" She hesitated, half expecting a little resistance, but she continued on, "I'll pray, if that's all right with you guys, since I've been named the designated "prayer warrior" and I don't see either of you, jumping at the chance! As, you alluded to earlier, Morgan, prayer never hurt anybody. It's a lot like chicken soup, remember, fellows?" Morgan looked really puzzled and they both shifted uneasily, but she proceeded to close her eyes and pray out loud, "Dear Heavenly Father, please help our friends to have good trip and a gentle landing in their new country. Please guide their steps and help them to place one foot, in front of the other and not to worry about anything, but to always depend on You. In the merciful Name of Jesus Christ, I pray, Amen." She wiped away a tear that ran down her blushed cheek, then silently stood up and commenced to make the boys some hot coco. James smiled at Morgan, as he sprawled back on the couch in exhaustion. Morgan eased out of the tight space, where he had been sitting and slipped down onto the couch, beside James.

"After you guys have your bedtime snack, it will be almost dawn and I'll be giving you the boot, over to the trawler, so we can all get a little sleep."

After a short while, all three friends were blissfully sipping their dark, creamy chocolate. Melted marshmallows floated like tiny prams, across the steamy surface of each mug of coco. The guys devoured more than their share of Amber's delectable, sweet breads and cakes. Looking like two satisfied Tom cats, ready to curl up, on a warm hearth, in front of a crackling fire, they grinned contentedly and closed their sleepy eyes. The winter rain began a gentle, pitter-patter on the fiberglass hull above their heads. They were all three relieved that the volatile fireworks and the thunder's fearsome growls had passed by, to the west of them, never making landfall in Key West.

Suddenly, loud thuds struck on the cabin door, again. Amber's expression appeared frozen and her eyes opened wide, darting back and forth, at James and Morgan. "Well, one thing we know for sure, it's not you doing it this time, Meredith." James cracked. Morgan rolled his china-blue eyes and conceded to the lame joke, by gesturing a sarcastic "thumbs up".

"I wonder who's out there," Amber whispered to James and

Morgan in a nervous voice. But, not waiting for their reply, she shockingly yelled out to the trespassers very loudly, "Who is it?"

"It's Manny, Mr. Sardis's security guard and my helpers. Sorry to bother you so late, Mrs. Albury. Can we come in? Mr. Sardis is looking for someone very important and he has ordered us to check out everyone who works for him. You know, to see if anybody has seen her. . . I mean the person Mr. Sardis is searching for."

"No, you're not coming in! Whoever, it is, you're out looking for, they're not here! You're disturbing me and I'm very sick! You and your buddies can go tell Mr. Sardis that I won't be reporting in to work and doing my show, tomorrow morning. Don't you ever sneak onboard my boat again! Get your butts off of my boat immediately! I need my sleep!"

"We'll tell Mr. Sardis what you said. Good night, Mrs. Albury. Didn't mean to disturb you." The boat heaved slightly, as they disembarked in a big hurry. Their feet scuffled abrasively down the wooden dock, as they retreated off into the damp night to hunt the crowded island, like loyal hounds. Sardis's dirty work came with rewards and the chase was on.

"Well, I think we might have one tough lady-captain on board this vessel! Does she seem to be, all that she appears, to be?" James teased. "Good job, Amber! You surprised us with that one!" Then they cracked up into a fit of liberating laughter, ringing from tip to stern.

Feeling the release from the pent up tension, Morgan stood up and helped weary James to his feet. Saying his parting *adieus* to Amber, Morgan headed up the stairs and opened the hatch door. It was only faintly misting, so he stepped out onto the deck, closed the hatch behind him and waited for James to join him.

James encircled Amber with his strong arms and gave her a hug good night. Laying his hands delicately on her rounded shoulders, he looked deep into her jade-green eyes and spoke in a hushed tone, "Remember, tomorrow night, you will unlock and open your locket for the very first time." James smiled at her, as he lifted the necklace up from her neck and kissed the rich pink luster of the flawless conch pearl gleaming in the cabin light. "I can't imagine anyone, in the world but you wearing my grandmother's locket. It enhances, only, how beautiful you are already. I can't help but admit. . . that I'll always envision you, just the way you look, tonight." He raised her surrendering hand and kissed it tenderly with his soft lips, as if she were a fragile piece of priceless porcelain. He captured the romantic moment and gave her a final caress. She entreated him to kiss her, once again. After fulfilling her request, Amber fluttered her dark, eye lashes, smiled at him, and sealed her farewell, by pressing her cheek firmly upon his broad chest. Her long, sun-streaked, auburn hair cascaded down over his torso. James slid his fingers smoothly through her silky tresses.

"We'll be together at the party, later on. . . Amber," James whispered her name, "and, I'll be counting the minutes 'til I see you again, my sweet lassie." He held her face up, just for a brief instant and looked deeply into her tear-filled eyes, as if searching for an answer to an unspoken question. And without another word, he then touched her nose with the end of his finger, turned away, hopped up the steps, darted through the cabin door and out onto the boat deck, where Morgan was impatiently, waiting for him. Finally, the two friends headed for the trawler to get some sleep.

Amber sang a song, wistfully to herself, as she locked the cabin door, behind them and turned off the electric lanterns. The pleasant rain shower had sadly ended for her, but the falling droplets, she discovered, had faithfully, left behind, a brand new awareness. A sparkling-clean feeling swept over her, washing her imagination with mysterious images of hopefulness and expectation. She paused for a minute, to look out the brass-trimmed portholes that James had so attentively, buttoned-down, earlier. With wonder, she beheld the silvery moonlight streaming through the rain-splattered, glass. Lacy, grey tracings rendered etched patterns of whimsy, on the wet panes and she marveled at the special masterpiece that God had fashioned for her. Thoughtfully, she lifted her little finger and drew a petite heart on the moist glass, followed by some scripted letters, placed in the center.

Pulling the window curtains down over the concealed creations, she fell blissfully into her warm bed.

Thirty-seven

"Hey Captain! Welcome aboard!" James called out across the incredible, entrance hall of Prescott's new, luxurious house located, on Shark Key. He strolled over across the brightly lit-up, glass floor, leading to where Morgan had just come through the tall, carved mahogany doors. Beneath his footsteps, under the immense, thick glass, were countless numbers of vibrant, tropical fish and multicolored invertebrates swimming in clear saltwater. The underground aquarium was fed by a tall, tumbling waterfall, flowing down a shear drop, in front of a magnificent wall of sparkling rocks, elevated three stories high above the bolder-lined pool. Lofty, leafy, elephant ear plants, vivid orchids, bouquets of bromeliads and blooming tillandsias bordered the aqua-green, cascading marvel. Morgan stood still, mesmerized, by the variety of colorful fish moving under his feet.

"This home is something else, isn't it, Morgan? This could be where the word "ambiance" got its start! A place, where, once, there was just sweet-smelling seawater and mangrove marshes! That's what I call renovation! I can't wait 'til Amber sees these fish swimming under her feet!" He hesitated and quickly looked around. "Hey! Please, don't tell me, you forgot to go by and pick her up!" He laughed ludicrously, swallowing the last gulp of his fruity concoction and exclaiming ecstatically, "I'm on break for awhile. I want her to get in, here, so I can tell her, the good news. Her snoopy, reporter friend, Heather, would be indebted to her the rest of her life, if she knew that Amber was behind, her new-found notoriety! The authorities gave Heather the scoop, today, but fortunately, Amber's identity is a total secret that Heather will never know about, sparing her a huge debt, she could not pay. Her story hits the Key West paper this weekend, plus some other major newspapers are picking it up, too. The case is closed, over, done and *fini*! Some of Sardis's thugs turned state's evidence, just as, Barlow expected they would. And, may I add, that they squealed big-time on their boss-man, completely sealing the future of Sardis and Sardis's enterprise. He got the just desserts that he deserves and none of us were implicated. For Amber, it's a done-deal. Tonight, Amber can celebrate 'til the sun rises. Dominique-the-freak, is locked up with a bunch of his buddies and crying the blues! This is so great, isn't it, Captain? I can't wait to see her face, when I tell her what happened. Where the heck, is she? When is she coming in?"

"Amber's not coming in, James."

"What do you mean, she's not coming in? The no-see-ums will eat her alive, out there?"

"I mean she's not coming in and she's not even here."

"Well, you better get the heck over there and pick her up. She's been waitin' on you, to come by since four o'clock to drive over and get her. I haven't had the pleasure of a lot of sleep, like you, but I do remember you were supposed to go to the marina and give her ride to the party!"

"I did go by and she was gone, James," Morgan held his out his hand. "Here, all I found was this." He presented a personalized, monogrammed, lime-green envelope, with *Morgan* written on the front. "She sealed a note inside this for me, to find, when I arrived to take her out here. It was secured with packing tape, in a plastic, zip-lock baggie, to the top of her dock-locker. The padlock on her locker was just hanging on the hinge . . . unlocked. Her note instructed me to go to the marina office and see the dock master, show him my driver's license for ID and collect this bag, from him and give it to you, as soon, as I saw you, this evening." He handed James a taupe, parchment bag. The jute handles were tied shut with a lavender ribbon. "Oh!" Morgan brandished his arms toward the red and gold macaws, sitting in suspended, ornate birdcages, far above their heads, "I almost forgot, this was inside the envelope with the note." He pulled a tiny trinket from his pastel, shirt pocket and gave it to James.

"Yeah, I recognize that polished, little key. It goes to her special Captain's box that she keeps her *unusual* photos in. Why would she be giving that to me?" His head pivoted back and forth, as his fiery, brown eyes frantically scanned the foyer and the yard, beyond. "Maybe, she's just late and driving over here, by herself."

"No, James. Read the note. There's more." James slid the paper out, unfolded it and read her message quietly to himself. Stunned, he lifted his gaze, staring at Morgan. "It says, she's not coming to the party, tonight. She's left Key West, for an indefinite time. The answers that I'm looking for are locked in her box."

"That's what it says, alright." Morgan flipped the worn key with his index finger. It spun in circles, dangling on James's finger from its silken ribbon. "So, open the bag. The box must be in the bag!"

"I will, Morgan, but not this minute. I'm more curious than

you are about what's going on with Amber's sudden decision to take off, but . . . "

"Not only did she take off, but so did her sailboat and her Jeep! They're gone! All gone! Vanished!"

"What are you talking about? She doesn't even know how to sail that boat by herself! Her Jeep is gone, too?" He ran his sun-tanned hand frantically through his thick, dark hair. His brown eyes filled with uncertainty, as unsolved questions, assailed his thoughts. "Whoa! Hold it a second!" he rolled his puzzled eyes. "This is crazy, Morgan! What's going on here?"

"Maybe, Sardis kidnapped her or something . . . that's possible! Perhaps, for a ransom!" Morgan gasped at the idea. "A lot of weird things are happening these days! I never did go back over to Amber's boat to check on her, after I got up, at noon. I just hailed a cab, outside the front of the marina and headed to your place to pick up the BMW. You never know, James, Sardis may have abducted her!"

"I told you that Sardis is already in jail! And, so is his stupid terrorist group. So, you can forget, working up your little con-spiracy theory!"

"Well, we should go out and try to find her, right now, or at least, investigate this box for clues."

"Don't worry, we are leaving, immediately. I will get Bow Diddle and her fiddle, together with Biggs and his drums. They can play without me, for the rest of the party. Prescott will understand. He knows, I'm barely, hanging-on-by-a-thread, from lack of sleep, anyway. He said, he didn't, even, care if I played, tonight, as long, as the fiddle player and drummer, could pull it off. They're both really talented musicians and Key West's best. I need to tell Prescott my problem and get my guitar and stuff packed up, right away. Wait for me in the banqueting hall."

He pointed to the lavish, catered tables, standing in the formal dining room. Each long table was decked with a different mermaid, ice sculpture, positioned perfectly, surrounded by the delectable creations. "Ask Paul, the owner of Conner's Connoisseurs Catering, for a dinner-to-go. He'll fix you up good. There are lots of exotic foods to choose from. Then, you can follow me back over to my place. I sure don't feel like eating anything."

James walked over to his gear and slowly withdrew the box from its wrapper. Turning the enigmatic box in different directions and studying the intricate carvings of the skillfully, inlaid wood, he grew very curious. Carefully, he inserted Amber's box back in the paper bag and deposited the small key into his guitar case. Replacing his new possession, securely under his arm, he hesitated and a baffled look spread across his face, his eyes filled with tears, as he quietly murmured to himself, "I thought we were falling in love. . . . "

Morgan pulled in the short driveway, behind James's truck, at the little cottage on Higgs Lane. He helped James unload the pickup and carry the guitar, case, stand, amplifier and all the equipment, into the cottage.

James headed to the kitchen and started a pot of fresh, shade-grown coffee. He placed the wooden box in the middle of the kitchen table, next to a cobalt-blue vase that was holding three, white orchids. Morgan trailed in behind him, balancing two, over-filled plates of food, in his hands. He set them down next to Amber's box. After, locating a clean fork in the dish-drainer, he sat down and proceeded to eat his catered dinner with pure pleasure.

Unconsciously, James opened the back door and let his mewing cat, in to eat. Pip greeted James with many "meows" mingled, with much profuse purring, while pushing his pointy ears and wispy whiskers, hard against his master's legs. The Pipster proudly waved his plume-of-a-tail, high in the air and his dark, furry paws kneaded James's bare feet, like pastry dough.

"Well, Pip, at least, you showed up, tonight," and he leaned over, scratched Pip's tawny chin and awarded him with his daily saucer of "creamy"! "Okay, let's open Amber's box," James proposed wryly, as he sat down with a mug of hot coffee. Morgan glanced up from his take-out plate, smelling the wafting aroma of James's strong coffee. "Get a cup if you want one," James offered dryly. Morgan looked slightly offended. "Here, you can have this one, then," James commiserated. "I'll pour another mug for myself." He got up, went to the tile counter and filled a big mug. After, doctoring it up, he sat down, at the table, once again. "I figured you were all set there, with your buffet-thing going on," James sighed, while observing Morgan's almost empty plates. "You sure didn't loose your appetite over this phenomenon, did you?" James pushed back in his chair and looked at Pip, lapping up the last drop of half and half cream from his bowl. "It doesn't seem to affect Pip's hunger either. Sorry, Captain, I guess I'm just reacting to Amber's surprise departure. I mean, I've got a major crush on this woman and she doesn't even call, to say, "goodbye"! I thought our relationship deserved more, than a scrap of paper and an old box. What's going on, Morgan?"

"I don't know, but we can start, by first, opening the stupid box."

"Yep! You're right! Amber said I would find the answers, I needed, inside the box. What are we waiting for?"

"What if its contents are personal and I shouldn't be here, seeing whatever, she's left in her precious box, for you. Maybe, that's why she had me bring it to you . . . she did instruct me, to give it particularly, just, to you. You know, it probably isn't for me to see or anyone else, for that matter, otherwise, she would have just left it, sitting by the locker, on the dock, with my note."

"Morgan, just, shut up and pass me the box." Morgan slid it past the blue vase and over to the end of the table, where James was sitting. James got up and fetched the key, from his guitar case. Returning to his seat, he inserted the key into the tiny lock and turned it. At a snail's pace, he opened the lid and peeked in.

"You're right, Morgan, maybe I better do this by myself. Go on, out in the living room and relax. Check out the new movie that's in the machine. The thing is way, over-the-top, over-due with late fees and I never, even, saw the whole thing. P.J.'s movie store won't mind, another night. Go for it!" James's eyes eagerly fell back upon Amber's gift and he gradually lowered the lid. "You understand, right?"

"Yeah, I'd much rather watch a movie, than see you, blubbering over some old crap that Amber left you in her infantile box. Even, watching Pip, wash his face will be a whole lot, more interesting, than seeing you, change colors." With that said, Morgan refilled his coffee cup, dumped in some cream and sugar and headed out, to join the cat, in the living room.

James raised the box lid again and removed a folded, sweet-scented letter and shut the lid. Carefully opening it, he read Amber's hand written message:

My Dearest James,
I regret that I had to leave so suddenly, today. My explanation will be hard for you to understand, as it is, even, more

difficult, for me, to comprehend. Colonel Benson came to my boat, early this morning. He motored here on a large, "privately" owned yacht. Marsha, his fiancée was with him, too. They shocked me, to say the least. I never returned the urgent phone calls he made to me to warn me that they were arriving, today, in Key West. Their arrival was a total surprise! They came to say that Secret Service operatives are almost positive that they have possibly located, my "so-called" late husband, Peter, somewhere, at a top-secret spot, in the Middle East and that he may be very much alive and in danger. They informed me that I had to leave immediately with them, today. I will, straight-away, be flying to an undisclosed place, over there in the Middle East. They tethered the Lady Poetry *behind their vessel and lowered my Jeep, on the front deck, next to a government helicopter. James, I truthfully promise that is everything I know. I will be briefed on the rest of the details later, on this trip and when I get to where I am going. I have been told that it is on a need-to-know basis. I trust the Lord Jesus, and that is all I can say. In the confusion and rush to leave, I took the time to think about you and me, and the sweet times we had together. You are so precious to me and your devotion, as a true friend, will be, forever, with me. You shall always live in a warm place in my heart. I have left some things in my old box, for you, with notes attached. I thought you would like them and the box is for you to keep, as well. We had something so special and I hope I have not broken your heart in two. My heart aches, also, and asks so many questions, but I know we are both strong and we can get through this. If not together, then it must be apart, but I know I will see you in my dreams. We can truly rely on God, to see us through. I must always remember the verse, "I can do all things through Christ, Who strengthens me." I hope that you will hold-fast to it, believing it, as I do. Please, tell Morgan, our Captain, goodbye for me and how much his friendship meant to me. I will always love you and pray for you, both. May God be with you and keep you, forever, James.*

Lovingly, Amber

He refolded the letter and placed it to the side. Then, he reached into the box and pulled out a piece of parchment paper. On the top edge, it read: *This is the poem I wrote, that I never got to recite for you on the* Lady Poetry. *We were at Yellow Rocks off of Key West and we got interrupted by a storm. Remember? I hope you like it:*

James looks down at the flowing, curvy handwriting and began to read softly, aloud:

FLIGHT

A brown leaf on the wind is born and that's me this frosty morn.
Crackly and brittle is my fragile, soft heart, as I take to the air to find my start.
Blow wind, blow! Breeze me along. Up high, down low, like notes in a song.
Give me a push—give me a swoosh. Twirl and whirl me, until I get my wish.
A windy quest, and then I rest. My blustery friend knows what's best.
He spins me where I do not know—with gentle stops, a scoot and go.
A sudden halt, a gusting start—my friend, the wind, consumes my heart.
From picking me up, he never tires, my peace and

hopes are his desires.
So, breathe, old wind, upon this tired soul.
Strengthen me, until I reach my goal.
To attain my dreams, is his dream, too. Oh! Invisible
friend, I do love you.
I think I'm going to make it. P.T.L.

AMBER ALBURY

James set the poem on top of the letter. Next, he brought out
the antique locket, fashioned from the pearl, of the queen conch
shell. It glistened with a shimmering pink color under the pale
overhead, kitchen light. There was a small, inscribed tag tied to
it with a thin, scarlet ribbon. It read:

Thank you, James, for allowing me to wear your beautiful,
heirloom necklace. It is your treasure, once again. I never
opened it up, for I promised to do that only with you, so what
is inside will always remain, a mystery to me. Thank you for
blessing me with your lovely locket to wear for the short time,
that I was able. I shall always feel like I was entrusted with a
valuable, buried treasure, of some kind, from your family's past.

Love, your good friend, Amber

James untied the personal tag from the old necklace. After,
sliding the locket, deep into the hiding place, of his shirt pocket,
he next discovered a small, leather-bound Bible lying down
inside the box. Removing it, he opened it up and read the
inscription inside the front cover:

Please, James, keep this Bible with you and read it often. It
is like food for a hungry spirit and water for a thirsty soul.

Remember, it's like chicken soup! Love and prayers for you,

Always, Amber

After skimming through a few pages, he laid the Bible on the table. Picking up a tissue, he dabbed his wet eyes and looked back into the box. There was only one thing left and it was wrapped in a black, velvet cloth. He took it out and unrolled the supple fabric. A chill crawled down his spine and crept over his whole body. There it was! The Saint Francis medal. She did not tag this item.

James blinked his eyes and his breathing became labored, as he turned it over between his thumb and fingers, feeling the raised embossment on the smooth metal. Leaning back in his kitchen chair, he looked up and stared for a few seconds, at the revolving fan blades, above his head.

Carefully, he put the letter and the poem, back into the small, wooden box, along with the miniature Bible. *The gold medal, that, once, was Doctor Herald Vickers's valuable possession, has been passed to me. But, why did she do this?* James scratched his head. He knew he was the new custodian, now. *Only, Amber and I, know what this little jewel contains. Perhaps, that it even truly exists. What was she thinkin' when she left this for me? Why didn't she dispose of this earlier?*

He reflected, a few moments, then, without further hesitation, he opened the clasp of the gold-linked chain and fastened it securely, around his neck. Impressed, by the effortless weight of the adornment, he got up and sauntered out to the old, fish-net-draped, dresser-mirror that was hanging behind the tiki bar, on his back porch. *Check it out*, he thought, as he admired the gold treasure, hanging against his suntanned chest. The light flickered unusually upon the figure of Saint Francis, as James held it up, to the mirror.

Studying his new ornament, he considered, *I'm not even Catholic, but here I am, wearing Vickers's special medal. Why would Amber give this to me? What could be the reason? Because, I like animals and Saint Francis is the patron Saint of animals? That's possible, but not likely . . . a real stretch! Ummmm . . . don't think so. Maybe, she thinks I'm the patron Saint of War Widows. Who knows? But, lately, things are not so much what they appear to be.*

James flipped the wooden box shut with a hard clunk. *No photos of Doctor Vickers, left in the box. . . . Wonder why?* He pondered, faintly, a few seconds on this puzzle, but, then he pushed the box back into the middle of the table, next to the cobalt-blue vase and the three, white orchids. After, a few minutes, he composed himself and stood up from the table, flicked off the coffee pot and strolled out into the living room.

"Hey Morgan," he grinned. Morgan was asleep in the easy chair and the movie was rolling on. "Morgan!" James called. The Captain's china-blue eyes, popped open and he shot James a puzzled look. James smirked and he walked over and turned off the DVD player. A fiery expression was ablaze in James's dark brown eyes and he gave Morgan a very hard stare.

Morgan yawned, and then whispered in a hoarse voice, "How does the Green Parrot sound to you, just about now?"

"I don't know, Morgan, maybe later. I read in the *Key West Soundings,* where there's a visiting, street ministry playing a bunch of music, down on Duval and Front Street. They'll be performing 'til late, tonight. I'm not sure, but I think the paper said, the guy's name is, Doctor Markee from Tennessee. The photo showed, a quartette of really pretty sisters that sing and play banjo, flute, piano and guitar. Let's go! Why not? It's something different to do and a new song can't hurt me . . . not any worse, than I'm hurtin', already. I could use an airy, new song. Besides, it may be Providential. What the heck! I'm dressed for it and I'm not even Catholic!" His fingers felt the embossed pattern of the Saint Francis medal hidden under his yellow hibiscus-flowered shirt.

"Right, James! Whatever you say! And, just, what exactly are you saying?"

"I got my flip-flops on and I'm ready to go!"

"Besides, *'flip-flops'*, is there more?"

"Yeah! I'm plannin' on drivin' to the marina in the morning, to get my skiff. And I may do a little *treasure-divin'* when I'm over there."

"Sounds like a plan!"

"Care to come along, Captain?"

"What are we waitin' on?"

"Sunrise, lad. A sweet Key West sunrise!"

PAMELA PINHOLSTER lives on Big Pine Key with her husband of forty years. After, home school-ing and raising their eight children in the Keys and beyond, she followed her dream of writing a book. She placed in the Key West Writer's Guild contest with a short story and that is when and where the idea for Key West Rhapsody *was born. She loves to enjoy the local sunrises and sunsets, speaking with nearby dolphins and deer, while spending time day dreaming of an imaginary world, for her readers to hopefully read about, later on, in the future.*

You can visit Pamela Pinholster at
www.keywestrhapsody.com